ith Brian
also the
ne of the
lon with

CHUNG KUO

ICE AND FIRE

CHUNG KUO

BOOK 4

DAVID WINGROVE

CORVUS

Ice and Fire was first published as *The Middle Kingdom* in Great Britain in 1989 by New English Library.

This revised and updated edition published in special edition hardback, trade paperback, and E-book in Great Britain in 2012 by Corvus, an imprint of Atlantic Books Ltd.

10 9 8 7 6 5 4 3 2 1

A CIP catalogue record for this book is available from the British Library.

Hardback ISBN: 978 1 84887 728 3
Trade paperback ISBN: 978 1 84887 729 0
E-book ISBN: 978 0 85789 799 2

Printed in Great Britain by the MPG Books Group.

Corvus
An imprint of Atlantic Books Ltd
Ormond House
26–27 Boswell Street
London
WC1N 3JZ

www.corvus-books.co.uk

CONTENTS

Is this the way the world ends?
Under ice
Under fire
Has there been some mistaken design?
Under ice
Got to find the human voice
Lord deliver us from Babel
—'Mr X Gets Tense', Peter Hammill, 1979

INTRODUCTION

Chung Kuo. The words mean 'Middle Kingdom' and, since 221 BC, when the First Emperor, Ch'in Shih Huang-ti, unified the seven Warring States, it is what the 'black-haired people', the Han, or Chinese, have called their great country. The Middle Kingdom – for them it was the whole world; a world bounded by great mountain chains to the north and west, by the sea to east and south. Beyond was only desert and barbarism. So it was for two thousand years and through sixteen great dynasties. Chung Kuo *was* the Middle Kingdom, the very centre of the human world, and its Emperor the 'Son of Heaven', the 'One Man'. But in the eighteenth century that world was invaded by the young and aggressive Western powers with their superior weaponry and their unshakeable belief in Progress. It was, to the surprise of the Han, an unequal contest and China's myth of supreme strength and self-sufficiency was shattered. By the early twentieth century China – *Chung Kuo* – was the sick old man of the East: 'a carefully preserved mummy in a hermetically sealed coffin', as Karl Marx called it. But from the disastrous ravages of that century grew a giant of a nation, capable of competing with the West and with its own Eastern rivals, Japan and Korea, from a position of incomparable strength. The twenty-first century, 'the Pacific century' as it was known even before it began, saw China become once more a world unto itself, but this time its only boundary was space.

David Wingrove
May 2012

PART 8   THE DOMAIN

SPRING 2201

With all its eyes the creature-world beholds
the open. But our eyes, as though reversed,
encircle it on every side, like traps
set round its unobstructed path to freedom.
What is outside, we know from the brute's face
alone; for while a child's quite small we take it
and turn it round and force it to look backwards
at conformation, not that openness
so deep within the brute's face. Free from death.
We alone see that; the free animal
has its decease perpetually behind it
and God in front, and when it moves, it moves
within eternity, like running springs.
We've never, no, not for a single day,
pure space before us, such as that which flowers
endlessly open into: always world,
and never nowhere without no: that pure,
unsuperintended element one breathes,
endlessly knows, and never craves. A child
sometimes gets quietly lost there, to be always
jogged back again. Or someone dies and is it.
—Rainer Maria Rilke, *Duino Elegies*: 'Eighth Elegy'

Chapter 35

THE DEAD RABBIT

Meg Shepherd, Hal Shepherd's daughter, was standing in the tall grass of the Domain, watching her brother. It was early evening and on the far side of the water, dense shadow lay beneath the thick cluster of trees. At this end the creek narrowed to a shallow, densely weeded spike of water. To her left, in the triangle of wild, uncultivated land between the meadow and the vast, overtowering whiteness of the Wall, the ground grew soft and marshy, veined with streams and pocked with tiny pools.

Ben was crouched at the water's edge, intensely still, staring at something in the tall, thick rushes to his right. For a moment there was only the stillness and the boy watching, the soft soughing of the wind in the trees across the water and the faint, lulling call of pigeons in the wood. Then, with an abrupt crash and spray and a strong beating of wings, the bird broke from cover. Ben's head went up, following the bird's steep ascent, his twelve-year-old eyes wide with watching.

'Look at it, Meg! Isn't it a beauty?'

'Yes,' she answered softly, but all the while she was watching him, seeing how his eyes cast a line to the climbing bird. Saw how he grasped every last detail of it and held that knowledge tight in his memory. His body was tensed, following the bird's flight, and his eyes burned. She shivered. It was astonishing to watch, that intensity of his. The world seemed to take form in his eyes: to grow bright and rich and real. As if, before he saw it, it was but a pale shadow of itself; a mere blueprint, uncreated until he saw and re-imagined it. So it was for her. She could see nothing unless he had seen it first.

The bird was gone. He turned and looked at her.

'Did you see it?'

'Yes,' she said, meaning something else. 'It was beautiful.'

He turned his head, looking away from her, towards the village. When he looked back his green eyes were dark, thoughtful.

'Things are different this year, Meg. Don't you feel it? Small things. Like the bird.'

She shrugged then pushed her way through the grass, out into the open. Standing there beside him at the water's edge, she looked down at his reflection, next to her own in the still, clear water.

'Why do you think that is? Why *should* it change?' He looked around him, his brow furrowing. 'I mean, this place has always been the same. Always. Unchanged. Unchanging but for the seasons. But now... ' He looked at her. 'What is it, Meg? What's happening?'

She looked up from his reflection and met his eyes.

'Does it worry you?'

He thought for a moment. 'Yes,' he said finally. 'And I don't know why. And I want to know why.'

She smiled at him and reached out to touch his arm. It was so typical of him, wanting to understand what he thought and why he thought it. Never happy unless he was worrying at the problem of himself.

'It's nothing,' she said reassuringly. 'They're only small things, Ben. They don't mean anything. Really they don't.'

But she saw he wasn't convinced. 'No,' he said. 'Everything has meaning. It's all signs, don't you see? It all *signifies*. And the small things... that's where it's to be seen first. Like the bird. It was beautiful, yes, but it was also...' He looked away and she said the word for him, anticipating him without quite knowing how, as she so often did.

'Frightening.'

'Yes.'

She followed his gaze a moment, seeing how his eyes climbed the Wall to its summit far overhead, then looked back at him again. He was more than a head taller than her, dark-haired and straight-boned. She felt a small warmth of pride kindle in her. So elegant he was. So handsome. Did he know how much she loved him? He knew so much, but did he know that? Maybe. But if he did he gave no sign.

'It was only a bird, Ben. Why should it frighten you?'

He almost smiled. 'It wasn't the bird, Meg. At least, not the outer thing, the cage of bone and flesh, sinew and feather. It was what was within the bird – the force that gave it such power, such vitality.' He looked down at his left hand, then turned it over, studying its back. 'That's where its beauty lies. Not in the outward show but in the shaping force. That... well, it's mystery. Pure mystery. And that frightens me, Meg. The thought of all that dark, unharnessed power simply existing in the world. I look at it and I want to know where it comes from. I want to know why it's there at all. Why it isn't mere mechanics and complexity of detail. Why all that fiery excess?'

'The force that through the green fuse drives the flower.'

And now he did smile, pleased by her recognition; by her quoting back at him the poem he had read to her only two days past. How rare that was, him smiling. And only for her. Never for mother or father. Or for those others that came so rarely to this place.

'I guess there's that too,' he said. 'That same force brings us on, from bud to flower to... well, to something browned and withered. And thus to clay.' He shrugged. 'It's all connected, isn't it? It uses us and then discards us. As if we're here only to flesh out its game – to give it form. Doesn't that frighten you, Meg?'

She shook her head. 'Why should it? There's plenty of time, Ben. A whole world of time before we have to think of that.'

He studied her intently for a moment, then bowed his head slightly. 'Perhaps.'

He began to walk, treading a careful path through the marshy ground, following a rising vein of rock that jutted from the sodden turf, until he came beneath the shadow of the Wall.

There, facing them not thirty paces away, was the Seal. Part of the Wall, it was the same dull pearl in colour, a great circle five times Ben's height, its base less than an arm's length above the surface of the ground, its outer edge a thick ridge of steel-tough plastic.

For a moment he stood there, staring at it, oblivious of all else.

Meg, watching him, understood. It was a gateway. A closed door. And beyond it was the darkness of the Clay. Primal, unadulterated Clay. Beyond it the contiguous earth was sun-deprived and barren. Here Heaven, there Hell. And only a Wall, a Seal, between the two.

She climbed up beside him on the ridge of rock. 'What's that?' She pointed outward to their left. There was something there. Something small and pale and grey against the green. Something that hadn't been there before.

He looked, then shrugged. 'I don't know. Let's see, eh?'

At once he scrambled down. Meg hesitated, then followed. The ground was soft and spongy and in only a few paces her canvas shoes were soaked. Ben had gone ahead of her, his feet sinking, squelching as he ran. Then she saw him crouch down and examine something.

She came up behind him and looked over his shoulder. It was a rabbit. A dead rabbit.

'What killed it?' she asked.

He prised the carcass up from out of the wet, clinging turf and turned it over, examining it.

'I don't know. There's no sign of external injury. But it's not been here long.' He looked up at her. 'Here, Meg, give me your jumper.'

She pulled her jumper off and handed it to him, then watched as he spread it out and laid the dead animal on it.

'What are you doing?'

Ben drew his hunting knife from its sheath, then cut the rabbit from chin to rump. For a moment he watched the blood well from the cut, staining the mottled grey fur, then laid the knife down and eased the flesh apart.

Meg watched, fascinated and horrified, as he probed inside the animal, the blood dark on his fingers. Then he lifted something small and wet; a pale, tiny sac attached by tubes and tendons to the rest. It glistened in his fingers as he bent to study it. Then he looked up at her.

'It's as I thought. Look. The liver's covered in dark blotches.'

She shook her head, not understanding, watching him bundle the rabbit in her jumper, then lift it and sling it over his shoulder.

'It's diseased,' he said, staring across at the Seal, then turned to look at her. 'It's part of the change in things. Don't you see that now? There's a sickness here in the Domain.'

★

Hal Shepherd stood at the turn of the road, his hands resting lightly on the low stone wall, looking down at the row of cottages and the bay beyond. To his right the hill rose up above where he stood, then fell again to meet the next turn of the river. It was dotted with old stone-built houses and cottages. At its summit was a small church.

It was almost three months since he had been home, but now, standing there, it seemed that he had never been away. This much at least remains unchanged, he thought; each hill, each tree, each house familiar to him from youth. *I see it as my grandfather saw it, and his grandfather before him.* In three hundred years only the trees had changed, growing older, dying, replaced by others of their own ancient seed. *Like us,* he thought. *We too are trees.*

He walked on. The road dipped steeply here then curved back wickedly upon itself. Where he had been standing had been a turning point for cars once upon a time – when there were still cars in the world – but this had never been a place for modern things. Even back then, when the world was connected differently, it had been seven miles by road to the nearest town of any size, and that easier to get to by the river. Time had stood still here even then. During the Madness, when the old world had heaved itself apart, this place had been a point of stillness at the centre of things. Now it was timeless.

There were walls, no more than a pace or two either side of him. White-washed walls, in heavy shadow now, their low-silled windows dark; only one cottage in the row lit up. He smiled, seeing it ahead of him; imagining Beth there in the low-beamed living room, the fire lit and the curtains drawn; seeing her, as he had so often seen her, go to the back door and call the children in from the meadow.

Home. It meant so many things, but only one to him. He would have withered inside long ago had there not been this to return to.

He stood outside the low, broad door, listening, then put his hand out flat against the wood and gently pushed. There was no need for locks here. No need for fear. The door swung back slowly, silently, and he went in.

Beth stood there in the doorway, framed by the soft light of the living room behind her and to her left. She smiled.

'I knew you were coming. I dreamed of you last night.'

He laughed and went to her, then held her tightly against him, kissing her tenderly. 'Your dreams...' He gazed into her eyes, loving the beauty, the measureless depth of them. 'They never fail you, do they?'

She smiled and kissed his nose. 'Never.'

He shivered and reached up to stroke her cheek then trace the contours of her lips with a fingertip. His whole body was alive with desire for her. 'Where's Ben and Meg?'

Her body was pressed hard against his own, her hands at his neck. Her eyes were dark with longing. 'They're outside. Down by the creek. But they'll not be back. Not just yet.'

She kissed him again, a harder, longer kiss this time.

He let his left hand rest gently on her waist a moment, then rucked up her skirt. Beneath it she was wearing nothing. He sought her mouth again, the kiss more urgent. His fingers traced the warm smoothness of her thighs and belly, then found the hot wetness at the core of her. She moaned and closed her eyes, her whole body trembling at his touch, then she reached down and freed him, grasping his swollen penis, her fingers softly tracing its length, once, then again, almost making him come, before drawing him up into her.

He groaned, then, grasping her by the buttocks, lifted her, backing her against the wall, thrusting up into her once, twice, a third time before he came explosively, feeling her shudder violently against him.

For a while, then, they were silent, watching each other. Then Beth smiled again. 'Welcome home, my love.'

The pine surface of the kitchen table was freshly scrubbed, the knives newly sharpened. Ben looked about him, then, leaving the bundled rabbit on the wide stone step outside, busied himself. He spread an oilcloth on the table then laid the big cutting board on top of it. He laid the knives out beside the board and then, because it was growing dark, brought the lamp from beside the old ceramic butler sink, trimming the wick before he lit it.

Meg stood in the garden doorway, her small figure silhouetted against the redness of the bay. She watched him roll back his sleeves, then fill a bowl with water and set it beside the knives.

'Why are you doing that?' she asked. 'You know it's diseased. Why not just burn it?'

Ben barely glanced at her. He turned and went down the four steps that led into the long, dark, low-ceilinged dining room, returning a moment later with a book from the shelves. An old thing, leather-bound and cumbersome.

'I've a hunch,' he said, putting the heavy volume down on the other side of the board to the knives and the water.

Meg stood beside him. It was a book of animal anatomy. One of their great-great-great-grandfather Amos's books. Ben flicked through the pages until he came to the diagram he was looking for. 'There,' he said, the heavy, glossy pages staying in place as he turned away to bring the rabbit.

She looked. Saw at once how like a machine it was. A thing of pumps and levers, valves and switches, controlled by chemicals and electric pulses. It was all there on the page, dissected for her. The whole of the mystery – there at a glance.

Ben came back. He placed the dead rabbit carefully on the block then turned and looked at her. 'You needn't stay, Meg. Not if you don't want to.'

But she stayed, fascinated by what he was doing, knowing that this had meaning for him. Something had caught his attention. Something she had missed but he had seen. Now she waited as he probed and cut and then compared what had been exposed against the diagram spread across the double page.

At last, satisfied, he went to the sink and washed his hands, then came back and threw a muslin cloth over the board and its bloodied contents.

'Well?'

He was about to answer her when there was the sound of footsteps in the dining room. Their mother's. Then a second set.

Meg pushed past him and jumped down the four steps in her haste.

'Daddy!'

Hal Shepherd gathered his daughter up, hugging her tight and kissing her, delighted to see her. Then he ducked under the lintel and climbed the steps up into the kitchen, Beth following.

'Gods, Ben, what have you been up to?'

Ben turned to face the table.

'It's a dead rabbit. We found it down by the Seal. It's diseased. But that's not all. It doesn't come from here. It was brought in.'

Hal put Meg down and went across. 'Are you sure, Ben?' But he knew that Ben was rarely if ever wrong.

Ben pulled back the cloth. 'Look. I made certain of it against Amos's book. This one isn't real. It's a genetic redesign. Probably GenSyn. One of the guards must have made a substitution.'

Hal studied the carcass a while, then nodded. 'You're right. And it won't be the only one, I'm sure. I wonder who brought it in?'

Ben saw the anger mixed with sadness on his father's face. There were two gates to the Domain, each manned by an elite squad of a dozen men, hand-picked by the T'ang himself. Over the years they had become friends of the family and had been granted privileges – one of which was limited entry to the Domain. Now that would have to stop. The culprit would have to be caught and made to pay.

Meg came up to him and tugged at his arm. 'But why would they do it? There's no great difference, is there?'

Hal smiled sadly. 'It's a kind of foolishness, my love, that's all. There are people in the City who would pay a vast sum of money to be able to boast they had real rabbit at one of their dinners.'

Ben stared at the carcass fixedly. 'How much is a vast sum?'

Hal looked down at his son. 'Fifty, maybe a hundred thousand yuan for each live animal. They would breed them, you see, then sell the doctored litters.'

Ben considered. Such a sum would be as nothing to his father, he knew, but to others it was a fortune. He saw at once how such an opportunity might have tempted one of the guards. 'I see,' he said. 'But there's another, more immediate worry. If they're all like this they could infect everything in the Domain. We'll need to sweep the whole area. Catch everything and test it. Quarantine whatever's sick.'

Hal nodded, realizing his son was right. 'Damn it! Such stupidity! I'll have the culprit's hide!' He laid a hand on his son's shoulder. 'But you're right, Ben, we'd best do something straight away. This can't wait for morning.'

He turned to Beth, anger turning to apology in his face. 'This complicates things, I'm afraid. I meant to tell you earlier, my love. We have a guest coming, tomorrow evening. An important guest. He'll be with us a few days. I can't say any more than that. I was hoping we could hunt, but this business buggers things.'

She frowned at him and made a silent gesture towards Meg.

Shepherd glanced at his daughter then looked back at his wife and gave a slight bow. 'I'm sorry. My language. I forget when I've been away. But this...' He huffed angrily, exasperated, then turned to his son again. 'Come, Ben, there's much to be done.'

★

It was calm on the river. Ben pulled easily at the oars, the boat moving swiftly through the water. Meg sat facing him, looking across at the eastern shore. Behind her, in the stern, sat Peng Yu-wei, tall, elderly and very upright, his staff held in front of him like an unflagged mast. It was ebb tide and the current was in their favour. Ben kept the boat midstream, enjoying the warmth of the midday sun on his bare shoulders, the feel of the mild sea breeze in his hair. He felt drowsy, for one rare moment almost lapsed out of consciousness, then Meg's cry brought him back to himself.

'Look!'

Meg was pointing out towards the far shore. Ben shipped oars and turned to look. There, stretching from the foreshore to the Wall, was a solid line of soldiers. Slowly, methodically, they moved between the trees and over the rough-grassed, uneven ground, making sure nothing slipped between them. It was their third sweep of the Domain and their last. What was not caught this time would be gassed.

Peng Yu-wei cleared his throat, his head held slightly forward in a gesture of respect to his two charges.

'What is it, Teacher Peng?' Ben asked coldly, turning to face him. Lessons had ended an hour back. This now was their time and Peng, though chaperone for this excursion, had no authority over the master and mistress outside his classroom.

'Forgive me, young master, I wish only to make an observation.'

Meg turned, careful not to make the boat tilt and sway, and looked up at Peng Yu-wei, then back at Ben. She knew how much Ben resented the imposition of a teacher. He liked to make his own discoveries and follow his own direction, but their father had insisted upon a more rigorous approach. What Ben did in his own time was up to him, but in the morning classes he was to do as Peng Yu-wei instructed; learn what Peng Yu-wei asked him to learn. With some reluctance Ben had agreed, but only on the understanding that outside the classroom the teacher was not to speak without his express permission.

'You understand what Teacher Peng really is?' he had said to Meg when they were alone one time. 'He's their means of keeping tabs on me. Of controlling what I know and what I learn. He's bit and bridle, ball and chain, a rope to tether me like any other animal.'

His bitterness had surprised her. 'Surely not,' she had answered. 'Father wouldn't want that, would he?'

Ben had not answered, only looked away, the bitterness in his face unchanged.

Now some of that bitterness was back as he looked at Teacher Peng. 'Make your observation then. But be brief.'

Peng Yu-wei bowed, then turned his head, looking across at the soldiers who were now level with them. One frail, thin hand went up to pull at his wispy grey goatee, the other moved slightly on the staff, inclining it towards the distant line of men. 'This whole business seems most cumbersome, would you not agree, Master Ben?'

Ben's eyes never left the teacher's face. 'Not cumbersome. Inefficient's a better word.'

Teacher Peng looked back at him and bowed slightly, corrected. 'Which is why I felt it could be made much easier.'

Meg saw the impatience in Ben's face and looked down. No good would come of this.

'You had best tell me *how*, Teacher Peng.' The note of sarcasm in Ben's voice was bordering on outright rudeness now. Even so, Peng Yu-wei seemed not to notice. He merely bowed and continued.

'It occurs to me that, before returning the animals to the land again, a trace could be put inside each animal. Then, if this happened again, it would be a simple thing to account for each animal. Theft and disease would both be far easier to control.'

Peng Yu-wei looked up at his twelve-year-old charge expectantly, but Ben was silent.

'Well, master?' he asked after a moment. 'What do you think of my idea?'

Ben looked away. He lifted the oars and began to pull at them again, digging heavily into the water to his right, bringing the boat back onto a straight course. He looked back at the teacher.

'It's a hideous idea, Peng Yu-wei. An unimaginative, small-minded idea. Just another way of keeping tabs on things. I can see it now. You would make a great electronic wall chart of the Domain, eh? And have each animal as a blip on it.'

The stretched olive skin of Peng Yu-wei's face was relaxed, his dark eyes, with their marked epicanthic fold, impassive. 'That would be a refinement, I agree, but...'

Ben let the oars fall and leaned forward in the boat. Peng Yu-wei reflex-ively moved back. Meg watched, horrified, as Ben scrabbled past her, the boat swaying violently, and tore at the teacher's *pau* , exposing his chest.

'Please, young master. You know that is not allowed.'

Peng Yu-wei still held his staff, but with his other hand he now sought to draw the two ends of the torn silk together. For a moment, however, the white circle of the control panel set into his upper chest was clearly visible.

For a second or two Ben knelt there in front of him threateningly, his whole body tensed as if to act.

'You'll be quiet, understand? And you'll say nothing of this. Nothing! Or I'll switch you off and drop you over the side. Understand me, Teacher Peng?'

For a moment the android was perfectly still, then it gave the slightest nod.

'Good,' said Ben, moving back and taking up the oars again. 'Then we'll proceed.'

As Ben turned the boat into the tiny, box-like harbour the two sailors looked up from where they sat on the steps mending their nets and smiled. They were both old men, in their late sixties, with broad, healthy, salt-tanned faces. Ben hailed them, then concentrated on manoeuvring between the moored fishing boats. There was a strong breeze now from the mouth of the river and the metallic sound of the lines flapping against the masts filled the air, contesting with the cry of gulls overhead. Ben turned the boat's prow with practised ease and let the craft glide between a big, high-sided fisher-boat and the harbour wall, using one of the oars to push away, first one side, then the other. Meg, at the stern, held the rope in her hand, ready to jump ashore and tie up.

Secured, Ben jumped ashore, then looked back into the boat. Peng Yu-wei had stood up, ready to disembark.

'You'll stay,' Ben said commandingly.

For a moment Peng Yu-wei hesitated, his duty to chaperone the children conflicting with the explicit command of the young master. Water slopped noisily between the side of the boat and the steps. Only paces away the two old sailors had stopped their mending, watching.

Slowly, with great dignity, the teacher sat, planting his staff before him. 'I'll do as you say, young master,' he said, looking up at the young boy on the quayside, 'but I must tell your father about this.'

Ben turned away, taking Meg's hand. 'Do what you must, tin man,' he muttered under his breath.

The quayside was cluttered with coils of rope, lobster pots, netting and piles of empty wooden crates – old, frail-looking things that awaited loads of fish that never came. The harbour was filled with fishing boats, but no one ever fished. The town beyond was full of busy-seeming people, but no one lived there. It was all false: all part of the great illusion Ben's great-great-grandfather, Augustus, had created here.

Once this had been a thriving town, prospering on fishing and tourism and the naval college. Now it was dead. A shell of its former self, peopled by replicants.

Meg looked about her, delighted, as she always was by this. Couples strolled in the afternoon sunshine, the ladies in crinolines, the men in stiff three-piece suits. Pretty little girls with curled blonde hair tied with pink ribbons ran here and there, while boys in sailor suits crouched, playing five-stones.

'It's so *real* here!' Meg said enthusiastically. 'So alive!'

Ben looked down at her and smiled. 'Isn't it?' He had seen pictures of the City. It seemed such an ugly, hideous place by comparison. A place of walls and cells and corridors – a vast, unending prison of a place. He turned his face to the breeze and drew in great lungfuls of the fresh salt air, then looked back at Meg. 'What shall we do?'

She looked past the strolling holidaymakers at the gaily painted shops along the front, then looked up at the hillside and, beyond it, the Wall, towering over all.

'I don't know...' She squeezed his hand. 'Let's just go where we want, Ben. Look wherever we fancy looking, eh?'

'Okay. Then we'll start over there, at the Chandler's.'

For the next few hours they went among the high-street shops, first searching through the shelves of Joseph Toms, Toys and Fancy Goods, for novelties, then looking among the tiny cupboards of Charles Weaver, Apothecary, sampling the sweet-tasting, harmless powders on their fingers and mixing the brightly coloured liquids in beakers. But Ben soon tired of such games and merely watched as Meg went from shop to shop, unchallenged by the android shopkeepers. In Nash's Coffee House they had their lunch, the food real but somehow unsatisfying, as if reconstituted.

'There's a whole world here, Meg. Preserved. Frozen in time. Sometimes I look at it and think it's such a waste. It should be used somehow.'

Meg sipped at her iced drink then looked up at him. 'You think we should let others come here into the Domain?'

He hesitated, then shook his head. 'No. Not that. But...'

Meg watched him curiously. It was unusual to see Ben so indecisive.

'You've an idea,' she said.

'No. Not an idea. Not as such.'

Again that uncertainty, that same slight shrugging of his shoulders. She watched him look away, his eyes tracing the row of signs above the shop fronts: David Wishart, Tobacconist; Arthur Redmayne, Couturier; Thomas Lipton, Vintner; Jack Delcroix, Dentist & Bleeder; Stagg & Mantle, Ironmongers; Verry's Restaurant; Jackson & Graham, Cabinet Makers; The Lambe Brothers, Linen-Drapers; and there, on the corner, facing Goode's Hostelry, Pugh's Mourning House.

Seeing Pugh's brought back a past visit. It had been months ago and Ben had insisted on going into Pugh's, though they had always avoided the shop before. She had watched him go amongst the caskets, then lift one of the lids, peering inside. The corpse looked realistic enough, but Ben had turned to her and laughed. 'Dead long before it was dead.' Somehow that had made him talk about things here. Why they were as they were, and what kind of man her great-great-grandfather had been to create a place like this. He had not skimped on anything. One looked in drawers or behind doors and there, as in real life, one found small, inconsequential things. Buttons and pins and photographs. A hatstand with an old, well-worn top hat on one peg, a scarf on another, as if left there only an hour past. Since then she had searched and searched, her curiosity unflagging, trying to catch him out – to find some small part of this world he had made that wasn't finished. To find some blank, uncreated part behind the superficial details.

Would she have thought to do this without Ben? Would she have searched so ardently to find that patch of dull revealing blankness? No. In truth she would never have known. But he had shown her how this, the most real place she knew, was in other ways quite hollow. Was all a marvellous sham. A gaudy, imaginative fake.

'If this is fake, then why is it so marvellous?' she had asked, and he had shaken his head in wonder at her question.

'Why? Because it's god-like! Look at it, Meg! It's so presumptuous! Such consummate mimicry! Such shameless artifice!'

Now, watching him, she knew he had a scheme. Some way of using this.

'Never mind,' she said. 'Let's move on. I'd like to try on some of Lloyd's hats.'

Ben smiled at her. 'Okay. Then we'll start back.'

They were upstairs in Edgar Lloyd, Hatters, when Ben heard voices down below. Meg was busy trying on hats at the far side of the room, the android assistant standing beside her at the mirror, a stack of round, candy-striped boxes in her arms.

Ben went to the window and looked down. There were soldiers in the passageway below. Real soldiers. And not just any soldiers. He knew the men at once.

Meg turned to him, a wide-brimmed creation of pale cream lace balanced precariously on top of her dark curls. 'What do you think, Ben? Do you...?'

He hushed her urgently.

'*What is it?*' she mouthed.

'*Soldiers,*' he mouthed back.

She set the hat down and came across to him.

'*Keep down out of sight,*' he whispered. '*They're our guards, and they shouldn't be here. They're supposed to be confined to barracks.*'

She looked up at him, wide-eyed, then knelt down, so that her head was below the sill. '*Tell me what's happening.*'

He watched. There were ten of them down there, their voices urgent, excited. For a moment Ben couldn't understand what was going on, then one of them turned. It was the captain, Rosten. He pointed down the passageway towards the open ground in front of the old inn and muttered something Ben couldn't quite make out.

'*What are they doing?*'

He looked down at Meg and saw the fear in her eyes.

'*Nothing. Hush now, Megs. It'll be all right.*'

He put his hand on her shoulder and looked out again. What he saw this time surprised him. Two of the men were being held and bound; their wrists and ankles taped together. One of the men started to struggle, then began to cry out. Meg tried to get up to see, but with a gentle pressure he pushed her back down.

There was the sound of a slap, then silence from below. A moment later Rosten's voice barked out. 'Out there! Quick now!'

Ben moved across to the other side of the window, trying to keep them in sight, but he lost them in a moment.

'Stay here, Meg. I'm going downstairs.'

'But, Ben...'

He shook his head. 'Do what I say. I'll be all right. I'll not let them see me.'

He had to move slowly, carefully on the stairs because, for a brief moment, he was in full sight of the soldiers through the big plate-glass window that looked out onto the narrow quay. At the bottom he moved quickly between the racks and tables until he was crouched between two mannequins, looking out through their skirts at the scene in front of the inn.

Two men held each of the prisoners. The other three stood to one side, in a line, at attention. Rosten had his back to Ben and stood there between the window and the prisoners. With an abrupt gesture that seemed to jerk his body forward violently, he gave an order. At once both prisoners were made forcibly to kneel and lower their heads.

Only then, as Rosten turned slightly, did Ben see the long, thin blade he held.

For a moment the sight of the blade held him; the way the sunlight seemed to flow like a liquid along the gently curved length of it, flickering brilliantly on the razor-sharp edge and at the tip. He had read how swords could seem alive – could have a personality, even a name – but he had never thought to see it.

He looked past the blade. Though their heads were held down forcibly, the two men looked up at Rosten, anxious to know what he intended. Ben knew them well. Gosse, to the left, was part Han, his broad, rough-hewn, Slavic features made almost Mongolian by his part-Han ancestry. Wolfe, to the right, was a southerner, his dark, handsome features almost refined; almost, but not quite, classical. Almost. For when he smiled or laughed, his eyes and mouth were somehow ugly. Brutish and unhealthy.

Rosten now stood between the two, his feet spread, his right arm out-stretched, the sword in his right hand, its tip almost touching the cobbled ground a body's length away.

'You understand why you're here? You've heard the accusations?'

'They're lies...' began Wolfe, but he was cuffed into silence by the man behind him.

Rosten shook his head. The long sword quivered in his hand. 'Not lies, Wolfe. You have been tried by a panel of your fellow officers and found guilty. You and Gosse here. You stole and cheated. You have betrayed our master's trust and dishonoured the Banner.'

Wolfe's eyes widened. The blood drained from his face. Beside him Gosse looked down, as if he had already seen where this led.

'There is no excusing what you did. And no solution but to excise the shame.'

Wolfe's head came up sharply and was pushed down brutally. 'No!' he shouted, beginning to struggle again 'You can't do this! You...'

A blow from one of the men holding him knocked him down onto the cobbles.

'Bring him here!'

The two guards grabbed Wolfe again and dragged him on his knees, until he was at Rosten's feet.

Rosten's voice was almost hysterical now. He half-shouted, half-screamed, his sword arm punctuating the words. 'You are scum, Wolfe! Faceless! Because of you your fellow officers have fallen under suspicion! Because of you, all here have been dishonoured!' Rosten shuddered violently and spat on the kneeling man's head. 'You have shamed your Banner! You have shamed your family name. And you have disgraced your ancestors!'

Rosten stepped back and raised the sword. 'Hold the prisoner down!'

Ben caught his breath. He saw how Wolfe's leg muscles flexed impotently as he tried to scrabble to his feet; how he squirmed in the two men's grip, trying to get away. A third soldier joined the other two, forcing Wolfe down with blows and curses. Then one of them grabbed Wolfe's topknot and, with a savage yank that almost pulled the man up off his knees, stretched his neck out, ready for the sword.

Wolfe was screaming now, his voice hoarse, breathless. 'No! No! Kuan Yin, Goddess of Mercy, help me! I did nothing! Nothing!' His face was torn with terror, his mouth twisted, his eyes moving frantically in their sockets, pleading for mercy.

Ben saw Rosten's body tauten like a compressed coil. Then, with a sharp hiss of breath, he brought the sword down sharply.

Wolfe's screams stopped instantly. Ben saw the head drop and roll, the body tumble forward like a sack of grain, the arms fall limp.

Ben looked across at Gosse.

Gosse had been watching all in silence, his jaw clenched, his neck muscles taut. Now, with a visible shudder, he looked down again, staring at the cobbles.

Rosten bent down and wiped the sword on the back of Wolfe's tunic, then straightened, facing Gosse.

'You have something to say, Gosse?'

Gosse was silent a moment, then he looked up at Rosten. His eyes, which, moments earlier, had been filled with fear and horror, were now clear, almost calm. His hands shook, but he clenched them to control their trembling. He took a deep breath, then another, like a diver about to plunge into the depths, and nodded.

'Speak then. You've little time.'

Gosse hunched his shoulders and lowered his head slightly, in deference to Rosten, but kept his eyes on him. 'Only this. It is true what you say. I am guilty. Wolfe planned it all, but I acted with him, and there is no excusing my actions. I accept the judgement of my fellow officers and, before I die, beg their forgiveness for having shamed them before the T'ang.'

Rosten stood there, expecting more, but Gosse had lowered his head. After a moment's reflection, Rosten gave a small nod, then spoke.

'I cannot speak for all here, but for myself I say this. You were a good soldier, Gosse. And you face death bravely, honestly, as a soldier ought. I cannot prevent your death now, you understand, but I can, at least, change the manner of it.'

There was a low gasp from the men on either side as Rosten took a pace forward and drew the short sword from his belt and cutting the bonds at Gosse's wrists, handed it to him.

Gosse understood at once. His eyes met Rosten's, bright with gratitude, then looked down at the short sword. With his left hand he tore open the tunic of his uniform and drew up the undershirt, baring the flesh. Then he gripped the handle of the short sword with both hands and turned it, so that the tip was facing his stomach. The two guards released him and stood back. Rosten watched him a moment, then took up his place, just behind Gosse and to one side, the long sword half raised.

Ben eased forward until his face was pressed against the glass, watching Gosse slow his breathing and focus his whole being upon the blade resting only a hand's length from his stomach. Gosse's hands were steady now, his eyes glazed. Time slowed. Then, quite abruptly, it changed. There was a sudden, violent movement in Gosse's face – a movement somewhere between ecstasy and extreme agony – and then his hands were thrusting the blade deep into his belly. With what seemed superhuman strength and control he drew the short sword to the left, then back to the right, his intestines spilling out onto the cobbles. For a moment his face held its expression of ecstatic agony, then it crumpled and his eyes looked down, widening, horrified by what he had done.

Rosten brought the sword down sharply.

Gosse knelt a moment longer. Then his headless body fell and lay there, motionless, next to Wolfe's.

Ben heard a moan behind him and turned. Meg was squatting at the top of the stairs, her hands clutching the third and fourth struts tightly, her eyes wide, filled with fright.

'Go up!' he hissed anxiously, hoping he'd not be heard; horrified that she had been witness to Gosse's death. He saw her turn and look at him, for a moment barely recognizing him or understanding what he had said to her. *Dear gods*, he thought, *how much did she see?*

'Go up!' he hissed again. '*For heaven's sake go up!*'

It was dark on the river, the moon obscured behind the Wall's north-western edge. Ben jumped ashore and tied the rowboat up to the small, wooden jetty, then turned to give a hand to Peng Yu-wei who stood there, cradling a sleeping Meg in one arm.

He let the teacher go ahead, reluctant to go in, wanting to keep the blanket of darkness and silence about him a moment longer.

There was a small rectangle of land beside the jetty, surrounded on three sides by steep clay walls. A set of old, wooden steps had been cut into one

side. Ben climbed them slowly, tired from the long row back. Then he was in the garden, the broad swathe of neat-trimmed grass climbing steadily to the thatched cottage a hundred yards distant.

'Ben!'

His mother stood in the low back doorway, framed by the light, an apron over her long dress. He waved, acknowledging her. Ahead of him, Peng Yu-wei strode purposefully up the path, his long legs showing no sign of human frailty.

He felt strangely separate from things. As if he had let go of oars and rudder and now drifted on the dark current of events. On the long row back he had traced the logic of the thing time and again. He knew he had caused their deaths. From his discovery things had followed an inexorable path, like the water's tight spiral down into the whirlpool's mouth. They had died because of him.

No. Not because of him. Because of his discovery. He was not to blame for their deaths. They had killed themselves. Their greed had killed them. That and their stupidity.

He was not to blame; yet he felt their deaths quite heavily. If he had said nothing. If he had simply burned the rabbit as Meg had suggested...

It would have solved nothing. The sickness would have spread; the discovery would have been made. Eventually. And then the two soldiers would have died.

It was not his fault. Not his fault.

His mother met him at the back door. She knelt down and took his hands. 'Are you okay, Ben? You look troubled. Has something happened?'

He shook his head. 'No. I...'

The door to the right of the broad, low-ceilinged passage-way opened and his father came out, closing the door behind him. He smiled at Ben, then came across.

'Our guest is here, Ben. He's been here all afternoon. I know I said earlier that you would be eating alone tonight, but he says he'd like to meet you. So I thought that maybe you could eat with us after all.'

Ben was used to his father's guests and had never minded taking his evening meal in his room, but this was unusual. He had never been asked to sit at table with a guest before.

'Who is it?'

His father smiled enigmatically. 'Wash your hands, then come through. I'll introduce you. But, Ben... be on your best behaviour, please.'

Ben gave a slight bow, then went to the small washroom. He washed his face and hands, then scrubbed his nails and tidied his hair in the mirror. When he came out his mother was waiting for him. She took his hands, inspecting them, then straightened his tunic and bent to kiss his cheek.

'You look fine, Ben. Now go in.'

'Who is it?' he asked again. 'Tell me who it is.'

But she only smiled and turned him towards the door. 'Go on in. I'll be there in a moment.'

Chapter 36

A CONVERSATION IN THE FIRELIGHT

In the light from the open fire the T'ang's strong, oriental features seemed carved in ancient yellowed ivory. He sat back in his chair, smiling, his eyes brightly dark.

'And you think they'll be happy with that, Hal?'

Li Shai Tung's hands rested lightly on the table's edge, the now-empty bowl he had been eating from placed to one side, out of his way. Ben, watching him, saw once again how the light seemed trapped by the matt black surface of the heavy iron ring he wore on the index finger of his right hand. The *Ywe Lung*. The seal of power.

Hal Shepherd laughed, then shook his head. 'No. Not for a moment. They all think themselves emperors in that place.'

They were talking about the House of Representatives at Weimar – 'That troublesome place', as the T'ang continually called it – and about ways of shoring up the tenuous peace that now existed between it and the Seven.

The T'ang and his father sat at one end of the long, darkwood table, facing each other, while Ben sat alone at the other end. His mother had not joined them for the meal, bowing in this regard to the T'ang's wishes. But in other respects she had had her own way. The T'ang's own cooks sat idle in her kitchen, watching with suspicion and a degree of amazement as she single-handedly prepared and served the meal. This departure from the T'ang's normal practices was remarkable enough in itself, but what had happened at the beginning of the meal had surprised even his father.

When the food taster had stepped up to the table to perform his normal duties, the T'ang had waved him away and, picking up his chopsticks, had taken the first mouthful himself. Then, after chewing and swallowing the fragrant morsel, and after a sip of the strong green Longjing *ch'a* – itself 'untasted' – he had looked up at Beth Shepherd and smiled broadly, complimenting her on the dish. It was, as Ben understood at once, seeing the surprised delight on his father's face and the astonished horror on the face of the official taster, quite unprecedented, and made him realize how circumscribed the T'ang's life had been. Not free at all, as others may have thought, but difficult; a life lived in the shadow of death. For Li Shai Tung, trust was the rarest and most precious thing he had to offer; for in trusting he placed his life – quite literally his life – in the hands of others.

In that small yet significant gesture, the T'ang had given his father and mother the ultimate in compliments.

Ben studied the man as he talked, aware of a strength in him that was somehow more than physical. There was a certainty – a vitality – in his every movement, such that even the slightest hesitancy was telling. His whole body spoke a subtle language of command; something that had developed quite naturally and unconsciously during the long years of his rule. To watch him was to watch not a man but a directing force; was to witness the channelling of aggression and determination into its most elegant and expressive form. In some respects Li Shai Tung was like an athlete, each nuance of voice or gesture the result of long and patient practice. Practice that had made these things second nature to the T'ang.

Ben watched, fascinated, barely hearing the words, but aware of their significance, and of the significance of the fact that he was there to hear them.

Li Shai Tung leaned forward slightly, his chin, with its pure white, neatly braided beard, formulating a slight upward motion that signalled the offering of a confidence.

'The House was never meant to be so powerful. Our forefathers saw it only as a gesture. To be candid, Hal, as a sop to their erstwhile allies and a mask to their true intentions. But now, a hundred years on, certain factions persist in taking it at face value. They maintain that the power of the House is sanctioned by "the People". And we know why, don't we? Not for "the People". Such men don't spare a second's thought for "the People". No, they think only of themselves. They seek to climb at our expense. To raise themselves by pulling down the Seven. They want control, Hal, and the House is the means through which they seek to get it.'

The T'ang leaned back again, his eyes half-lidded now. He reached up with his right hand and grasped the tightly furled queue at the back of his head, his fingers closing about the coil of fine white hair. It was a curious, almost absent-minded gesture; yet it served to emphasize to Ben how at ease the T'ang was in his father's company. He watched, aware of a whole vocabulary of gesture there in the dialogue between the two men: conscious not just of what they said but of how they said it; how their eyes met or did not meet; how a shared smile would suddenly reveal the depths of their mutual understanding. All served to show him just how much the T'ang depended on his father to release these words, these thoughts, these feelings. Perhaps because no other could be trusted with them.

'I often ask myself, is there any way we might remove the House and dismantle the huge bureaucratic structure that has grown about it? But each time I ask myself I know beforehand what the answer is. No. At least, not now. Fifteen, maybe twenty years ago it might have been possible. But even then it might simply have pre-empted things. Brought us quicker to this point.'

Hal Shepherd nodded. 'I agree. But perhaps we should have faced it back then. We were stronger. Our grip on things was firmer. Now things have changed. Each year's delay sees them grow at our expense.'

'You'd counsel war, then, Hal?'

'Of a kind.'

The T'ang smiled. 'And what kind is that?'

'The kind we're best at. A war of levels. Of openness and deception. The kind of war the Tyrant, Tsao Ch'un, taught us how to fight.'

The T'ang looked down at his hands, his smile fading. 'I don't know. I really don't, Hal. Sometimes I question what we've done.'

'As any man must surely do.'

Li Shai Tung looked up at him and shook his head. 'No, Hal. For once I think you're wrong. Few actually question their actions. Most are blind to their faults. Deaf to the criticisms of their fellow men.' He laughed sourly. 'You might say that Chung Kuo is filled with such individuals – blind, wicked, greedy creatures who see their blindness as strength, their wickedness as necessity, their greed as historical process.'

'That's so...'

For a moment the two men fell silent, their faces solemn in the flickering light from the fire. Before either could speak again, the door at the far end of the room opened and Ben's mother entered, carrying a tray. She set it down on a footstool beside the open fire, then leaned across to take something from a bowl on the mantelpiece and sprinkle it on the burning logs.

At once the room was filled with the sweet, fresh smell of mint.

The T'ang gave a gentle laugh, delighted, and took a long, deep breath.

Ben watched his mother turn from the fire, drawing her long dark hair back from her face, smiling. 'I've brought fresh *ch'a*,' she said simply, then lifted the tray and brought it across to them.

As she set it down the T'ang stood and, reaching across, put his hand over hers, preventing her from lifting the kettle.

'Please. I would be honoured if you sat a while with us and shared the *ch'a*.'

She hesitated then, smiling, did as he bid her; watching the strange sight of a T'ang pouring *ch'a* for a commoner.

'Here,' he said, offering her the first bowl. '*Ch'a* from the dragon's well.'

The T'ang's words were a harmless play on the name of the Longjing *ch'a*, but for Ben they seemed to hold a special meaning. He looked at his mother, seeing how she smiled self-consciously and lowered her head, for a moment the youthful look of her reminding him terribly of Meg – of how Meg would be a year or two from now. Then he looked back at the T'ang, standing there, pouring a second bowl for his father.

Ben frowned. The very presence of the T'ang in the room seemed suddenly quite strange. His silks, his plaited hair, his very foreignness seemed out of place amongst the low oak beams and sturdy yeoman furniture. That contrast, that curious juxtaposition of man and room, brought home to Ben how strange this world of theirs truly was. A world tipped wildly from its natural balance.

The dragon's well. It made him think of fire and darkness, of untapped potency. *Is that what's missing from our world?* he asked himself. *Have we done with fire and darkness?*

'And you, Ben? Will you drink of the dragon's well?'

Li Shai Tung looked across at him, smiling; but behind the smile – beyond it, in some darker, less accessible place – lay a deep disquiet.

Flames danced in the glass of each eye, flickered wet and evanescent on the dark surface of his vision. But where was the fire on the far side of the glass? Where the depths that made of Man a man? In word and gesture, the T'ang was great and powerful – a T'ang, unmistakably a king among men – but he had lost contact with the very thing that had made – had shaped – his outer form. He had denied his inner self once too often and now the well was capped, the fire doused.

He stared at the T'ang, wondering if he knew what he had become; if the doubt that he professed was as thorough, as all-inclusive as it ought to be. Whether, when he looked at his reflection in the mirror, he saw beyond the glass into that other place behind the eyes. Ben shivered. No. It could not be so. For if it were the man himself would crumble. Words would fail, gestures grow hesitant. No. This T'ang might doubt what they had done, but not what he was. That was innate – was bred into his bones. He would die before he doubted himself.

The smile remained, unchallenged, genuine; the offered bowl awaited him.

'Well, Ben?' his father asked, turning to him. 'Will you take a bowl with us?'

Li Shai Tung leaned forward, offering the boy the bowl, conscious that he had become the focus of the child's strange intensity; of the intimidating ferocity of his stare.

Hal was right. Ben was not like other children. There was something wild in his nature; some part of him that remained untamed, unsocialized. When he sat there at table it was as if he held himself in check. There was such stillness in him that when he moved it was like something dead had come alive again. Yet he was more alive – more vividly alive – than anyone the T'ang had ever met.

As he handed Ben the bowl he almost expected to receive some kind of shock – a violent discharge of the child's unnatural energy – through the medium of the bowl. But there was nothing. Only his wild imagining.

The T'ang looked down, thoughtful. Ben Shepherd was a breed of one. He had none of those small refinements that fitted a man for the company of his fellows. He had no sense of give and take; no idea of the concessions one made for the sake of social comfort. His stare was uncompromising, almost proprietorial. As if all he saw was his.

Yes, Li Shai Tung thought, smiling inwardly. You should be a T'ang, Ben Shepherd, for you'll find it hard to pass muster as a simple man.

He lifted his bowl and sipped, thinking back to earlier that afternoon. They had been out walking in the garden when Hal had suggested he go with him and see Ben's room.

He had stood in the centre of the tiny, cluttered upstairs room, looking at the paintings that covered the wall above the bed.

Some were lifelike studies of the Domain. Lifelike, at least, but for the dark, unfocused figures who stood in the shadows beneath the trees on the far side of the water. Others were more abstract, depicting strange distortions of the real. Twins figured largely in these latter compositions; one twin quite normal – strong and healthy – the other twisted out of shape, the eyes blank, the mouth open as if in pain. They were disturbing, unusually disturbing, yet their technical accomplishment could not be questioned.

'These are good, Hal. Very good indeed. The boy has talent.'

Hal Shepherd gave a small smile, then came alongside him. 'He'd be pleased to hear you say that. But if you think those are good, look at this.'

The T'ang took the folder from him and opened it. Inside was a single ultra-thin sheet of what seemed like pure black plastic. He turned it in his hands and then laughed. 'What is it?'

'Here,' Shepherd indicated a viewer on the table by the window, then drew the blind down. 'Lay it in the tray there, then flick that switch.'

Li Shai Tung placed the sheet down in the viewer. 'Does it matter which way up?'

'Yes and no. You'll see.'

The T'ang flicked the switch. At once the tank-like cage of the viewer was filled with colour. It was a hologram. A portrait of Hal Shepherd's wife, Beth.

'He did this?'

Shepherd nodded. 'There are one hundred and eighty cross-sectional layers of information. Ninety horizontal, ninety vertical. He hand drew each sheet and then compressed them. It's his own technique. He invented it.'

'Hand drew... ?'

'And from memory. Beth wouldn't sit for him, you see. She said she was too busy. But he did it anyway.'

Li Shai Tung shook his head slowly. 'It's astonishing, Hal. It's like a camera image of her.'

'You haven't seen the half of it. Wait...' Shepherd switched the hologram off, then reached in and lifted the flexible plate up. He turned it and set it down again. 'Please...'

The T'ang reached out and pressed the switch. Again the viewing cage was filled with colour. But this time the image was different.

The hologram of Hal Shepherd was far from flattering. The flesh was far cruder, much rougher than the reality, the cheeks ruddier. The hair was thicker, curlier, the eyebrows heavier and darker. The nose was thick and fleshy, the ears pointed, the eyes larger, darker. The lips were more sensual than the original, almost licentious. They seemed to sneer.

Shepherd moved closer and looked down into the viewer. 'There's something of the satyr about it. Something elemental.'

The T'ang turned his head and looked at him, not understanding the allusion.

Shepherd laughed. 'It was a Greek thing, Shai Tung. In their mythology satyrs were elementary spirits of the mountains and the forests. Part-goat, part-man. Cloven-hooved, thickly-haired, sensual and lascivious.'

Li Shai Tung stared at the urbane, highly sophisticated man standing at his side and laughed briefly, bemused that Shepherd could see himself in that brutal portrait. 'I can see a slight likeness. Something in the eyes, the shape of the head, but...'

Shepherd shook his head slowly. He was staring at the hologram intently. 'No. Look at it, Shai Tung. Look hard at it. He sees me clearly. My inner self.'

Li Shai Tung shivered. 'The gods help us that our sons should see us thus!'

Shepherd turned and looked at him. 'Why? Why should we fear that, old friend? We know what we are. Men. Part mind, part animal. Why should we be afraid of that?'

The T'ang pointed to the image. 'Men, yes. But men like that? You really see yourself in such an image, Hal?'

Shepherd smiled. 'It's not the all of me, I know, but it's a part. An important part.'

Li Shai Tung shrugged – the slightest movement of his shoulders – then looked back at the image. 'But why is the other as it is? Why aren't both alike?'

'Ben has a wicked sense of humour.'

Again the T'ang did not understand, but this time Shepherd made no attempt to enlighten him.

Li Shai Tung studied the hologram a moment longer then turned from it, looking all about him. 'He gets such talent from you, Hal.'

Shepherd shook his head. 'I never had a tenth of his ability. Anyway, even the word "talent" is unsatisfactory. What he has is genius. In that he's like his great-great-grandfather.'

The T'ang smiled at that, remembering his father's tales of Augustus Shepherd's eccentricity. 'Perhaps. But let us hope that that is all he has inherited.'

He knew at once that he had said the wrong thing. Or, if not the wrong thing, then something that touched upon a sensitive area.

'The resemblance is more than casual.'

The T'ang lowered his head slightly, willing to drop the matter at once, but Shepherd seemed anxious to explain. 'Ben's schizophrenic too, you see. Oh, nothing as bad as Augustus. But it creates certain incongruities in his character.'

Li Shai Tung looked back at the pictures above the bed with new understanding. 'But from what you've said the boy is healthy enough.'

'Even happy, I'd say. Most of the time. He has bouts of it, you understand. Then we either dose him up heavily or leave him alone.'

Shepherd leaned across and switched off the viewer, then lifted the thin black sheet and slipped it back into the folder. 'They used to think schizophrenia was a simple malfunction of the brain; an imbalance in certain chemicals – dopamine, glutamic acid and gamma-amino-butyric acid. Drugs like largactil, modecate, disipal, priadel and haloperidol were used, mainly as tranquillizers. But they simply kept the thing in check and had the side-effect of enlarging the dopamine system. Worst of all, at least as far as Ben is concerned, they damp down the creative faculty.'

The T'ang frowned. Medicine, like all else, was based on traditional Han ways. The development of Western drugs, like Western ideas of progress, had been abandoned when Tsao Ch'un had built his City. Many such drugs were, in fact, illicit now. One heard of them, normally, only in the context of addiction – something that was rife in the lowest levels of the City. Nowadays all serious conditions were diagnosed before the child was born and steps taken either to correct them or to abort the foetus. It thus surprised him, first to hear that Ben's illness had not been diagnosed beforehand, second that he had even considered taking drugs to keep the illness in check.

'He has not taken these drugs, I hope.'

Shepherd met his eyes. 'Not only has but still does. Except when he's working.'

The T'ang sighed deeply. 'You should have told me, Hal. I shall arrange for my herbalist to call on Ben within the next few days.'

Shepherd shook his head. 'I thank you, Shai Tung. Your kindness touches me. But it would do no good.'

'No good?' The T'ang frowned, puzzled. 'But there are numerous sedatives – things to calm the spirit and restore the body's yin-yang balance. Good, healthy remedies, not these... drugs!'

'I know, Shai Tung, and again I thank you for your concern. But Ben would have none of it. Oh, I can see him now – "Dragon bones and oyster shells!" he'd say scornfully. "What good are they against this affliction?"'

The T'ang looked down, disturbed. In this matter he could not insist. The birthright of the Shepherds made them immune from the laws that governed others. If Ben took drugs to maintain his mental stability there was little he, Li Shai Tung, could do about it. Even so, he could not stop himself from feeling it was wrong. He changed the subject.

'Is he a good son, Hal?'

Shepherd laughed. 'He is the best of sons, Shai Tung. Like Li Yuan, his respect is not a matter of rote, as it is with some of this new generation, but a deep-rooted thing. And as you've seen, it stems from a thorough knowledge of his father.'

The T'ang nodded, leaving his doubts unexpressed. 'Good. But you are right, Hal. These past few years have seen a sharp decline in morality. The li – the rites – they mean little now. The young mouth the old words but they mean nothing by them. Their respect is an empty shell. We are fortunate, you and I, that we have good sons.'

'Indeed. Though Ben can be a pompous, intolerant little sod at times. He has no time for fools. And little enough for cleverness, if you see what I mean. He loathes his machine-tutor, for instance.'

Li Shai Tung raised his eyebrows. 'That surprises me, Hal. I would have thought he cherished knowledge. All this...' he looked about him at the books and paintings and machines '...it speaks of a love of knowledge.'

Shepherd smiled strangely. 'Perhaps you should talk to him yourself, Shai Tung.'

The T'ang smiled. 'Perhaps I should.'

Now, watching the boy across the length of the dinner table, he understood.

'What do you think, Ben? Do you think the time has come to fight our enemies?'

Unexpectedly, the boy laughed. 'That depends on whether you know who or what your enemies are.'

The T'ang lifted his chin slightly. 'I think I have a fair idea.'

Ben met his eyes again, fixing that same penetrating stare on him. 'Maybe. But you must first ask yourself what exactly you are fighting against. When you think of your enemies your first thought is of certain identifiable men and groups of men, is that not so?'

The T'ang nodded. 'That is so, Ben. I know my enemies. I can put names to them and faces.'

'There, you see. And you think that by waging war against them you will resolve this present situation.' Ben set his bowl down and sat back, his every gesture momentarily – though none but Ben himself realized it – the mirror image of the T'ang's. 'With respect, Li Shai Tung, you are wrong.'

The T'ang laughed fiercely, enjoying the exchange. 'You think their ideology will outlive them? Is that it, Ben? If it were not so false in the first place, I would agree with you. But their sole motivation is greed. They don't really want change. They want power.'

Ben shook his head. 'Ah, but you're still thinking of specific men. Powerful men, admittedly, even men of influence, but only men. Men won't bring Chung Kuo down, only what's inside Man. You should free yourself from thinking of them. To you they seem the greatest threat, but they're not. They're the scum on the surface of the well. And the well is deep.'

Li Shai Tung took a deep breath. 'With respect, Ben, in this you are wrong. Your argument presupposes that it does not matter who rules – that things will remain as they are whoever is in power. But that's not so. Their ideology is false, but, forgive me, they are *Hung Mao*.'

Across from him Hal Shepherd smiled, but he was clearly embarrassed. It was more than two decades since he had taken offence at the term – a term used all the while in court, where the Han were predominant and the few Caucasians treated as honorary Han – yet here, in the Domain, he felt the words incongruous, almost – surprisingly – insulting.

'They have no sense of harmony,' continued the T'ang, unaware. 'No sense of li. Any change they brought would not be for the good. They are men of few principles. They would carve the world up into principalities and then there would be war again. Endless war. As it was before.'

There was the faintest of smiles on Ben's lips. 'You forget your own history, Li Shai Tung. No dynasty can last forever. The wheel turns. Change comes, whether you will it or no. It is the way of Mankind. All of Mankind, even the Han.'

'So it may have been, but things are different now. The wheel no longer turns. We have done with history.'

Ben laughed. 'But you cannot stop the world from turning!'

He was about to say more but his mother touched his arm. She had sat there, perfectly still and silent, watching the fire while they talked, her dark hair hiding her face. Now she smiled and got up, excusing herself.

'Perhaps you men would like to go through into the study. I've lit the fire there.'

Shepherd looked to the T'ang, who gave the slightest nod of agreement before standing and bowing to his hostess. Again he thanked her warmly for the meal and her hospitality, then, when she had gone, went before Shepherd and his son into the other room.

'Brandy?' Shepherd turned from the wall cabinet, holding the decanter up. The T'ang was usually abstemious, but tonight his mood seemed different. He seemed to want to talk – to encourage talk. As if there were some real end to all this talking: some problem which, though he hadn't come to it, he wished to address. Something he found difficult; that worried him profoundly.

The T'ang hesitated, then smiled. 'Why not? After all, a man ought to indulge himself now and then.'

Shepherd poured the T'ang a fingernail's measure of the dark liquid and handed him the ancient bowled glass. Then he turned to his son. 'Ben?'

Ben smiled almost boyishly. 'Are you sure mother won't mind?'

Shepherd winked at him. 'Mother won't know.'

He handed the boy a glass, then poured one for himself and sat, facing the T'ang across the fire. Maybe it was time to force the pace; time to draw the T'ang out of himself.

'Something's troubling you, Shai Tung.'

The T'ang looked up from his glass almost distractedly and gave a soft laugh. 'Everything troubles me, Hal. But that's not what you mean, is it?'

'No. No visit of yours is casual, Shai Tung. You had a specific reason for coming to see me.'

The T'ang's smile was filled with gratitude. 'As ever, Hal, you're right. But I'll need no excuse to come next time. I've found this very pleasant.'

'Well?'

The T'ang took a long inward breath, steeling himself, then spoke. 'It's Tolonen.'

For some time now the T'ang had been under intense pressure from the House to bring the General to trial for the murder of Under Secretary Lehmann. They wanted Tolonen's head for what he'd done. But the T'ang had kept his thoughts to himself about the killing. No one – not the Seven or Hal Shepherd – knew how he really felt about the matter, only that he had refused to see Tolonen since that day; that he had exiled him immediately and appointed a new General, Vittorio Nocenzi, in his place.

Shepherd waited, conscious of how tense Li Shai Tung had suddenly become. Tolonen had been of the same generation as the T'ang and they shared the same unspoken values. In their personal lives there had been parallels that had drawn them close and formed a bond between them; not least the loss of both their wives some ten years back. In temperament, however, they were ice and fire.

'I miss him. Do you understand that, Hal? I really miss the old devil. First and foremost for himself. For all that he was. Loyal. Honest. Brave.' He looked up briefly, then looked down again, his eyes misting. 'I felt he was my champion, Hal. Always there at my side. From my eighteenth year. My General. My most trusted man.'

He shuddered and was silent for a while. Then he began again, his voice softer, yet somehow stronger, more definite than before.

'Strangely I miss his rashness most of all. He was like Han Ch'in in that. What he said was always what part of me felt. Now I feel almost that that part of me is missing – is unexpressed, festering in the darkness.'

'You want him back?'

Li Shai Tung laughed bitterly. 'As if I could. No, Hal, but I want to see him. I need to speak to him.'

Shepherd was silent for a time, considering, then he leaned forward and set his glass down on the table at his side. 'You should call him back, Shai

Tung. For once damn the House and its demands. Defy them. You are T'ang, and thus above their laws.'

Li Shai Tung looked up and met Shepherd's eyes. 'I am T'ang, yes, but I am also Seven. I could not act so selfishly.'

'Why not?'

The T'ang laughed, surprised. 'This is unlike you, Hal. For more than twenty years you have advised me to be cautious, to consider the full implications of my actions, but now, suddenly, you counsel me to rashness.'

Shepherd smiled. 'Not rashness, Shai Tung. Far from it. In fact, I've thought of little else this past year.' He got up and went across to a bureau in the corner furthest from the fire, returning a moment later with a folder which he handed to the T'ang.

'What is this, Hal?'

Shepherd smiled, then sat again. 'My thoughts on things.'

Li Shai Tung stared thoughtfully at Shepherd a moment, then set his glass down and opened the folder.

'But this is handwritten.'

Shepherd nodded. 'It's the only copy. I've said things in there that I'd rather not have fall into the hands of our enemies.'

He looked briefly at his son as he said the last few words, conscious that the boy was watching everything.

Li Shai Tung looked up at him, his face suddenly hawk-like, his eyes fiercer than before. 'Why did you not mention this before?'

'It was not my place. In any case, it was not ready before now.'

The T'ang looked back down at the folder and at the summary Shepherd had appended to the front of his report. This was more than a simple distillation of the man's thoughts on the current political situation. Here, in its every detail, was the plan for that 'War of Levels' Shepherd had mentioned earlier. A scheme which would, if implemented, bring the Seven into direct confrontation with the House.

Li Shai Tung flicked through the pages of the report quickly, skimming, picking out phrases that Shepherd had highlighted or underlined, his pulse quickening as he read. Shepherd's tiny, neat handwriting filled almost forty pages, but the meat of it was there, in that opening summary. He read once more what Shepherd had written.

Power is defined only through the exercise of power. For too long now we have refrained from openly exercising our power and that restraint has been taken for weakness by our enemies. In view of developments it might be argued that they have been justified in this view. However, our real weakness is not that we lack the potential, but that we lack the will to act.

We have lost the initiative and allowed our opponents to dictate the subject – even the rules – of the debate. This has resulted in the perpetuation of the belief that change is not merely desirable but inevitable. Moreover, they believe that the natural instrument of that change is the House, therefore they seek to increase the power of the House.

The logic of this process is inexorable. There is nothing but House and Seven, hence the House can grow only at the expense of the Seven.

War is inevitable. It can be delayed but not avoided. And every delay is henceforth to our opponents' advantage. They grow while we diminish. It follows that we must pre-empt their play for power.

We must destroy them now, while we yet have the upper hand.

Li Shai Tung closed the file with a sigh. Shepherd was right. He knew, with a gut certainty, that this was what they should do. But he had said it already. He was not simply T'ang, he was Seven, and the Seven would never act on this. They saw it differently.

'Well?'

'I can keep this?'

'Of course. It was meant for you.'

The T'ang smiled sadly, then looked across at the boy. He spoke to him as he would to his own son, undeferentially, as one adult to another. 'Have you seen this, Ben?'

Shepherd answered for his son. 'You've heard him already. He thinks it nonsense.'

Ben corrected his father. 'Not nonsense. I never said that. I merely said it avoided the real issue.'

'Which is?' Li Shai Tung asked, reaching for his glass.

'Why men are never satisfied.'

The T'ang considered a moment, then laughed softly. 'That has always been so. How can I change what men are?'

'You could make it better for them. They feel boxed in. Not just physically, but mentally, too. They've no dreams. Not one of them feels real any more.'

There was a moment's silence, then Hal Shepherd spoke again. 'You know this, Ben? You've talked to people?'

Ben stared at his father momentarily, then turned his attention back to the T'ang. 'You can't miss it. It's there in all their eyes. There's an emptiness there. An unfilled, unfulfilled space deep inside them. I don't have to talk to them to see that. I have only to watch the media. It's like they're all dead but they can't see it. They're looking for some purpose for it all and they can't find it.'

Li Shai Tung stared back at the boy for a moment, then looked down, chilled by what Ben had said. Was it so? Was it really so? He looked about the room, conscious suddenly of the lowness of the ceiling, of the dark oak beams that divided up the whitewashed walls, the fresh-cut roses in a silver bowl on the table in the corner. He could feel the old wood beneath his fingers, smell the strong pine scent of the fire. All this was real. And he, he too was real, surely? But sometimes, just sometimes...

'And you think we could give them a purpose?'

'No. But you might give them the space to find one for themselves.'

'Ah. Space. Well, Ben, there are more than thirty-nine billion people in Chung Kuo. What practical measures could we possibly take to give space to so many?'

'You mistake me, Li Shai Tung. You take my image too literally.' He put a finger to his brow. 'I meant space up here. That's where they're trapped. The City's only the outward, concrete form of it. But the blueprint – the paradigm – is inside their heads. That's where you've got to give them room. And you can only do that by giving them a sense of direction.'

'Change. That's what you mean, isn't it?'

'No. You need change nothing.'

'Then I don't understand you, Ben. Have you some magic trick in mind?'

'Not at all. I mean only that if the problem is in their heads then the solution can be found in the same place. They want outwardness. They want space, excitement, novelty. Well, why not give it to them? But not out there, in the real world. Give it to them up here, in their heads.'

'But don't they get that? Doesn't the media give them that now?'

'No. I'm talking of something entirely different. Something that will make the walls dissolve. That will make it real to them.' Again he tapped his brow. 'Up here, where it counts.'

The T'ang was about to answer him when there was a knock on the door.

'Come in!' said Shepherd, half turning in his seat.

It was the T'ang's steward. He bowed low to Shepherd and his son, then turned, his head still lowered, to his master. 'Forgive me, *Chieh Hsia*, but you asked me to remind you of your audience with Minister Chao.' Then, with a bow, the steward backed away, closing the door behind him.

Li Shai Tung looked back at Shepherd. 'I'm sorry, Hal, but I must leave soon.'

'Of course...' Shepherd began, but his son interrupted him.

'One last thing, Li Shai Tung.'

The T'ang turned, patient, smiling. 'What is it, Ben?'

'I saw something. This afternoon, in the town.'

'You *saw* something?'

'An execution. And a suicide. Two of the elite guards.'

'Gods!' The T'ang sat forward. 'You saw that?'

'We were upstairs in one of the shops.'

Shepherd broke in. '*We*. You mean Meg was with you?'

Ben nodded, then told what he had seen. At the end Li Shai Tung, his face stricken, turned to Shepherd. 'Forgive me, Hal. This is all my fault. Captain Rosten was acting on my direct orders. However, had I known Ben and Meg would be there...' He shuddered, then turned back to the boy. 'Ben, please forgive me. And ask Meg to forgive me, too. Would that I could undo what has been done.'

For a moment Ben seemed about to say something, then he dropped his eyes and made a small movement of his head. A negation. But what it signified neither man knew.

There was another knock on the door; a signal that the T'ang acknowledged with a few words of Mandarin. Then the two men stood, facing each other, smiling, for a brief moment in perfect accord.

'It has been an honour to have you here, Li Shai Tung. An honour and a pleasure.'

The T'ang's smile broadened. 'The pleasure has been mine, Hal. It is not often I can be myself.'

'Then come again. Whenever you need to be yourself.'

Li Shai Tung let his left hand rest on Shepherd's upper arm a moment, then nodded. 'I shall. I promise you. But come, Hal, I've a gift for you.'

The door opened and two of the T'ang's personal servants came in, carrying the gift. They set it down on the floor in the middle of the room, as the T'ang had instructed them earlier, then backed away, heads lowered. It was a tree. A tiny, miniature apple tree.

Shepherd went across and knelt beside it, then turned and looked back at Li Shai Tung, clearly moved by the T'ang's gesture.

'It's beautiful. It really is, Shai Tung. How did you know I wanted one?'

The T'ang laughed softly. 'I cheated, Hal. I asked Beth. But the gift is for you both. Look carefully. The tree is a twin. It has two intertwined trunks.'

Shepherd looked. 'Ah, yes.' He laughed, aware of the significance. Joined trees were objects of good omen; symbols of conjugal happiness and marital fidelity. More than that, an apple – p'ing, in Mandarin – was a symbol of peace. 'It's perfect, Li Shai Tung. It really is.' He shook his head, overwhelmed, tears forming in his eyes. 'We shall treasure it.'

'And I this.' Li Shai Tung held up Shepherd's file. He smiled, then turned to the boy. 'It was good to talk with you, Ben. I hope we might talk again some time.'

Ben stood and, unexpectedly, gave a small bow to the T'ang.

'My father's right, of course. You should destroy them. Now, while you still can.'

'Ah...' Li Shai Tung hesitated, then nodded. *Maybe so*, he thought, surprised yet again by the child's unpredictability. But he said nothing. Time alone would prove them right or wrong.

He looked back at Shepherd who was standing now. 'I must go, Hal. It would not do to keep Minister Chao waiting.' He laughed. 'You know, Chao has been in my service longer than anyone but Tolonen.'

It was said before he realized it.

'I forget...' he said, with a small, sad laugh.

Shepherd, watching him, shook his head. 'Bring him back, Shai Tung,' he said softly. 'This once, do as your heart bids you.'

The T'ang smiled tightly and held the file more firmly. 'Maybe,' he said. But he knew he would not. It was as he had said. He was T'ang, yes, but he was also Seven.

When the T'ang had gone they stood at the river's edge. The moon was high overhead – a bright, full moon that seemed to float in the dark mirror of the water. The night was warm and still, its silence broken only by the sound – a distant, almost disembodied sound – of the soldiers working on the cottage.

Shepherd squatted down, looking out across the water into the darkness on the other side.

'What did you mean, Ben, earlier? All that business about dissolving walls and making it real. Was that just talk or did you have something real in mind?'

Ben was standing several paces from his father, looking back up the grassy slope to where they had set up arc lamps all around the cottage. The dark figures of the suited men seemed to flit through the glare like objects seen peripherally, in a dream.

'It's an idea I have. Something I've been working on.'

Shepherd turned his head slightly and studied his son a moment. 'You seemed quite confident. As if the thing existed.'

Ben smiled. 'It does. Up here.'

Shepherd laughed and looked down, tugging at the long grass. 'So what is it? I'm interested. And I think the T'ang was interested, too.'

'What did he want?'

A faint breeze ruffled the water, making the moon dance exaggeratedly on the darkness. 'What do you mean?'

'Why was I there?'

Shepherd smiled to himself. He should have known better than to think Ben would not ask that question.

'Because he wanted to see you, Ben. Because he thinks that one day you might help his son.'

'I see. And he was assessing me?'

'You might put it that way.'

Ben laughed. 'I thought as much. Do you think he found me strange?'

'Why should you think that?'

Ben looked directly at his father. 'I know what I am. I've seen enough of the world to know how different I am.'

'On a screen, yes. But not everything's up there on the screen, Ben.'

'No?' Ben looked back up the slope towards the cottage. They were hauling the first of the thin, encasing layers over the top of the frame, the heavily suited men pulling on the guide ropes. 'What don't they show?'

Hal laughed, but let the query pass. Ben was right. He did know what he was, and he *was* different. There was no point in denying that.

'You've no need to follow in my footsteps.'

Ben smiled but didn't look at him. 'You think I'd want that?'

Shepherd felt a twinge of bitterness, then shook his head. 'No, I guess not. In any case, I'd never force that on you. You know that, don't you?'

Ben turned and stared out across the water fixedly. 'Those things don't interest me. The political specifics. The who-runs-what and who-did-what. I would be bored by it all. And what good is a bored advisor? I'd need to care about those things, and I don't.'

'You seemed to care. Earlier, when we were talking about them.'

'That was something different. That was the deeper thing.'

Shepherd laughed. 'Of course. The *deeper* thing.'

Ben looked back at him. 'You deal in surfaces, father, both of you. But the problem's deeper than that. It's inside. Beneath the surface of the skin. It's bred in the blood and bone of men, in the complex web of nerve and muscle and organic tissue. But you... Well, you persist in dealing with only what you see. You treat the blemished skin and let the inner man corrupt.'

Shepherd was watching his son thoughtfully, aware of the gulf that had grown between them these last few years. It was as if Ben had outgrown them all. Had done with childish things. He shrugged. 'Maybe. But that doesn't solve the immediate problem. Those surfaces you dismiss so readily have hard edges. Collide with them and you'll realize that at once. People get hurt, lives get blighted, and those aren't superficial things.'

'It wasn't what I meant.'

'No. Maybe not. And maybe you're right. You'd make a lousy advisor, Ben. You've been made for other things than politics and intrigue.'

He stood, wiping his hands against his trousers. 'You know, there were many things I wanted to do, but I never had the time for them. Pictures I wanted to paint, books I wanted to write, music I wanted to compose. But in serving the T'ang I've had to sacrifice all those and much else besides. I've seen much less of you and Meg than I ought – and far, far too little of your mother. So...' He shrugged. 'If you don't want that kind of life, I understand. I understand only too well. More than that, Ben, I think the world would lose something were you to neglect the gifts you have.'

Ben smiled. 'We'll see.' Then he pointed up the slope. 'I think they've almost finished. That's the third of the isolation skins.'

Shepherd turned and looked back up the slope. The cottage was fully encased now, its cosy shape disguised by the huge, white insulating layers. Only at the front, where the door to the garden was, was its smooth, perfectly geometric shape broken. There they had put the seal-unit; a big cylinder containing the air-pump and the emergency generator.

A dozen suited men were fastening the edges of the insulator to the brace of the frame. The brace was permanently embedded in the earth surrounding the cottage; a crude, heavy piece of metal a foot wide and three inches thick with a second, smaller 'collar' fixed by old-fashioned wing-screws to the base.

The whole strange apparatus had been devised by Ben's great-great-great-grandfather, Amos – the first of the Shepherds to live here – as a precaution against nuclear fallout. But when the Great Third War – 'The War To End It All' as the old man had written in his journal – had failed to materialize, the whole cumbersome isolation unit had been folded up and stored away, only the metal brace remaining, for the amusement of each new generation of Shepherd children.

'Gift-wrapped!' Shepherd joked, beginning to climb the slope.

Ben, following a few paces behind, gave a small laugh, but it was unrelated to his father's comment. He had had an insight. It had been Amos who had designed City Earth. His preliminary architectural sketches hung in a long glass frame on the passage wall inside the cottage, alongside a framed cover of the best-selling PC game, *World Domination*, he'd created.

Nearer the cottage the soldiers had set up an infestation grid, the dull mauve light attracting anything small and winged from the surrounding meadows. Ben stood and watched as a moth, its wings like the dull gauze of an old and faded dress, its body thick and stubby like a miniature cigar, fluttered towards the grid. For a moment it danced in the blue-pink light, mesmerized by the brightness, its translucent wings suffused with purple. Then its wing-tip brushed against the tilted surface. With a spark and a hiss the moth fell, senseless, into the grid, where it flamed momentarily, its wings curling, vanishing in an instant, its body cooking to a dark cinder.

Ben watched a moment, conscious of his own fascination; his ears filled with the brutal music of the grid – the crack and pop and sizzle of the dying creatures, his eyes drawn to each brief, sudden incandescence. And in his mind he formed a pattern of their vivid after-images against the dull mauve light.

'Come, Ben. Come inside.'

He turned. His mother was standing in the doorway, beckoning to him. He smiled then sniffed the air. It was filled with the tart, sweet scent of ozone and burnt insects.

'I was watching.'

'I know.' She came across to him and put her hand on his shoulder. 'It's horrible, isn't it? But necessary, I suppose.'

'Yes.'

But he meant something other by the word: something more than simple agreement. It was both horrible and necessary, if only to prevent the spread of the disease throughout the Domain; but it was just that – the horrible necessity of death – that gave it its fascination. *Is all of life just that?* he asked himself, looking away from the grid, out across the dark, moonlit water of the bay. *Is it all merely one brief, erratic flight into the burning light? And then nothing?*

Ben shivered, not from fear or cold, but from some deeper, more complex response, then turned and looked up at his mother, smiling. 'Okay. Let's go inside.'

The captain of the work party watched the woman and her son go in, then signalled to his men to complete the sealing-off of the cottage. It was nothing to him, of course – orders were orders – yet it had occurred to him several times that it would have been far simpler to evacuate the Shepherds than go through with all this nonsense. He could not for the life of him understand why they should wish to remain inside the cottage while the Domain was dusted with poisons. Still, he had to admit, it was a neat job. Old man Amos had known what he was up to.

He walked across and inspected the work thoroughly. Then, satisfied that the seal was airtight, he pulled the lip-mike up from under his chin. 'Okay. We're finished here. You can start the sweep.'

Six miles away, at the mouth of the estuary, the four big transporters, converted specially for the task, lifted one by one from the pad and began to form up in a line across the river. Then, at a signal, they began, moving slowly down the estuary, a thin cloud – colourless, like fine powdered snow – drifting down behind them.

Chapter 37

AUGUSTUS

I t was just after ten in the morning, yet the sun already blazed down from a vast, deep blue sky that seemed washed clean of all impurities. Sunlight burnished the surface of the grey-green water, making it seem dense and yet clear, like melted glass. The tide was high but on the turn, lapping sluggishly against the rocks at the river's edge.

In midstream Meg let Ben take the oars from her, changing seats with him nimbly as the boat drifted slowly about. Then she sat back, watching him as he strove to right their course, his face a mask of patient determination, the muscles of his bare, tanned arms tensing and untensing. Ben clenched his teeth then pulled hard on the right-hand oar, turning the prow slowly towards the distant house, the dark, slick-edged blade biting deep into the glaucous, muscular flow as he hauled the boat about in a tight arc.

'Are you sure it's all right?'

Ben grimaced, concentrating, inwardly weighing the feel of the boat against the strong pull of the current. 'She'll never know,' he answered. 'Who'll tell her?'

It wasn't a threat. He knew he could trust her to say nothing to their mother. Meg looked down briefly, smiling, pleased that he trusted her. Then she sat there, quiet, content to watch him, to see the broad river stretching away beyond him, the white-painted cottages of the village dotted against the broad green flank of the hill, while at her back the house grew slowly nearer.

Solitary, long abandoned, it awaited them.

The foreshore was overgrown. Weeds grew waist-high in the spaces between the rocks. Beyond, the land was level for thirty yards or so then climbed, slowly at first, then steeply. The house wasn't visible from where they stood, in the cool beneath the branches, and even further along, where the path turned, following the contours of the shoreline, they could see only a small part of it, jutting up, white between the intense green of the surrounding trees.

The land was strangely, unnaturally silent. Meg looked down through the trees. Below them, to their right, was the cove, the dark mouth of the cave almost totally submerged, the branches of the overhanging trees only inches above the surface of the water. It made her feel odd. Not quite herself.

'Come on,' said Ben, looking back at her. 'We've not long. Mother will be back by two.'

They went up. A path had been cut from the rock. Rough-hewn steps led up steeply, hugging an almost sheer cliff face. They had to force their way through a tangle of bushes and branches. At the top they came out into a kind of clearing. There was concrete underfoot, cracked but reasonably clear of vegetation. It was a road. To their left it led up into the trees. To their right it ended abruptly, only yards from where they stood, at an ornate cast-iron gate set into a wall.

They went across and stood there, before the gate, looking in.

The house lay beyond the gate; a big, square, three-storey building of white stone, with a steeply pitched roof of grey slate. They could see patches of it through the overrun front garden. Here, more noticeably than else-where, nature had run amok. A stone fountain lay in two huge grey pieces, split asunder by an ash that had taken seed long ago in the disused fissure at its centre. Elsewhere the regular pattern of a once elaborate garden could be vaguely sensed, underlying the chaotic sprawl of new growth.

'Well?' she said, looking up at him. 'What now?'

The wall was too high to climb. The gate seemed strong and solid, with four big hinges set into the stone. A big, thick-linked steel chain was wrapped tightly over the keyhole, secured by a fist-sized padlock.

Ben smiled. 'Watch.'

Taking a firm hold of two of the upright bars, he shook the gate vigor-ously, then gave it one last sharp forward thrust. With a crash it fell inward, then swung sideways, twisting against the restraining chain.

Ben stepped over it, then reached back for her. 'The iron was rotten,' he said, pointing to the four places in the stone where the hinges had snapped sheer off.

She nodded, understanding at once what he was really saying to her. *Be careful here. Judge nothing by its appearance.*

He turned from her.

She followed, more cautious now, making her way through the thick sprawl of greenery towards the house.

A verandah ran the length of the front of the house. At one end it had collapsed. One of the four mock-doric pillars had fallen and now lay, like the broken leg of a stone giant, half-buried in the window frame behind where it had previously stood. The glass-framed roof of the verandah was cracked in several places where branches of nearby trees had pushed against it, and the whole of the wooden frame – the elaborately carved side pieces, the stanchions, rails and planking – was visibly rotten. Ben stood before the shallow flight of steps that led up to the main entrance, his head tilted back as he studied the frontage.

'It's not what I expected,' he said as she came alongside him. 'It seems a lot grander from the river. And bigger. A real fortress of a place.'

She took his arm. 'I don't know. I think it is rather grand. Or was.'

He turned and looked at her. 'Did you bring the lamp?'

She nodded.

'Good. Though I doubt there'll be much to see. The house has been boarded up more than eighty years now.'

She was silent a moment, thoughtful, and knew he was thinking the same thing. Augustus. The mystery of this house had something to do with their great-uncle, Augustus.

'Well?' she prompted after a moment. 'Shall we go inside?'

'Yes. But not this way. There's another door round the side. We'll get in there, through the kitchens.'

She stared at him a moment, then understood. He had already studied plans of the old house. Which meant he had planned this visit for some while. But why this morning? Was it something to do with the soldiers' deaths? Or was it something else? She knew they had had a visitor last night, but no one had told her who it was or why they'd come. Whatever, Ben had seemed disturbed first thing when she had gone to wake him. He had been up already. She had found him sitting there, hunched up on his bed, his arms wrapped about his knees, staring out through the open window at the bay. That same mood was on him even now as he stood there looking up at the house.

'What exactly are we looking for?'

'Clues...'

She studied his face a moment longer but it gave nothing away. His answer was unlike him. He was always so specific, so certain. But today he was different. It was as if he was looking for something so ill defined, so vaguely comprehended that even he could not say what it was.

'Come on, then,' he said suddenly. 'Let's see what ghosts we'll find.'

She laughed quietly, that same feeling she had had staring down at the cove through the trees – that sense of being not quite herself – returning to her. It was not fear, for she was never afraid when she was with Ben, but something else. Something to do with this side of the water. With the wildness here. As if it reflected something in herself. Some deeper, hidden thing.

'What do you think we'll find?' she called out to him as she followed him, pushing through the dense tangle of bushes and branches. 'Have you any idea at all?'

'None,' he yelled back. 'Maybe there's nothing at all. Maybe it's an empty shell. But then why would they board it up? Why bother if it's empty? Why not just leave it to rot?'

She caught up with him. 'From the look of it it's rotted anyway.'

Ben glanced at her. 'It'll be different inside.'

A broad shaft of daylight breached the darkness. She watched Ben fold the shutter into its recess, then move along to release and fold back another, then another, until all four were open. Now the room was filled with light. A big room. Much bigger than she'd imagined it in the dark. A long wooden worksurface filled most of the left-hand wall, its broad top cleared. Above it, on the wall itself, were great tea-chest-sized oak cupboards. At the far end four big ovens occupied the space, huge pipes leading up from them into the ceiling overhead. Against the right-hand wall, beneath the windows, was a row of old machines and, beside the door, a big enamel sink.

She watched Ben bend down and examine the pipes beneath the sink.

They were green with moss, red with rust. He rubbed his finger against the surface of one of them, then put the finger gingerly to his lips. She saw him frown then sniff the finger, his eyes intense, taking it all in.

He turned, then, surprisingly, he laughed. 'Look.'

There, in the middle of the white-tiled floor, was a beetle. A rounded, black-shelled thing the size of a brooch.

'Is it alive?' she asked, expecting it to move at any moment.

He shrugged, then went across and picked it up. But it was only a husk, the shell of a beetle. 'It's been dead years,' he said.

Yes, she thought, *maybe since the house was sealed*.

There was another door behind them, next to an old, faded print that was rotten with damp beneath its mould-spattered glass. Beyond the door was a narrow corridor that led off to the right. They went through, moving slowly, cautiously, side by side, using their lamps to light the way ahead.

They explored, throwing open the shutters in each of the big rooms, but there was nothing. The rooms were empty, their dusty floorboards bare, only the dark outlines of long-absent pictures interrupting the blankness of the walls.

No sign of life. Only the husk, the empty shell of what they'd come for.

Augustus. Not Amos's son, Augustus, but his namesake. His grandson. No one talked of that Augustus. Yet it was that very absence that made him so large in their imaginations. Ever since Ben had first found that single mention of him in the journals. But what had he been? What had he done that he could not be talked of?

She shivered and looked at Ben. He was watching her, as if he knew what she was thinking.

'Shall we go up?'

She nodded.

Upstairs it was different. There the rooms were filled with ancient furniture, preserved under white sheets, as if the house had been closed up for the summer, while its occupant was absent.

In one of the big rooms at the front of the house, Meg stood beside one of the huge, open shutters, staring out through the trees at the river. Light glimmered on the water through gaps in the heavy foliage. Behind her she could hear Ben, pulling covers off chairs and tables, searching, restlessly searching for something.

'What happened here?'

Ben stopped and looked up from what he was doing. 'I'm not sure. But it's the key to things. I know it is.'

She turned and met his eyes. 'How do you know?'

'Because it's the one thing they won't talk about. Gaps. Always look for the gaps, Meg. That's where the truth is. That's where they hide all the important stuff.'

'Like what?'

His face hardened momentarily, then he looked away.

She looked down, realizing just how keyed up he was; how close he had come to snapping at her.

'There's nothing here,' he said. 'Let's go up again.'

She nodded, then followed, knowing there would be nothing. The house was empty. Or as good as. But she was wrong.

Ben laughed, delighted, then stepped inside the room, shining his lamp about the walls. It was a library. Or a study maybe. Whichever, the walls were filled with shelves, and the shelves with books. Old books, of paper and card and leather. Ben hurried to the shutters and threw them open, then turned and stared back into the room. There was a door, two windows and a full-length mirror on the wall to his left. Apart from that there were only shelves. Books and more books, filling every inch of the wall-space.

'Whose were they?' she asked, coming alongside him; sharing his delight.

He pulled a book down at random, then another. The bookplates were all the same. He showed her one.

She read the words aloud. 'This book is the property of Augustus Raedwald Shepherd.' She laughed, then looked up into Ben's face. 'Then he lived here. But I thought...'

Ben shrugged. 'I don't know. Maybe he used this house to work in.'

She turned, looking about her. There were books scattered all about their cottage, but not a tenth as many as were here. There must have been five, maybe ten thousand of them. She laughed, astonished. There were probably more books here – *real* books – than there were in the rest of Chung Kuo.

Ben was walking slowly up and down the room, looking about him curiously. 'It's close,' he said softly. 'It's very close now.'

What's close? she wanted to ask. But the question would only anger him. He knew no better than she.

Then, suddenly, he stopped and turned and almost ran outside into the corridor again. 'There!' he said, exultant, and she watched him pace out the distance from the end of the corridor to the doorway. Fifteen paces. He went inside and did the same. Twelve. Only twelve!

She saw at once. The mirror. The mirror was a door. A way through.

He went to it at once, looking for a catch, a way of releasing it, but there was nothing. Frustrated, he pulled books down from the shelf and knocked at the wall behind them. It was brick, solid brick.

For a moment he stood before the mirror, staring into it. Then he laughed. 'Of course!'

He turned and pointed it out to her. 'Level with the top of the mirror. That row of books opposite. Look, Meg. Tell me what you see.'

She went across and looked. They were novels. Famous novels. *Ulysses, Nostromo, Tess of the D'Urbervilles, Vanity Fair, Howard's End, Bleak House, Daniel Martin, Orlando* and others. She turned back to him. 'I don't understand. What am I looking for?'

'It's a cryptogram. Look at the order. The first letter of the titles.'

She looked, doing as he said. D.A.E.H.R.E. V.O.N.O.T.T.U.B. Then she understood. It was mirrored. You had to reverse the letters.

He laughed, ahead of her, and reached up to find the button.

With a faint hiss of escaping air the mirror sprang free. Beyond it was a room. Ben shone his lamp inside. It seemed like a smaller version of the library, the walls covered with books. But in its centre, taking up most of the floor space, was a desk.

He shone his lamp over the desk's surface, picking out four objects. A letter knife, an ink-block, a framed photograph and a large, folio-sized journal. The light rested on the last of these for some while, then moved upward, searching the end wall.

Meg came alongside him. 'What are you looking for?'

'A window. There must have been a window.'

'Why? If he really wanted to keep this room a secret, having no window onto the outside would be the best way, surely?'

He looked at her, then nodded. But she, watching him, was surprised that he hadn't seen it for himself. It was as if, now that he'd found it, he was transfixed by his discovery. She shone her lamp into his face.

'Meg...' He pushed her hand away.

She moved past him, into the room, then turned back, facing him.

'Here.' She handed him the journal, knowing, even before he confirmed it, whose it was. Augustus. There was a space for it on the shelf on her father's study, amongst the others there. She recognized the tooled black leather of its cover.

Ben opened it. He turned a page, then smiled and looked up at her.

'Am I right?' she asked.

In answer he turned the book and showed her the page. She laughed uneasily, shocked, then looked back up at him. It was a picture of Ben. An almost perfect portrait of him. And underneath, in Ben's own handwriting, was a name and a date.

'Augustus Shepherd. Anno Domini 2120.'

'But that's you. Your handwriting.'

He shook his head. 'No. But it's a clue. We're getting close, Meg. Very close.'

Beth Shepherd set the two bags down on the kitchen table then went to the garden door and undid the top catch. Pushing the top half back, she leaned out and called to the children.

'Ben! Meg! I'm back!'

She went inside again and busied herself, filling the cupboards from the bags. Only when she had finished did she go to the door again and, releasing the bottom catch, go out into the rose garden.

There was no sign of them. Perhaps they're indoors, she thought. But then they would have heard her, surely? She called again, moving out through the gate until she stood at the top of the lower garden that sloped down to the bay. She put her hand up to her eyes, searching the sunlit meadows for a sign of them.

'Strange...' she muttered, then turned and went back inside. She knew she was back quite early, but they usually came when she called, knowing she would have brought something special for each of them.

She took the two gifts from her handbag and set them on the table. An old-fashioned paper book for Ben – one he had specifically asked for – on sensory deprivation. And for Meg a tiny Han ivory. A delicately carved globe.

Beth smiled to herself, then went down the steps, into the relative darkness of the dining room.

'Ben...? Meg?'

She stopped at the bottom of the steps and listened. Strange. Very strange. Where could they be? Ben had said nothing about going into town. In any case, it was only a little after twelve. They weren't due to finish their lessons for another twenty minutes.

Curious, she went upstairs and searched the rooms. Nothing. Not even a note on Ben's computer.

She went out and put her hand up to her brow a second time, searching the meadows more thoroughly this time. Then she remembered Peng Yu-wei. The android tutor had a special location unit. She could trace where they were by pinpointing him on Hal's map.

Relieved, she went back upstairs, into Hal's study, and called the map up onto the screen. She waited a moment for the signal to appear somewhere on the grid, then leaned forward to key the search sequence again, thinking she must have made a mistake. But no. There was no trace.

Beth felt her stomach flip over. 'Gods...'

She ran down the stairs and out.

'Ben! Meg! Where are you?'

The meadows were silent, empty. A light breeze stirred the waters of the bay. She looked. Of course, the bay. She set off down the slope, forcing herself not to run, telling herself again and again that it was all right; that her fears were unfounded. They were sensible children. And, anyway, Peng Yu-wei was with them.

Where the lawn ended she stopped and looked out across the bay, scanning the water for any sign of life. Then she turned and eased herself over the lip, clambered down the old wooden steps set into the clay wall, and ran across towards the jetty.

The rowboat was gone.

Where? She couldn't understand it. Where? Then, almost peripherally, she noticed something. Off to the far left of her, jutting from the water, revealed by the ebb of the tide.

She climbed up again, then ran along the shoreline until she was standing at the nearest point to it. It lay there, fifteen, maybe twenty ch'i from the shore, part-embedded in the mudbank, part-covered by the receding water. She knew what it was at once. And knew, for a certainty, that Ben had done this to it.

The android lay unnaturally in the water, almost sitting up, one shoulder, part of its upper arm and the side of its head projecting above the surface. It did not float, like a corpse would float, but rested there, solid and heavy, its torn clothing flapping about it like weeds.

'Poor thing,' she might have said another time, but now any sympathy she had for the machine was swamped by her fears for her children.

She looked up sharply, her eyes going immediately to the far shore and to the house on the crest above the cove. They had been forbidden. But that would not stop Ben. No. The sight of Peng Yu-wei in the water told her that.

She turned, her throat constricted now, her heart pounding in her breast, and began to run back up the slope towards the cottage. And as she ran her voice hissed from her, heavy with anxiety and pain.

'Let them be safe! Please, gods, let them be safe!'

Ben sat at the desk, reading from the journal. Meg stood behind him, at his shoulder, holding the two lamps steady above the page, following Ben's finger as it moved from right to left, up and down the columns of cyphers.

Ben had explained it to her. He had shown her how the frontispiece illustration was the key to it. In the illustration a man sat by a fireplace, reading a newspaper, his face obscured, the scene reflected at an angle in the mirror over the mantelpiece. Using the magnifying glass he had found in the left-hand drawer, Ben had shown her how the print of the reflected newspaper was subtly different from the one the man held. Those differences formed the basis of the cypher. She understood that – even the parts about the governing rules that made the cypher change – but her mind was too slow, too inflexible to hold and use what she'd been shown.

It was as if all this was a special key – a coded lexicon – designed for one mind only. Ben's. It was as if Augustus knew that Ben would come. As if he had seen it clearly, as in a glass. It reminded her of the feeling she had had in the room below this one, stood there amongst the shrouded furniture; that the house was not abandoned, merely boarded up temporarily, awaiting its occupant's return.

And now he was back.

She shuddered, and the light danced momentarily across the page, making Ben look up.

He smiled and closed the journal, then stood and moved past her, leaving the big, leather-bound book on the desk.

Meg stood there a moment, staring at the journal, wondering what it said, knowing Ben would tell her when he wanted to. Then she picked it up and turned, following Ben out.

Always following, she realized. But the thought pleased her. She knew he needed her to be there – a mirror for his words, his thoughts, his dark, unworded ambitions. She, with her mere nine years of experience, knew him better than anyone. Understood him as no one else could understand him. No one living, anyway.

He was standing there, at the window, looking down thoughtfully through the broad crowns of the trees.

'What is it?' she asked.

'I'm trying to work out where the garden is.'

She understood at once. There had been a picture towards the back of the journal – a portrait of a walled garden. She had thought it fanciful, maybe allegorical, but Ben seemed to think it was an actuality – somewhere here, near the house.

She stared at the book-filled wall above the desk, then turned back, seeing how he was looking past her at the same spot. He smiled and moved his eyes to her face.

'Of course. There was a door at the end of the bottom corridor.'

She nodded. 'Let's go down.'

The door was unlocked. Beyond it lay the tiny garden, the lawn neatly trimmed, delphinia and gladioli, irises and hemerocallis in bloom in the dark earth borders. And there, beneath the back wall, the headstone, the white marble carved into the shape of an oak, its trunk exaggeratedly thick, its crown a great cumulus.

'Yes,' Ben said softly. 'I knew he would be here.'

He bent down beside the stone and reached out to touch and trace the indented lettering.

AUGUSTUS RAEDWALD SHEPHERD

Born December 7 2106

Deceased August 15 2122

Oder jener stirbt und ists.

Meg frowned. 'That date is wrong, surely, Ben?'

He shook his head, not looking at her. 'No. He was fifteen when he killed himself.'

'Then...' But she still didn't understand. Only fifteen? Then, belatedly, she realized what he had said: the *whole* of what he had said. 'Killed himself?'

There was a door set into the wall behind the stone. A simple wooden door, painted red, with a latch high up. Ben had stood up, facing it, and was staring at it in his usual intent manner.

Doors, she thought, *always another door*. And behind each door something new and unexpected. Augustus, for instance. She had never dreamed he would be so much like Ben. Like a twin.

'Shall we?' Ben asked, looking at her. 'Before we set off back? There's time.'

She looked down at the headstone, a strange feeling of unease nagging at her. She was tempted to say no, to tell him to leave it, but why not? Ben was right. There was time. Plenty of time before they'd be missed.

'Okay,' she said quietly. 'But then we go straight back. All right?'

He smiled at her and nodded, then went to the door, stretching to reach the latch.

It was a workroom. There were shelves along one wall on which were a number of things: old-fashioned screwdrivers and hammers, saws and pliers; a box of nails and an assortment of glues; locks and handles, brackets and a tray of different keys. A spade and a pitchfork stood against the wall beneath, beside a pair of boots, the mud on them dried, flaky to the touch.

Meg looked around her. At the far end, against the wall, was a strange upright shape, covered by an old bedspread. Above it, hanging from an old iron chain, hung a bevelled mirror. As she watched, Ben went across and threw the cloth back. It was a piano. An old upright piano. He lifted the lid and stared at the keys a while.

'I wonder if it's...'

Some sense – not precognition, nor even the feeling of danger – made her speak out. 'No, Ben. Please. Don't touch it.'

He played a note. A chord. Or what should have been a chord. Each note was flat, a harsh, cacophonic noise. The music of the house. Discordant.

She heard the chain break with a purer note than any sounded by her brother; heard the mirror slither then crash against the top of the piano;

then stepped forward, her hand raised to her mouth in horror, as the glass shattered all about him.

'Ben!!!'

Her scream echoed out onto the water beyond the house.

Inside the room there was a moment of utter stillness. Then she was at his side, sobbing breathlessly, muttering to him again and again. 'What have you done, Ben? What have you done?'

Shards of glass littered his hair and shoulders. His cheek was cut and a faint dribble of blood ran towards the corner of his mouth. But Ben was staring down at where his left hand had been only a moment before, sounding the chord. It still lay there on the keys, the fingers extended to form the shape. But the arm now ended in a bloodied stump. Cut clean, the blood still pumping.

For a moment she did nothing, horrified, her lips drawn back from her teeth, watching how he turned the stump, observing it, his eyes filled with wonder at the thing he had accidentally done. He was gritting his teeth against the pain, keeping it at bay while he studied the stump, the severed hand.

Then, coming to herself again, she pressed the stud at her neck and sounded the alarm.

Much later Meg stood at the bottom of the slope, looking out across the water.

Night had already fallen, but in one place its darkness was breached. Across the bay flames leapt high from the burning house and she could hear the crackling of burning vegetation, the sudden sharp retorts as wood popped and split.

Smoke lay heavy on the far side of the water, laced eerily with threads of light from the blaze. She could see dark shapes moving against the brilliance; saw one of the Security craft rise up sharply, its twin beams cutting the air in front of it.

'Meg? Come inside!'

She turned, looking back up the slope towards the cottage. Lamps burned at several of the windows, throwing faint spills of light across the white-painted stonework. Her father stood there, a dark, familiar figure, framed in the light of the doorway.

'I'm coming, daddy. Just a moment longer. *Please.*'

He nodded, somewhat reluctantly, then turned away.

Meg faced the blaze again, looking out across the dark glass of the bay. She thought she could see small shapes in the uprush of flame, like insects burning, crackling furiously as their shells ignited in a sudden flare of brilliance. *Books*, she thought, *all those books...*

Ben was upstairs, in his bed. They had frozen the stump but they had not saved the hand. He would need a new one now.

She could still hear the chord he had sounded; still see his fingers spreading to form the shape. She looked away from the blaze. After-images flickered in the darkness. The eye moved on, but the image remained. For a time.

She went indoors. Went up and saw him where he lay, propped up with a mound of pillows behind his back. He was awake, fully conscious. She sat at his bedside and was silent for a time, letting him watch her.

'What's it like?'

'Beautiful. The way the light's reflected in the dark water. It's...'

'I know,' he said, as if he'd seen it too.

She looked away, noticing how the fire's light flickered in the window pane; how it cast a mottled, ever-changing pattern against the narrow opening.

'I'm glad you did what you did,' he said, more softly than before. 'I would have stood there and watched myself bleed to death. I owe you my life.'

It was not entirely true. He owed his life to their mother. If Beth had not come back early then what she had done would not have mattered.

'I only wrapped it with the sheet,' she said. But she saw how he was looking at her, his eyes piercing her. She could see he was embarrassed. Yet there was something else there, too – something that she had never seen in him before – and it touched her deeply. She felt her lips pucker and her eyes grow moist.

'Hey, little sis, don't cry.'

He had never called her that before; neither had he ever touched her as he touched her now, his good right hand caressing both of hers where they lay atop the bedclothes. She shuddered and looked down.

'I'm fine,' he said, as if in answer to something she had said, his hand squeezing both of hers. 'Father says they can graft a new hand onto the nerve ends. It'll work as good as new. Maybe better.'

She found she could not look up at him. If she did she would burst into tears, and she didn't want him to see her weakness. He had been so strong, so brave. The pain – it must have been awful.

'You know, the worst thing was that I missed it.'

'Missed what?'

'I didn't see it,' he said, and there was genuine surprise in his voice. 'I wasn't quick enough. I heard the chain break and I looked up, but I missed the accident. It was done before I looked down again. My hand was no longer part of me. When I looked it was already separate, there on the keyboard.'

He laughed. A queer little sound.

Meg looked at him. He was staring at the stub of his left arm. It was neatly capped, like the end of an old cane. Silvered and neutral. Reduced to a thing.

'I didn't see it,' he insisted. 'The glass. The cut. And I felt... only a sudden absence. Not pain, but...'

She could see that he was searching for the right words, the very thing that would describe what he had felt, what he had experienced at that moment. But it evaded him. He shrugged and gave up.

'I love you, Ben.'

'I know,' he said, and seemed to look at her as if to gauge how love looked in a person's eyes. As if to place it in his memory.

After Meg had gone he lay there, thinking things through.

He had said nothing to her about what was in the journal. For once he felt no urge to share his knowledge with her. It would harm her, as it had harmed him: not on the surface, as the mirror had, but deeper, where his true self lived. In the darkness.

He felt angered that he had not been told; that Hal had not trusted him enough. More than that, he felt insulted that they had hidden it from him. Oh, he could see why it was important for Meg not to know; she responded to things in a different way. But to hide it? He clenched his fists, feeling the ghostly movement in the hand he had lost. Didn't they know? Didn't they understand him, even now? How could he make sense of it all unless he could first solve the riddle of himself?

It was all there, in the journal. Some of it explicit, the rest hidden teasingly away – cyphers within cyphers – as if for his eyes alone.

He had heard Augustus's voice, speaking clearly in his head, as if direct across the years. 'I am a failed experiment,' he had said. 'Old Amos botched me when he made me from his seed. He got more than he bargained for.'

It was true. They were all an experiment. All the Shepherd males. Not sons and fathers, uncles and grandfathers, but brothers every last one of them – all the fruit of Amos's seed.

Ben laughed bitterly. It explained so much. For Augustus was his twin. Ben knew it for a certainty. He had proof.

There, in the back of the journal, were the breeding charts – a dozen complex genetic patterns, each drawn in the tiniest of hands, one to a double page; each named and dated, Ben's own amongst them. A whole line of Shepherds, each one the perfect advisor for his T'ang.

Augustus had known somehow. Had worked it out. He had realized what he was meant for. What task he had been bred for.

But Augustus had been a rebel. He had defied his father; refusing to be trained as the servant of a T'ang. Worse, he had sired a child by his own sister, in breach of the careful plans Amos had laid. His mirror had become his mate. Furious, his 'father', Robert, had made him a prisoner in the house, forbidding him the run of the Domain until he changed his ways, but Augustus had remained defiant. He had preferred death to compromise.

Or so it seemed. There was no entry for that day.

There were footsteps on the stairs. He tensed, then made himself relax. He had been expecting this; had been rehearsing what he would say.

Hal stood in the doorway, looking in 'Ben? Can I come in?'

Ben stared back at him, unable to keep the anger from his face. 'Hello, elder brother.'

Hal seemed surprised. Then he understood. He had confiscated the journal, but he could not confiscate what was in Ben's head. It did not matter that Ben could not physically see the pages of the journal: in his mind he could turn them anyway and read the tall columns of cyphers.

'It isn't like that,' he began, but Ben interrupted him, a sharp edge to his voice.

'Don't lie to me. I've had enough of lies. Tell me who I am.'

'You're my son.'

Ben sat forward, but this time Hal got in first. 'No, Ben. You're wrong. It ended with Augustus. He was the last. You're my son, Ben. Mine and your mother's.'

Ben made to speak, then fell silent, watching the man. Then he looked down. Hal was not lying. Not intentionally. He spoke as he believed. But he was wrong. Ben had seen the charts, the names, the dates of birth. Amos's great experiment was still going on.

He let out a long, shuddering breath. 'Okay... But tell me. How did Augustus die? Why did he kill himself?'

'He didn't.'

'Then how did he die?'

'He had leukaemia.'

That too was a lie, for there was no mention of ill health in the journal. But again Hal believed it for the truth. His eyes held nothing back from Ben.

'And the child? What happened to the child?'

Hal laughed. 'What child? What are you talking about?'

Ben looked down. Then it was all a lie. Hal knew nothing. Nor would he learn anything from the journal unless Meg gave him the key to it; for the cypher was a special one, transforming itself constantly page by page as the journal progressed.

'Nothing,' he said finally. 'I was mistaken.'

He lifted his eyes. Saw how concerned Hal was.

'I'm sorry,' he said. 'I didn't mean to trouble anyone.'

'No...'

Then, strangely, Hal looked down and laughed. 'You know, Ben, when I saw Peng Yu-wei stuck there in the mud, all my anger drained from me.' He looked up and met Ben's eyes, his voice changing, becoming more serious. 'I understand why you did it. Believe me. And I meant what I said the other night. You can be your own man. Live your own life. It's up to you whether you serve or not. Neither I nor the great T'ang himself will force you.'

Ben studied his brother – the man he had always thought of as his father – and saw suddenly that it did not matter what he was in reality, for Hal Shepherd had become what he believed he was. His father. A free man, acting freely, choosing freely. For him the illusion was complete. It had become the truth.

It was a powerful lesson. One Ben could use. He nodded. 'Then I choose to be your son, if that's all right?'

Hal smiled and reached out to take his good hand. 'That's all I ever wanted.'

PART 9 ICE AND FIRE

SUMMER 2201

'War is the highest form of struggle for resolving contradictions, when they have developed to a certain stage, between classes, nations, states, or political groups, and it has existed ever since the emergence of private property and of classes.'
—Mao Tse Tung, *Problems Of Strategy in China's Revolutionary War* (December 1936)

'It is our historical duty to eradicate all opposition to change. To cauterize the cancers that create division. The future cannot come into being until the past is dead. Chung Kuo cannot live until the world of petty nation states, of factions and religions, is dead and buried beneath the ice. Let us have no pity then. Our choice is made. Ice and fire. The fire to cauterize, the ice to cover over. Only by such means will the world be freed from enmity.'
—Tsao Ch'un, *Address to his Ministers*, (May 2068)

CHUNG KUO

Chapter 38

THE SADDLE

The old T'ang backed away, his hands raised before him, his face rigid with fear.

'Put down the knife, *erh tzu!* For pity's sake!'

A moment before there had been laughter; now the tension in the room seemed unendurable. Only the hiss and wheeze of Tsu Tiao's laboured breathing broke the awful silence.

In the narrow space between the pillars, Tsu Ma circled his father slowly, knife in hand, his face set, determined. On all sides T'ang and courtier alike – all Han, all Family – were crowded close, looking on, their faces tense, unreadable. Only one, a boy of eight, false whiskered and rouged up, his clothes identical to those of the old T'ang, showed any fear. He stood there, wide-eyed, one hand gripping the arm of the taller boy beside him.

'Erh Tzu!' the old man pleaded, falling to his knees. *My son!* He bowed his head, humbling himself. 'I beg you, Tsu Ma! Have mercy on an old man!'

All eyes were on Tsu Ma now. All saw the shudder that rippled through the big man like a wave; the way his chin jutted forward and his face contorted in agony as he steeled himself to strike. Then it was done and the old man slumped forward, the knife buried deep in his chest.

There was a sigh like the soughing of the wind, then Tsu Ma was surrounded. Hands clapped his back or held his hand or touched his shoulder briefly. 'Well done, Tsu Ma,' each said before moving on, expecting no answer; seeing how he stood there, his arms limp at his sides, his broad chest heaving, his eyes locked on the fallen figure on the floor beneath him.

Slowly the great room emptied until only Tsu Ma, the six T'ang and the two young boys remained.

Li Shai Tung stood before him, staring into his face, a faint smile of sadness mixed with satisfaction on his lips. He spoke softly, 'Well done, Tsu Ma. It's hard, I know. The hardest thing a man can do...'

Slowly Tsu Ma's eyes focused on him. He swallowed deeply and another great shudder racked his body. Pain flickered like lightning across the broad, strong features of his face, and then he spoke, his voice curiously small, like a child's. 'Yes... but it was so hard to do, Shai Tung. It... it was just like him.'

Li Shai Tung shivered but kept himself perfectly still, his face empty of what he was feeling. He ached to reach out and hold Tsu Ma close, to comfort him, but knew it would be wrong. It was hard, as Tsu Ma now realized, but it was also necessary.

Since the time of Tsao Ch'un it had been so. To become T'ang the son must kill the father. Must become his own man. Only then would he be free to offer his father the respect he owed him.

'Will you come through, Tsu Ma?'

Tsu Ma's eyes had never left Li Shai Tung's face, yet they had not been seeing him. Now they focused again. He gave the barest nod, then, with one last, appalled look at the body on the floor, moved towards the dragon doorway.

In the room beyond, the real Tsu Tiao was laid out atop a great, tiered pedestal on a huge bed spread with silken sheets of gold. Slowly and with great dignity, Tsu Ma climbed the steps until he stood there at his dead father's side. The old man's fine grey hair had been brushed and plaited, his cheeks delicately rouged, his beard brushed out straight, his nails painted a brilliant pearl. He was dressed from head to foot in white. A soft white muslin that, when Tsu Ma knelt and gently brushed it with his fingertips, reminded him strangely of springtime and the smell of young girls.

You're dead, Tsu Ma thought, gazing tenderly into his father's face. *You're really dead, aren't you?* He bent forward and gently brushed the cold lips with his own, then sat back on his heels, shivering, toying with the ring that rested, heavy and unfamiliar, like a saddle on the first finger of his right hand. *And now it's me.*

He turned his head, looking back at the six T'ang standing amongst the pillars, watching him. *You know how I feel*, he thought, looking from face to face. *Each one of you. You've been here before me, haven't you?*

For the first time he understood why the Seven were so strong. They had this in common: each knew what it was to kill their father; knew the reality of it in their bones. Tsu Ma looked back at the body – the real body, not the lifelike GenSyn copy he had 'killed' – and understood. He had been blind to it before, but now he saw it clearly. It was not life that connected them so firmly, but death. Death that gave them such a profound and lasting under-standing of each other.

He stood again and turned, facing them, then went down amongst them. At the foot of the steps they greeted him; each in his turn bowing before Tsu Ma; each bending to kiss the ring of power he now wore; each embracing him warmly before repeating the same eight words.

'Welcome, Tsu Ma. Welcome, T'ang of West Asia.'

When the brief ceremony was over, Tsu Ma turned and went across to the two boys. Li Yuan was much taller than when he had last seen him. He was entering that awkward stage of early adolescence and had become a somewhat ungainly-looking boy. Even so, it was hard to believe that his birthday in two days' time would be only his twelfth. There was something almost unnatural in his manner that made Tsu Ma think of childhood tales of changelings and magic spells and other such nonsense. He seemed so old, so knowing. So unlike the child whose body he wore. Tsu Tao Chu, in contrast, seemed younger than his eight years and wore his heart embroi-dered like a peacock on his sleeve. He stood there in his actor's costume, bearded, his brow heavily lined with black make-up pencil, yet still his youth shone through, in his eyes and in the quickness of his movements.

Tsu Ma reached out and ruffled his hair, smiling for the first time since the killing. 'Did it frighten you, Tao Chu?'

The boy looked down, abashed. 'I thought...'

Tsu Ma knelt down and held his shoulders, nodding, remembering how he had felt the first time he had seen the ritual, not then knowing what was happening, or why.

Tao Chu looked up and met his eyes. 'It seemed so real, Uncle Ma. For a moment I thought it was Grandpa Tiao.'

Tsu Ma smiled. 'You were not alone in that, Nephew Chu.'

Tao Chu was his dead brother's third and youngest son and Tsu Ma's favourite; a lively, ever-smiling boy with the sweetest, most joyful laugh. At the ritual earlier Tao Chu had impersonated Tsu Tiao, playing out scenes from the old T'ang's life before the watching Court. The practice was as old as the Middle Kingdom itself and formed one link in the great chain of tradition, but it was more than mere ritual, it was a living ceremony, an act of deep respect and celebration, almost a poem to the honoured dead. For the young actor, however, it was a confusing, not to say unnerving experience, to find the dead man unexpectedly there, in the seat of honour, watching the performance.

'Do you understand why I had to kill the copy, Tao Chu?'

Tao Chu glanced quickly at Li Yuan, then looked back steadily at his uncle. 'Not at first, Uncle Ma, but Yuan explained it to me. He said you had to kill the guilt you felt at Grandpa Tiao's death. That you could not be your own man until you had.'

'Then you understand how deeply I revere my father? How hard it was to harm even a copy of him?'

Tao Chu nodded, his eyes bright with understanding.

'Good.' He squeezed the boy's shoulders briefly, then stood. 'But I must thank you, Tsu Tao Chu. You did well today. You gave me back my father.'

Tao Chu smiled, greatly pleased by his uncle's praise, then, at a touch from Li Yuan, he joined the older boy in a deep bow and backed away, leaving the T'ang to their Council.

From the camera's vantage point, twenty li out from the spaceship, it was hard to tell its scale. The huge sphere of its forward compartments was visible only as a nothingness in the star-filled field of space – a circle of darkness more intense than that which surrounded it. Its tail, so fine and thin that it was like a thread of silver, stretched out for ten times its circumference, terminating in a smaller, silvered sphere little thicker than the thread.

It was beautiful. Li Shai Tung drew closer, operating the remote from a distance of almost three hundred thousand li, adjusting the camera image with the most delicate of touches, the slight delay in response making him cautious. Five li out he slowed the remote and increased the definition.

The darkness took on form. The sphere was finely stippled, pocked here and there with hatches or spiked with communication towers. Fine, almost invisible lines covered the whole surface, as if the sphere were netted by the frailest of spiders' webs.

Li Shai Tung let the remote drift slowly towards the starship and sat back, one hand smoothing through his long beard while he looked about him at the faces of his fellow T'ang.

'Well?'

He glanced across at the waiting technicians and dismissed them with a gesture. They had done their work well in getting an undetected remote so close to *The New Hope*. Too well, perhaps. He had not expected it to be so beautiful.

'How big is it?' asked Wu Shih, turning to him. 'I can't help thinking it must be huge to punch so big a hole in the star field.'

Li Shai Tung looked back at him, the understanding of thirty years passing between them. 'It's huge. Approximately two li in diameter.'

'Approximately?' It was Wei Feng, T'ang of East Asia, who picked up on the word.

'Yes. The actual measurement is one kilometre. I understand that they have used the old *Hung Mao* measurements throughout the craft.'

Wei Feng grunted his dissatisfaction, but Wang Hsien, T'ang of Africa, was not so restrained. 'But that's an outrage!' he roared. 'An insult! How dare they flout the Edict so openly?'

'I would remind you, Wang Hsien,' Li Shai Tung answered quietly, seeing the unease on every face. 'We agreed that the terms of the Edict would not apply to the starship.'

He looked back at the ship. The fine web of lines was now distinct. In its centre, etched finer than the lines surrounding it, were two lines of bead-like figures spiralling about each other, forming the double helix of heredity, symbol of the Dispersionists.

Three years ago – the day after Under Secretary Lehmann had been killed in the House by Tolonen – he had summoned the leaders of the House before him, and there, in the Purple Forbidden City where they had murdered his son, had granted them concessions, amongst them permission to build a generation starship. It had prevented war. But now the ship was almost ready and though the uneasy peace remained intact, soon it

would be broken. The cusp lay just ahead. Thus far on the road of concession he had carried the Seven. Thus far but no further.

He stared at the starship a moment longer. It was beautiful, but both House
and Seven knew what *The New Hope* really was. No one was fooled by the mask
of rhetoric. The Dispersionists talked of it being an answer – 'the only guarantee of a future for our children' – but in practical terms it did nothing to
solve the problem of over-population that was supposedly its *raison d'être*. Fully
laden, it could carry no more than five thousand settlers. In any case, the ship,
fast as it was, would take a thousand years to reach the nearest star. No, *The
New Hope* was not an answer, it was a symbol, a political counter – the thin end
of the great wedge of Change. It heralded not a new age of dispersal but a
return to the bad old days of technological free-for-all – a return to that
madness that had once before almost destroyed Chung Kuo.

He cleared the image and sat there, conscious that they were waiting for
him to say what was on his mind. He looked from face to face, aware that the
past three years had brought great changes in his thinking. What had once
seemed certain was no longer so. His belief in peace at all costs – in a policy
of concession and containment – had eroded in the years since Han Ch'in's
death. He had aged, and not only his face. Some days there was an air of
lethargy about him, of having done with things. *Yes*, he thought, looking
down at his own long hands, *the tiger's teeth are soft now, his eyes grown dull. And
they know this. Our enemies know it and seek advantage from it. But what might we
do that we have not already done? How can we stem the tidal flow of change?*

Tsu Ma broke into his thoughts. 'Forgive me, Li Shai Tung. But what of
Tolonen?'

Li Shai Tung looked up, surprised, meeting the new T'ang's eyes.

'Tolonen? I don't understand you, Tsu Ma. You think I should accede to
the House's demands?' He looked away, a bitter anger in his eyes. 'You
would have me give them that satisfaction too?'

Tsu Ma answered him softly. 'Not at all, Shai Tung. You mistake my
meaning. Things have changed. Many who were angry three years ago have
cooled. They see things differently now, even in the House.'

Li Shai Tung looked about him, expecting strong disagreement with Tsu
Ma's remarks, but there was nothing. They looked at him expectantly.

'I still don't follow you. You mean they'd have him back? After what he did?'

Tsu Ma shook his head. 'Not as General, no. But in some other role.'

Li Shai Tung looked down sharply. It was more than he could have hoped for. But dare he say yes? Dare he call the old rogue back?

'We are not alone in thinking things have gone too far,' said Wu Shih, picking up on what Tsu Ma had said. 'There are many at First Level – even among the *Hung Mao* – who feel we gave too much; were too timid in our dealings with the Dispersionists. They would see the changes to the Edict reversed, *The New Hope* melted down.'

'We daren't go so far. There would be war, surely?'

Tsu Ma leaned forward. 'Not if we challenge them in their own sphere.'

'You mean the House?'

There were nods all around. So, they had discussed this between them. Why? Had he been so preoccupied? So unreachable?

Wei Feng spoke for them all. 'We know the last three years have been hard for you, Shai Tung. You have tasted bitterness and we have had to watch in silence. But we shall watch no longer, or hold our tongues for fear of hurting you. We have seen the plan your advisor, Shepherd, drew up and...'

Li Shai Tung sat forward jerkily. 'Impossible! No one has seen those papers!'

Wei Feng waited a moment then continued. 'Not impossible, old friend. Not at all. Shepherd merely took advantage of his right as equal to appeal to us. He knew you would not act as your heart dictated, so he sent us copies.'

Li Shai Tung stared back at him, astonished. Then they knew...

'And we agree.' Wei Feng was smiling now. 'Don't you see, Li Shai Tung. We agree with *Shih* Shepherd's proposals. Our enemies have gone too far. To kill your son and take advantage from it – it was too much for any man to bear. And a T'ang is not just any man. A T'ang is one of Seven.'

'And the Seven?'

Wei Feng looked about him, then back at Li Shai Tung. 'In this the Seven shall do as Li Shai Tung decides.'

As the door at the far end of the room hissed open, steam billowed out into the corridor beyond. Berdichev shivered but stood straighter, his skin still tingling from the shower.

An armed guard stood there in the doorway, head bowed, a clean silk *pau* folded over one arm. Behind him stood two Han servants who, after a moment's hesitation, entered the room and began to dry Berdichev with soft towels. When they had done, he went over to the guard and took the full-length gown from him, pulling it on and tying it at the waist.

'You have my charm?'

The guard's head moved fractionally, but remained bowed. 'I'm sorry, excellency. I was given only the *pau*.'

Berdichev huffed impatiently and looked up at the overhead camera. Moments later an official appeared at the far end of the corridor and hurried to him. The man bowed deeply, his face flushed with embarrassment, and held out one hand, offering the necklace.

'My humble apologies, Excellency. I did not understand.'

Berdichev took the silver chain and fastened it about his neck, closing his hand over the smooth surface of the charm a moment. *The impertinence of these little men*, he thought, making a mental note of the official's number – so prominently displayed on his chest – before he waved him away. Then he waited as one of the two Han brought him anti-static slippers while the other combed and plaited his hair. Only then, when they were finished, did Director Clarac make his appearance.

Clarac embraced him lightly and then stepped back, smiling pleasantly, his appearance and manner the very model of elegance and charm. Berdichev smiled tightly and gave the barest of nods in response to Clarac's respectful bow. As ever, he was in two minds about Clarac's value to the project. He was a good front man, but the real work was done by his team of four assistants. Clarac had only to step out of line once and he would be out, family connections or no.

Clarac's voice oozed warmth and friendliness. 'Soren! It's a real delight to have you here as our guest.'

Yes, thought Berdichev, *but I'm the last person you expected to see up here today. I bet you were shitting your elegant white pants when you heard I was here.* That said, Berdichev was impressed by what he had seen. The defences about The New Hope left nothing to be desired. Neither had he had any reason to complain about the security measures surrounding visitors to the base. He had been forced to undergo the full body search and decontamination procedure. And when he had tried to bully the guards into making an exception in his case, their officer had politely but firmly stated that there could be no exceptions – hadn't *Shih* Berdichev insisted as much?

'Shih Clarac,' he answered, distancing the man at once and subtly reminding him of their relative status. 'I'm delighted to be here. But tell me, what are you doing about the spy camera?'

Clarac's momentary hesitation was telling. He was a man who prided himself on having everything at his fingertips, but he had not counted on Berdichev's directness. Clarac was used to social nicety. It was how he functioned. He approached such matters slowly, obliquely, over wine and sweetmeats. But Berdichev had no time for such 'niceties'.

'We know about the remote,' Clarac answered, recovering quickly. 'In fact, if you'll permit me, Shih Berdichev, I'll take you to our tracking room.'

Berdichev nodded tersely and walked on, not waiting for Clarac, who had to hurry to catch up with him.

'And that gap in your defences – the blind spot on darkside – how do you account for that?'

Clarac did not hesitate this time. 'Our defence experts have assured me that nothing of any real size could get through undetected. The blind spot, as you call it, is a mere 30 degrees of arc. Our central sensors would detect any ship coming in from five thousand li out. In any case, no one would come from that direction. There's nothing out there. You would have to orbit the moon in a one-man craft to get into position. And who would do that?'

Berdichev stopped and stared at him a moment.

'Besides which,' Clarac added quickly, facing Berdichev, 'there's the question of cost. To extend our defence satellite system to cover the darkside channel would cost a further one hundred and twenty million. The budget is already two hundred and eighty-five per cent over original costings. Our investors are justifiably concerned...'

'And if one man did just what you say is impossible and slipped in on the darkside?'

Clarac laughed. 'If he did it would make no difference. Every airlock is linked to central security. There are seals at every level. And more than a thousand security men guarding the outer shell alone. The inner shell is a self-sufficient unit which can be cut off at once from the outer shell. As the engines and life-support systems are there, there's no possibility of them being under threat. No, the only way the Seven could get at *The New Hope* would be to try to blow it out of the sky from below. And we've designed our defence system to prevent just that possibility.'

Berdichev sniffed, then, satisfied, nodded and began to walk on. Beside him, Clarac began to talk about the progress they had made, the difficulties they had overcome, but Berdichev was hardly listening. He had seen the reports already. What he wanted were answers to some of the things they might not have thought of. He wanted to make certain for himself that nothing had been overlooked.

In the tracking room he took a seat at the desk and listened while Clarac explained the system. But all the time he was looking about him, noting things.

Interrupting Clarac he pointed to the screen that showed the remote spy camera. 'You're certain it's not a weapon?'

Clarac laughed. A laugh which, to Berdichev's ear, was just a touch too self-confident.

'We've scanned it thoroughly, of course. There's an engine unit at the back of it and a whole system of foils and anti-jamming devices, and though the central core of it is lead-screened, our experts have calculated that there's barely enough room for the camera unit, let alone any kind of weaponry.'

'Unless they've developed something new, neh?'

Clarac looked at him and gave a slight bow, understanding that he would be allowed nothing today. He would need answers for everything.

'I've assumed that that might be the case. Which is why I personally ordered that the thing should be tracked twenty-four hours a day. I've two lasers trained on the aperture constantly. At the smallest sign of unusual activity they'll blow the thing apart.'

'Before it can damage *The New Hope*?'

'The lasers are set for automatic response. The remote would be blasted out of the sky in less than a fiftieth of a second.'

Berdichev turned his head and looked at Clarac, for the first time letting a brief smile signal his satisfaction.

'Good. I want nothing to stop *The New Hope* from making its maiden flight three months from now.'

He saw the surprise on Clarac's face, followed an instant later by a broad smile of unfeigned delight. 'But that's excellent, *Shih* Berdichev! That's marvellous news! When did the Seven agree to this?'

'They haven't. But they will. Very soon now. By the week's end there will be a proposal in the House. We're going to push them on this one. We're going to make them fulfil the promises they made three years ago. And then we'll push some more. Until there's a whole fleet of these ships. You understand me? But this is the first, the most important of them. *The New Hope* will break their stranglehold. They know that and they'll try to prevent it – but we must pre-empt their every move. That's why it's so important things are right up here. That's why I came to see things for myself.'

Clarac bowed. 'I understand, Shih Berdichev. You think, then, that we should extend the satellite system?'

Berdichev shook his head. 'No. I'm satisfied with your reasoning. As you say, it would be impossible for a single man to do any real damage to the craft. Let us worry about more direct approaches, eh? And for a start let's destroy that remote. I'm sure one of our ferry craft could have a little accident, eh? A technical malfunction, perhaps, that would place it on a collision course?'

Clarac smiled. 'Of course, Shih Berdichev. It shall be done at once.'

Fei Yen stood in the shade of the willow, waiting for the two princes to come along the path that led to the bridge. She had seen their craft land only minutes earlier and had placed herself deliberately here where they would have to pass her. Her maids stood off at a slight distance, amongst the trees, talking quietly amongst themselves and pretending not to watch her, but she knew they were as inquisitive as she. For the past three years they had shared her tedious exile on her father's estate, where she had seen no one but her brothers and aunts. Today, however, for the first time since the period of mourning had ended, she had been granted permission to call upon the young prince – to stay a week and celebrate his birthday.

Seeing movement among the trees at the far end of the stone-flagged path, she turned and signalled to the maids to be quiet. *Here they come!* she mimed exaggeratedly.

The maids giggled then, obedient, fell silent.

Fei Yen turned back to watch the two approach. But as they came closer she drew her sandalwood fan and waved it impatiently, certain there must be a mistake. Where was Tao Chu? Where was Tsu Ma's strapping young nephew?

She saw the taller of the boys hesitate, then touch the arm of the other and lean close to whisper something. The smaller of them seemed to stare at her a moment, then turn to the other and nod. Only then did the older boy come on.

Three paces from her he stopped. At first she didn't recognize him, he was so much taller, so much gawkier than when she had seen him last.

'Li Yuan?'

Li Yuan swallowed and then bowed; an awkward, stilted movement that betrayed his unease. When he straightened up and looked at her again she saw his face was scarlet with embarrassment. His lips moved as if he was about to say something, but he had not formed the words when she interrupted him.

'Where is Tao Chu? I was told Tao Chu would be with you.'

There were giggles from the trees behind her, and she turned sharply, furious with her maids, then turned back in time to see Li Yuan summon the small boy forward.

'Fei Yen?' said the boy, bowing elegantly like a tiny courtier. Then, in a lilting yet hesitant voice that betrayed his unfamiliarity with English, he added, 'I am most honoured to meet you, Lady Fei. My uncle told me you were beautiful, but he did not tell me how beautiful.'

She laughed, astonished. 'And who have I the pleasure of addressing?'

The boy bowed again, enjoying her astonishment in the same way he had enjoyed the applause of the T'ang earlier that day when he had played Tsu Tiao. 'I am Tsu Tao Chu, son of Tsu Wen, and third nephew of the T'ang, Tsu Ma.'

The fan that she had been waving stopped in mid-motion and clicked shut. 'Tao Chu?' She laughed – a different, shorter laugh, expressing a very different kind of surprise – then shook her head. 'Oh, no. I mean, you can't be. I was told...'

Then she understood. She heard the giggling from the trees topple over into laughter. Flushing deeply, she lowered her head slightly. 'Tsu Tao Chu. I... I'm delighted to meet you. Forgive me if I seemed confused. I...' Then, forgetting her disappointment, she too burst into laughter.

'What is it?' asked the eight-year-old, delighted that he had somehow managed to amuse this mature woman of nineteen.

'Nothing,' she said quickly, fanning herself and turning slightly, so that the shadow of the willow hid her embarrassment. 'Nothing at all.' She turned quickly to Li Yuan, finding it easier, suddenly, to talk to him. 'Li Yuan, forgive me. My father, Yin Tsu, sends his deep regards and best wishes on your forthcoming birthday. I have come on his behalf to celebrate the day.'

Li Yuan's smile was unexpectedly warm. Again he bowed, once more colouring from neck to brow. His awkwardness made her remember the last time they had met – that time he had come to her and cried upon her shoulder, four days after Han Ch'in's death. Then, too, his reaction had been unexpected. Then, too, he had seemed to shed a skin.

'I... I...' He stuttered, then looked down, seeming almost to laugh at himself. 'Forgive me, Fei Yen. I was not told you were coming.'

She gave the slightest bow. 'Nor I until this morning.'

He looked up at her, a strange expectation in his eyes. 'Will you be staying long?'

'A week.' She turned and signalled to her maids who at once came out from beneath the trees and hurried along the path to her. Then, turning back, she added, 'We had best be getting back, don't you think? They'll be expecting us in the house.' And, before they could answer, she turned away, heading back towards the bridge.

Li Yuan stood there a while, watching her. Only when he turned to speak to Tao Chu did he realize how avidly the boy was studying him.

'What are you staring at, Squib?' he said, almost angrily, conscious that his cheeks were warm for the third time that afternoon.

'At you, Great Yuan,' answered Tao Chu with a mock earnestness that made Li Yuan relent. Then, in a softer voice, the small boy added, 'You love her, don't you?'

Li Yuan laughed awkwardly then turned and looked back up the path. 'What does it matter? She was my brother's wife.'

The Overseer's House dominated the vast plain of the East European plantation. Three tiers high, its roof steeply pitched, it rested on stilts over the meeting point of the two broad irrigation canals that ran north-south and east-west, feeding the great latticework of smaller channels. To the south lay the workers' quarters; long, low huts that seemed embedded in the earth. To the north and east were store-houses; huge, covered reservoirs of grain and rice. West, like a great wave frozen at its point of turning under, lay the City, its walls soaring two li into the heavens.

It was late afternoon and the shadow of the Overseer's House lay like a dark, serrated knife on the fields to the east. There, in the shadow, on a bare earth pathway that followed the edge of one of the smaller north-south channels, walked three men. One walked ahead, alone and silent, his head down, his drab brown clothes, with their wide, short trousers, indicative of his status as field worker. The two behind him joked and laughed as they went along. Their weapons – lethal *deng* rifles, 'lantern guns' – slung casually over their shoulders. They were more elegantly dressed, the kingfisher blue of their jackets matching the colour of the big sky overhead. These were the Overseer's men, Chang Yan and Teng Fu; big, brutal men who were not slow to chastise their workers and beat them if they fell behind with quotas.

'What does he want?' Teng asked, lifting his chin slightly to indicate the man plodding along in front of them but meaning the Overseer when he said 'he'. No one requested to see the Overseer. He alone chose who came to see him.

'The man's a thief,' said Chang. He spat out into the channel, below and to his left, and watched the off-white round of spittle drift away slowly on the water. Then he looked back at Teng. 'One of the patrol cameras caught him in the Frames making harvest.'

The Frames were where they grew the special items – strawberries and lychees, pineapples and oranges, grapes and peaches, cherries and almonds, pears and melons.

'Stupid,' Teng said, looking down and laughing. 'These peasant types – they're all stupid.'

Chang shrugged. 'I don't know. I thought this one was different. He was supervisor. A trusted man. We'd had no trouble with him before.'

'They're all trouble,' said Teng, scratching his left buttock vigorously. 'Stupid and trouble. It's genetic. That's what it is.'

Chang laughed.

They had come to a bridge. The first man had stopped, his head still bowed, waiting for the others. He was forbidden to cross the bridge without a permit.

'Get on!' said Teng, drawing the long club from his belt and jabbing the man viciously in the small of the back. 'The Overseer wants to see you. Don't keep him waiting, now!'

The man stumbled forward onto the bridge, then got up and trudged on again, wiping his dirtied hands against his thighs as he went and glancing up briefly, fearfully, as the big house loomed over him.

More guards lounged at the foot of the steps. One of them, a tall Hung Mao seated apart from the rest, looked up as the three men approached, then, with the vaguest movement of his head to indicate that they should go on up, looked back down at the rifle in his lap, continuing his meticulous inspection of the weapon.

'Good day, Shih Peskova,' said Teng, acknowledging the Overseer's lieutenant with a bow. But Peskova paid him no attention. Teng was Han and Han were shit. It didn't matter whether they were guard or peasant. Either way they were shit. Hadn't he heard as much from The Man himself often enough?

When they had gone, Peskova turned and looked up at the house again. He would have to watch that Teng. He was getting above himself. Thinking himself better than the other men. He would have to bring him down a level. Teach him better manners.

With a smile he put the rifle down and reached for the next in the stack at his side. Yes, it would be fun to see the big Han on his knees and begging. A lot of fun.

Overseer Bergson looked across as the three men entered.

'What is it, Teng Fu?'

The big Han knelt in the doorway and bowed his head. 'We have brought the man you asked for, Overseer.'

Bergson turned from the bank of screens that took up one whole wall of the long room and got up from his chair. 'You can go, Teng Fu. You too, Chang Yan. I'll see to him myself.'

When they were gone and he was alone with the field supervisor, Bergson came across and stood there, no more than an arm's length from the man.

'Why did you do it, Field Supervisor Sung?'

The man swallowed, but did not lift his head. 'Do what, Shih Bergson?'

Bergson reached out almost tenderly and took the man's cheek between the fingers of his left hand and twisted until Sung fell to his feet, whimpering in pain.

'Why did you do it, Sung? Or do you want me to beat the truth out of you?'

Sung prostrated himself, holding on to Bergson's feet. 'I could not bear it any longer, Overseer. There is barely enough to keep a child alive, let alone men and women who have to toil in the fields all day. And when I heard the guards were going to cut our rations yet again...'

Bergson stepped back, shaking Sung's hands off. 'Barely enough? What nonsense is this, Sung? Isn't it true that the men steal from the rice fields? That they eat much of the crop they are supposed to be harvesting?'

Sung went to shake his head, but Bergson brought his foot down firmly on top of his left hand and began to press down. 'Tell me the truth, Sung. They steal, don't they?'

Sung cried out, then nodded his head vigorously. 'It is so, *Shih* Bergson. There are many who do as you say.'

Bergson slowly brought his foot up, then stepped away from Sung, turning his back momentarily, considering.

'And you stole because you had too little to eat?'

Sung looked up, then quickly looked back down, keeping his forehead pressed to the floor. 'No... I...'

'Tell me the truth, Sung!' Bergson barked, turning sharply. 'You stole because you were hungry, is that it?'

Sung miserably shook his head. 'No, *Shih* Bergson. I have enough.'

'Then why? Tell me why.'

Sung shuddered. A sigh went through him like a wave. Then, resigned to his fate, he began to explain. 'It was my wife, Overseer. She is a kindly woman, you understand. A good woman. It was her suggestion. She saw how it was for the others: that they were suffering while we, fortunate as we were, had enough. I told her we could share what we had, but she would not have it. I pleaded with her not to make me do as she asked...'

'Which was?'

'I stole, Overseer. I took fruit from the Frames and gave it to the others.'

Bergson laughed coldly. 'Am I meant to believe this, Sung? An honest thief? A *charitable* thief? A thief who sought no profit from his actions?'

Sung nodded his head once but said nothing.

Bergson moved closer. 'I could have you flogged senseless for what you did, Sung. Worse, I could have you thrown into the Clay. How would you like that, Field Supervisor Sung? To be sent into the Clay?'

Sung stared up at Bergson, his terror at the thought naked in his eyes. 'You'd not do that, *Shih* Bergson. Please. I beg you. Anything but that.'

Bergson was silent a moment. He turned and went across to the desk. When he returned he was holding a thin card in one hand. He knelt down and held it in front of Sung's face a moment.

'Do you know what this is, Sung?'

Sung shook his head. He had never seen the like of it. It looked like a piece of Above technology – something they never saw out in the fields – but he would not have liked to have guessed just what.

'This here, Sung, is the evidence of your crime. It's a record of the hour you spent harvesting in the Frames. A hidden camera took a film of you.'

Again Sung shuddered. 'What do you want, *Shih* Bergson?'

Bergson smiled and slipped the thin sliver of ice into his jacket pocket, then stood up again. 'First I want you to sit down over here and write down the names of all those who shared the stolen fruit with you.'

Sung hesitated. 'And then?'

'Then you'll go back to your barracks and send your wife to me.'

Sung stiffened but did not look up. 'My wife, Overseer?'

'The good woman. You know, the one who got you into all this trouble.'

Sung swallowed. 'And what will happen to my wife, *Shih* Bergson?'

Bergson laughed. 'If she's good – if she's *very* good to me – then nothing. You understand? In fact – and you can tell her this – if she's *exceptionally* good I might even give her the tape. Who knows, eh, Sung?'

Sung looked up, meeting Bergson's cold grey eyes for the first time in their interview, then looked down again, understanding perfectly.

'Good. Then come. There's paper here and ink. You have a list of names to write.'

She came when it was dark. Peskova took her up to the top room – the big room beneath the eaves – and locked her in as he had been told to. Then he went, leaving the house empty but for the woman and the Overseer.

For a time DeVore simply watched her, following her every movement with the hidden cameras, switching from screen to screen, zooming in to focus on her face or watching her from the far side of the room. Then, when he was done with that, he nodded to himself and blanked the screens.

She was much better than he had expected. Stronger, prettier, more attractive than he'd anticipated. He had thought beforehand that he would have to send her back and deal with Sung some other way, but now he had seen her he felt the need in him, like a strong, dark tar in his blood, and knew he would have to purge himself of that. He had not had a woman for weeks – not since that last trip to the Wilds – and that had been a sing-song girl, all artifice and expertise. No, this would be different; something to savour.

Quickly he went to the wall safe at the far end of the room and touched the combination. The door irised open and he reached inside, drawing out the tiny phial before the door closed up again. He hesitated a moment then gulped the drug down, feeling its warmth sear his throat and descend quickly to his stomach. It would be in his blood in minutes.

He climbed the stairs quickly, almost eagerly now, but near the top he slowed, calming himself, waiting until he had complete control. Only then did he reach out and thumb the lock.

She turned, surprised. A big woman, bigger than her husband, nothing cowed or mean about the way she stood. *You married below yourself*, DeVore thought at once, knowing that Sung would never have made Field Supervisor without such a woman to push him from behind.

Her bow was hesitant. 'Overseer?'

He closed the door behind him, then turned back to her, trying to gauge her response to him. Would she do as he wanted? Would she try to save her husband? She was here. That, at least, augured well. But would she be compliant? Would she be *exceptionally* good to him?

'You know why you're here?' he asked, taking a step closer to her.

Her eyes never left him. 'I'm here because my husband told me to be here, Shih Bergson.'

DeVore laughed. 'From what I'm told old Sung is a docile man. He does what he's told. Am I wrong in thinking that? Does Sung roar like a lion within his own walls?'

She met his gaze fiercely, almost defiantly, making the blood run thicker, heavier in his veins. 'He is my husband and I a dutiful wife. He wished me here, so here I am.'

DeVore looked down, keeping the smile from his face. He had not been wrong. She had spirit. He had seen that when he had been watching her;

had seen how she looked at everything with that curious, almost arrogant stare of hers. She had strength. The strength of twenty Sungs.

He took another step then shook his head. 'You're wrong, you know. You're here because I said you should be here.'

She did not answer him this time, but stared back at him almost insolently, only a slight moistening of her lips betraying her nervousness.

'What's your name, Sung's wife?'

She looked away, then looked back at him, as if to say, Don't toy with me. Do what you are going to do and let me be.

'Your name?' he insisted, his voice harder now.

'My name is Si Wu Ya,' she answered proudly.

This time he smiled. Si Wu Ya. *Silk Raven*. He looked at her and understood why her parents had given her the name. Her hair was beautifully dark and lustrous. 'Better an honest raven than a deceitful magpie, eh?' he said, quoting the old Han adage.

'What do you want me to do?'

He shook his head. 'Don't be impatient, Si Wu Ya. We'll come to that. But tell me this – is Sung a good man? Is he good in bed? Does he make you sing out with pleasure?'

He saw how she bridled at the question, but saw also how the truth forbade her to say yes. So, Sung was a disappointment. Well, he, DeVore, would make her sing tonight. Of that he had no doubt. He took a step towards her, then another, until he stood before her, face to face.

'Is he hard like bamboo, or soft like a rice frond? Tell me, Si Wu Ya. I'd like to know.'

For a moment her eyes flared with anger, but then she seemed to laugh deep inside herself and her eyes changed, their anger replaced by a hard amusement. 'Don't mock me, *Shih* Bergson. I'm here, aren't I? Do what you want. I'll be good to you. I'll be very good. But don't mock me.'

He looked back at her a moment, then reached down and took her left hand in his own, lifting it up to study it. It was a big, strong hand, roughly calloused from field-work, but she had made an effort. It was clean and the nails were polished a deep brown.

He met her eyes again. 'My friends tell me you Han women wear no underclothes. Is it true?'

In answer she took his hand and placed it between her legs. His fingers met the soft, masking texture of cloth, but beneath them he could feel her warmth, the firm softness of her sex.

'Well?' she asked, almost smiling now, determined not to be cowed by him.

'Strip off,' he said, standing back a pace. 'I want to see what you look like.'

She shrugged, slipped the one-piece off and kicked off her briefs, then stood there, her hands at her sides, making no effort to cover her nakedness.

DeVore walked round her, studying her. She was a fine woman, unspoilt by childbirth, her body hardened by fieldwork. Her breasts were large and firm, her buttocks broad but not fat. Her legs were strongly muscled yet still quite shapely, her stomach flat, her shoulders smooth. He nodded, satisfied. She would have made a good wife for a T'ang, let alone a man like Sung.

'Good. Now over there.'

She hesitated, her eyes showing a momentary unease, then she did as she was told, walking over to the corner where he had indicated. He saw how she looked about her; how her eyes kept going to the saddle. As if she knew.

'What do you want me to do?'

DeVore smiled coldly. He had watched her earlier. Had seen, through the camera's hidden eye, how fascinated she had been with the saddle. Had witnessed her puzzlement and then her shocked surprise as she realized what it was.

It was a huge thing, almost half a man's height and the same in length. At first glance it could be mistaken for an ornately carved stool, its black and white surfaces for a kind of sculpture. And in a way it was. Ming craftsmen had made the saddle more than seven hundred years before, shaping ivory and wood to satisfy the whim of a bored nobleman.

'Have you seen my saddle?'

She watched him, eyes half-lidded now, and nodded.

'It was a custom of your people, you know. They would place a saddle in the gateway to the parental home before the bride and bridegroom entered it.'

She wet her lips. 'What of it?'

He shrugged. 'An, it was. A saddle. An. Almost the same sound as for peace.'

He saw her shiver, yet the room was warm.

'Have you studied my saddle?'

She nodded briefly.

'And did it amuse you?'

'You're mocking me again, *Shih* Bergson. Is that what you want me to do? To play that game with you?'

He smiled. So she had worked it out. He went across and stood there beside the saddle, smoothing his hand over its finely polished surfaces. What at first seemed a mere tangle of black and white soon resolved itself. Became a man and woman locked in an embrace that was, some said, unnatural; the man's head buried between the woman's legs, the woman's head between the man's.

He looked across at her, amused. 'Have you ever done that with Sung?'

She blinked. Then, unexpectedly, she shook her head.

'Would you like to do that, now, with me?'

He waited, watching her like a hawk watching its prey. Again she hesitated, then she nodded.

'You think you'd like it, don't you?'

This time she looked away, for the first time the faintest colour appearing at her neck.

Ah, he thought. *Now I have you. Now I know your weakness. You are dissatisfied with Sung. Perhaps you're even thinking what this might lead to. You've ambitions, Si Wu Ya. For all your social conscience you're a realist. And, worse for you, you enjoy sex. You want to be made love to. You want the excitement that I'm offering here.*

'Come here.'

He saw how her breathing changed. Her nipples were stiff now and the colour had not left her neck. Slowly, almost fearful now, she came to him.

He took her hand again, guiding it down within the folds of his *pau* , then heard her gasp as her hand closed on him; saw her eyes go down and look.

DeVore laughed, knowing the drug would last for hours yet – would keep him at this peak until he had done with her. He leaned closer to her, drawing her nearer with one hand, his voice lowering to a whisper.

'Was he ever this hard, Si Wu Ya? Was he ever this hot?'

Her eyes went to his briefly, the pupils enlarged, then returned to the splendour she held. Unbidden, she knelt and began to stroke him and kiss him. He put his hands on her shoulders now, forcing her to take him in her mouth, her whole body shuddering beneath his touch, a soft moaning in her throat. Then he pushed her off, roughly, almost brutally and moved away from her.

She knelt there, her breasts rising and falling violently, her eyes wide, watching him. Almost. She was almost ready. One more step. One more step and she would be there.

He threw off the *pau* and stood there over her, naked, seeing how eagerly she watched him now. How ready she was for him to fuck her. With one foot he pushed her back, then knelt and spread her legs, watching her all the while, one hand moving between her legs, seeing how her eyes closed, how her breath caught with the pleasure of it.

'Gods,' she moaned, reaching up for him. 'Goddess of mercy, put it there! Please, Shih Bergson! Please put it there!'

His fingers traced a line from her groin up to her chin, forcing her to look back at him.

'Not like this,' he said, putting her hands on him again. 'I know a better way.'

Quickly he led her to the saddle, pushing her face down onto its hard smooth surface, his hands caressing her intimately all the while, keeping her mind dark, her senses inflamed. Then, before she realized what was happening, he fastened her in the double stirrups, binding her hands and feet.

He stood back, looking at his handiwork, then crossed to the wall and switched off all the lights but one – the spot that picked out her naked rump.

She was shaking now. He could see the small movement of the muscles at the top of her legs. 'What's happening?' she asked in a tiny, sobered voice. 'What are you doing?'

He went over to her and placed his hand on the small of her back, running his fingers down the smooth channel that ended in the tight hole of her anus, feeling her shudder at his touch.

Pleasure or fear? he wondered. Did she still believe it would all turn out all right?

The thought almost made him laugh. She had mistaken him. She had thought he wanted ordinary satisfactions.

He reached beneath the saddle and dipped his fingers in the shelf of scented unguents, then began to smear them delicately about the tiny hole, pushing inward, the unguents working their magic spell, making the muscles relax.

He felt her breathing change again, anticipating pleasure; knew, without looking, that she would have been newly aroused by his ministrations; that her nipples would be stiff, her eyes wide with expectation.

He reached under the saddle a second time and drew out the steel-tipped phallus that was attached by a chain to the pommel. The chain was just long enough. Longer and there would not be that invigorating downward pull – that feeling of restraint – shorter and penetration would not be deep enough to satisfy. He smiled, holding the hollowed column lovingly between his hands and smoothing his fingers over the spiralling pattern of the *wu-tu*, the 'five noxious creatures' – toad, scorpion, snake, centipede and gecko – then drew it on, easing himself into its oiled soft-leather innards and fastening its leather straps about his waist.

For a moment he hesitated, savouring the moment, then centred the metal spike and pushed. His first thrust took her by surprise. He felt her whole body stiffen in shock, but though she gasped, she did not cry out.

Brave girl, he thought, *but that's not what you're here for. You're not here to be brave. You're here to sing for me.*

The second thrust tore her. He felt the skin between her anus and vagina give like tissue and heard her cry out in agony.

'Good,' he said, laughing brutally. 'That's good. Sing out, Si Wu Ya! It's good to hear you sing out!'

He thrust again.

When he was done he unstrapped himself, then took one of the white sheets from the side and threw it over her, watching as the blood spread out from the centre of the white; a doubled circle of redness that slowly formed into an ellipse.

Hearing her moan, he went round and knelt beside her, lifting her face gently, almost tenderly, and kissing her brow, her nose, her lips.

'Was that good, Si Wu Ya? Was it hard enough for you?' He laughed softly, almost lovingly. 'Ah, but you were good, Si Wu Ya. The best yet. And for that you'll have your tape. But later, neh? In the morning. We've a whole night ahead of us. Plenty of time to play our game again.'

Sung was kneeling on the top of the dyke, staring across at the House as the dawn broke. He was cold to the bone and his clothes were wet through, but still he knelt there, waiting.

He had heard her cries in the night. Had heard and felt his heart break inside his chest. Had dropped his head, knowing, at last, how small he was, how powerless.

Now, as the light leached back into the world, he saw the door open at the head of the steps and a figure appear.

'Si Wu Ya...' he mouthed, his lips dry, his heart, which had seemed dead in him, pounding in his chest. He went to get up but his legs were numb from kneeling and he had to put his hand out to stop himself from tumbling into the water far below. But his eyes never left her distant, shadowed figure, seeing at once how slowly she moved, how awkwardly, hobbling down the steps one by one, stopping time and again to rest, her whole body crooked, one hand clutching the side rail tightly, as if she'd fall without it.

He dragged himself back, anxious now, and began to pound the life back into his legs. Once more he tried to stand and fell back, cursing, almost whimpering now in his fear for her. 'Si Wu Ya,' he moaned, 'Si Wu Ya.'

Once more he tried to stand, gritting his teeth, willing his muscles to obey him. For one moment he almost fell again, then he thrust one leg forward, finding his balance.

'Si Wu Ya...' he hissed.

Forcing his useless legs to work, he made his way to the bridge, awkwardly at first, hobbling, as if in some grotesque mimicry of his wife, then with more confidence as the blood began to flow, his muscles come alive again.

Then, suddenly, he was running, his arms flailing wildly, his bare feet thudding against the dark earth. Until he was standing there, before her, great waves of pain and fear, hurt and anger washing through him like a huge black tide.

He moaned, his voice an animal cry of pain. 'What did he do, Si Wu Ya? Gods save us, what did he do?'

She stared back at him almost sightlessly.

'Your face...' he began, then realized that her face was unmarked. The darkness was behind her eyes. The sight of it made him whimper like a child and fall to his knees again.

Slowly, each movement a vast, unexplored continent of pain, she pushed out from the steps and hobbled past him. He scrambled up and made to help her but she brushed him off, saying nothing, letting the cold emptiness of her face speak for her.

On the narrow bridge he stood in front of her again, blocking her way, looking back past her at the House.

'I'll kill him.'

For the first time she seemed to look at him. Then she laughed; her laughter so cold, so unlike the laughter he had known from her, that it made his flesh tingle with fear.

'He'd break you, little Sung. He'd eat you up and spit you out.'

She leaned to one side and spat. Blood. He could see it, even in this half light. She had spat blood.

He went to touch her, to put his hands on her shoulders, but the look in her eyes warned him off. He let his arms fall uselessly.

'What did he do, Si Wu Ya? Tell me what he did.'

She looked down, then began to move on, forcing him to move aside and let her pass. He had no will to stop her.

At the first of the smaller channels she turned and began to ease herself down the shallow bank, grunting, her face set against the pain she was causing herself. Sung, following her, held out his hand and for the first time she let him help her, gripping his hand with a force that took his breath, her fingers tightening convulsively with every little jolt she received.

Then she let go and straightened up, standing there knee deep in the water at the bottom of the unlit channel, the first light lain like a white cloth over the latticework of the surrounding fields, picking out the channel's lips, the crouching shape of Sung. The same clear light that rested in the woman's long dark hair like a faintly jewelled mist.

She looked up at him. 'Have you your torch, Sung?'

He nodded, not understanding why she should want it, but took it from his pocket and, edging down the bank, reached out and handed it to her, watching as she unscrewed the top, transforming it into a tiny cutting tool. Then she took something from the pocket of her one-piece. Something small enough to fold inside her palm.

The card. The tape that had the record of his theft. Sung swallowed and looked at her. So she had done it. Had saved them both. He shivered, wanting to go down to her, to stroke her and hold her and thank her, but what he wanted wasn't somehow right. He felt the coldness emanate from her, a sense of the vast distance she had travelled. It was as if she had been beyond the sky. Had been to the place where they said there was no air, only the frozen, winking nothingness of space. She had been there. He had seen it in her eyes.

She put the card against the bank and played the cutting beam upon it. Once, twice, three times she did it, each time picking up the card and examining it. But each time it emerged unscathed, unmarked.

She looked up at him, that same cold distance in her eyes, then let the card fall from her fingers into the silt below the water. *Yes*, he thought, *they'll not find it there. They could search a thousand years and they'd not find it.*

But she had forgotten about the card already. She was bent down now, unbuttoning the lower half of her one-piece, her fingers moving gingerly, as if what she touched were flesh not cloth.

'Come down,' she said coldly, not looking at him. 'You want to know what he did, don't you? Well, come and see. I'll show you what he did.'

He went down and stood there, facing her, the water cold against his shins, the darkness all around them. He could see that the flap of cloth gaped open, but in the dark could make out no more than the vague shape of her legs, her stomach.

'Here.' She handed him the two parts of the torch and waited for him to piece the thing together.

He made to shine the torch into her face, but she pushed his hand down. 'No,' she said. 'Not there. Down here, where the darkness is.'

He let her guide his hand, then tried to pull back as he saw what he had previously not noticed, but she held his hand there firmly, forcing him to look. Blood. The cloth was caked with her blood. Was stained almost black with it.

'Gods...' he whispered, then caught his breath as the light moved across onto her flesh.

She had been torn open. From her navel to the base of her spine she had been ripped apart. And then sewn up. Crudely, it seemed, for the stitches were uneven. The black threads glistened in the torchlight, blood seeping from the wound where she had opened it again by walking.

'There,' she said, pushing the torch away. 'Now you've seen.'

He stood there blankly, not knowing what to say or do, remembering only the sound of her crying out in the darkness and how awful he had felt, alone, kneeling there on the dyke, impotent to act.

'What now?'

But she did not answer him, only bent and lowered herself into the water, hissing as the coldness burned into the wound, a faint moan escaping through her gritted teeth as she began to wash.

At dawn on the morning of his official birthday – in the court annals his thirteenth, for they accorded with ancient Han tradition in calling the day of the child's birth its first 'birth day' – Li Yuan was woken by his father and, when he was dressed in the proper clothes, led down to the stables of the Tongjiang estate.

It was an informal ceremony. Even so, there was not one of the six hundred and forty-eight servants – man, woman or girl – who was not present. Neither had any of the guests – themselves numbering one hundred and eighty – absented themselves on this occasion.

The grounds surrounding the stable buildings had been meticulously swept and tidied, the grooms lined up, heads bowed, before the great double doors. And there, framed in the open left-hand doorway of the stalls, was the T'ang's birthday gift to his son.

It was an Andalusian; a beauty of a horse, sixteen hands high and a perfect mulberry in colour. It was a thick-necked, elegant beast, with the strong legs of a thoroughbred. It had been saddled up ready for him and as Li Yuan stood there, it turned its head curiously, its large dark eyes meeting the prince's as if it knew its new owner.

'You have ridden my horses for too long now,' Li Shai Tung said to his son quietly. 'I felt it was time you had your own.'

Li Yuan went across to it and reached up gently, stroking its neck, its dappled flank. Then he turned and bowed to his father, a fleeting smile on his lips. The chief groom stood close by, the halter in his hand, ready to offer it to the prince when he was ready. But when Li Yuan finally turned to him it was not to take the halter from him.

'Saddle up the Arab, Hung Feng-Chan.'

The chief groom stared back at him a moment, open-mouthed, then looked across at the T'ang as if to query the instruction. But Li Shai Tung stood there motionless, his expression unchanged. Seeing this, Hung Feng-Chan bowed deeply to his T'ang, then to the prince, and quickly handed the halter to one of the nearby grooms.

When he had gone, Li Yuan turned back to his father, smiling, one hand still resting on the Andalusian's smooth, strong neck.

'He's beautiful, father, and I'm delighted with your gift. But if I am to have a horse it must be Han Ch'in's. I must become my brother.'

Throughout the watching crowd there was a low murmur of surprise, but from the T'ang himself there was no word, only the slightest narrowing of the eyes, a faint movement of the mouth. Otherwise he was perfectly still, watching his son.

The chief groom returned a minute later, leading the Arab. The black horse sniffed the air, and made a small bowing movement of its head, as if in greeting to the other horse. Then, just when it seemed to have settled, it made a sharp sideways movement, tugging against the halter. Hung Feng-Chan quieted the horse, patting its neck and whispering to it, then brought it across to where Li Yuan was standing.

This was the horse that General Tolonen had bought Han for his seventeenth birthday; the horse Han Ch'in had ridden daily until his death. A dark, spirited beast; dark-skinned and dark-natured, her eyes full of fire. She was smaller than the Andalusian by a hand, yet her grace, her power were undeniable.

'Well, father?'

All eyes were on the T'ang. Li Shai Tung stood there, bare-headed, a bright blue quilted jacket pulled loosely about his shoulders against the morning's freshness, one foot slightly before the other, his arms crossed across his chest, his hands holding his shoulders. It was a familiar stance to those who knew him, as was the smile he now gave his son; a dark, ironic smile that seemed both amused and calculating.

'You must ride her first, Li Yuan.'

Li Yuan held his father's eyes a moment, bowing, then he turned and, without further hesitation, swung up into the saddle. So far so good. The Arab barely had time to think before Li Yuan had leant forward and, looping the reins quickly over his hands, squeezed the Arab's chest gently with both feet.

Li Yuan's look of surprise as the Arab reared brought gasps as well as laughter from all round. Only the T'ang remained still and silent. Hung Feng-Chan danced round the front of the horse, trying to grab the halter, but Li Yuan shouted at him angrily and would have waved him away were he not clinging on dearly with both hands.

The Arab pulled and tugged and danced, moving this way and that, bucking, then skittering forward and ducking its head, trying to throw the rider from its back. But Li Yuan held on, his teeth gritted, his face determined. And slowly, very slowly, the Arab's movements calmed. With difficulty Li Yuan brought the Arab's head round and moved the stubborn beast two paces closer to the watching T'ang.

'Well, father, is she mine?'

The T'ang's left hand went from his shoulder to his beard. Then he laughed; a warm, good-humoured laugh that found its echo all around.

'Yes, Li Yuan. In name, at least. But watch her. Even your brother found her difficult.'

They met by accident, several hours later, in one of the bright, high-ceilinged corridors leading to the gardens.

'Li Yuan.'

Fei Yen bowed deeply, the two maids on either side of her copying her automatically.

The young prince had showered and changed since she had last seen him. He wore red now, the colour of the summer, his *ma k'ua*, the waist-length ceremonial jacket, a brilliant carmine, his loose silk trousers poppy, his suede boots a delicate shade of rose. About his waist he wore an elegant *ta lien*, or girdle pouch, the border a thick band of russet, the twin heart-shaped pockets made of a soft peach cloth, the details of trees, butterflies and flowers picked out in emerald green and blue and gold. On his head he wore a Ming-style summer hat, its inverted bowl lined with red fur and capped with a single ruby. Three long peacock feathers hung from its tip, reminder that Li Yuan was a royal prince.

'Fei Yen...' It might only have been the light reflected from his costume, yet once again he seemed embarrassed by her presence. 'I... was coming to see you.'

She stayed as she was, looking up at him from beneath her long black lashes, allowing herself the faintest smile of pleasure.

'I am honoured, Li Yuan.'

Fei Yen had dressed quite simply, in a peach *ch'i p'ao*, over which she wore a long embroidered cloak of white silk, decorated with stylized bamboo leaves of blue and green and edged in a soft pink brocade that matched the tiny pink ribbons in her hair, setting the whole thing off quite perfectly.

She knew how beautiful she looked. From childhood she had known her power over men. But this was strange, disturbing. It was almost as if this boy, this child...

Fei Yen rose slowly, meeting the prince's eyes for the first time and seeing how quickly he re-directed his gaze. Perhaps it was just embarrassment – the memory of how he had shamed himself that time when she had comforted him. Men were such strange, proud creatures. It was odd what mattered to them. Like Han Ch'in that time, when she had almost bettered him at archery...

Li Yuan found his tongue again. But he could only glance at her briefly as he complimented her.

'May her name be preserved on bamboo and silk.'

She laughed prettily at that, recognizing the old saying and pleased by his allusion to her cloak. 'Why, thank you, Li Yuan. May the fifteen precious things be yours.'

It was said before she fully realized what she had wished for him. She heard her maids giggle behind her and saw Li Yuan look down, the flush returning to his cheeks. It was a traditional good-luck wish, for long life and prosperity. But it was also a wish that the recipient have sons.

Her own laughter dispelled the awkwardness of the moment. She saw Li Yuan look up at her, his dark eyes strangely bright, and was reminded momentarily of Han Ch'in. As Han had been, so Li Yuan was now. One day he would be Head of his family – a powerful man, almost a god. She was conscious of that as he stood there, watching her. Already, they said, he had the wisdom of an old man, a sage. Yet that brief reminder of her murdered husband saddened her. It brought back the long months of bitterness and loneliness she had suffered, shut away on her father's estate.

Li Yuan must have seen something in her face, for what he said next seemed almost to read her thoughts.

'You were alone too long, Fei Yen.'

It sounded so formal, so old-mannish, that she laughed. He frowned at her, not understanding.

'I mean it,' he said, his face earnest. 'It isn't healthy for a young woman to be locked away with old maids and virgins.'

His candidness, and the apparent maturity it revealed, surprised and amused her. She had to remind herself again of his precocity. He was only twelve. Despite this she was tempted to flirt with him. It was her natural inclination, long held in check, and, after a moment's hesitation, she indulged it.

'I'm gratified to find you so concerned for my welfare, Li Yuan. You think I should have been living life to the full, then, and not mourning your brother?'

She saw immediately that she had said the wrong thing. She had misread his comment. His face closed to her and he turned away, suddenly cold, distant. It troubled her and she crossed the space between them, touching his shoulder. 'I didn't mean...'

She stood there a moment, suddenly aware of how still he was. Her hand lay gently on his shoulder, barely pressing against him, yet it seemed he was gathered there at the point of contact, his whole self focused in her touch. It bemused her. What *was* this?

She felt embarrassed, felt that she ought to remove her hand, but did not know how. It seemed that any movement of hers would be a snub.

Then, unexpectedly, he reached up and covered her hand with his own, pressing it firmly to his shoulder. 'We both miss him,' he said. 'But life goes on. I too found the customs too... strict.'

She was surprised to hear that. It was more like something Han Ch'in might have said. She had always thought Li Yuan was in his father's mould. Traditional. Bound fast by custom.

He released her and turned to face her.

Li Yuan was smiling now. Once more she found herself wrong-footed. What was happening? Why had his mood changed so quickly? She stared at him, finding the likeness to Han more prominent now that he was smiling. But then, Han had always been smiling. His eyes, his mouth, had been made for laughter.

She looked away, vaguely disturbed. Li Yuan was too intense for her taste. Like his father there was something daunting, almost terrible about him: an austerity suggestive of ferocity. Yet now, standing there, smiling at her, he seemed quite different – almost quite likeable.

'It was hard, you know. This morning... to mount Han's horse like that.'

Again the words were unexpected. His smile faded, became a wistful, boyish expression of loss.

It touched her deeply. For the first time she saw through his mask of precocious intelligence and saw how vulnerable he was, how frail in spite of all. Not even that moment after Han's death had revealed that to her. Then she had thought it grief, not vulnerability. She was moved by her insight and, when he looked up at her again, saw how hurt he seemed, how full of pain his eyes were. Beautiful eyes. Dark, hazel eyes. She had not noticed them before.

Han's death had touched him deeply. He had lost more – far more – than her. She was silent, afraid she would say the wrong thing, watching him, this man-boy, her curiosity aroused, her sympathies awoken.

He frowned and looked away.

'That's why I came to see you. To give you a gift.'

'A gift?'

'Yes. The Andalusian.'

She shook her head, confused. 'But your father...'

He looked directly at her now. 'I've spoken to my father already. He said the horse is mine to do with as I wish.' He bowed his head and swallowed. 'So I'd like to give him to you. In place of the Arab.'

She laughed shortly. 'But the Arab was Han's, not mine.'

'I know. Even so, I'd like you to have him. Han told me how much you enjoyed riding.'

This time her laughter was richer, deeper, and when Li Yuan looked up again he saw the delight in her face.

'Why, Li Yuan, that's...' She stopped and simply looked at him, smiling broadly. Then, impulsively, she reached out and embraced him, kissing his cheek.

'Then you'll take him?' he whispered softly in her ear.

Her soft laughter rippled through him. 'Of course, Li Yuan. And I thank you. From the bottom of my heart I thank you.'

When she was gone he turned and looked after her, feeling the touch of her still, the warmth on his cheek where she had kissed him. He closed his eyes and caught the scent of her, *mei hua* – plum blossom – in the air and on his clothes where she had brushed against him. He shivered, his thoughts in turmoil, his pulse racing.

The plum. Ice-skinned and jade-boned, the plum. It symbolized winter and virginity. But its blossoming brought the spring.

'*Mei hua...*' He said the words softly, like a breath, letting them mingle with her scent, then turned away, reddening at the thought that had come to mind. *Mei hua*. It was a term for sexual pleasure, for on the bridal bed were spread plum blossom covers. So innocent a scent, and yet...

Shivering, he took a long, slow breath of her. Then he turned and hurried on, his fists clenched at his sides, his face the colour of summer.

'There have been changes since you were last among us, Howard.'

'So I see.'

DeVore turned briefly to smile at Berdichev before returning his attention to the scene on the other side of the one-way mirror that took up the whole of one wall of the study.

'Who are they?'

Berdichev came up and stood beside him. 'Sympathizers. Money men, mainly. Friends of our host, Douglas.'

The room the two men looked into was massive; was more garden than room. It had been landscaped with low hills and narrow walks, with tiny underlit pools, small temples, carefully placed banks of shrub and stone, shady willows, cinnamon trees and delicate *wu-tong*. People milled about casually, talking amongst themselves, eating and drinking. But there the similarities with past occasions ended. The servants who went amongst them were no longer Han. In fact, there was not a single Han in sight.

DeVore's eyes took it all in with great interest. He saw how, though they still wore silks, the style had changed; had been simplified. Their dress seemed more austere, both in its cut and in the absence of embellishment. What had been so popular only three years ago was now conspicuous by its absence. There were no birds or flowers, no dragonflies or clouds, no butterflies or pictograms. Now only a single motif could be seen, worn openly on chest or collar, on hems or in the form of jewellery, on pendants about the neck or emblazoned on a ring or brooch: the double helix of heredity. Just as noticeable was the absence of the colour blue – the colour of imperial service. DeVore smiled appreciatively; that last touch was the subtlest of insults.

'The Seven have done our work for us, Soren.'

'Not altogether. We pride ourselves on having won the propaganda war. There are men out there who, three years ago, would not have dreamed of

coming to a gathering like this. They would have been worried that word
would get back – as, indeed, it does – and that the T'ang would act through
his Ministers to make life awkward for them. Now they have no such
fears. We have educated them to the fact of their own power. They are many,
the Seven few. What if the Seven close one door to them? Here, at such
gatherings, a thousand new doors open.'

'And The New Hope?'

Berdichev's smile stretched his narrow face against its natural grain. The
New Hope was his brainchild. 'In more than one sense it is our flagship. You
should see the pride in their faces when they talk of it. We did this, they
seem to be saying. Not the Han, but us, the Hung Mao, as they call us. The
Europeans.'

DeVore glanced at Berdichev. It was the second time he had heard the term.
Their host, Douglas, had used it when he had first arrived. 'We Europeans
must stick together,' he had said. And DeVore, hearing it, had felt he had used
it like some secret password; some token of mutual understanding.

He looked about him at the decoration of the study. Again there were
signs of change – of that same revolution in style that was sweeping the
Above. The decor, like the dress of those outside, was simpler – the design
of chairs and table less extravagant than it had been. On the walls now hung
simple rural landscapes. Gone were the colourful historical scenes that had
been so much in favour with the Hung Mao. Gone were the lavish screens
and bright floral displays of former days. But all of this, ironically, brought
them only further into line with the real Han – the Families – who had always
preferred the simple to the lavish, the harmonious to the gaudy.

These tokens of change, superficial as they yet were, were encouraging,
but they were also worrying. These men – these Europeans – were not Han,
neither had they ever been Han. Yet the Han had destroyed all that they had
once been – had severed them from their cultural roots as simply and as
thoroughly as a gardener might snip the stem of a chrysanthemum. The
Seven had given them no real choice: they could be Han or they could be
nothing. And to be nothing was intolerable. Now, however, to be Han was
equally untenable.

DeVore shivered. At present their response was negative: a reaction against
Han ways, Han dress, Han style. But they could not live like this for long. At
length they would turn the mirror on themselves and find they had no real

identity, no positive channel for their newborn sense of racial selfhood. *The New Hope* was a move to fill that vacuum, as was this term 'European'; but neither was enough. A culture was a vast and complex thing and, like the roots of a giant tree, went deep into the rich, dark earth of time. It was more than a matter of dress and style. It was a way of thinking and behaving. A thing of blood and bone, not cloth and architecture.

Yes, they needed more than a word for themselves, more than a central symbol for their pride; they needed a focus – something to restore them to themselves. But what? What on earth could fill the vacuum they were facing? It was a problem they would need to address in the coming days. To ignore it would be fatal.

He went to the long table in the centre of the room and looked down at the detailed map spread out across its surface.

'Has everyone been briefed?'

Berdichev came and stood beside him. 'Not everyone. I've kept the circle as small as possible. Douglas knows, of course. And Barrow. I thought your man, Duchek, ought to know, too, considering how helpful he's been. And then there's Moore and Weis.'

'Anton Weis? The banker?'

Berdichev nodded. 'I know what you're thinking, but he's changed in the last year or so. He fell out with old man Ebert. Was stripped by him of a number of important contracts. Now he hates the T'ang and his circle with an intensity that's hard to match.'

'I understand. Even so, I'd not have thought him important enough.'

'It's not him so much as the people he represents. He's our liaison with a number of interested parties. People who can't declare themselves openly. Important people.'

DeVore considered a moment, then smiled. 'Okay. So that makes seven of us who know.'

'Eight, actually.'

DeVore raised his eyebrows in query, but Berdichev said simply, 'I'll explain later.'

'When will they be here?'

'They're here now. Outside. They'll come in when you're ready for them.'

DeVore laughed. 'I'm ready now.'

'Then I'll tell Douglas.'

DeVore watched Berdichev move among the men gathered there in the garden room, more at ease now than he had ever been; saw too how they looked to him now as a leader, a shaper of events, and noted with irony how different that was from how they had formerly behaved. And what was different about the man? Power. It was power alone that made a man attractive. Even the potentiality of power.

He stood back, away from the door, as they filed in. Then, when the door was safely closed and locked, he came forward and exchanged bows with each of them. Seeing how closely Weis was watching him, he made an effort to be more warm, more friendly in his greeting there, but all the while he was wondering just how far he could trust the man.

Without further ado, they went to the table.

The map was of the main landmass of City Europe, omitting Scandinavia, the Balkans, Southern Italy and the Iberian Peninsula. Its predominant colour was white, though there was a faint, almost ivory tinge to it, caused by the fine yellow honeycombing that represented the City's regular shape – each tiny hexagon a hsien, an administrative district.

All Security garrisons were marked in a heavier shade of yellow, Bremen to the north-west, close to the coast, Kiev to the east, almost off the map, Bucharest far to the south; these three the most important of the twenty shown. Weimar, to the south-east of Bremen, was marked with a golden circle, forming a triangle with the Berlin garrison to the north-east.

Two large areas were marked in red, both in the bottom half of the map. One, to the left, straddled the old geographic areas of Switzerland and Austria; the other, smaller and to the right, traced the border of old Russia and cut down into Romania. In these ancient, mountainous regions – the Alps and the Carpathians – the City stopped abruptly, edging the wilderness. They formed great, jagged holes in its perfect whiteness.

Again in the top right-hand section of the map the dominant whiteness ceased abruptly in a line extending down from Gdansk hsien to Poznan, and thence to Krakow and across to Lviv, ending on the shores of the Black Sea, at Odessa. This, shaded the soft green of springtime, was the great growing area, where the Hundred Plantations – in reality eighty-seven – were situated; an area that comprised some twenty-eight per cent of the total land mass of City Europe. DeVore's own plantation was in the northwest of this area, adjoining the garrison at Lodz.

He let them study the map a while, accustoming themselves once again to its details, then drew their attention to the large red-shaded area to the bottom left of the map.

To him the outline of the Swiss Wilds always looked the same. That dark red shape was a giant carp turning in the water, its head facing east, its tail flicking out towards Marseilles *hsien*, its cruel mouth open, poised to eat Lake Balaton which, like a tiny minnow, swam some three hundred li to the east. Seven of the great Security garrisons ringed the Wilds – Geneva, Zurich, Munich and Vienna to the north, Marseilles, Milan and Zagreb to the south. Strategically that made little sense, for the Wilds were almost empty, yet it was as if the City's architect had known that this vast, jagged hole – this primitive wilderness at the heart of its hive-like orderliness – would one day prove its weakest point.

As, indeed, it would. And all the preparedness of architects would not prevent the City's fall. He leaned forward and jabbed his finger down into the red, at a point where the carp's backbone seemed to twist.

'Here!' he said, looking about him and seeing he had their attention. 'This is where our base will be.'

He reached into the drawer beneath the table and drew out the transparent template, then laid it down over the shaded area. At once that part of the map seemed to come alive; was overlaid with a fine web of brilliant gold, the nodes of which sparkled in the overhead light.

They leaned closer, attentive, as he outlined the details of his scheme. Three nerve centres, built deep into the mountainside, joined to a total of eighteen other fortresses, each linked by discreet communication systems to at least two other bases, yet each capable of functioning independently. The whole thing hidden beneath layers of ice and rock, untraceable from the air: a flexible and formidable system of defences from which they would launch their attack on the Seven.

And the cost?

The cost they knew already. It was a staggering sum. Far more than any one of them could contemplate. But together...

DeVore looked from face to face, gauging their response, coming to Weis last of all.

'Well, *Shih* Weis? Do you think your backers would approve?'

He saw the flicker of uncertainty at the back of Weis's eyes, and smiled inwardly. The man was still conditioned to think like a loyal subject of the T'ang. Even so, if he could be pushed to persuade his backers...

DeVore smiled encouragingly. 'You're happy with the way funds will be channelled through to the project, I assume?'

Weis nodded, then leaned forward, touching the template.

'This is hand drawn. Why's that?'

DeVore laughed. 'Tell me, *Shih* Weis, do you trust all your dealings to the record?'

Weis smiled and others about the table laughed. It was a common business procedure to keep a single written copy of a deal until it was considered safe for the venture to be announced publicly. It was too easy to gain access to a company's computer records when everyone used the same communications web.

'You want the T'ang to know our scheme beforehand?'

Weis withdrew his hand, then looked at DeVore again and smiled. 'I think my friends will be pleased enough, Major.'

DeVore's face did not change immediately, but inwardly he tensed. It had been agreed beforehand that they would refer to him as *Shih* Scott. Weis, he was certain, had not forgotten that, neither had he mentioned his former Security rank without some underlying reason.

You're dead, thought DeVore, smiling pleasantly at the man as if amused by his remark. *As soon as you're expendable, you're dead.*

'I'm delighted, *Shih* Weis. Like yourself, they will be welcome any time they wish to visit. I would not ask them to fund anything they cannot see with their own eyes.'

He saw the calculation at the back of Weis's eyes that greeted his comment – saw how he looked for a trap in every word of his – and smiled inwardly. At least the man was wise enough to know how dangerous he was. But his wisdom would not help him in this instance.

DeVore turned to Barrow. 'And you, Under Secretary? Have you anything to add?'

Barrow had succeeded to Lehmann's old position, and whilst his contribution to this scheme was negligible, his role as leader of the Dispersionist faction in the House made his presence here essential. If he approved then First Level would approve, for he was their mouthpiece, their conscience in these times of change.

Barrow smiled sadly, then looked down. 'I wish there were some other way, *Shih* Scott. I wish that pressure in the House would prove enough, but I am realist enough to know that change – real change – will only come now if we push from every side.' He sighed. 'Your scheme here has my sanction. My only hope is that we shall never have to use it against the Seven.'

'And mine, Barrow Chen,' DeVore assured him, allowing no trace of cynicism to escape into his voice or face. 'Yet, as you say, we must be realists. We must be prepared to use all means to further our cause. We Europeans have been denied too long.'

Afterwards, alone with Berdichev and Douglas, he talked of minor things, concealing his pleasure that his scheme had their sanction and – more important – their financial backing. Times have certainly changed, he thought, admiring a small rose quartz snuff bottle Douglas had handed him from a cabinet to one side of the study. Three years ago they would have hesitated before speaking against the Seven; now – however covertly – they sanctioned armed rebellion.

'It's beautiful,' he said. And indeed it was. A crane, the emblem of long life, stood out from the surface of the quartz, flanked by magpies, signifying good luck; while encircling the top of the bottle was a spray of peonies, emblematic of spring and wealth. The whole thing was delightful, almost a perfect work of art, yet small enough to enclose in the palm of his hand.

'One last thing, Howard.'

DeVore raised his head, aware of the slight hesitation in Berdichev's voice. 'Is there a problem?'

'Yes and no. That is, there is only if you feel there's one.'

DeVore set the rose quartz bottle down and turned to face his friend. 'You're being unusually cryptic, Soren. Are we in danger?'

Berdichev gave a short laugh. 'No. It's nothing like that. It's... Well, it's Lehmann's son.'

DeVore was silent a moment. He looked at Douglas, then back at Berdichev. 'Lehmann's *son*? I didn't know Pietr had a son.'

'Few did. It was one of his best-kept secrets.'

Yes, thought DeVore, *it certainly was. I thought I knew everything about you all – every last tiny little, dirty little thing – but now you surprise me.*

'Illegitimate, I suppose?'

Berdichev shook his head. 'Not at all. The boy's his legal heir. On Lehmann's death he inherited the whole estate.'

'Really?'

That too was news to him. He had thought Lehmann had died intestate – that his vast fortune had gone back to the Seven. It changed things dramatically. Lehmann must have been worth at least two billion yuan.

'It was all done quietly, of course, as Lehmann wished.'

DeVore nodded, masking his surprise. There was a whole level of things here that he had been totally unaware of. 'Explain. Lehmann wasn't even married. How could he have a son and heir?'

Berdichev came across and stood beside him. 'It was a long time ago. Back when we were at college. Pietr met a girl there. A bright young thing, but unconnected. His father, who was still alive then, refused to even let Pietr see her. He threatened to cut him off without a yuan if he did.'

'And yet he did, secretly. And married her.'

Berdichev nodded. 'I was one of the witnesses at the ceremony.'

DeVore looked away thoughtfully; looked across at the window wall and at the gathering in the garden room beyond it. 'What happened?'

For a moment Berdichev was quiet, looking back down the well of years to that earlier time. Then, strangely, he laughed; a sad, almost weary laugh. 'You know how it is. We were young. Far too young. Pietr's father was right: the girl wasn't suitable. She ran off with another man. Pietr divorced her.'

'And she took the child with her?'

The look of pain on Berdichev's face was unexpected. 'No. It wasn't like that. You see, she was four months pregnant when they divorced. Pietr only found out by accident, when she applied to have the child aborted. Of course, the official asked for the father's details, saw there was a profit to be made from the information and went straight to Lehmann.'

DeVore smiled. It was unethical, but then so was the world. 'And Pietr made her have the child?'

Berdichev shook his head. 'She refused. Said she'd kill herself first. But Pietr hired an advocate. You see, by law the child was his. It was conceived within wedlock and while she was his wife any child of her body was legally his property.'

'I see. But how did hiring an advocate help?'

'He had a restraining order served on her. Had her taken into hospital and the foetus removed and placed in a MedFac nurture unit.'

'Ah. Even so, I'm surprised. Why did we never see the child? There was no reason to keep things secret.'

'No. I suppose not. But Pietr was strange about it. I tried to talk to him about it several times, but he would walk out on me. As for the boy, well, he never lived with his father, never saw him, and Pietr refused ever to see the child. He thought he would remind him too much of his mother.'

DeVore's mouth opened slightly. 'He loved her, then? Even after what she did?'

'Adored her. It's why he never married again, never courted female company. I think her leaving killed something in him.'

'How strange. How very, very strange.' DeVore looked down. 'I would never have guessed.' He shook his head. 'And the son? How does he feel about his father?'

'I don't know. He's said nothing, and I feel it impertinent to ask.'

DeVore turned and looked directly at Berdichev. 'So what's the problem?'

'For the last three years the boy has been my ward. As Pietr's executor I've handled his affairs. But now he's of age.'

'So?'

'So I'd like you to take charge of the boy for a while.'

DeVore laughed, genuinely surprised by Berdichev's request. 'Why? What are you up to, Soren?'

Berdichev shook his head. 'I've nothing to do with this, Howard. It's what the boy wants.'

'The boy...' DeVore felt uncomfortable. He had been wrong-footed too many times already in this conversation. He was used to being in control of events, not the victim of circumstance; even so, the situation intrigued him. What could the boy want? And, more to the point, how had Lehmann's son heard of him?

'Perhaps you should meet him,' Berdichev added hastily, glancing across at Douglas as if for confirmation. 'Then you might understand. He's not... Well, he's not perhaps what you'd expect.'

'Yes. Of course. When?'

'Would now do?'

DeVore shrugged. 'Why not?'

But his curiosity was intense. Why should the boy be not what he'd expect? 'Is there something I should know beforehand, Soren? Is there something strange about him?'

Berdichev gave a brief laugh. 'You'll understand. You more than anyone will understand.'

While Berdichev went to get the boy he waited, conscious of Douglas's unease. It was clear he had met the boy already. It was also clear that something about the young man made him intensely uncomfortable. He glanced at DeVore, then, making up his mind, gave a brief bow and went across to the door.

'I must be getting back, Howard. You'll forgive me, but my guests...'

'Of course.' DeVore returned the bow, then turned, intrigued, wondering what it was about the boy that could so thoroughly spook the seemingly imperturbable Douglas.

He did not have long to wait for his answer.

'Howard, meet Stefan Lehmann.'

DeVore shivered. Despite himself, he felt an overwhelming sense of aversion towards the young man who stood before him. It wasn't just the shocking, skull-like pallor of his face and hair, or the unhealthy pinkness of his eyes, both signs of albinism, but something to do with the unnatural coldness of the youth. When he looked at you it was as if an icy wind blew from the far north. DeVore met those eyes and saw through them to the emptiness beyond. But he was thinking, *Who are you? Are you really Lehmann's son? Were you really taken from your mother's womb and bred inside a nurture unit until the world was ready for you?*

Red in white, those eyes. Each eye a wild, dark emptiness amidst the cold, clear whiteness of the flesh.

He stepped forward, offering his hand to the albino but looking at Berdichev as he did so. 'Our eighth man, I presume.'

'I'm sorry?' Then Berdichev understood. 'Ah, yes, I said I'd explain, didn't I? But you're right, of course. Stefan was the first to be briefed. He insisted on it. After all, he's responsible for sixty per cent of the funding.'

DeVore looked down at the hand that held his own. The fingers were long, unnaturally thin, the skin on them so clear it seemed he could see right through them to the bone itself. But the young man's grip was firm, his skin surprisingly warm.

He looked up, meeting those eyes again, suddenly curious; wanting to hear the boy speak.

'So. You want to stay with me a while?'

Stefan Lehmann looked at him – looked through him – then turned and looked across at Berdichev.

'You were right, Uncle Soren. He's like me, isn't he?'

DeVore laughed, uncomfortable, then let go of the hand, certain now. The boy's voice was familiar – unnaturally familiar. It was Pietr Lehmann's voice.

The albino was standing behind where he was sitting, studying the bank of screens, when Peskova came into the room. DeVore saw how his lieutenant hesitated – saw the flicker of pure aversion, quickly masked, that crossed his face – before he came forward.

'What is it, Peskova?'

DeVore sat back, his eyes narrowed.

Peskova bowed, then glanced again at the albino. 'There's been unrest, *Shih* Bergson. Some trouble down on Camp Two.'

DeVore looked down at the desk. 'So?'

Peskova cleared his throat, self-conscious in the presence of the stranger. 'It's the Han woman, Overseer. Sung's wife. She's been talking.'

DeVore met his lieutenant's eyes, his expression totally unreadable. 'Talking?'

Peskova swallowed. 'I had to act, *Shih* Bergson. I had to isolate her from the rest.'

DeVore smiled tightly. 'That's fine. But you'll let her go now, neh? You'll explain that it was all a mistake.'

Peskova's mouth opened marginally then closed without a sound. Bowing deeply, and with one last, brief look at the albino, he turned and left, to do at once what the Overseer had ordered.

'Why did you tell him that?'

DeVore turned and looked at Lehmann's son. He was eighteen, but he seemed ageless, timeless. Like death itself.

'To make him do as I say, not as he thinks he should do.'

'And the woman?'

DeVore smiled into that empty, mask-like face. He had no need to answer. The boy knew already what would happen to the woman.

The moon was huge and monstrous in the darkness: a full, bright circle, like a blind eye staring down from nothingness. Si Wu Ya looked up at it and shivered, anxious now. Then, as the rope tightened again, tugging at her, she stumbled on, the tops of her arms chafing where the rope bit into them.

Ahead of her Sung was whimpering again. 'Be quiet!' she yelled, angry with him for his weakness, but was rewarded with the back of Teng's hand. Then Teng was standing over her, his breathing heavy and irregular, a strange excitement in his face. Groaning, the pain in her lower body almost more than she could bear, she got to her feet, then spat blood, unable to put her hand up to her mouth to feel the damage he had done to her.

Ahead lay the water-chestnut fields, glimmering in the reflected light from Chung Kuo's barren sister.

We are cursed, she thought, staggering on, each step sending a jolt of pain through her from arse to abdomen. *Even Teng and Chang. Even Peskova and that bastard Bergson. All cursed. Every last one of us. All of us fated to go this way; stumbling on in darkness, beneath the gaze of that cold, blind eye.*

She tried to laugh but the sound died in her before it reached her lips. Then, before she realised it, they had stopped and she was pushed down to the ground next to Sung, her back to him.

She lay there, looking about her, the hushed voices of the four men standing nearby washing over her like the senseless murmur of the sea.

Smiling, she whispered to her husband, 'The sea, Sung. I've never seen the sea. Never really seen it. Only on vidcasts...'

She rolled over and saw at once that he wasn't listening. His eyes were dark with fear, his hands, bound at his sides like her own, twitched convulsively, the fingers shaking uncontrollably.

'Sung...' she said, moved by the sight of him. 'My sweet little Sung...'

She wanted to reach out and hold him to her, to draw him close and comfort him, but it was too late now. All her love for him, all her anguish welled up suddenly, overwhelming her.

'Kuan yin!' she said softly, tearfully. 'Oh, my poor Sung. I didn't mean to be angry with you. Oh, my poor, poor darling. I didn't mean...'

Teng kicked her hard in the ribs, silencing her.

'Which one first?'

The voice was that of the simpleton, Seidemann. Si Wu Ya breathed slowly, deeply, trying not to cry out again, letting the pain wash past her, over her; trying to keep her mind clear of it. In case. Just in case...

She almost shook her head; almost laughed. In case of what? It was done with now. There was only pain ahead of them now. Pain and the end of pain.

Peskova answered. 'The woman. We'll do the woman first.'

She felt them lift her and take her over to the low stone wall beside the glimmering field of water-chestnuts. *The woman*, she thought, vaguely recognizing herself in the words. *Not Si Wu Ya now, no longer Silk Raven, simply 'the woman'.*

She waited, the cold stone of the wall pushed up hard against her breasts, her knees pushing downward into the soft, moist loam, while they unfastened the rope about her arms. There was a moment's relief, a second or two free of pain, even of thought, then it began again.

Teng took one arm, Chang the other, and pulled. Her head went down sharply, cracking against the top of the wall, stunning her.

There was a cry followed by an awful groan, but it was not her voice. Sung had struggled to his feet and now stood there, only paces from where the Overseer's man, Peskova was standing, a big rock balanced in both hands.

Sung made a futile struggle to free his arms, then desisted. 'Not her,' he pleaded. 'Please, gods, not her. It's me you want. I'm the thief, not her. She's done nothing. Nothing. Kill me, Peskova. Do what you want to me, but leave her be. Please, gods, leave her be...' His voice ran on a moment longer, then fell silent.

Teng began to laugh, but a look from Peskova silenced him. Then, with a final look at Sung, Peskova turned and brought the rock down on the woman's upper arm.

The cracking of the bone sounded clearly in the silence. There was a moment's quiet afterwards, then Sung fell to his knees, vomiting.

Peskova stepped over the woman and brought the heavy stone down on the other arm. She was unconscious now. It was a pity, that; he would have liked to have heard her groan again, perhaps even to cry out as she had that night when The Man had played his games with her.

He smiled. Oh, yes, they'd all heard that. Had heard and found the echo in themselves. He looked across at Sung. Poor little Sung. Weak little Sung. All his talk meant nothing now. He was powerless to change things. Powerless to save his wife. Powerless even to save himself. It would be no fun killing him. No more fun than crushing a bug.

He brought the stone down once again; heard the brittle sound of bone as it snapped beneath the rock. So easy it was. So very, very easy.

Teng and Chang had stepped back now. They were no longer necessary. The woman would be going nowhere now. They watched silently as he stepped over her body and brought the stone down once again, breaking her other leg.

'That's her, then.' Peskova turned and glanced at Sung, then looked past him at Seidemann. 'Bring him here. Let's get it over with.'

Afterwards he stood there beside the wall, staring at Sung's body where it lay, face down on the edge of the field of water-chestnuts. *Strange,* he thought. *It was just like a machine. Like switching off a machine.*

For a moment he looked out across the water meadow, enjoying the night's stillness, the beauty of the full moon overhead. Then he heaved the stone out into the water and turned away, hearing the dull splash sound behind him.

Chapter 39

CASTING A SPELL OUT OF ICE

K im lay on his back in the water, staring up at the ceiling of the pool.
Stars hung like strung beads of red and black against the dull gold
background, the five sections framed by Han pictograms. It was a
copy of part of the ancient Tun Huang star map of AD 940. According to the
Han it was the earliest accurate representation of the heavens; a cylindrical
projection that divided the sky into twenty-eight slices – like the segments
of a giant orange.

There was a game he sometimes played, floating there alone. He would
close his eyes and clear his mind of everything but darkness. Then, one by
one, he would summon up the individual stars from within a single section
of the Tun Huang map; would set each in its true place in the heavens of his
mind, giving them a dimension in time and space that the inflexibility – the
sheer flatness – of the map denied them. Slowly he would build his own small
galaxy of stars. Then, when the last of them was set delicately in place, like a
jewel in a sphere of black glass, he would try to give the whole thing motion.

In his earliest attempts this had been the moment when the fragile sphere
had shattered, as if exploded from within; but experiment and practice had
brought him beyond that point. Now he could make the sphere expand or
contract along the dimension of time; could trace each separate star's unique
and unrepeated course through the nothingness he had created within his
skull. It gave him a strong feel for space – for the relationships and per-
spectives of stars. Then, when he opened his eyes again, he would see – as

if for real – the fine tracery of lines that linked the bead-like stars on the Tun Huang map, and could see, somewhere beyond the dull gold surface, where their real positions lay – out there in the cold, black eternity beyond the solar system.

Kim had cleared his mind, ready for the game, when he heard the doors at the far end of the pool swing open and the wet slap of bare feet on the tiles, followed moments later by a double splash. He knew without looking who it was, and when they surfaced, moments later, close to him, acknowledged them with a smile, his eyes still closed, his body stretched out in the water.

'Daydreaming?' It was Anton's voice.

'That's right,' he said, assuming a relaxed, almost lazy tone of voice. He had told no one of his game, knowing how the other boys responded to the least sign of eccentricity. Both Anton and Josef were some three years older than he and shared a tutorial class with him, so knew how brilliant he was; but brilliance inside the classroom was one thing, how one behaved outside it was another. Outside they took care to disguise all sign of what had brought them here.

At times Kim found this attitude perverse. They should be proud of what they were – proud of the gifts that had saved them from the Clay. But it was not so simple. At the back of it they were ashamed. Ashamed and guilty. They had survived, yes, but they knew that they were here on sufferance. At any moment they could be cast down again, into darkness. Or gassed, or simply put to sleep. That knowledge humbled them; bound them in psychological chains far stronger than any physical restraint. Outside the classroom they were rarely boastful.

Josef sculled backwards with his hands, his head tilted back, his knees bent, experimenting with his balance in the water. 'Are you going to see the film tonight?'

Kim lifted his head and looked back at his friend, letting his feet drift slowly down. He was nine now but, like all of them, much smaller, lither than normal boys his age. He combed his hair back with his fingers, then gave his head a tiny shake. 'What film is it?'

Anton laughed. 'What do you think?'

'Ah...' Kim understood at once. They had been joking about it only yesterday. 'Pan Chao...'

Pan Chao! It sometimes seemed as if half the films ever made had been about Pan Chao! He was the great hero of Chung Kuo – the soldier turned diplomat turned conqueror. In AD 73 he had been sent, with thirty-six followers, as ambassador to the King of Shen Shen in Turkestan. Ruthlessly defeating his rival for influence, the ambassador from the Hsiung Nu, he had succeeded in bringing Shen Shen under Han control. But this, his first triumph, had been eclipsed by what had followed. Over the next twenty-four years, by bluff and cunning and sheer force of personality, Pan Chao had brought the whole of Asia under Han domination. In AD 97 he had stood on the shore of the Caspian Sea, an army of 70,000 vassals gathered behind him, facing the great Ta Ts'in, the Roman Empire. The rest was history, known to every schoolboy.

For a moment the three boys' laughter echoed from the walls.

In the silence that followed, Kim asked, 'Do you think he really existed?'

'What do you mean?' It was Anton who answered him, but he spoke for both the boys. How could Pan Chao not have existed? Would Chung Kuo *be* Chung Kuo were it not for Pan Chao? It would be *Ta Ts'in* instead. A world ruled by the *Hung Mao*. And such a world was an impossibility. The two boys laughed, taking Kim's comment for dry humour.

Kim, watching them, saw at once how meaningless such questions were to them. None of them shared his scepticism. They had been bewitched by the sheer scale of the world into which they had entered; a world so big and broad and rich – a world so deeply and thoroughly embedded in time – that it could not, surely, have been invented? So grateful were they to have escaped the darkness of the Clay, they were loath to question the acts and statements of their benefactors.

No, it was more than that: they had been *conditioned* not to question it.

'Forget it,' he said, and realized that even in that he differed from them. They *could* forget. In fact, they found it easy to forget. But he could not. Everything – even his mistakes – were engraved indelibly in his memory, almost as if his memory had greater substance – was more *real* – than their own.

'Well?' Anton persisted. 'Are you going to come? It's one we haven't seen before. About the Fall of Rome and the death of Kan Ying.'

Kim smiled, amused, then nodded. 'Okay, I'll...'

He stopped.

The three boys turned in the water, looking.

The doors at the far end had swung open. Momentarily they stayed open, held there by a tall, spindly youth with long arms, a mop of unruly yellow hair and bright blue, staring eyes. It was Matyas.

'Shit!' said Josef under his breath and ducked beneath the water.

Matyas smiled maliciously then came through, followed by two other boys, smaller, much younger than himself. 'Greaser' and 'Sucker', Anton called them, though not in Matyas's hearing: names that captured not only the subservient nature of their relationship to Matyas but also something of their physical appearance. Greaser – his real name was Tom – had a slick, rat-like look to him, especially in the water, while Sucker, a quiet boy named Carl, had a small, puckered face dominated by thick, fleshy lips.

It was whispered that the two of them 'serviced' Matyas in a most original manner; but how much of that was truth and how much it was influenced by Anton's persuasively apt names was hard to gauge. All that was certain was that the two younger boys accompanied Matyas everywhere; were shadow and mirror to his twisted image.

Kim watched Matyas lope arrogantly along the edge of the pool, his head lowered, an unhealthy smile on his thin lips, until he stood across from him. There Matyas turned and, his smile broadening momentarily, threw himself forward into the water in an ungainly dive.

Kim glanced briefly at the two boys at his side. Like him, they had tensed in the water, expecting trouble. But it was always difficult to know with Matyas. He was no ordinary bully. Neither would he have got here and stayed here had he been. No, his deviousness was part of the fabric of his clever mind. He was a tormentor, a torturer, a master of the implicit threat. He used physical force only as a last resort, knowing he could generally accomplish more by subtler means.

However, Matyas had one weakness. He was vain. Not of his looks, which, even he would admit, tended towards ugliness, but about his intelligence. In that respect he had been cock of the roost until only a year ago, when Kim had first come to the Centre. But Kim's arrival had eclipsed him. Not at once, for Kim had been careful to fit in, deferring to the older boy whenever they came into contact, but as the months passed and word spread that the new boy was something special, Kim saw how Matyas changed towards him.

Matyas surfaced directly in front of Kim, less than a forearm's length away, and shook his head exaggeratedly, sending the spray into Kim's face. Then he laughed and began to move around him in a leisurely but awkward breaststroke. Kim turned, keeping the older boy in front of him at all times.

'And how's golden boy, then?' Matyas asked quietly, looking up and sideways, one intensely blue eye fixing the nine-year-old.

Matyas himself was fifteen, almost sixteen. On his birthday, in a month's time, he would leave the Centre and begin his service in the Above, but until then he was in a kind of limbo. He had outgrown the Centre, yet the thought of losing his 'position' as senior boy both frightened and angered him. *Ning wei chi k'ou mo wei niu hou,* the Han said – 'Rather be the mouth of a chicken than the hindquarters of a cow' – and so it was with Matyas. He did not relish becoming a small fish once again – a 'cow's arse'. As a result, he had been restless these last few weeks – dangerous and unpredictable, his sarcasm tending towards open cruelty. Several times Kim had caught Matyas staring at him malevolently and knew the older boy would never forgive the newcomer for robbing him – unjustly, Matyas believed – of his intellectual crown.

It was why Matyas was so dangerous just now. It was more than jealousy or uncertainty or restlessness. He had lost face to Kim, and that loss burned in him like a brand.

Kim looked past him, noting how his followers, Tom and Carl, had positioned themselves at the pool's edge, crouched forward, watching things closely, ready to launch themselves into the water at any moment. Then he looked back at Matyas and smiled.

'*Ts'ai neng t'ung shen,*' he said provocatively and heard Anton, behind him, splutter with surprise.

'Shit!' Josef exhaled softly, off to his right. 'That's done it!'

Kim kept the smile on his face, trying to act as naturally as he could, but the hair on his neck had risen and he could feel a tension in his stomach that had not been there a moment earlier. *A golden key opens every door,* he had said playing on Matyas' use of 'golden'. It seemed simple enough, innocuous enough, but the jibe was clear to them all. It was Kim to whom doors would open, not Matyas.

It seemed a reckless thing to say – a deliberate rubbing of salt into the open wound of Matyas' offended pride – but Kim hoped he knew what he was doing. There was no avoiding this confrontation. He had half expected it for days now. That admitted, it was still possible to turn things to his advantage. A calm Matyas was a dangerous Matyas. Infuriated, he might prove easier to beat. And beat him Kim must.

Matyas had turned in the water, facing him, the leering smile gone, his cheeks red, his eyes wide with anger. Kim had been right – the words acted on him like a goad. Without warning he lashed out viciously with one arm, but the weight and resistance of the water slowed his movement and made the blow fall short of Kim, who had pushed out backwards, anticipating it.

There was a loud splash as Tom and Carl hit the water behind Kim. Without a moment's hesitation Anton and Josef launched themselves into Kim's defence, striking out to intercept the two boys. As he backed away, Kim saw Anton plough into Carl and, even as the boy surfaced, thrust his head savagely down into the water again before he could take a proper breath. But that was all he saw, for suddenly Matyas was on him, struggling to push Kim down beneath the surface, his face blind with fury.

Kim kicked out sharply, catching Matyas painfully on the hip, then wriggled out under him, twisting away and down. He kicked hard, thrusting himself down through the water, then turned and pushed up from the floor of the pool, away from the figure high above him.

For the moment Kim had the advantage. He spent far more time in the pool than Matyas and was the better swimmer. But the pool was only so big, and he could not avoid Matyas indefinitely. Matyas had only to get a firm grip on him and he was done for.

He broke surface two body lengths from the older boy and kicked out for the steps. He had to get out of the water.

Kim grabbed the metal rungs and hauled himself up, but he had not been quick enough. Desperation and anger had made Matyas throw himself through the water, and as Kim's back foot lifted up out of the water, Matyas lunged at it and caught the ankle. He was ill balanced in the water and could not hold it, but it was enough. Tripped, Kim sprawled forward, slamming his forearm painfully against the wet floor and skidding across to the wall.

Kim lay there, stunned, then rolled over and sat up. Matyas was standing over him, his teeth bared, eyes blazing, water running from him. In the water the others had stopped fighting and were watching.

'You little cockroach,' Matyas said, in a low, barely controlled voice. He jerked forward and pulled Kim to his feet, one hand gripping Kim's neck tightly, as if to snap it. 'I should kill you for what you've done. But I'll not give you that satisfaction. You deserve less than that.'

A huge shudder passed through Matyas. He pushed Kim down, onto his knees. Then, his eyes never leaving Kim's face, his other hand undid the cord to his trunks and drew out his penis. As they watched, it unfolded slowly, growing huge, engorged.

'Kiss it,' he said, his face cruel, his voice low but uncompromising.

Kim winced. Matyas' fingers bit into his neck, forcing Kim's face down into his groin. For a brief moment he considered not resisting. Did it matter? Was it worth fighting over such a thing as face? Why not kiss Matyas' prick and satisfy his sense of face? But the thought was fleeting. Face mattered here. He could not bow to such as Matyas and retain the respect of those he lived with. It would be the rod the other boys would use to beat him. And beat him they would – mercilessly – if he capitulated now. He had not made these callous, stupid rules of behaviour, but he must live by them or be cast out.

'I'd as soon bite it,' he said hoarsely, forcing the words out past Matyas' fingers.

There was laughter from the water. Matyas glared round, furious, then turned back to Kim, yanking him up onto his feet. Anger made his hand shake as he lifted Kim off the floor and turned, holding him out over the water.

Kim saw in his eyes what Matyas intended. He would let him fall, then jump on him, forcing him down, keeping him down, until he drowned.

It would be an accident. Even Anton and Josef would swear to the fact. That too was how things were.

Kim tried to swallow, suddenly, unexpectedly afraid, but Matyas' fingers pressed relentlessly against his windpipe, making him choke.

'Don't, Matyas. Please don't...' It was Josef's voice. But none of the boys made to intercede. Things were out of their hands now.

Kim began to struggle, but Matyas tightened his grip, almost suffocating him. For a moment Kim thought he had died – a great tide of blackness swept through his head – then he was falling.

He hit the water gasping for breath and went under. His chest was suddenly on fire. His eyes seemed to pop. Pain lanced through his head like lightning. Then he surfaced, coughing, choking, flailing about in the water, and felt someone grab hold of him tightly. He began to struggle, then convulsed, spears of heated iron ripping his chest apart. For a moment the air seemed burnished a dull gold, flecked with tiny beads of red and black. Lights danced momentarily on the surface of his eyes, fizzling and popping like firecrackers, then the blackness surged back – a great sphere of blackness, closing in on him with the sound of great wings pulsing, beating in his head...

And then there was nothing.

'Have you heard about the boy?'

T'ai Cho looked up from his meal, then stood, giving the Director a small bow. 'I'm sorry, *Shih* Andersen. The boy?'

Andersen huffed impatiently, then glared at the other tutors so that they looked back down at their meals. 'The boy! Kim! Have you heard what happened to him?'

T'ai Cho felt himself go cold. He shook his head. He had been away all day on a training course and had only just arrived back. There had been no time for anyone to tell him anything.

Andersen hesitated, conscious of the other tutors listening. 'In my office, T'ai Cho. Now!'

T'ai Cho looked about the table, but there were only shrugs.

Andersen came to the point at once. 'Kim was attacked. This morning, in the pool.'

T'ai Cho had gone cold. 'Is he hurt?'

Andersen shook his head. He was clearly angry. 'No. But it might have been worse. He could have died. And where would we be then? It was only Shang Li-Yen's prompt action that saved the boy.'

Shang Li-Yen was one of the tutors. Like all the tutors, part of his duties entailed a surveillance stint. Apparently he had noted a camera malfunction in the pool area and, rather than wait for the repair crew, had gone to investigate.

'What did Shang find?'

Andersen laughed bitterly. 'Six boys sky-larking! What do you think? You know how they are – they'd sooner die than inform on each other! But Shang thinks it was serious. Matyas was involved. He was very agitated when Shang burst in on them; standing at the poolside, breathing strangely, his face flushed. Kim was in the water nearby. Only the quick actions of one of the other boys got him out of the water.' Anger flared in the Director's eyes. 'Fuck it, T'ai Cho, Shang had to give him the kiss of life!'

'Where is he now?' T'ai Cho asked, trying to keep his emotions in check.

'In his room. But let me finish. We had Kim examined and there were marks on his throat and arms and on his right leg consistent with a fight. Matyas also had some minor bruises. But both boys claim they simply fell while playing in the pool. The other boys back them up, but all six stories differ widely. It's clear none of them is telling the truth.'

'And you want me to try to find out what really happened?'

Andersen nodded. 'If anyone can get to the bottom of it, you can, T'ai Cho. Kim trusts you. You're like a father to him.'

T'ai Cho lowered his eyes, then shook his head. 'Maybe so, but he'll tell me nothing. As you said, it's how they are.'

Andersen was quiet a moment, then he leaned across his desk, his voice suddenly much harder, colder than it had been. 'Try anyway, T'ai Cho. Try hard. It's important. If Matyas was to blame I want to know. Because if he was I want him out. Kim's too important to us. We've got too much invested in him.'

T'ai Cho rose from his seat and bowed, understanding perfectly. It wasn't Kim – the boy – Andersen was so concerned about, it was Kim-as-investment. Well, so be it. He would use that in Kim's favour.

Kim's room was empty. T'ai Cho felt his stomach tighten, his pulse quicken. Then he remembered. Of course. The film. Kim would have gone to see the film. He glanced at his timer. It was just after ten. The film was almost finished. Kim would be back in fifteen minutes.

He looked about the room, noting as ever what was new, what old. The third-century portrait of the mathematician Liu Hui remained in its place of honour on the wall above Kim's terminal, and on the top, beside the keyboard, lay Hui's *Chiu Chang Suan Shu*, his 'Nine Chapters On The Mathematical Art'. T'ai Cho smiled and opened its pages. Kim's notations filled the margins. Like the book itself, they were in Mandarin, the tiny, perfectly formed pictograms in red, black and green inks.

T'ai Cho flicked through inattentively and was about to close the book when one of the notations caught his attention. It was right at the end of the book, amongst the notes to the ninth chapter. The notation itself was un-remarkable – something to do with ellipses – but beside it, in green, Kim had printed a name and two dates. Tycho Brahe. 1546 – 1601.

He frowned, wondering if the first name was a play on his own. But then, what did the other mean? Bra He... It made no sense. And the dates? Or were they dates? Perhaps they were a code.

For a moment he hesitated, loath to pry, then set the book down and switched on the terminal.

A search of the system's central encyclopedia confirmed what he had believed. There was no entry, either on Tycho or Brahe. Nothing. Not even on close variants of the two names.

T'ai Cho sat there a moment, his fingers resting lightly on the keys, a vague suspicion forming in his head.

He shook his head. No. It wasn't possible, surely? The terminal in T'ai Cho's room was secretly 'twinned' with Kim's. Everything Kim did on his terminal was available to T'ai Cho. Everything. Work files, diary, jottings, even his messages to the other boys. It seemed sneaky, but it was necessary. There was no other way of keeping up with Kim. His interests were too wide ranging, too quicksilver to keep track of any other way. It was their only means of controlling him – of anticipating his needs and planning ahead.

But what if?

T'ai Cho typed his query quickly, then sat back.

The answer appeared on the screen at once.

'SUB-CODE?'

T'ai Cho leaned forward and typed in the dates, careful to include the spacing and the dash.

There was the briefest hesitation, then the file came up. 'BRAHE, Tycho.' T'ai Cho scanned it quickly. It was a summary of the man's life and achieve-ments in the manner of a genuine encyclopedia entry.

T'ai Cho sat back again, astonished, then laughed, remembering the time long before when Kim had removed the lock from his cell without their knowing. *And so again*, he thought. But this was much subtler, much more clever than the simple removal of a lock. This was on a wholly different level of evasiveness.

He read the passage through, pausing thoughtfully at the final line, then cleared the file and switched the terminal off. For a moment he sat there, staring sightlessly at the screen, then he stood up and moved away from the terminal.

'T'ai Cho?'

He turned with a start. Kim was standing in the doorway, clearly surprised to see him. He seemed much quieter than normal, on his guard. There was an eri-silk scarf around his neck and his wrist was bandaged. He made no move to come into the room.

T'ai Cho smiled and sat down on the bed. 'How was the film?'

Kim smiled briefly, unenthusiastically. 'No surprises,' he said after a moment. 'Pan Chao was triumphant. As ever.'

T'ai Cho saw the boy look across at the terminal, then back at him, but there was no sign that Kim had seen what he'd been doing.

'Come here,' he said gently. 'Come and sit with me, Kim. We need to talk.'

Kim hesitated, understanding at once why T'ai Cho had come. Then he shook his head. 'Nothing happened this morning.'

'Nothing?' T'ai Cho looked deliberately at the scarf, the bandage.

Kim smiled but said nothing.

'Okay. But it doesn't matter. We already know what happened. There's a hidden camera in the ceiling of the pool. One Matyas overlooked when he sabotaged the others. We saw him attack you. Saw him grab you by the throat, then try to drown you.'

Still Kim said nothing, gave nothing away.

T'ai Cho shrugged then looked down, wondering how closely the scenario fitted. Was Kim quiet because it was true? Or was he quiet because it had happened otherwise? Whichever, he was certain of one thing. Matyas *had* attacked Kim. He had seen for himself the jealous envy in the older boy's eyes. But he had never dreamed it would come to this.

He stood up, inwardly disturbed by this side of Kim. This primitive, savage side that all the Clayborn seemed to have. He had never understood this aspect of their behaviour: this perverse tribal solidarity of theirs. Where they came from it was a strength, no doubt – a survival factor – but up here, in the Above, it was a failing, a fatal flaw.

'You're important, Kim. Very important. You know that, don't you? And Matyas should have known better. He's out for what he did.'

Kim looked down. 'Matyas did nothing. It was an accident.'

T'ai Cho took a deep breath, then stood and went across to him. 'As you say, Kim. But we know otherwise.'

Kim looked up at him, meeting his eyes coldly. 'Is that all?'

That too was unlike Kim. That hardness. Perhaps the experience had shaken him. Changed him in some small way. For a moment T'ai Cho studied him, wondering whether he should bring up the matter of the secret files, then decided not to. He would investigate them first. Find out what Kim was up to. Then, and only then, would he confront him.

He smiled and looked away. 'That's all.'

Back in his room T'ai Cho locked his door, then began to summon up the files, beginning with the master file, referred to in the last line of the BRAHE.

The Aristotle File.

The name intrigued him, because, unlike Brahe, there had been an Aristotle: a minor Greek philosopher of the fourth century BC. He checked the entry briefly on the general encyclopedia. There was less than a hundred and fifty words on the man. Like T'ai Cho, he had been a tutor, in his case to the Greek King, Alexander. As to the originality of his thinking, he appeared to be on a par with Hui Shih, a contemporary Han logician who had stressed the relativity of time and space and had sought to prove the existence of the 'Great One Of All Things' through rational knowledge. Now, however, both men existed only as tiny footnotes in the history of science. Greece had been conquered by Rome and Rome by the Han. And the Han had abandoned the path of pure logic with Hui Shih.

T'ai Cho typed in the three words, then leaned back. The answer appeared on the screen at once.

'SUB-CODE?'

He took a guess. ALEXANDER, he typed, then sat back with a laugh as the computer accepted the codeword.

There was a brief pause, then the title page came up on the screen.

THE ARISTOTLE FILE
Being The True History Of Western Science

T'ai Cho frowned. What *was* this? Then he understood. It was a game. An outlet for Kim's inventiveness. Something Kim had made up. Yes, he understood at once. He had read somewhere how certain young geniuses invented worlds and peopled them, as an exercise for their intellects. And this was Kim's. He smiled broadly and pressed to move the file on.

Four hours later, at three bells, he got up from his seat and went to relieve himself. He had set the machine to print and had sat there, reading the copy as it emerged from the machine. There were more than two hundred pages of copy in the tray by now and the file was not yet exhausted.

T'ai Cho went through to the kitchen, the faint buzz of the printer momentarily silenced, and put on a kettle of *ch'a*, then went back out and stood there by the terminal, watching the paper spill out slowly.

It was astonishing. Kim had invented a whole history; a fabulously rich, incredibly inventive history. So rich that at times it seemed almost real. All that about the Catholic Church suppressing knowledge and the great Renaissance – was that the word? – that split Europe into two camps. Oh, it was wild fantasy, of course, but there was a ring of truth – of universality – behind it that gave it great authority.

T'ai Cho laughed. 'So that's what you've been up to in your spare time,' he said softly. Yes, it made sense now. Kim had been busy reshaping the world in his own image – had made the past the mirror of his own logical, intensely curious self.

But it had not been like that. Pan Chao had conquered *Ta Ts'in*. Rome had fallen. And not as Kim had portrayed it, to Alaric and the Goths in the fifth century, but to the Han in the first. There had been no break in order, no decline into darkness. No Dark Ages and no Christianity – Oh, and what a lovely idea *that* was: organized religion! The thought of it...

He bent down and took the last few sheets from the stack. Kim's tale had reached the twentieth century now. A century of war and large-scale atrocity. A century in which scientific 'progress' had become a headlong flight. He glanced down the highlighted names on the page – Röntgen, Planck, Curie, Einstein, Bohr, Heisenberg, Baird, Schrödinger – recognizing none of them. Each had its own sub-file, like the BRAHE. And each, he knew, would prove consistent with the larger picture.

'Remarkable!' he said softly, reading a passage about the development of radio and television. In Kim's version they had appeared only in the twentieth century – a good three centuries after the Han had really invented them. It was through such touches – by arresting some developments and accelerating others – that Kim made his story live. In his version of events, Han science had stagnated by the fourth century AD, and Chung Kuo had grown insular, until, in the nineteenth century, the Europeans – and what a strange, alien ring that phrase had; not *Hung Mao*, but 'Europeans' – had kicked the rotten door of China in.

Ah, and that too. Not Chung Kuo. Kim called it China. As if it had been named after the First Emperor's people, the Ch'in. Ridiculous! And yet, somehow, strangely convincing, too.

T'ai Cho sat back, rubbing his eyes, the sweet scent of the brewing *ch'a* slowly filling the room. Yes, much of it was ridiculous. A total fantasy – like the strange idea of Latin, the language of the *Ta Ts'in*, persisting fifteen hundred years after the fall of their Empire. For a moment he thought of that old, dead language persisting through the centuries by means of that great paradox, the Church – at one and the same time the great defender and destroyer of knowledge – and knew such a world as the one Kim had dreamed up was a pure impossibility. A twisted dream of things.

While the printer hummed and buzzed, T'ai Cho examined his feelings. There was much to admire in Kim's fable. It spoke of a strong, inventive mind, able to grasp and use broad concepts. But beyond that there was something problematic about what Kim had done – something that troubled T'ai Cho greatly.

What disturbed him most was Kim's reinterpretation of the Ch'ing or, as Kim called it, the Manchu period. There, in his notion of a vigorous, progressive West and a decadent, static East was the seed of all else. That was his starting point: the focus from which all else radiated out, like some insidious disease, transforming whatever it touched. Kim had not simply changed history, he had inverted it. Turned black into white, white into black. It was clever, yes, but it was also somehow diabolical.

T'ai Cho shook his head and stood up, pained by his thoughts. On the surface the whole thing seemed the product of Kim's brighter side; a great edifice of shining intellect; a work of considerable erudition and remarkable imaginative powers. Yet in truth it was the expression of Kim's darker self; a curiously distorted image; envious, almost malicious.

Is this how he sees us? T'ai Cho wondered. *Is this how the Han appear to him?*

It pained him deeply, for *he* was Han; the product of the world Kim so obviously despised. The world he would replace with his own dark fantasy.

T'ai Cho shuddered and stood up, then went out and switched off the *ch'a*. *No more*, he thought, hearing the printer pause, then beep three times – signal that it had finished printing. No, he would show this to Director Andersen. See what the *Hung Mao* in charge made of it. And then what?

Then I'll ask him, T'ai Cho thought, switching off the light. *Yes. I'll ask Kim why.*

The next morning he stood before the Director in his office, the file in a folder under his arm.

'Well, T'ai Cho? What did you find out from him?'

T'ai Cho hesitated. He knew Andersen meant the matter of the fight between Kim and Matyas, yet for a moment he was tempted to ignore that and simply hand him the folder.

'It was as I said. Kim denies there was a fight. He says Matyas was not to blame.'

Andersen made a noise of disbelief, then, placing both hands firmly on the desk, leaned forward, an unexpected smile lighting his features.

'Never mind. I've solved the problem anyway. I've got RadTek to take Matyas a month early. We've had to provide insurance cover for the first month – while he's under age – but it's worth it if it keeps him from killing Kim, neh?'

T'ai Cho looked down. He should have guessed Andersen would be ahead of him. But for once he could take him by surprise.

'Good. But there's something else.'

'Something else?'

T'ai Cho held out the folder.

Andersen took the folder and opened it. 'Cumbersome,' he said, his face crinkling with distaste. He was the kind of administrator who hated paperwork. Head-Slot spoken summaries were more his thing. But in this instance there was no alternative: a summary of the Aristotle File could not possibly have conveyed its richness, let alone its scope.

Andersen read the title page, then looked up at T'ai Cho. 'What is this? Some kind of joke?'

'No. It's something Kim put together.'

Andersen looked back down at the document, leafing through a few pages, then stopped, his attention caught by something he had glimpsed. 'You knew about this?'

'Not until last night.'

Andersen looked up sharply. Then he gave a tiny little nod, seeing what it implied. 'How did he keep the files hidden?'

T'ai Cho shook his head. 'I don't know. I thought it was something you might want to investigate.'

Andersen considered a moment. 'Yes. It has wider implications. If Kim can keep files secret from a copycat system...' He looked back down at the stack of paper. 'What exactly is this, T'ai Cho? I assume you've read it?'

'Yes. But as to what it is... I suppose you might call it an alternative history. Chung Kuo as it might have been had the Ta Ts'in legions won the Battle of Kazatin.'

Andersen laughed. 'An interesting idea. Wasn't that in the film they showed last night?'

T'ai Cho nodded, suddenly remembering Kim's words. '*Pan Chao was triumphant. As ever.*' In Kim's version of things Pan Chao had never crossed the Caspian. There had been no Battle of Kazatin. Instead, Pan Chao had met the *Ta Ts'in* legate and signed a pact of friendship. An act which, eighteen centuries later, had led to the collapse of the Han Empire at the hands of a few 'Europeans' with superior technology.

'There's more, much more, but the drift of it is that the West – the *Hung Mao* – got to rule the world, not the Han.'

The Director turned a few more pages, then frowned. 'Why should he want to invent such stuff? What's the point of it?'

'As an exercise, maybe? A game to stretch his intellect?'

Andersen looked up at him again. 'Hmm. I like that. It's good to see him exercising his mind. But as to the idea itself...' He closed the file and pushed it aside. 'Let's monitor it, neh, T'ai Cho? See it doesn't get out of hand and take up too much time. I'd say it was harmless enough, wouldn't you?'

T'ai Cho was about to disagree, but saw the look in Andersen's eyes. He was not interested in pursuing the matter. Set against the business of safeguarding his investment it was of trivial importance. T'ai Cho nodded and made to retrieve the file.

'No. Leave it with me, T'ai Cho. *Shih* Berdichev is calling on me tomorrow. The file might amuse him.'

T'ai Cho backed away and made as if to leave, but Andersen called him back.

'One last thing.'

'Yes, Director?'

'I've decided to bring forward Kim's socialization. He's to start in the Casting Shop tomorrow.'

'Tomorrow? Don't you think... ?' He was about to say he thought Kim too young, but saw that Andersen was looking at him again, that same expression in his eyes. *I have decided*, it said. *There is to be no argument.* T'ai Cho swallowed, then bowed. 'Very well, *Shih* Andersen. Should I make arrangements?'

Andersen smiled. 'No. It's all been taken care of. My secretary will give you the details before you leave.'

T'ai Cho bowed again, humbled, then backed away.

'And T'ai Cho...'

'Yes, Director?'

'You'll say nothing of this file to anyone, understand?'

T'ai Cho bowed low. 'Of course.'

For a moment Kim studied the rust-coloured scholar's garment T'ai Cho had given him, then he looked back at his tutor. 'What's this?'

T'ai Cho busied himself, clearing out his desk. 'It's your work *pau*.'

'Work? What kind of work?'

Still T'ai Cho refused to look at him. 'You begin this morning. In the Casting Shop.'

Kim was silent a moment, then, slowly, he nodded. 'I see.' He shrugged out of his one-piece and pulled the loose-fitting *pau* over his head. It was a simple, long-sleeved *pau* with a chest-patch giving the Project's name in pale green pictograms and, beneath that, in smaller symbols, Kim's ownership details – the contract number and the SimFic symbol.

T'ai Cho looked fleetingly across at him. 'Good. You'll be going there every day from now on. From eight until twelve. Your normal classes will be shifted to the afternoon.'

He had expected Kim to complain – the new arrangements would cost him two hours of his free time every day – but Kim gave no sign. He simply nodded.

'Why are you clearing your desk?'

T'ai Cho paused. The anger he had felt on finishing the Aristotle File had diminished somewhat, but still he felt resentful towards the boy. He had thought he knew him. But he had been wrong. The File had proved him wrong. Kim had betrayed him. His friendliness was like the tampered lock, the hidden files – a deception. The boy was Clayborn and the Clayborn were cunning by nature. He should have known that. Even so, it hurt to be proved wrong. Hurt like nothing he had felt in years.

'I'm asking to be reposted.'

Kim was watching him intently. 'Why?'

'Does it matter?' He could not keep the bitterness from his voice, yet when he turned and looked at Kim he was surprised to see how shocked, how hurt the boy was.

Kim's voice was small, strangely vulnerable. 'Is it because of the fight?'

T'ai Cho looked down, pursing his lips. 'There was no fight, Kim. You told me that.'

'No.' The word was barely audible.

T'ai Cho looked up. The boy was looking away from him now, his head slightly turned to the right. For a moment he was struck by how cruel he was being, not explaining why he was going. Surely the child deserved that much? Then, as he watched, a tear formed in Kim's left eye and slowly trickled down his cheek.

He had never seen Kim cry. Neither, he realized, had he ever really thought of him as a child. Not as a true child, anyway. Now, as he stood there, T'ai Cho saw him properly for the first time. Saw how fragile Kim was. A nine-year-old boy, that was all he was. An orphan. And all the family Kim had in the world was himself.

He closed the desk, then went across and knelt at Kim's side. 'You want to know why?'

Kim could not look at him. He nodded. Another tear rolled slowly down his cheek. His voice was small and hurt. 'I don't understand, T'ai Cho. What have I done?'

For a moment T'ai Cho was silent. He had expected Kim to be cold, indifferent to his news. But this? He felt his indignation melt and dissipate like breath, then reached out and held the boy to him fiercely.

'Nothing,' he said. 'You've done nothing.'

The boy gave a little shudder, then turned his head slowly, until he was looking into T'ai Cho's face. 'Then why? Why are you going away?'

T'ai Cho looked back at him, searching the child's dark eyes for evidence of betrayal – for some sign that this was yet another act – but he saw only hurt there and incomprehension.

'I've seen your secret files,' he said quietly. 'Brahe and Aristotle.'

There was a small movement in the dark pupils, then Kim dropped his eyes. 'I see.' Then he looked up again, and the expression of concern took T'ai Cho by surprise. 'Did it hurt you, reading them?'

T'ai Cho shivered, then answered the boy honestly. 'Yes. I wondered why you would create a world like that.'

Kim's eyes moved away, then back again. 'I never meant to hurt you. You must believe me, T'ai Cho. I'd never deliberately hurt you.'

'And the File?'

Kim swallowed. 'I thought Matyas would kill me. He tried, you see. That's why I left the note in the book. I knew that if I was killed you'd find it. But I didn't think...'

T'ai Cho finished it for him. 'You didn't think I'd find it before you were dead, is that it?'

Kim nodded. 'And now I've hurt you...' He reached out and gently touched T'ai Cho's face, stroking his cheek. 'Believe me, T'ai Cho. I wouldn't hurt you. Not for anything.' Tears welled in his big dark eyes. 'I thought you knew. Didn't you see it? Don't you understand it, even now?' He hesitated, a small shudder passing through his frail, thin body, then spoke the words almost in a whisper. 'I love you, T'ai Cho.'

T'ai Cho shivered, then drew Kim against him once more. 'Then I'd best stay, hadn't I?'

The Casting Shop was a long, wide room with a high ceiling. Along its centre stood six tall, spiderish machines with squat bases and long, segmented arms; each machine three times the height of a grown man. To the sides were a series of smaller machines, no two of them the same, but all resembling to some degree or other their six identical elders. Between the big machines in the centre and the two rows of smaller ones at the sides ran two gangways, each with an overhead track. Young men moved between the machines, readying them, or stood in groups, talking casually in these last few minutes before the work bell rang.

Kim stood in the doorway, looking in, and felt at once a strange affinity with the machines. He smiled and looked up at T'ai Cho. 'I think I'll like it here.'

The Supervisor was a Han; a small man named Nung, who bowed and smiled a lot as he led them through to his office at the far end of the Casting Shop. As he made his way between the machines, Kim saw heads turn and felt the eyes of the young men on his back, but his attention was drawn to the huge, mechanical spiders that stretched up to the ceiling.

'What are they?' Kim asked the Supervisor once the partition door had slid shut behind them.

Supervisor Nung smiled tightly and looked to T'ai Cho. 'Forgive my unpreparedness, *Shih* T'ai. I was only told of this yesterday evening.'

It was clear from the manner in which he ignored Kim's question that he felt much put out by the circumstances of Kim's arrival.

'What are they?' T'ai Cho asked, pointedly repeating Kim's question. 'The boy would like to know.'

He saw the movement in Nung's face as he tried to evaluate the situation. Nung glanced at Kim, then gave the slightest bow to T'ai Cho. 'Those are the casting grids, *Shih* T'ai. One of the boys will give a demonstration in a while. Kim...' He smiled insincerely at the boy. 'Kim will be starting on one of the smaller machines.'

'Good.' T'ai Cho took the papers from the inner pocket of his er-satin jacket and handed them to the Supervisor. 'You must understand from the outset that while Kim is not to be treated differently from any other boy, he is also not to be treated badly. The boy's safety is of paramount importance. As you will see, Director Andersen has written a note under his own hand to this effect.'

He saw how mention of the Director made Nung dip his head, and thought once more how fortunate he was to work in the Centre, where there were no such men. Yet it was the way of the Above, and Kim would have to learn it quickly. Here status counted more than mere intelligence.

The qualms he had had in Andersen's office returned momentarily. Kim was too young to begin this. Too vulnerable. Then he shrugged inwardly, knowing it was out of his hands. *Mei fa tzu*, he thought. *It's fate*. At least there was no Matyas here. Kim would be safe, if nothing else.

When T'ai Cho had gone, the Supervisor led Kim halfway down the room to one of the smallest and squattest of the machines and left him in the care of a pleasant-looking young Han named Chan Shui.

Kim watched the partition door slam shut, then turned to Chan Shui, his eyebrows forming a question.

Chan Shui laughed softly. 'That's Nung's way, Kim. You'll learn it quickly enough. He does as little as he can. As long as we meet our production schedules he's happy. He spends most of his day in his room, watching the screens. Not that I blame him, really. It must be dreadful to know you've reached your level.'

'His level?'

Chan Shui's eyes widened with surprise. Then he laughed again. 'I'm sorry, Kim. I forgot. You're from the Clay, aren't you?'

Kim nodded, suddenly wary.

Chan Shui saw this and quickly reassured him. 'Don't get me wrong, Kim. What you were – where you came from – that doesn't worry me like it does some of them round here.' He looked about him pointedly, and Kim realized that their conversation was being listened to by the boys at the nearby machines. 'It's what you are that really counts. And what you could be. At least, that's what my father always says. And he should know. He's climbed the levels.'

Kim shivered. *Fathers...* He gave a little smile and reached out to touch one of the long, thin arms of the machine.

'Careful!' Chan Shui warned. 'Always make sure the machine's switched off before you touch it. They've cut-outs built into their circuits, but they're not absolutely safe. You can get a nasty burn.'

'How does it work?'

Chan Shui studied Kim a moment. 'How old are you?'

Kim looked back at him. 'Nine. So they say.'

Chan Shui looked down. He himself was eighteen, the youngest of the other boys sixteen. Kim looked five, maybe six at most. But that was how they were. He had seen one or two of them before, passing through. But this was the first time he had been allocated one to 'nursemaid'.

The dull, hollow tones of the work bell filled the Shop. At once the boys stopped talking and made their way to their machines. There was a low hum as a nearby machine was switched on, then a growing murmur as others added to the background noise.

'It's rather pleasant,' said Kim, turning back to Chan Shui. 'I thought it would be noisier than this.'

The young Han shook his head, then leaned forward and switched their own machine on. 'They say they can make these things perfectly silent, but they found that it increased the number of accidents people had with them. If it hums a little you can't forget it's on, can you?'

Kim smiled, pleased by the practical logic of that. 'There's a lesson in that, don't you think? Not to make things too perfect.'

Chan Shui shrugged, then began his explanation.

The controls were simple and Kim mastered them at once. Then Chan Shui took a slender phial from the rack beside the control panel.

'What's that?'

Chan Shui hesitated, then handed it to him.

'Be careful with it. It's ice. Or at least, the constituents of ice. It slots in there.' He pointed to a tiny hole low down on the control panel. 'That's what these things do. They spin webs of ice.'

Kim laughed, delighted by the image. Then he looked down at the transparent phial, studying it, turning it in his fingers. Inside was a clear liquid with a faint blue colouring. He handed it back, then watched closely as Chan Shui took what he called a 'template' – a thin card stamped with a recognition code in English and Mandarin – and slotted it into the panel. The template was the basic computer programme that gave the machine its instructions.

'What do we do, then?' Kim asked, his expression as much as to say, *Is that all there is to it?* It was clear he had expected to control the grid manually.

Chan Shui smiled. 'We watch. And we make sure nothing goes wrong.'

'And does it?'

'Not often.'

Kim frowned, not understanding. There were something like a hundred boys tending the machines in the Casting Shop, when a dozen, maybe less, would have sufficed. It made no sense.

'Is all of the Above so wasteful?'

'Wasteful? What do you mean?'

Kim stared at him a moment longer, then saw he didn't understand. This, too, was how things were. Then he looked around and saw that many of the boys working on the smaller machines wore headwraps, while those on the central grids chatted, keeping only a casual eye on their machines.

'Don't you get bored?'

Chan Shui shrugged. 'It's a job. I don't plan to be here forever.'

Kim watched as the machine began to move, the arms to extend, forming a cradle in the air. Then, with a sudden hiss of air, it began.

It was beautiful. One moment there was nothing in the space between the arms, the next something shimmered into existence. He shivered, then clapped his hands together in delight.

'Clever, neh?' said Chan Shui, smiling. He lifted the wide-bodied chair from the grid with one hand. Its perfectly transparent shape glimmered wetly in the overhead light. 'Here,' he said, handing it to Kim.

Like most of the furniture in the Above, it weighed nothing. Or almost nothing. Yet it felt solid, unbreakable.

Kim handed the chair back, then looked at the spiderish machine with new respect. Jets of air from the segmented arms had directed the fine, liquid threads of ice as they shot out from the base of the machine, but the air had only defined the shape.

He looked at Chan Shui, surprised that he didn't understand – that he had so readily accepted their explanation for why the machines hummed. They did not hum to stop their operators forgetting they were switched on; the vibration of the machine had a function. It set up standing waves – like the tone of a bell or a plucked string, but perfect, unadulterated. The uncongealed ice rode those waves, forming a skin, like the surface of a soap bubble, but a million times stronger because it was formed of thousands of tiny corrugations – the menisci formed by those standing waves.

Kim saw the beauty of it at once. Saw how East and West had come together here. The Han had known about standing waves since the fifth century BC: had understood and utilized the laws of resonance. He had seen an example of one of their 'spouting bowls' which, when its handles were rubbed, had formed a perfect standing wave – a shimmering, perfect hollow cone of water that rose a full half ch'i above the bowl's bronze rim. The machine, however – its cybernetics, its programming, even its basic engineering – was a product of Western science. The Han had abandoned those paths millennia before the West had found and followed them.

Kim looked around; watching as forms shimmered into life in the air on every side. Tables, cupboards, benches and chairs. It was like magic. Boys moved between the machines, gathering up the objects and stacking them on the slow-moving collection trays that came along the gangways, hung on cables from the overhead tracks. At the far end, beyond the door where Kim had entered, was the paint shop. There the furniture was finished – the permapaint bonded to the ice – before it was packed for despatch.

At ten they took a break. The refectory was off to their right, with a cloak-room leading off from it. There were toilets there and showers. Chan Shui showed Kim around, then took him back to one of the tables and brought him *ch'a* and a soypork roll.

'I see they've sent us a dwarf this time!'

There was a loud guffaw of laughter. Kim turned, surprised, and found himself looking up into the face of a beefy, thick-set youth with cropped brown hair and a flat nose. A *Hung Mao*, his pale, unhealthy skin heavily pitted. He stared down at Kim belligerently, the mean stupidity of his expression balanced by the malevolence in his eyes.

Chan Shui, beside Kim, leaned forward nonchalantly, unimpressed by the newcomer's demeanour.

'Get lost, Janko. Go and play your addle-brained games on someone else and leave us alone.'

Janko sniffed disdainfully. He turned to the group of boys who had gathered behind him and smiled, then turned back, looking at Kim again, ignoring Chan Shui.

'What's your name, rat's arse?'

Chan Shui touched Kim's arm. 'Ignore him, Kim. He'll only trouble you if you let him.' He looked up at the other boy. '*Se li nei jen*, neh, Janko?' *Stern in appearance, weak inside.* It was a traditional Han rebuttal of a bully.

Kim looked down, trying not to smile. But Janko leaned forward threateningly. 'None of your chink shit, Chan. You think you're fucking clever, don't you? Well, you'll get yours one day, I promise.'

Chan Shui laughed and pointed to the camera over the counter. 'Best be careful, Janko. Uncle Nung might be watching. And you'd be in deep shit then, wouldn't you?'

Janko glared at him, infuriated, then looked down at Kim. 'Fucking little rat's arse!'

There was a ripple of laughter from behind him, then Janko was gone.

Kim watched the youth slope away, then turned back to Chan Shui. 'Is he always like that?'

'Most of the time.' Chan Shui sipped his ch'a, thoughtful a moment, then he looked across at Kim again and smiled. 'But don't let it get to you. I'll see he doesn't worry you.'

Berdichev sat back in Director Andersen's chair and surveyed the room. 'Things are well, I hope?'

'Very well, Excellency,' Andersen answered with a bow, knowing that Berdichev was referring to the boy; that he had no interest whatsoever in his own well-being.

'Good. Can I see him?'

Andersen kept his head lowered. 'I am afraid not, Shih Berdichev. Not at the moment, anyway. He began socialization this morning. However, he will be back by one o'clock, if you'd care to wait.'

Berdichev was silent a moment, clearly put out by this development. 'Don't you feel that might be slightly premature?'

Andersen swallowed. He had decided to say nothing of the incident with Matyas. 'Kim is a special case, as you know. He requires different handling. Normally we wouldn't dream of sending a boy out so young, but we felt there would be too much of an imbalance were we to let his intellectual development outstrip his social development.'

He waited tensely. After a while Berdichev nodded. 'I see. And you've taken special precautions to see he'll be properly looked after?'

Andersen bowed. 'I have seen to matters personally, Shih Berdichev. Kim is in the hands of one of my most trusted men, Supervisor Nung. He has my personal instructions to take good care of the boy.'

'Good. Now tell me, is there anything I should know?'

Andersen stared back at Berdichev, wondering for a moment if it was possible he might know something. Then he relaxed. 'There is one thing, Excellency. Something you might find very interesting.'

'Something to do with the boy, I hope.'

'Yes. Of course. It's something he produced in his free time. A file. Or rather a whole series of files.'

Berdichev's slight movement forward revealed his interest. 'A file?'

Andersen smiled and turned. On cue his secretary appeared and handed him the folder. He had added the sub-files since T'ai Cho had brought the matter to his attention, and the stack of paper was now almost twice the size it had been. He turned back to Berdichev, then crossed the room and deposited the folder on the desk beside Berdichev before withdrawing with a bow.

'"The Aristotle File",' Berdichev read aloud. '"Being The True History Of Western Science".'

He laughed. 'Says who?'

Andersen echoed his laughter. 'It is amusing, I agree. But fascinating, too. His ability to fuse ideas and extrapolate. The sheer breadth of his vision...'

Berdichev silenced him with a curt gesture of his hand, then turned the page, reading. After a moment he looked up. 'Would you bring me some *ch'a*, Director?'

Andersen was about to turn and instruct his secretary when Berdichev interrupted him. 'I'd prefer it if you did it yourself, Director. It would give me a few moments to digest this.'

Andersen bowed deeply. 'Whatever you say, Excellency.'

Berdichev waited until the man had gone, then sat back, removing his glasses and wiping them on the old-fashioned cotton handkerchief he kept for that purpose in the pocket of his satin jacket. Then he picked up the sheet he had been reading and looked at it again. There was no doubt about it. This was it. The real thing. What he had been unearthing fragments of for the last fifteen or twenty years. Here it was – complete!

He felt like laughing, or whooping for joy, but knew hidden cameras were watching his every movement, so he feigned disinterested boredom. He flicked through, as if only casually interested, but behind the mask of his face he could feel the excitement course through him, like fire in his blood.

Where in the gods' names had Kim got all this? Had he invented it? No. Berdichev dismissed the thought instantly. Kim *couldn't* have invented it. Just a glance at certain details told him it was genuine. This part about Charlemagne and the Holy Roman Empire, for instance. And here, this bit about the subtle economic influence of the Medici family. And here, about the long-term effects of the great sea battle of Lepanto – the deforestation of the Mediterranean and the subsequent shift of the shipbuilding industry to the Baltic where wood was plentiful. Yes. He had seen shards of this before – bits and pieces of the puzzle – but here the picture was complete.

He shuddered. Andersen was a fool. And thank the gods for it. If he had known what he had in his possession. If he'd had but the slightest inkling...

Berdichev looked down, stifling the laugh that came unbidden to his lips. Gods, he felt elated! He flicked back to the title page again. *The Aristotle File.* Yes! That was where it all started. Back there in the Yes/No logic of the Greek.

He tapped the stack of papers square, then slid them back into the folder. What to do? What to do? The simple possession of such information was treasonous. Was punishable by death.

There was a knock on the door.

'Come in!'

Andersen bowed, then brought the tray over to the desk and set it down on one side, well away from the folder. Then he poured the *ch'a* into a bowl and held it out, his head slightly lowered.

Berdichev took the bowl and sipped.

'How many people know about this?'

'Four, including yourself and Kim.'

'The boy's tutor... T'ai Cho, isn't it? I assume he's the other?'

'That's correct, Excellency. But I've already instructed him to mention it to no one else.'

'Good. Very good. Because I want you to destroy the files at once. Understand?'

Andersen's smile drained away, replaced by a look of utter astonishment. He had thought Berdichev would be pleased. 'I'm sorry?'

'I want all evidence of this foolishness destroyed at once, understand me, Director? I want the files closed and I want you to warn Kim not to indulge in such idle fancies any longer.' He banged the file violently with the flat of his hand, making Andersen jump. 'You don't realize how much this worries me. I already have several quite serious misgivings about the whole venture, particularly regarding the matter of the boy's safety. I understand, for instance, that there was a fight, and that you've had to send one of the older boys away. Is that right?'

Andersen blanched, wondering who Berdichev's spy was. 'That is so, Excellency.'

'And now this.' Berdichev was silent a moment, the threat implicit in his silence. The purpose of his visit today had been to make the latest stage payment on Kim's contract. There had been no mention of the matter so far, but now he came to it. 'My feeling is that the terms of our contract have not been fully met. You are in default, Director Andersen. You have failed to adequately protect my investment. In the circumstances, I feel I must insist on some... *compensation*. A reduction of the stage payment, perhaps?'

Andersen lowered his head even further. His voice was apologetic. 'I am afraid I have no discretion, *Shih* Berdichev. All contractual matters have to be referred to the board.'

He glanced at Berdichev, expecting anger, but the Head of SimFic was smiling. 'I know. I spoke to them before I came here. They have agreed to a reduction of one hundred thousand yuan.' He held out the document for Andersen to take. 'I understand it requires only your signature to make it valid.'

Andersen shivered, suppressing the anger he felt, then bowed and, taking the brush from the stand, signed the paper.

'We'll verify this later,' Berdichev said, his smile fading. 'But with regard to the files, you'll do as I say. Yes?'

'Of course, Excellency.'

He reached for the folder, but Berdichev held on to it. 'I'll keep this copy. I'd like my company psychiatrists to evaluate it. They'll destroy it once they've done with it.'

Andersen looked at him, open-mouthed, then hastily backed off a pace, bowing his head.

'Good,' said Berdichev, reaching across for the *ch'a* kettle. 'Then bring another bowl, Director. I believe you have some money to collect from me.'

'And how's little rat's arse this morning?'

Kim kept his eyes on his plate, ignoring the figure of Janko, who stood beside him. Chan Shui had gone off to the toilets, saying he would only be a moment, but Janko must have seen him go and had decided this was his chance.

He felt Janko's hand on his shoulder, squeezing, not hard as yet but enough to make him feel uncomfortable. He shrugged it off, then reached out to take the biscuit. But Janko beat him to it. Laughing, he crammed it in his mouth, then picked up Kim's bowl to wash it down.

Kim went very still. He heard Janko's cronies laugh, then heard the unmistakable sound of the boy hawking into his bowl.

Janko set it down in front of him with a bang, then poked him hard. 'Drink up, rat's arse! Got to keep our strength up, haven't we?'

The inane laughter rang out once again from beyond Janko. Kim looked at the bowl. A nasty greenish gob of spit floated on the surface of the *ch'a*.

Kim stared at it a moment, then half turned in his seat and looked up at Janko. The youth was more than half as big as him again. He would have made Matyas look a weakling by comparison. But unlike Matyas, he wasn't dangerous. He was merely flabby and stupid and a touch ridiculous.

'Go fuck yourself, windbag,' Kim said, loud enough for Janko alone to hear.

Janko grabbed at Kim, half lifting him from his seat, then thrust the bowl at his face. 'Drink, you little piece of shit! Drink, if you know what's good for you!'

'Put him down!'

Janko turned. Chan Shui had come back and was standing there on the far side of the room. Several of the boys glanced up at the cameras nervously, as if expecting Nung to come in and break things up. But most of them knew Nung well enough to guess he'd be jerking off to some PornoStim, not checking up on what was happening in the refectory.

Janko released Kim, then, with an exaggerated delicacy, let the bowl fall from his fingers. It shattered on the hard tile floor.

'Best clear it up, rat's arse. Before you get into trouble.'

Kim looked across at Chan Shui, a faint smile on his lips, then turned and went to the counter to get a brush and pan.

Chan Shui was standing there when he came back. 'You don't have to do that, Kim.'

Kim nodded, but got down anyway and started collecting the shattered pieces. He looked up at Chan Shui. 'Why don't they make these out of ice?'

Chan Shui laughed, then knelt down and began to help him. 'Have you ever tasted *ch'a* from an ice bowl?'

Kim shook his head.

'It's revolting. Worse than Janko's phlegm!' Chan Shui leaned closer, whispering. 'What did you say to him, Kim? I've never seen Janko so mad.'

Kim told him what he had said.

Chan Shui roared with laughter, then grew quiet. 'That's good. But you'd better watch yourself from now on. He's a fool and a windbag, yes, but he doesn't want to lose face. When I go for a pee, you come too. And fuck what these bastards think about that.'

When T'ai Cho met him, just after twelve, he had two guards with him.

'What's happening?' Kim asked when they were outside.

T'ai Cho smiled reassuringly. 'It's okay, Kim. Just a measure the Director is insisting on from now on. He's concerned for your safety outside the Centre, that's all.'

'So we've got them every day?'

T'ai Cho shook his head. 'No. It's not necessary for the Casting Shop, but we're going somewhere special this afternoon, Kim. There's something I want to show you. To set the record straight, if you like.'

'I don't understand.'

'I know. But you will. At least, much better after this.'

They went up another twelve decks – a full one hundred and twenty levels – until they were in the heart of the Mids, at Level 181. Stepping out of the lift, Kim noticed at once how different things were from the level where the Casting Shop was. It was cleaner here, tidier, less crowded; even the pace at which people moved seemed more sedate, more orderly.

They waited at a Security barrier while a guard checked their permits, then went inside. An official greeted them and took them along a corridor, then up a narrow flight of stairs into a viewing gallery, its front sealed off from the hall below by a pane of transparent ice.

In the hall below five desks were set out in a loose semi-circle. In front of them were a number of chairs, grouped in a seemingly random fashion. Five grey-haired Han sat behind the desks, a small comset – or portable computer – in front of each.

'What is this?'

T'ai Cho smiled and indicated two seats at the front of the gallery. When they were sitting, he turned to Kim and explained. 'This is a deck tribunal, Kim. They have them once a week throughout the levels. It is the Han way of justice.'

'Ah...' Kim knew the theory that lay behind Han justice, but he had never seen it in action.

T'ai Cho leaned forward. 'Note how informal it all is, Kim. How relaxed.'

'A family affair,' Kim said, rather too patly.

'Yes,' T'ai Cho said at once. 'Exactly that.'

They watched the hall fill up, until not a chair was free and latecomers had to squat or sit on the floor. Then, without anyone calling anything to order, it began. One of the elders leaned forward across his desk and began to speak, his voice rising above the background murmur. The other voices dropped away until the elder's voice sounded alone.

He was reading out the circumstances of the first case. Two cousins had been fighting. The noise had woken neighbours who had complained to Deck Security. The elder looked up, his eyes seeking out the two Han youths. They stood at once.

'Well? What have you to say for yourselves?'

Beside them an old man, grey-haired like the elders, his long beard plaited, stood and addressed the elder.

'Forgive me, Hsien Judge Hong, but might I speak? I am Yung Pi-Chu, Head of the Yung family.'

'The tribunal waits to hear from you, Shih Yung.'

The old man bowed his thanks, then brought his two great-nephews out into the space in front of the desks and had them strip off their tops. Their backs were striped from recent punishment. He made the two youths turn, showing the elders first and then the gathered audience. Then, bidding them return to their seats, he faced the elders.

'As you see, respected elders, my great-nephews have been punished for their thoughtlessness. But the matter of my neighbours' inconvenience remains. In that regard I propose to offer compensation of six hundred yuan, to be shared equally amongst the complainants.'

Hsien Judge Hong bowed, pleased, then looked out past the old man. 'Would the complainants stand.'

Three men got to their feet and identified themselves.

'Are you willing to accept Shih Yung's generous compensation?'

All three nodded. Two hundred yuan was a very generous figure.

'Good. Then the matter is settled. You will pay the clerk, *Shih Yung.*'

Without preamble, and before the old man had returned to his seat, another of the elders began reading out the circumstances of the second case. Again it involved two young men, but this time they had been charged with unsocial behaviour. They had vandalized a row of magnolia trees while drunk.

At the elder's request the two men stood. They were *Hung Mao*, their dress neat, respectable, their hair cut in the Han style.

'Well?' the elder asked. 'What have you to say for yourselves?'

The two men hung their heads. One looked momentarily at the other, who swallowed, then looked up, acting as spokesman for the two.

'Respected elders, we make no excuses for our behaviour and are deeply ashamed of what we did. We accept full responsibility for our actions and would fully understand if the respected elders should punish us to the full severity for what we did. However, we ask you to consider our past exemplary record and would humbly submit the testimony of our employers as to our conduct. We propose to pay for the damage in full and, in respect of the damage to the harmony of the community we ask that we should be given a month's community service.'

The elder looked briefly at his fellows, who all nodded, then faced the two youths again.

'We have read the submissions of your employers and take into account your past exemplary conduct. Your shame is clear and your repentance obvious. In the circumstances, therefore, we accept your proposals, your term of public service to commence in two weeks' time. However, should you come before this tribunal a second time on a similar charge it will result in immediate demotion. You understand?'

Both men bowed deeply and looked to each other briefly.

Two more cases followed. The first was an accusation of theft. Two men claimed that another had robbed them, but a Security film showed they had falsely accused the man. The two men, protesting violently, found themselves held by Security guards and sentenced. They were to be demoted five decks. Amidst wailing from the two men and their families and rejoicing from the falsely accused man and his, the permits of the two were taken from them and they were led away.

The fourth case involved a charge of violent assault by a middle-aged man on his wife's father. Both families were in court, and for the first time there was real tension in the air. The matter was in dispute and it seemed there was no way to resolve it. Both men were deeply respected members of the community. Both swore their version of events was the truth. There was no Security film to solve the matter this time and no impartial witnesses.

The elders conferred a moment, then *Hsien* Judge Hong called the two men forward. He addressed the older of them first.

'What began this dispute?'

The old man bristled and pointed contemptuously at the younger. 'He insulted my family.'

Judge Hong was patient. It was, after all, a matter of face. For the next half hour he slowly, cleverly, drew the threads of circumstance out into the daylight. At the core of it all lay a trivial remark – an off-hand comment that the younger man's wife was like her mother, idle. It had been said heatedly, carelessly, in the course of a disagreement about something entirely different, but the old woman had taken great offence and had called upon her husband to defend her honour.

'Do you not both think that things have got out of hand? You, *Shih* T'eng,' he looked at the younger man, 'Do you really believe your mother-in-law an idler? Do you really have so little respect for your wife's mother?'

Shih T'eng lowered his head, then shook it. 'No, Elder Hong. She is a good, virtuous woman. What I said, I said heatedly. It was not meant. I...' He hesitated, then looked at his father-in-law. 'I unreservedly apologize for the hurt I caused his family. I assure him, it was not intended.'

Judge Hong looked at the old man and saw at once, from his bearing, that he was satisfied. Their dispute was at a close. But the Elder had not finished with the two men. He leaned forward angrily.

'I am appalled that two such good, upright men should have come before me with such a... a petty squabble. Both of you should feel deeply shamed that you let things come to this.'

Both men lowered their heads, chastened. The hall was deathly silent as Judge Hong continued.

'Good. In the circumstances I fine you each five hundred yuan for wasting the time of this tribunal.' He looked at the two men sternly. 'If I hear any more of this matter I shall have you up before us again. And that, I guarantee you, *chun tzu*, will be to neither of your likings.'

The two 'gentlemen' bowed deeply and thanked the court, then went meekly to the clerk to pay their fines.

T'ai Cho turned to his pupil. 'Well, Kim? Do you still think the Han way so bad?'

Kim looked down, embarrassed. T'ai Cho's discovery had made things difficult between them. It would have been easier had he been able to say, *No. I did not invent the world you read about*, but sometimes the truth was stranger than a lie and far harder to accept.

'I have never thought the Han way a bad way, T'ai Cho. Whatever you believe, I find you a highly civilized people.'

T'ai Cho stared at him a moment, then shrugged and looked back down into the body of the hall. The crowd had dispersed now and only the five elders remained, talking amongst themselves and tying up any remaining items of business. T'ai Cho considered a moment, then smiled and looked back at Kim.

'There are no prisons in Chung Kuo. Did you realize that, Kim? If a man wishes to behave badly he may do so, but not among those who wish to behave well. Such a man must find his own level. He is demoted.'

He paused, then nodded to himself. 'It is a humane system, Kim. The most severe penalties are reserved for crimes against the person. We might be traders, but our values are not wholly venal.'

Kim sighed. It was a direct reference to something in the File – to the greedy and corrupt *Hoi Po*, or Hoppos, as the Europeans knew them, who had run the Canton trade in the nineteenth century. He had not meant his comment to stand for all the Han, but saw how T'ai Cho could easily have mistaken it for such.

Damn Matyas! he thought. *And damn the man who left the files for me to find and piece together!*

T'ai Cho continued. 'There are exceptions, naturally. Treason against the T'ang, for instance, is punishable by death. The traitor and all his family, to the third generation. But ours is a fair system, Kim. It works for those who wish it to work. For others there are other levels of existence. In Chung Kuo a man must find his own level. Is that not fair?'

Kim was tempted to argue, to ask whether it was fair for those born into the Net, or into the Clay like himself, but after all the damage he had done with the File he felt it would be churlish to disagree. He looked past T'ai Cho at the elders.

'What I saw today, that seemed fair.'

T'ai Cho looked at Kim and smiled. It was not a full capitulation but, still, there was good in the boy. A great deal of good. When he smiled, for instance, it was such a fierce, sincere smile – a smile from the very depths of him. T'ai Cho sniffed and nodded to himself. He realized now he had taken it too personally. Yes, he understood it now. Kim had been talking of systems. Of philosophies. He had let the abstract notion carry him away. Even so, he had been wrong.

'About the files, Kim. I had to tell the Director.'

Kim looked across at him, his eyes narrowed. 'And?'

T'ai Cho lowered his head. 'And he has ordered their destruction, I'm afraid. We must forget they ever were. Understand?'

Kim laughed, then bowed his head. 'I am ordered to forget?'

T'ai Cho looked up at him, sudden understanding in his eyes. Then, unexpectedly, he laughed. 'Why, yes. I never thought...'

Forget, Kim thought, then laughed again, a deep, hearty laughter. As if I could forget.

CHUNG KUO

Chapter 40

THE SCENT OF PLUM BLOSSOM

The big man came at Chen like an automaton, swinging and punching, kicking and butting, making Chen duck and bob and jump to evade the furious rain of blows. Back and back he was pushed until his shoulders thudded painfully against the wall. He ducked then kicked off from the wall, head first, aiming for the stomach of the big man. But he was too slow. The big man parried him, linking both hands to form a shield and thrust him down into the floor. Then, before Chen could get his breath, he was yanked up by one huge hand and pinned against the wall.

Chen chopped down against the arm desperately, but it was like hitting an iron bar. The arm quivered but held him firm. Chen swallowed and met the big man's eyes, conscious of the power there, the control.

The big man drew back his free arm, his fist forming a phoenix eye – a *feng huang yen ching* – the knuckle of the first finger extended, ready to strike and shatter Chen's skull.

Chen closed his eyes, then laughed. 'It's no good, my friend. I have no counter to your strength and skill.'

Karr held him there a moment longer, his fist poised as if to strike, then relaxed, letting Chen slide down onto the floor again.

'Then we must work at it until you do.'

Chen squatted on his haunches, getting his breath. He looked up at Karr, smiling now. 'I can't see why. There's only one of you, *Shih* Karr. And you're on my side. For which I thank the gods.'

Karr's sternness evaporated. 'Maybe now, Chen, but one day they'll make machines like me. I guarantee it. Things like those copies that came from Mars. Even now, I'd warrant, they're working on them somewhere. I'd rather find an answer now than wait for them to come, wouldn't you?'

They had spent the morning working out extensively, first with stick and sword and spear – *kuai chang shu, tao shu* and *ch'iang shu* – then with their bare hands, concentrating on the 'hand of the wind' – *feng shou kung fu* – style that Karr favoured. It was the first time the two men had seen each other in several months and they had enjoyed the friendly tussle, but Karr had not asked Chen here simply to polish his skills.

After they had showered they sat in the refectory, a large jug of hot sweet almond *ch'a* on the table between them – a delicacy Chen's wife, Wang Ti, had introduced them to.

'How is young Jyan?' Karr asked. 'I've meant to visit, but the T'ang has kept me busy these past months.'

Chen smiled and bowed his head slightly, but his eyes lit at the mention of his son. 'Jyan is well. Only four and already he knows all the stances. You should see how well he executes the *kou shih*. Such balance he has! And when he kicks he really kicks! You should see the bruises on my legs!'

Karr laughed. 'And Wang Ti?'

Chen looked down, his smile broadening. 'Wang Ti is Wang Ti. Like the sun she is there each morning. Like the moon she shines brilliantly at night.'

Again the big man laughed, then grew quiet. 'I hear you have news, Chen. The very best of news.'

Chen looked up, surprised, then smiled broadly. 'Who told you, *Shih* Karr? Who ruined my moment? I wanted to tell you myself!'

Karr tilted his head. 'Well... Let's just say I heard, neh? You know me, Chen. There's little that escapes my notice.'

'Or your grasp!'

Both men laughed.

'Anyway,' said Karr, lifting his bowl in salute. 'Here's to your second child! May he be strong and healthy!'

Chen raised his bowl. 'Thank you, my friend.' He sipped, then looked directly at Karr. 'This is very pleasant, *Shih* Karr. We do this too little these days. But tell me, why am I here? Is there a job for me? Something you want me to do?'

Karr smiled. 'There might be.'

'Might be? Why only might?'

The big man looked down, then reached across and filled his bowl again. 'I've a lead on DeVore. I think I know where he is.'

Chen laughed, astonished. 'DeVore? We've found him?'

'Maybe. I've trailed him three years since he evaded us at Nanking space-port. Three years, Chen. I've tracked down eight of the ten men who helped him get away that day, but not one of them knew a thing, not one of them helped me get a fraction closer. But now things have changed – now I think I have him.'

'Then what's the problem? Why don't you just go in and finish him off?'

Karr sniffed deeply. 'It's difficult. The T'ang wants him alive. He wants DeVore to stand trial. If possible to provide us with conclusive evidence against the other Dispersionists.'

'I see. Even so, what stops you from taking him?'

'The House. The stink they would make if we went in and took the wrong man.'

Chen shook his head. Still he didn't understand.

'The man we believe to be DeVore is an overseer. Understand me, Chen? On one of the big East European plantations. And that's a House appointment. If we go barging in there mistakenly the Dispersionists would have a field day attacking us for our heavy-handedness. And things are critical at the moment. The House is finely balanced and the Seven daren't risk that balance, even for DeVore. So we must be certain this Overseer Bergson is our man.'

'How certain?'

'As certain as a retinal print could make us.'

Chen looked down into his ch'a and laughed. 'And how do we do that? Do you think DeVore will sit there calmly while we check him out?'

Karr gave a tiny laugh and nodded, meeting his friend's eyes again. 'Maybe. Maybe that's just what he'll do. You see, Chen, that's where I thought you might come in.'

Tolonen watched his nine-year-old daughter run from the sea, her head thrown back, exhilarated. Behind her the waves broke white on the dark sand. Beyond, the distant islands were dim shapes of green and brown in the haze. Jelka stood there at the water's edge, smoothing her small, delicate hands through her hair. Long, straight hair like her mother's, darkened by the water. Her pure white costume showed off her winter tan, her body sleek, childlike.

She saw him there and smiled as she came up the beach towards him. He was sitting on the wide, shaded patio, the breakfast things still on the table before him. The Han servant had yet to come and clear it all away. He set down his book, returning her smile.

'What's it like?'

'Wonderful!' Her laughter rippled in the air. 'You should join me. It would do you good.'

'Well...' He shrugged. Maybe he would.

She sprawled in the lounger opposite him. A young animal, comfortable in her body. Unselfconscious. He looked at her, conscious more than ever that she was the image of her mother. Especially now, like this.

He had met her mother on an island similar to here. On the far side of the world from where he now sat. One summer almost thirty years before.

He had been a General even then. The youngest in the service of the Seven and the ablest. He had gone to Goteborg to see his father's sister, Hanna. In those days he made the trip twice a year, mindful of the fact that Hanna had looked after him those times his mother had been ill.

For once he had had time to stay more than a day, and when Hanna had suggested they fly up to Fredrikstad and visit the family's summer home, he had agreed at once. From Fredrikstad they had taken a motor cruiser to the islands south of the City.

He had thought they would be alone on the island – he, Hanna, and her two sons. But when the cruiser pulled up at the jetty, he saw that there were others there already. He had gone inside, apprehensive because he had not been warned there would be other guests, and was delighted to find not strangers but his oldest friend, Pietr Endfors, there in the low-ceilinged front cabin, waiting to greet him.

Endfors had married a girl from the far north. A cold, elegant beauty with almost-white hair and eyes like the arctic sea. They had an eight-year-old daughter, Jenny.

It had not happened at once. At first she was merely the daughter of an old friend; a beautiful little girl with an engaging smile and a warmth her mother seemed to lack. From the start, however, she had taken to him and by that evening was perched immovably in his lap. He liked her from that first moment, but even he could not tell how attached he would become.

When Pietr and his wife had died eight years later, he had become Jenny's guardian. Four years later he had married her. He had been thirty years her senior.

He returned from the bitter-sweet reverie and focused on his daughter.

'You've not been listening to a word, have you?'

He laughed and shook his head. 'Just reminiscing.' He sat up in his chair and reached across to feel the *ch'a* kettle. It was lukewarm. He grunted, then shouted for the servant.

'I was just saying. We ought to go home. It seems time. Don't you think?'

He looked sharply at her, then, confused by what she had said, shook his head. It was not so much a negative as an acknowledgment that he had not considered the matter. *Go home? Why? Why was it time?*

'Are you tired of all this?' he asked, almost incredulous. She seemed so happy here.

'I'm happy enough. But it's not me I'm thinking of, it's you. You're going soft here. Wasting away.' She looked up at him, concern in her young eyes. 'I want you to be as you were. I don't want you to be like this. That's all...'

He couldn't argue with that. He felt it in himself. Each day it seemed to get worse. Sitting here with nothing to do. Ordered to do nothing. He felt more and more restless as the months passed; more and more impotent. That was the worst of exile.

'What can I do? I *have* to be here.'

She could feel the bitterness in his voice, see the resignation in his hunched shoulders. It hurt her to be witness to such things. But for once she could help him.

'Where is that bloody servant!' he cried out, anger and frustration boiling over. She waited for him to finish, then told him that she had sent the servant away earlier.

'I want to talk to you.'

He looked at her, surprised by the grown-up tone of her voice. 'Talk, eh? What about?'

She looked away, stared out at the sea, the distant islands of the Kepu-lauan Barat Daya. 'This is beautiful, isn't it? The colours of the sky and sea.

But it's the wrong kind of beauty. It doesn't...' She struggled for some way of expressing what she was feeling, then shook her head.

He knew what she meant, though. It *was* beautiful. But it was a soft, pearled beauty. It didn't touch his soul the way the fjords, the mountains touched him. The unvarying warmth, the mists, the absence of seasonal change – these things irked him.

'I wish...' he began, then shook his head firmly. There was no use wishing. Li Shai Tung had exiled him here. He would live out his days on this island.

'What?' she asked. She had stood and was waiting at his side, looking at him, her head on the level of his own.

He reached out a hand and caressed her cheek, then let his hand rest on her bare shoulder. The skin was cool and dry.

'Why should I wish for anything more than what I have?' He frowned, thinking that he might have been killed for what he had done; and then she would have been alone, an orphan. Or worse. He had acted without understanding that. In his anger he had gambled that the T'ang would act as he had. Yet it pained him greatly now to think what might have been: the hurt he could have caused her – maybe even her death.

She seemed to sense this. Leaning forward she kissed his brow, his cheek. 'You did what you had to. Li Shai Tung understood that.'

He laughed at that. 'Understood? He was furious!'

'Only because he had to be.'

He removed his hand, leaned back in his chair. 'What is this, Jelka? What have you heard?'

She laughed. 'You were sleeping when he came. I didn't want to disturb you. I know how bad the nights are for you.'

He reached out. 'Who? Who has come?'

She reached up and took his hands from where they lay on her shoulders, then held them, turning them over. Strong, fine hands.

'Well?' he prompted, impatient now, but laughing too. 'Tell me!'

'General Nocenzi.'

He sat back heavily.

'He's in the house. Shall I bring him?'

He looked up at her distractedly, then nodded. 'Yes. It will be good to see Vittorio again.'

He watched her go, then let his gaze drift out over the surface of the sea. Nocenzi. It could mean only one thing. They had come for his head.

Friends had kept him informed. They had told him of the growing demand for 'justice' in the Lehmann case. Lately there had been rumours that the House was about to indict him for the murder. Well, now the T'ang had succumbed to that pressure. And he, Tolonen, would be made to account for what he'd done.

He shivered, thinking of Jelka, then turned to see that Nocenzi was already there, standing on the sand by the corner of the house, his cap under his arm.

'Knut...'

The two men embraced warmly and stood there a moment simply looking at each other. Then Tolonen looked down.

'I know why you've come.'

Nocenzi laughed strangely. 'You've read my orders, then, General?'

Tolonen met his eyes again, then shook his head. 'Just *Shih* Tolonen. You're General now, Vittorio.'

Nocenzi studied him a while, then smiled. 'Let's sit, neh? Jelka said she'd bring fresh *ch'a*.'

They sat, not facing each other but looking outward at the sea.

Nocenzi noted the book that lay face down on the table. 'What are you reading?'

Tolonen handed him the old, leather-bound volume and watched him smile. It was Sun Tzu's *Chan Shu*, his 'Art of War', dating from the third century BC. The Clavell translation.

'They say the Ch'in warriors were mad. They ran into battle without armour.'

Tolonen laughed. 'Yes, Vittorio, but there were a million of them. Nor had they ever tasted defeat.'

There was a moment's tense silence, then Tolonen turned to face his old friend. 'Tell me straight, Vittorio. Is it as I fear? Am I to pay for what I did?'

Nocenzi looked back at him. 'Lehmann deserved what you did to him. There are many who believe that.'

'Yes,' Tolonen insisted. 'But am I to pay?'

Tolonen's successor gazed back at the man he had served under for almost a quarter of a century and smiled. 'You said you knew why I had come, Knut. But you were wrong. I haven't come for your head. I've come because the T'ang has asked to see you.'

Li Yuan cried out and woke in the semi-darkness, his heart beating wildly, the feeling of the dark horse beneath him still vivid, the scent of plum blossom filling his nostrils.

He shivered and sat up, aware of the warm stickiness of his loins. Sweat beaded his brow and chest. The satin sheets were soaked about him. He moaned softly and put his head in his hands. Fei Yen... He had been riding with Fei Yen. Faster and faster they had ridden, down, down the long slope until, with a jolt and a powerful stretching motion he could feel in his bones even now, his horse had launched itself at the fence.

He threw the sheets back and, in the half-light, looked down at himself. His penis was still large, engorged with blood, but it was flaccid now. With a little shudder he reached down and touched the wetness. The musty smell of his own semen was strong, mixed with the lingering scent of plum blossom. He sniffed deeply, confused, then remembered. The silk she had given him lay on the bedside table, its perfume pervading the air.

He looked across at the broad ivory face of the bedside clock. It was just after four. He stood, about to go through and shower, when there were noises outside the door, then a muted knocking.

Li Yuan threw the cover back, then took a robe from the side and drew it on. 'Come!'

Nan Ho stood in the doorway, head bowed, a lantern in one hand.

'Are you all right, Prince Yuan?'

Nan Ho was his body servant; his head man, in charge of the eight juniors in his household-within-a-household.

'It was...' He shuddered. 'It was only a dream, Nan Ho. I'm fine.'

He glanced round at the bed, then, slightly embarrassed by the request, added, 'Would you bring clean sheets, Nan Ho. I... '

He turned away sharply, realizing he was holding Fei Yen's silk.

Nan Ho looked to him then to the bed and bowed. 'I'll be but a moment, Prince Yuan.' Then he hesitated. 'Is there...?' He moved his head slightly to one side, as if finding difficulty with what he was about to say. 'Is there anything I can arrange for you, Prince Yuan?'

Li Yuan swallowed, then shook his head. 'I don't understand you, Nan Ho? What might you arrange at this hour?'

Nan Ho came into the room and closed the door behind him. Then, in a softer voice, he said, 'Perhaps the Prince would like Pearl Heart to come and see to him?'

Pearl Heart was one of the maids. A young girl of fifteen years.

'Why should I want Pearl Heart... ?' he began, then saw what Nan Ho meant and looked away.

'Well, Highness?'

He held back the anger he felt, keeping his voice calm; the voice of a prince, a future T'ang.

'Just bring clean sheets, Nan Ho. I'll tell you when I need anything else.'

Nan Ho bowed deeply and turned to do as he was bid. Only when he was gone did Li Yuan look down at the wet silk in his hand and realize he had wiped himself with it.

Chen stood there in the queue, naked, waiting his turn. The sign over the doorway read DECONTAMINATION. The English letters were black. Beneath them, in big red pictograms was the equivalent Mandarin. Chen looked about him, noting that it was one of the rare few signs here that had an English translation. The Lodz Clearing Station handled more than three hundred thousand people a day, and almost all of them were Han. It was strange that. Unexpected.

Beyond the doorway were showers and disinfectant baths: primitive but effective solutions to the problem of decontaminating millions of workers every week. He shuffled along, ignoring his nakedness and the nakedness of those on every side, resisting the temptation to scratch at the skin patch beneath his left ear.

A Hung Mao guard pushed him through the doorway brutally and, like those in front of him, Chen bowed his head and walked on slowly through the stinging coldness of the showers, then down the steps into the bath, holding his breath as he ducked underwater.

Then he was outside, in daylight, goose-pimples on his flesh. A guard thrust clothes into his arms – a loincloth, a drab brown overall and a coolie hat – and then he was queueing again.

'Tong Chou?'

He answered to his alias and pushed through to the front to collect his ID card and his pack, checking briefly to make sure they had not confiscated the viewing-tube. Then he found a space and, holding the card between his teeth, the pack between his feet, got quickly dressed.

He followed the flow of people through, one of thousands, identically dressed. At the end of a long walled roadway the crowd spilled out into a wide arena. This was the embarkation area. Once more the signs were all in *Kuo-yu*, or Mandarin. Chen turned and looked back, seeing, for the first time, the wall of the City towering over them, stretching away whitely into the distance to either side. Then he looked down, searching for the pictogram he had learned – *Hsia*, the crab. Seeing it, he made his way across and up the ramp, stopping at the barrier to show his ID.

The train was packed. He squeezed in, smiling apologetically as he made his way through, then turned, waiting.

He had not long to wait. The train was crowded and extremely stuffy, the smell of disinfected bodies overpowering, but it was fast. Within the hour he was at *Hsia* Plantation, stumbling from the carriage, part of the crowd that made its way slowly down the ramp and out into the open.

There was a faint, unpleasant scent to the air, like something stale or over-cooked. Chen looked up, then looked down again quickly, his eyes unused to the brightness. The sun blazed down overhead; a huge, burning circle of light – bigger, much brighter than he remembered it. Ahead of him the land stretched away forever – flat and wide and green. Greener, much greener, than he'd ever imagined.

He smiled. Wang Ti would have liked to have seen this. She had always said she would love to live outside, beneath the sun and the stars, her feet planted firmly on the black earth. As their forefathers had once lived.

For a moment Chen's smile broadened, thinking of her and Jyan and the child to come, then his face cleared as he put all thought of her behind. He was Tong Chou now and had no family. Tong Chou, demoted from the levels. Tong Chou. Until this was over.

The crowd slowed. Another queue formed. Chen waited, patient, knowing that patience alone would carry him through the coming days. When he came to the barrier a guard babbled at him in *Kuo-yu*. He shook his head. 'I'm new,' he said. 'I only speak English. You know, *Ying Kuo*.'

The guard laughed and turned to say something to one of his fellows, again in Mandarin. The other guard laughed and looked Chen up and down, then said something that made the first guard laugh crudely. They were both *Hung Mao*.

He handed the guard his permit, then waited while the man scrutinized it thoroughly and, with a show of self-importance, used his comset to double-check. He seemed almost disappointed to find nothing wrong with it.

'Take care, *Han*,' the guard said, thrusting his card back at him.

He moved on, keeping his head down, following the flow.

'*Chiao shen me ming tsu?*'

Chen looked up, expecting another guard, but the young man who had addressed him wore the drab brown of a field worker. Moreover, he was *Hung Mao*. The first *Hung Mao* he had seen here who was not a guard.

He looked the youth up and down, then answered him. 'I'm sorry. My Mandarin is very poor.'

The young man had a long face and round, watery blue eyes. His hair was dark but wispy and his mouth was crooked, as if he had suffered a stroke. But he was far too young, too fit, to be suffering from heart troubles. The crooked mouth smiled and the eyes gave Chen the same scrutiny Chen had given him.

'I'm Pavel,' the youth said, inclining his head the slightest degree. 'I was asking what they called you.'

'Tong Chou,' Chen answered, then realized how easily it had come to his lips.

Pavel took one of his hands and turned it over, examining it. 'I thought so,' he said. 'You're new to this.'

Chen smiled. There were things that could not be faked, like calluses on the palms. 'I'm a refugee from the levels,' he said. 'When my father died I got into debt over his funeral. Then I got in with a shark. You know how it is.'

Pavel looked at him a moment, his watery blue eyes trying to figure him; then his crooked mouth smiled again. 'Come on, Tong Chou. You'll need someone to show you the ropes. There's a spare bed in our hut. You can kip down there.'

Pavel set off at once, moving away from the slow moving column of new recruits. Only as he turned did Chen notice something else about him. His back was hunched, the spine bent unnaturally. What Chen had taken for a bow of politeness was the young man's natural gait. Chen followed him quickly, catching up with him. As they walked along the dirt path Pavel began to talk, explaining how things worked on the plantation.

'How did you know I was new?'

Pavel glanced sideways at him. 'The way you walk. The way you're wearing those clothes. The way you squint against the sun. Oh, a hundred little signs. What were you up above? You've strong hands. They're not an office-worker's hands.'

'But not a peasant's either?'

Pavel laughed, throwing his head back to do so. Chen, watching him, decided he liked the youth. He looked a dull-wit, but he was sharp. Very sharp.

'And where are you from, Pavel?'

Pavel sniffed, then looked away across the vast plain. 'Me? I was born here.'

'Here?'

Pavel smiled crookedly and nodded. 'Here. In these fields.'

Ahead of them was a break in the green. A long black line that cut right across their path. The dirt track led out onto a wooden bridge. Halfway across the bridge Chen stopped, looking down.

Pavel came back to him and looked where he was looking, as if expecting to see something unusual in the water. 'What is it?'

Chen laughed. 'It's nothing.' But he had realized that he had never seen water flow like this before. Taps and baths and pools, that was all he had ever seen. It had made him feel strange. Somehow incomplete.

Pavel looked at him, then laughed. 'What did you say you were?'

They went on. The field they had crossed had been empty, but beyond the bridge it was different. Long lines of workers – five hundred, maybe a thousand to each line – were stretched out across the vast green, hunched forward, huge wicker baskets on their backs, their coolie hats making them seem a thousand copies of the same machine. Yet each was a man or woman – a person, like himself.

Where the path met another at a crossroads, a group of men were lounging by an electric cart. They were dressed differently, in smart black trousers and kingfisher blue jackets. They wore black, broad-rimmed hats with silk tassels hanging from the back and most of them had guns – Deng rifles, Chen noted – strapped to their shoulders. As Chen and Pavel approached, they seemed to stir expectantly.

Pavel touched Chen's arm, his voice a whisper. 'Keep your head down and keep walking. Don't stop unless they specifically order you to.'

Chen did as Pavel said. Even so, two of the men detached themselves from the group and came across onto the path, blocking their way. They were big, brutal-looking. Han, both of them.

'Who's this, Pavel?' one of them asked.

The youth kept his head lowered. 'This is Tong Chou, *Shih* Teng. I am taking him to register.'

Teng laughed caustically and looked at his fellow. 'You're quite a bit out of your way then, Pavel. Registration is back there, where you've just come from. Or have they moved it since I was last there?'

There was laughter from the men by the cart.

Chen glanced at the youth and saw how he swallowed nervously. But he wasn't finished yet. 'Forgive me, *Shih* Teng. That would be so normally. But Tong Chou is a replacement. He has been drafted to fill the place left by Field Supervisor Sung's unfortunate death. I was told to take him direct to Acting Supervisor Ming. Ming is to fill out a special registration form.'

Teng was silent a moment, then he stepped aside. 'Get moving, then. I want to see you both in the fields within the hour, understand me?'

Pavel dipped his head, then hurried on. Chen followed, keeping his eyes on the ground.

'Who were they?' Chen asked, when they were out of hearing.

'Teng Fu and Chang Yan. They're the Overseer's men. Chang's fairly docile. Teng's the one you need to watch. He's a vicious piece of work. Thinks he's something special. Fortunately he knows very little about how this place works. But that's true of most of them. There's not one of those guards has any brains. Providing you keep your nerve you can convince them of anything.'

Chen nodded. 'You were frightened, though. You took a risk for me. I'm grateful for that, Pavel.'

Pavel breathed deeply. 'Not for you, so much, Tong Chou, but for all of us. They say the spirits of the dead have no shadows, but the death of Field Supervisor Sung and his wife have left a darkness here that no man can dispel.'

Chen looked thoughtfully at him. 'I see.'

'I'll tell you some time,' the youth said, glancing at him.

They walked on. Up ahead of them, maybe ten li or so in the distance, the straight line of the horizon was broken by a building; a huge, three-tiered pagoda.

'What's that?' Chen asked.

Pavel didn't even bother to look up. 'That? That's the Overseer's House.'

As he watched a faint speck lifted from the fields close by the building and came towards them. A Security cruiser. The sound of its engines followed seconds later; muted at first, but growing louder by the moment. Minutes later it passed overhead, the shadow of the big craft sweeping across the fields.

Chen looked back at the Overseer's House and nodded to himself. So that was where he was. *Well, Shih Bergson,* he thought, *I'll find out all I can about this place. Then I'll pay you a visit. And find out if you are who we think you are.*

DeVore looked down from the window of the craft as it swept south over the fields, the fingers of one hand absently tracing the surface of the object in the other.

'What is that?'

The voice was cold, chillingly free of intonation, but DeVore was used to it by now. It was the voice of his dead friend. He turned and looked at Lehmann's albino son, then handed him the tiny rose quartz snuff bottle.

'It was a first meeting gift from Douglas. He saw me admiring it.'

Lehmann examined it, then handed it back. 'What did you give him?'

'I sent him a copy of Pecorini and Shu's *The Game Of Wei Chi*. The Longman edition of 1929.'

Lehmann was silent a moment, considering. 'It seems an odd gift. Douglas doesn't play.'

'No, but he should. All men – men of any ability – should play.' DeVore tucked the bottle away in the pocket of his jacket. 'Do you play, Stefan?'

Lehmann turned his head slowly, until he was facing DeVore. The albino's dead eyes seemed to stare straight through him. 'What do you think?'

DeVore smiled coldly. 'I think you do. I'd say you were a good player. Unorthodox, but good.'

Lehmann made no reaction. He turned his head back, facing the front of the craft.

Like a machine, DeVore thought, chilled and yet strangely delighted by the boy. *I could make something of you, given time.*

They were flying down to the Swiss Wilds, to meet Weis and see how work was going on the first of the fortresses.

DeVore looked back out the window. Two figures trudged along one of the paths far below. Field workers, their coolie hats making them seem like two tiny, black *wei chi* stones against the criss-cross pattern of the fields. Then they were gone and the craft was rising, banking to the right.

He had been busy since the meeting at Douglas's. The business with Lehmann's son had taken him totally by surprise, but he had recovered quickly. Using his contacts in Security he had had the mother traced; had investigated her past and discovered things about her that no one in her immediate circle knew. His man had gone to her and confronted her with what they knew.

And now she was his. A handle. A way, perhaps, of controlling Stefan Lehmann should he prove troublesome.

DeVore smiled and turned back to the youth. 'Perhaps we should play a game some time?'

Lehmann did not even look at him. 'No.'

DeVore studied the youth a moment, then looked away. *So he understands,* he thought. *He knows how much of a man's character is reflected in the mirror of the board, the stones. Yet his refusal says a lot about him. He's more cautious than his father. Colder. More calculating. Yes, I bet he's very good at the game. It's a shame he won't play. It would have been a challenge.*

The journey took them less than an hour. Weis met them in the landing dome, furred and gloved, anxious to complete his business and get away. DeVore saw this and decided to keep him – to play upon his fears, his insecurity.

'You'll eat with us, I hope, *Shih* Weis?'

He saw Weis's inner hesitation; saw how he assessed the possible damage of a refusal and weighed it against his own discomfort. A banker. Always, first and foremost, a banker.

'Well?' DeVore insisted, loading the scales against refusal.

'I have a meeting at six.'

It was just after one. DeVore took his elbow lightly and turned him towards the exit. 'Then we have plenty of time, neh? Come. I don't know about you, *Shih* Weis, but I'm famished.'

They were high up, almost thirteen thousand feet, and it was cold outside the dome of the landing platform, the sun lost behind thick cloud cover. Landeck Base was some way above them on the mountainside, a vast, flattened hemisphere, its brilliant whiteness blending with the snow and ice surrounding it. Beneath its cover, work had begun already on the fortress.

'It's a beautiful sight, don't you think, Major?' Weis said as he stepped out onto the snow, his breath pluming in the chill air.

DeVore smiled, then looked about him. 'You're right, Weis,' he said, noting how Weis had used his real identity yet again. 'It is beautiful.' But he knew Weis was talking about the base up ahead of them, not the natural beauty of their surroundings.

They were on the eastern slope of a great glacial valley – a huge trench more than two li deep and one across. It ran north-west, ringed on all sides by the brutal shapes of mountains. Cloud obscured the distance, but it could not diminish the purity of the place. This land was untouched, elemental. He felt at home here.

He stopped in the snow field just beneath the Base and studied the great, shield-like dome, thinking of the seven great Security garrisons ringing the Swiss Wilds, like seven black stones placed on a giant board. The T'ang's handicap. He laughed softly. Well, now he had placed the first white stone. The great game had begun.

Guards wearing full snow camouflage let them inside, then searched them. DeVore submitted patiently, smiling at the guard when he handed back the tiny snuff bottle. Only Weis seemed upset by the routine.

'Is this really necessary?' he huffed irritably, turning to DeVore as the soldier continued his body search.

'It's necessary, I assure you, Shih Weis. One small device could tear this place apart. And then your backers would be very angry that we had not taken such precautions.' He laughed. 'Isn't that how you bankers think? Don't you always assume the worst possible case and then act accordingly?'

Weis bowed his head, ceding the point, but DeVore could see he was still far from happy.

A door from the Secure Area led out into the dome itself. Mobile factories had been set up all over the dome floor and men were hard at work on every side – manufacturing the basic equipment for the Base. But the real work was being done beneath their feet – in the heart of the mountain. Down there they were hewing out the tunnels and chambers of Landeck Base from the solid rock. When it was finished there would be no sign from the air.

They crossed the dome floor. On the far side was an area screened off from the rest of the dome. Here the first of DeVore's recruits were temporarily housed. Here they slept and ate and trained, until better quarters were hewn from the rock for them.

DeVore turned to Weis and Lehmann, and indicated that they should go through. 'We'll be eating with the men,' he said, and saw – as he had expected – how discomfited Weis was by the news. He had thought that other arrangements – special arrangements – had been made.

DeVore studied him, thinking, *Yes, you like your comforts, don't you, Weis? And all this – the mountains, the cold, the busy preparations – mean very little by comparison. Your heart's in Han opera and little boys, not revolution. I'll watch you, Weis. Watch you like a hawk. Because you're the weakest link. If things go wrong, you'll be the first to break.*

He went inside after them and was greeted by the duty officer. Normally the man would have addressed him as Major, but, seeing Weis, he merely bowed deeply, then turned and led them across to the eating area.

Good, thought DeVore. *Though it matters little now, I like a man who knows when to hold his tongue.*

They sat on benches at one of the scrubbed wooden tables.

'Well, *Shih* Weis? What would you like to eat?'

The cook bowed and handed Weis the single sheet menu. DeVore kept his amusement hidden, knowing what was on the paper. It was all very basic fare – soldier's food – and he saw Weis's face crinkle with momentary disgust. He handed the sheet back and turned to DeVore.

'If you don't mind, I'd rather not. But you two go ahead.'

DeVore ordered, then turned and looked at Lehmann.

'I'll have the same.'

'Good.' He looked back at Weis. 'So. Tell me, *Shih* Weis, what *has* been happening?'

Weis leaned forward, lowering his voice. 'There's been a problem.'

'A problem?'

'Duchek. He's refused to pass the funds through the plantation accounts.'

'I see. So what have you done?'

Weis smiled broadly, clearly pleased by his own ingenuity. 'I've re-routed them – through various Security ordnance accounts.'

DeVore considered it a moment, then smiled. 'That's good. Much better, in fact. They'd never dream we'd use their own accounts.'

Weis leaned back, nodding. 'That's what I thought.'

Because of the vast sums involved they had had to take great care in setting up the routes by which the money got to DeVore. The finances of Chung Kuo were closely knit and any large movement was certain to be noted by the T'ang's Ministry, the Hu Pu, responsible for monitoring all capital transfers and ensuring the T'ang received the fifty per cent due him on the profit of each and every transaction.

It had been decided from the outset that it would be safest to be open about the movements. Any attempt to siphon away sums of this size would be noticed and investigated, but normal movements – if the T'ang received his cut from them – would not be commented upon. It had meant that the T'ang would actually receive almost seventy-five per cent of everything they allocated, but this had been budgeted for.

Weis and his small team had worked directly with the sponsors to set things up. First they had had to break the transfers down into smaller, less noticeable sums, then disguise these as payments to smaller companies for work done. From there they were re-routed and broken down into yet smaller payments – this process being repeated anything between ten and fifteen times before they finally got to DeVore. Again, it was an expensive process, but necessary to protect the seven major sponsors from being traced. Palms had had to be greased all the way down the line, 'squeeze' to be paid to greedy officials.

Funded directly it would have cost a quarter of the sum DeVore had asked for. But the risk of discovery would have been a hundred times greater.

'You've done an excellent job, Shih Weis,' DeVore said, leaning back to let the cook set his plate down in front of him. 'I have asked Shih Douglas if he could not show our appreciation in some small way.'

He saw how much that pleased Weis, then looked down and picked up his chopsticks, tucking into the heaped plate of braised beancurd and vegetables.

★

DeVore watched Weis's craft lift and accelerate away, heading north, back to the safety of the City. The man's impatience both irritated and amused him. He was so typical of his kind. So unimaginative. All his talk about *The New Hope*, for instance – it was all so much hot air. But that was fortunate, perhaps. For if they'd guessed – if any of them had had the foresight to see where all this really led...

He laughed, then turned to the youth. 'Do you fancy a walk, Stefan? The cold is rather exhilarating, I find.'

'I'd like that.'

The answer surprised him. He had begun to believe there was nothing the young man liked.

They went down past the landing dome and out onto a broad lip of ice-covered rock which once, long ago, had been a road. From that vantage point they could see how the valley began to curve away to the west. Far below them the mountainside was forested, but up here there was only snow and ice. They were above the world.

Standing there in the crisp air, surrounded by the bare splendour of the mountains, he saw it clearly. *The New Hope* was much more than a new start. For the Seven it would be the beginning of the end. His colleagues – Weis, Moore, Duchek, even Berdichev – saw it mainly as a symbol, a flagship for their cause, but it was more than that. It was a practical thing. If it succeeded – if new worlds could be colonized by its means – then control would slip from the hands of the Seven.

They knew that. Li Shai Tung had known it three years ago when he had summoned the leaders of the House to him and, unexpectedly, granted the concession. But the old man had had no choice. Lehmann's murder had stirred the hornet's nest. It was the only thing the T'ang could have done to prevent war.

Even so, none of his fellow conspirators had grasped what it *really* meant. They had not fully envisaged the changes that would come about – the vast, rapid metamorphosis that would sweep through their tight-knit community of thirty-nine billion souls. Science, kept in check by the Edict for so long, would not so much blossom as explode. When Mankind went out into the stars it would not, as so many had called it, be a scattering, but a shattering. All real cohesion would be lost. The Seven knew this. But few others had understood as yet. They thought the future would be an extension of the past. It would not. It would be something new. Something utterly, disturbingly new.

The new age, if it came, would be an age of grotesque and gothic wonders. Of magical transformations. Mutation would be the norm.

If it came.

'What were you up to with Weis back there?'

DeVore turned and looked at the young man. He seemed perfectly suited to this environment. His eyes, the pallor of his flesh; neither seemed out of place here. He was like some creature of the wild – a pine marten or a snow fox. A predator.

DeVore smiled. 'I've been told Weis is a weak man. A soft man. I wanted confirmation of that.'

'What had you heard?'

DeVore told him about the tape he had acquired. It showed Weis in bed with two young boys – well-known Han opera stars. That was his weakness; a weakness he indulged in quite often, if the reports were accurate.

'Can he be trusted?'

'We have no option. Weis is the only one with both the know-how and the contacts.'

'I see.'

DeVore turned and looked back at the view. He remembered standing here with Berdichev, almost a year before, when they had first drawn up their scheme; recalled how they had stood and watched the sunset together; how frightened Soren had been; how the sudden fall of dark had changed his mood entirely. But he had expected as much. After all, Berdichev was typical of the old Man.

Beneath it all they were still the same primitive creatures. Still forest dwellers, crouched on the treeline, watching the daylight bleed away on the plain below, fearful of the dark. Their moods, their very beings, were shaped by patterns older than the race. By the Earth's slow rotation about the sun. By the unglimpsed diurnal round – cycles of dark and light, heat and cold. They could not control how they were, how they felt.

In the new age it would be different. There would be a creature free of this. Unshackled. A creature of volition, unshaped by its environment. A creature fit for space.

Let them have their romantic image of dispersion; of new, unblemished worlds. Of Edens. His dreams were different and rode upon their backs. His dream was of new men. Of better, finer creatures. *Cleaner* creatures.

He thought back to the tape of Weis; to the image of the financier standing there, naked, straddling the young boy, his movements urgent, his face tight with need. *Such weakness*, he thought. So pitiful to be a slave to need.

In his dream of the new age he saw all such weaknesses eradicated. His new Man would be purged of need. His blood would flow clean and pure like the icy streams of the far north.

'It's magnificent. So pure.'

He looked across at the youth, surprised, then laughed. Yes, they were all much the same – all the same, primitive Man, unchanged by long millennia of so-called civilization. All, perhaps, but this one. 'Yes,' he said, after a moment, feeling himself drawn to the boy. 'It is magnificent, isn't it?'

The gateway was an arch of darkness, leading out into a vast and dimly lit hall. For a moment Tolonen thought he had come out into the Clay itself. Broad steps led down onto bare earth. The ceiling was high above him. But it was too bright, however dim, too clean, however bare, to be the Clay. And there, less than half a *li* from where he stood, was the ancient stadium, its high, curved walls in partial shadow, the great curved arches of its mighty windows black as a moonless night.

The Colosseum. Heart of the old *Ta Ts'in* empire.

He went down and crossed the space, choosing one of the tall archways at random, knowing they all led inward to the centre.

Feeling exposed. Feeling like a man walking in death's shadow.

He went inside, conscious of the sheer weight of stone above him as he stepped beneath the arch. The arch dwarfed him; was five times or more his height. Three great layers of arches, one above another, capped by a vast, uneven wall of ancient stone.

He had a sense of time, of power as old as time itself. This millennia-old edifice, monument to power and death and empire, awed him slightly, and he understood why the T'ang had chosen it for their meeting place.

'So you've come...'

Tolonen stopped on the edge of the inner arch, squinting into the darkness at the centre, trying to make out the shape of his master.

'Heavy-handed monsters, weren't they?'

Li Shai Tung stepped out from the next archway. At a signal from him the lights were raised and the central amphitheatre was suddenly revealed. It was huge, monstrous, barbaric. It spoke of a crude brutality.

Tolonen was silent, waiting. And while he waited, he thought about the pain and death this place had been built to hold. So much raw aggression had been moulded into darkness here. So much warm blood spilled for entertainment.

'You understand, then?' said the T'ang, turning to face him for the first time. There were tears in his eyes.

He found he could barely answer him. 'What is it, *Chieh Hsia*? What do you want from me?'

Li Shai Tung drew a deep breath, then raised a hand, indicating the building all about them. 'They would have me believe you are like this place. As unthinkingly callous. As brutal. Did you know that?'

He wanted to ask, *Who? Who would have you believe this?*, but he merely nodded, listening.

'However... I know you too well, Knut. You're a caring man. A loving man.'

Tolonen shivered, moved by his T'ang's words.

The T'ang moved closer; stood face to face with his ex-General, their breaths mingling. 'What you did was wrong. Very wrong.' Then, surprisingly, he leaned forward and kissed Tolonen's cheek, holding him a moment, his voice lowered to a whisper. 'But thank you, Knut. Thank you, dearest friend. You acted like a brother to my grief.'

Tolonen stood there, surprised, looking into his master's face, then bowed his head, all the old warmth welling up inside him. It had been so long, so hard being exiled.

He went down onto his knees at Li Shai Tung's feet, his head bowed in submission. 'Tell me what you want, *Chieh Hsia*. Let me serve you again.'

'Get up, old friend. Get up.'

'Not until you say I am forgiven.'

There was a moment's silence, then Li Shai Tung placed his hands on Tolonen's shoulders. 'I cannot reinstate you. You must realize that. As for forgiveness, there is nothing to forgive. You acted as I felt. I would need to forgive myself first.' He smiled sadly. 'Your exile is at an end, Knut. You can come home. Now get up.'

Tolonen stayed on his knees.

'Get up, you foolish man. Get up. You think I'd let my ablest friend rot in inactivity?' He was laughing now; a soft, almost childlike laughter. 'Yes, you foolish old man. I have a job for you.'

It was a hot night. Nan Ho had left the door to the garden open. A gentle breeze stirred the curtains, bringing the scents of night flowers and the sound of an owl in the orchard. Li Yuan woke and stretched, then grew very still.

'Who is it?' he said, his voice very small.

There was a touch of warmth against his back and a soft, muted giggle, then he felt her pressed against him – undoubtedly *her* – and heard her voice in his ear.

'Hush, little one. Hush. It's only me, Pearl Heart. I'll not bite you.'

He turned and, in the moon's light, saw her naked there beside him in his bed.

'What are you doing here, Pearl Heart?' he asked, but his eyes were drawn to the firmness of her breasts, the soft, elegant slope of her shoulders. Her dark eyes seemed to glisten in the moonlight and she lay there, unashamed, enjoying the way he looked at her.

She reached out and took his hand and pressed it gently to her breast, letting him feel the hardness of the nipple, then moved it down, across the silken smoothness of her stomach until it rested between her legs.

He shivered, then looked to her eyes again. 'I shouldn't...'

She smiled and shook her head, her eyes filled with amusement. 'No, perhaps you shouldn't, after all? Shall I go away?'

She made to move but his hand held her where she was, pressing down against the soft down of her sex. 'No... I...'

Again she laughed, a soft, delicious laughter that increased his desire, then she sat up and pushed him down, pulling back the sheet from him.

'What have we here? Ah, now here's the root of all your problems.'

She lifted his stiff penis gently between her fingers, making him catch his breath, then bent her head and kissed it. A small, wet kiss.

'There,' she said gently, looking up the length of his body into his eyes. 'I can see what you need, my little one. Why didn't you tell Pearl Heart before now?' She smiled and her eyes returned to his penis.

For a moment he closed his eyes, a ripple of pure pleasure passing through him as she stroked and kissed him. Then, when he could bear it no longer, he pulled her up against him, then turned her over, onto her back, letting her hand help him as he struggled to find the mouth of her sex with the blind eye of his penis.

Then, with a sudden sense of her flesh parting before his urgent pressure, he was inside her and she was pushing back up against him, her face suddenly different, her movements no longer quite so gentle, her legs wrapped about his back. He thrust and thrust and then cried out, his body stiffening, a great hot wave of blackness robbing him momentarily of thought.

He slept for a while and when he woke she was there still, not a dream as he had begun to imagine but real and warm, her body beautiful, naked in the moonlight beside him, her dark eyes watching him. The thought – the reality of her – made his penis stir again and she laughed and stroked his cheek, his neck, his shoulder, her fingers moving down his body until they were curled about the root of him again.

'Pearl Heart?' he said, looking up from where her fingers played with him, into her face.

'Hush,' she said, her smile like balm. 'Lie still and close your eyes, my little one. Pearl Heart will ease the darkness in you.'

He smiled and closed his eyes, letting the whole of him be drawn like a thread of fine silk into the contact of her fingers with his flesh. He gave a little shudder as her body brushed against his own, moving down him, then groaned as he felt her tiny, rosebud lips close wetly about the end of his penis.

'Pearl Heart,' he said softly, almost inaudibly. And then the darkness claimed him once again.

Chen leaned on his hoe, then looked up into the sky and wiped his brow with the cloth Pavel had given him.

'This is harder than I thought it would be,' he said, laughing.

The young man smiled back at him. 'Would you like some water, Tong Chou?'

He hesitated, then gave a small bow. 'That would be good. I've a thirst on me such as I've never had.'

'It's hot,' Pavel said kindly. 'You're not used to it yet, that's all. You'll get the hang of it.'

Chen rubbed his back then laughed again. 'Gods! Let's hope so. I've a feeling I'm not so much breaking the earth as the earth's breaking me.'

He watched Pavel go, then got down to it again, turning the dark, hard earth, one of a long line of workers stretching out across the huge, two-li-wide field. Then, only moments later, he looked up, hearing raised voices from the direction Pavel had gone. He turned and saw the youth had been stopped by the guards – the same two men who had stopped them on the path the day before.

'What is it?' he asked the woman next to him, then realized she didn't speak English, only Mandarin. But the woman seemed to understand. She made a drinking gesture with one cupped hand, then shook her head.

'But I thought...'

Then he remembered something Pavel had said earlier. They were only allowed three cups of water a day – at the allotted breaks. Curse him, the stupid boy! Chen thought, dropping his hoe and starting across the field towards the noise, but two of the field workers ran after him and held his arms until he returned to the line.

'Fa!' one of them kept saying. 'Fa!' Then, in atrocious English, he translated the word. 'Pah-nis-men.'

Chen went cold. 'I've got to stop it.'

One of the older men – a peasant in his late forties or fifties, his face deeply tanned and creased – stepped forward. 'You cannot stop it,' he said in a clipped but clear English. 'Watch. They will summon some of us. They will make us form a circle. Then the punishment will begin.' He sighed resignedly. 'It is their way.'

On the far side of the field the shouting had stopped now and he could see Pavel, his arm held tightly by one of the men, his head bowed under the coolie hat.

'Shit!' he said under his breath. But the old man was right. He could not afford to get involved; neither, probably, would his involvement change anything. He was a field worker here, not kwai, and his job was to get at DeVore. He could not risk that, even to prevent this injustice.

The bigger of the two guards – the one Pavel had identified as Teng – strode out towards them. He stopped and, hands on his hips, ordered a number of them over to the water wagon.

Chen felt sick. This was his fault. But he could do nothing.

Pavel did not look at him. It was clear he had chosen not to say why he had gone to the wagon. Without being told, the ku – the field workers – formed a circle about the youth and the two guards. There was an awful silence. Chen looked around the circle and saw how most of them looked down or away, anything but look at what was happening at the circle's heart.

Teng's voice barked out again. 'This man was disobedient. He knew the rules and yet he broke them.' He laughed; a curt, brutal laughter. 'He was stupid. Now he will be punished for his stupidity.'

Teng drew the long club from his belt and turned to face Pavel. Chang smiled and thrust the young man forward at his fellow.

Without warning, Teng lashed out, the club hitting Pavel on the back of the legs, making him fall down. The sound the boy made was awful; a frightened whimper.

Chen shuddered and gritted his teeth.

Teng stood over the youth now, smiling down at him. 'Get up, Pavel. It's not over yet.'

Slowly, his eyes never leaving Teng's face, Pavel got to his feet again. Teng's smile never wavered, but seemed to burn fiercely. It was clear he was enjoying himself hugely. He looked down at the club, then let fly again, this time catching Pavel across the side of the head.

The boy went down with a groan of pain. Chen could feel the indignation ripple about the circle. But still they were all silent. No one moved. No one did a thing.

Teng put the tip of the club against the young man's head and pushed gently, making him fall backwards. Then he looked across at his fellow guard.

'Chang! Pass me the rod!'

This time there was a low murmur from the circle. Teng turned, looking from face to face, then laughed. 'If there's anyone else who'd like a taste of this, just say.'

Chang went across and took the club from him, handing him a long, thin pole that was attached by a wire to a small box. Teng clipped the box to one of his jacket pockets, then pressed a button on the side of the rod. It hissed wickedly.

Teng looked across at Pavel. 'Drop your trousers, boy!'

Chen saw Pavel swallow awkwardly. The youth was petrified. His fingers fumbled at the strings that held up his trousers, then managed to untie the knot. Then he stood, his head drooping, letting his trousers fall around his ankles.

Under the trousers he was quite naked. He trembled uncontrollably. His penis had shrivelled up with fear.

Teng looked at him and laughed. 'We're a fine big boy, aren't we, Pavel? No wonder we've no girlfriend yet!' Again his brutal laugh rang out. Then, cruelly, he touched the rod against the tip of the boy's penis.

Pavel jerked back, but Teng had not activated the rod.

Teng looked across at Chang and both men laughed loudly at the joke. Then Teng pressed the button and thrust the rod into the young man's groin. Pavel doubled up convulsively, then lay there as if dead. Teng must have had the rod set high, for the smell of burnt flesh was suddenly sharp in the warm, still air.

'You dirty bastard!'

The words came from Chen's left. He turned and saw it was the old man who had spoken to him earlier.

Teng had also turned and was looking at the man. 'What is it, Fang Hui? You want to join the fun?'

Chang's voice sounded urgently from behind Teng. 'Use the club, Teng Fu. The rod will kill the old fool.'

But Teng wasn't listening. He walked slowly across to the old man and stood there, facing him, head and shoulders bigger than him.

'What did you say, old man? What did you call me?'

Fang Hui smiled bleakly. 'You heard me, Teng.'

Teng laughed. 'Yes, I heard you, Fang.' He reached forward and grabbed the man's face in one hand, forcing his mouth open, then thrust the rod inside, closing Fang Hui's teeth upon it. Then he moved his hand away. One finger hovered above the button of the box.

'You'd like a taste of this, Fang Hui?'

Fang's eyes were wide with terror. Slowly Teng withdrew the rod from the old man's mouth, a sadistic smile of enjoyment lighting his big, ugly features.

'A good peasant is a quiet peasant, eh, Fang?'

The old man nodded exaggeratedly.

'Good,' Teng said quietly, then kicked out, sending Fang sprawling.

The old man lay there, gasping. Chen looked across at him, relieved he had come to no greater harm, then turned and looked back at Teng.

It had been hard. Hard not to add his voice to Fang Hui's. Harder still just to stand there in the circle and do nothing. Pavel was stirring now. He lifted his head from the ground and looked up, his eyes unfocused, then let it fall back again.

Chang stepped up behind him, a cup of water in one hand, and poured it over the youth's head. 'Is this what you came for, Pavel?' His action brought guffaws of laughter from the watching Teng.

Yes, thought Chen. *I may have done nothing here today, but watch me, Teng. Be careful how you treat me. For I've every reason to kill you now for what you've done.*

He thought of what Pavel had told him of the murders and knew now it was more than rumour. It was what had happened. He was sure of it.

Yes. Every reason.

The sound of laughter carried from the garden into the house through the wide, open doorway. Outside the morning was bright and warm; inside, where Li Yuan sat with his eight-year-old nephew, Tsu Tao Chu, it was cooler and in shadow.

They were playing *wei chi*, practising openings and corner plays, but Li Yuan seemed distracted. He kept looking out into the garden where the maids were playing ball.

The younger boy's high, sing-song voice broke the silence that had lain between them for some time. 'Your heart's not in this, is it Yuan? It's a lovely morning. Why don't we go riding instead?'

Li Yuan turned and looked at him. 'I'm sorry, Tao Chu. What did you say?'

'I said...' He laughed sweetly, then leaned forward conspiratorially. 'Tell me, Yuan. Which one is it?'

Li Yuan blushed and set a white stone down. 'I don't know what you mean, Tao Chu.'

Tao Chu raised his eyebrows, then placed a black stone on the board, removing the six white captives he had surrounded.

'I thought Fei Yen was your sweetheart, Yuan. It's clear, though, that some other maiden has won your heart. Or if not your heart...'

'Tao Chu!' Li Yuan looked down at the board and saw the position was lost, his forces disrupted. He laughed. 'Is it so obvious?'

Tao Chu busied himself removing the stones and returning them to the bowls, then set the situation up anew. He looked up. 'Again?'

Li Yuan shook his head. Then he stood up and went over to the open doorway. The maids were out beyond the ornamental pool, playing catch with a ball of stitched silk. He watched them for a while, his eyes going time and again to Pearl Heart. At first he didn't think she'd seen him, but then he saw her pick up the ball and turn, looking directly at him; her smile holding a special meaning, for him alone.

He lifted his head slightly, smiling back at her, and saw her pause, then throw the ball to one of the other maids, saying something that he couldn't catch. Then he saw her go, between the magnolia and out down the pathway, heading towards his room.

He caught up with her in the corridor outside his room, and turned her, pulling her against him.

'Not here,' she said, laughing. 'Inside, Li Yuan. Let's get inside.'

He could barely wait for her. As she undressed he ran his hands across her skin, and pressed his face against her hair, which smelled of ginger and cinnamon. He would have taken her then, while he was still fully clothed, but she stopped him and began to undress him, her hands lingering against his painfully stiff penis. In daylight her body seemed different; harder, firmer, less melting than it had seemed in the darkness, but no less desirable. He let her draw him down onto the bed, then he was inside her, spilling his seed at once.

She laughed tenderly, no trace of mockery in her laughter. 'I see I'll have to teach you tricks, Li Yuan. Ways of holding back.'

'What do you mean?' He lay there against her, his eyes closed, letting her caress his neck, his shoulders, the top of his back.

'There are books we can get. *Chun hua*. And devices.'

He shivered. The light touch of her fingers on his flesh was delicious, making him want to purr like a cat. '*Chun hua*?' He had not heard of such things. 'Spring pictures? What kind of spring pictures?'

She laughed again, then whispered in his ear. 'Pictures of men and women doing things to each other. All kind of things. You'd not believe the number of ways it can be done, Li Yuan. And not just with two.'

She saw his interest and laughed. 'Ah, yes, I thought as much. There's no man living who has not desired two girls in bed with him.'

He swallowed. 'What do you mean, Pearl Heart?' But he was answered almost at once. From behind a screen on the far side of the room came the unmistakable sound of suppressed laughter.

Li Yuan sat up and looked across. 'Who's there? I demand to know...'

He fell silent. It was Sweet Rose, the youngest of his maids. She stepped out from behind the screen, demure but naked, a faint blush on her cheeks and at her neck. 'May I join you on the bed, Li Yuan?'

Li Yuan shuddered, then turned and looked mutely at Pearl Heart. She was smiling broadly at him. 'That's what we're here for. Didn't you realize it, Li Yuan? For this time. For when you woke to your manhood.'

Pearl Heart leaned forward and summoned the younger girl, then drew Li Yuan back onto the bed, making Sweet Rose lie the other side of him. Then, with a shared, sisterly exchange of laughter, they began their work, stroking and kissing him, their skin like silk, their breath like almonds, enflaming his senses until he blossomed and caught fire again.

Nan Ho stood there outside the room, his head bowed, his manner apologetic but firm. 'I am sorry, Lady Fei, but you cannot go inside.'

She looked at him, astonished. It was the second time he had defied her. 'What do you mean, cannot? I think you forget yourself, Nan Ho. If I wish to see Li Yuan, I have every right to call on him. I want to ask him if he will ride with me this afternoon, that's all. Now, please, stand out of my way.'

He saw it was hopeless to try to deny her any further and stood to one side, his head lowered. 'I beg you, Lady Fei...' But she brushed past him and opened the door to Li Yuan's rooms.

'Ridiculous man...' she had started to say, then fell silent, sniffing the air. Then she noticed the sounds, coming from beyond the screen. Unusual sounds to be coming from the bedroom of a twelve-year-old boy. She crept up to the screen, then put her hand to her mouth to stifle her surprise.

It was Li Yuan! Gods! Li Yuan with two of his maids!

For a moment she stood there, mesmerized by the sight of his firm, almost perfect bottom jutting and rutting with one of the maids while the other caressed and stroked the two of them. Then she saw him stiffen and groan and saw the maid's legs tighten momentarily about his back, drawing him down into her.

She shuddered and began to back away, then put her hand to her mouth to stop the laughter that had come unbidden to her lips. Li Yuan! Of all the cold fishes in the sea of life, imagine Li Yuan, rutting with his maids! The dirty little beggar!

Outside she looked at Nan Ho sternly. 'I was not here, Nan Ho. Do you understand me?'

The servant bowed deeply. 'I understand you, Lady Fei. And I will leave your message for the young prince. I am sure he would welcome the chance to ride with you this afternoon.'

She nodded, then turned, conscious of the blush that had come to her cheeks and neck, and walked quickly away.

Li Yuan! She gave a brief laugh, then stopped dead, remembering the sight of those small, perfectly formed buttocks clenching at the moment of his orgasm.

'And I thought you so cold, so passionless. So above all this.'

She laughed again; a strange, querulous laugh, then walked on, surprised by what she was thinking.

'Do you remember this place, Karr?'

Karr smiled and looked out from their private box into the pit with its surrounding tiers.

'How could I forget it, General?'

Tolonen leaned back and sighed. 'Men forget many things they'd do best to remember. They forget their roots. And when that happens they lose their ability to judge things true and clear.'

Karr smiled. 'This business...' He pointed to the brilliantly lit combat circle. 'It had a way of clearing the mind of everything but truth.'

'I can see that.'

Karr turned and faced Tolonen. 'I'm glad you're back, General. I mean no disrespect to General Nocenzi, but things haven't been the same without you at the helm.'

The old man sniffed and tilted his head slightly. 'I've missed it too, Karr. Missed it badly. But, listen, I'm not at the helm. Not in the sense that you're probably thinking. No. This is something else. Something secret that the T'ang has asked me to organize.'

He spelled it out quickly, simply, letting Karr understand that he would be briefed more fully later.

'This is a contingency plan, you understand. We hope never to have to use it. If the House votes in favour of the veto on space exploration – as it should – we can put this little scheme to the flame – throw it on the fire, so to speak.'

'But you don't believe that, do you, General?'

Tolonen shook his head. 'I'm afraid not. I think the T'ang hopes against hope. The House is no friend to the Seven.'

Below them, in the pit, the two contestants came out and took their places. The fight marshal read out the rules and then stepped back. The pit went deathly silent.

The fight was brief but brutal. In less than a minute one of the two men was dead. The crowd went mad, roaring its approval. Karr watched the stewards carry the body away, then shivered.

'I'm glad I let you buy my contract out. That could have been me.'

'No,' Tolonen said. 'You were the exception. No one would have carried you from the circle. Not in a hundred fights. I knew that at once.'

'The first time you saw me?' Karr turned to face the older man.

'Almost...'

Karr was smiling. 'I remember even now how you looked at me that first time – so dismissive, it was, that look – and then you turned your back on me.'

Tolonen laughed, remembering. 'Well, sometimes it's best not to let a man know all you're thinking. But it was true. It was why I welcomed your offer. I knew at once I could use you. The way you stood up to young Hans. I liked that. It put him on his mettle.'

Karr looked down. 'Have you heard that I've traced DeVore?'

Tolonen's eyes widened. 'No! Where?'

'I'm not certain, but I think he's taken an overseer's job on one of the big plantations. My man, Chen, is investigating him right now. As soon as he has proof we're going in.'

Tolonen shook his head. 'Not possible, I'm afraid.'

'I'm sorry, General, but what do you mean?'

Tolonen leaned forward and held the top of one of Karr's huge arms. 'I need you at once, that's why. I want you training for this operation from this evening. So that we can put the scheme into operation at a moment's notice.'

'Is there no one else?'

'No. There's only one man in the whole of Chung Kuo who could carry out this scheme, and that's you, Gregor. Chen will be all right. I'll see he has full back-up. But I can't spare you. Not this time.'

Karr considered a moment, then looked up again, smiling. 'Then I'd best get busy, neh, General?'

Overseer Bergson looked up as Chen entered. The room was dark but for a tight circle of light surrounding where he sat at a table in the centre. He was bare-headed, his dark hair slicked back wetly, and he was wearing a simple silk *pau*, but Chen thought he recognized him at once. It was DeVore. He was almost certain of it. On the low table in front of him a *wei chi* board had been set up, seven rounded black stones placed on the handicap points, forming the outline of a huge letter H in the centre of the grid. On either side of the board was a tray, one filled with white stones, the other with black.

'Do you play, Tong Chou?'

Chen met DeVore's eyes, wondering for a moment if it was possible he too would see through the disguise, then dismissed the thought, remembering how DeVore had killed the man he, Chen, had hired to play himself that day five years ago when Kao Jyan had died. No, he thought, *to you I am Tong Chou, the new worker. A bright man. Obedient. Quick to learn. But nothing more.*

'My father played, Shih Bergson. I learned a little from him.'

DeVore looked past Chen at the two henchmen and made a small gesture of dismissal with his chin. They went at once.

'Sit down, Tong Chou. Facing me. We'll talk as we play.'

Chen moved into the circle of light and sat. DeVore watched him a moment, relaxed, his hands resting lightly on his knees, then smiled.

'Those two who've just gone. They're useful men, but when it comes to this game they've shit in their heads instead of brains. Have you got shit in your head, Tong Chou? Or are you a useful man?'

'I'm useful, Shih Bergson.'

DeVore stared back at him a moment, then looked down.

'We'll see.'

He took a white stone from the tray and set it down, two lines in, six down at the top left-hand corner of the board from where Chen sat – in *shang*, the South. Chen noticed how firmly yet delicately DeVore had held the stone between thumb and forefinger; how sharp the click of stone against wood had been as he placed it; how crisp and definite that movement had seemed. He studied the board a while, conscious of his seven black stones, like fortresses marking out territory on the uncluttered battle-ground of the board. His seven and DeVore's one. That one so white it seemed to eclipse the dull power of his own.

Chen took a black stone from the tray and held it in his hand a moment, turning it between his fingers, experiencing the smooth coolness of it, the perfect roundness of its edges, the satisfyingly oblate feel of it. He shivered. He had never felt anything like it before; had never played with stones and board. It had always been machines. Machines, like the one in Kao Jyan's room.

He set the stone down smartly, taking his lead from DeVore, hearing once more that sharp, satisfying click of stone against wood. Then he sat back.

DeVore answered his move at once. Another white stone in the top left corner. An aggressive, attacking move. Unexpected. Pushing directly for the corner. Chen countered almost instinctively, his black stone placed between the two whites, cutting them. But at once DeVore clicked down another stone, forming a tiger's mouth about Chen's last black stone, surrounding it on three sides and threatening to take it unless...

Chen connected, forming an elbow of three black stones – a weak formation, though not disastrous, but already he was losing the initiative; letting DeVore's aggressive play force him back on the defensive. Already he had lost the corner. Six plays in and he had lost the first corner.

'Would you like *ch'a*, Tong Chou?'

He looked up from the board and met DeVore's eyes. Nothing. No trace of what he was thinking. Chen bowed. 'I would be honoured, *Shih* Bergson.'

DeVore clapped his hands and, when a face appeared around the door, simply raised his right hand, two fingers extended. At the same time his left hand placed another stone. Two down, two in, strengthening his line and securing the corner. Only a fool would lose it now, and DeVore was no fool.

DeVore leaned back, watching him again. 'How often did you play your father, Tong Chou?'

'Often enough when I was a child, *Shih* Bergson. But then he went away. When I was eight. I only saw him again last year. After his funeral.'

Chen placed another stone, then looked back at DeVore. Nothing. No response at all. And yet DeVore, like the fictional Tong Chou, had 'lost' his father as an eight-year-old.

'Unfortunate. And you've not played since?'

Chen took a breath, then studied DeVore's answer. He played so swiftly, almost as if he wasn't thinking, just reacting. But Chen knew better than to believe that. Every move DeVore made was carefully considered; all the possibilities worked out in advance. To play him one had to be as well prepared as him. And to beat him... ?

Chen smiled and placed another stone. 'Occasionally. But mainly with machines. It's been some years since I've sat and played a game like this, *Shih* Bergson. I am honoured that you find me worthy.'

He studied the board again. The corner was lost, almost certainly now, but his own position was much stronger and there was a good possibility of making territory on the top edge, in *shang* and chu, the west. Not only that, but DeVore's next move was forced. He had to play on the top edge, two in. To protect his line. He watched, then smiled inwardly as DeVore set down the next white stone exactly where he had known he would.

Behind him he heard the door open quietly. 'There,' said DeVore, indicating a space beside the play table. At once a second, smaller table was set down and covered with a thin cloth. A moment later a serving girl brought the kettle and two bowls, then knelt there, to Chen's right, wiping out the bowls.

'*Wei chi* is a fascinating game, don't you think, Tong Chou? Its rules are simple – there are only seven things to know – and yet mastery of the game is the work of a lifetime.' Unexpectedly he laughed. 'Tell me, Tong Chou, do you know the history of the game?'

Chen shook his head. Someone had once told him it had been developed at the same time as the computers, five hundred years ago, but the man who had told him that had been a know-nothing; a shit-brains, as DeVore would have called him. He had a sense that the game was much younger. A recent thing.

DeVore smiled. 'How old do you think the game is, Tong Chou? A hundred years? Five hundred?'

Again Chen shook his head. 'A hundred, Shih Bergson? Two hundred, possibly?'

DeVore laughed and then watched as the girl poured the ch'a and offered him the first bowl. He lowered his head politely, refusing, and she turned, offering the bowl to Chen. Chen also lowered his head slightly, refusing, and the girl turned back to DeVore. This time DeVore took the bowl in two hands and held it to his mouth to sip, clearly pleased by Chen's manners.

'Would it surprise you, Tong Chou, if I told you that the game we're playing is more than four and a half thousand years old? That it was invented by the Emperor Yao in approximately 2,350 BC?'

Chen hesitated, then laughed as if surprised, realizing that DeVore must be mocking him. Chung Kuo itself was not that old, surely? He took the bowl the girl was now offering him and, with a bow to DeVore, sipped noisily.

DeVore drained his bowl and set it down on the tray the girl was holding, waiting for the girl to fill it again before continuing.

'The story is that the Emperor Yao invented wei chi to train the mind of his son, Tan-Chu, and teach him to think like an emperor. The board, you see, is a map of Chung Kuo itself, of the ancient Middle Kingdom of the Han, bounded to the east by the ocean, to the north and west by deserts and great mountain ranges, and to the south by jungles and the sea. The board, then, is the land. The pieces men, or groups of men. At first the board, like the land, is clear, unsettled, but then as the men arrive and begin to grow in numbers, the board fills. Slowly but inexorably these groups spread out across the land; occupying territory. But there is only so much territory – only so many points on the board to be filled. Conflict is inevitable. Where the groups meet there is war: a war which the strongest and cleverest must win. And so it goes on, until the board is filled and the last conflict resolved.'

'And when the board is filled and the pieces still come?'

DeVore looked at him a moment, then looked away. 'As I said, it's an ancient game, Tong Chou. If the analogy no longer holds it is because we have changed the rules. It would be different if we were to limit the number of pieces allowed instead of piling them on until the board breaks from the weight of stones. Better yet if the board were bigger than it is, neh?'

Chen was silent, watching DeVore drain his bowl a second time. *I'm certain now,* he thought. *It's you. I know it's you. But Karr wants to be sure. More than that, he wants you alive. So that he can bring you before the T'ang and watch you kneel and beg for mercy.*

DeVore set his bowl down on the tray again, but this time he let his hand rest momentarily over the top of it, indicating he was finished. Then he looked at Chen.

'You know, Tong Chou, sometimes I think these two – *ch'a* and *wei chi* – along with silk, are the high points of Han culture.' Again he laughed, but this time it was a cold, mocking laughter. 'Just think of it, Tong Chou! *Ch'a* and *wei chi* and silk! All three of them some four and a half thousand years old! And since then? Nothing! Nothing but walls!'

Nothing but walls. Chen finished his *ch'a* and set it down on the tray the girl held out for him. Then he placed his stone and, for the next half-hour, said nothing, concentrating on the game.

At first the game went well for him. He lost few captives and made few trivial errors. The honours seemed remarkably even and, filled with confidence in his own performance, he began to query what Karr had told him about DeVore being a master of *wei chi.* But then things changed. Four times he thought he'd had DeVore's stones trapped. Trapped with no possibility of escape. Each time he seemed within two stones of capturing a group; first in *ping,* the east, at the bottom left-hand corner of the board, then in *tsu,* the north. But each time he was forced to watch, open-mouthed, as DeVore changed everything with a single unexpected move. And then he would find himself backtracking furiously; no longer surrounding but surrounded, struggling desperately to save the group which, only a few moves before, had seemed invincible – had seemed a mere two moves from conquest.

Slowly he watched his positions crumble on all sides of the board until, with a small shrug of resignation, he threw the black stone he was holding back into the tray.

'There seems no point.'

DeVore looked up at him for the first time in a long while. 'Really? You concede, Tong Chou?'

Chen bowed his head.

'Then you'll not mind if I play black from this position?'

Chen laughed, surprised. The position was lost. By forty, maybe fifty pieces. Irredeemably lost. Again he shrugged. 'If that's your wish, *Shih* Bergson.'

'And what's your wish, Tong Chou? I understand you want to be field supervisor.'

'That is so, *Shih* Bergson.'

'The job pays well. Twice what you earn now, Tong Chou.'

Yes, thought Chen, *so why does no one else apply? Because it is an unpopular job, being field supervisor under you, that's why. And so you wonder why I want it.*

'That's exactly why I want the job, *Shih* Bergson. I want to get on. To clear my debts in the Above and climb the levels once again.'

DeVore sat back, watching him closely a moment, then he leaned forward, took a black stone from the tray and set it down with a sharp click.

'All right. I'll consider the matter. But first there's something you can do for me, Tong Chou. Two nights back the storehouse in the western meadows was broken into and three cases of strawberries, packed ready for delivery to one of my clients in First Level, were taken. You'll understand how inconvenienced I was.' He sniffed and looked at Chen directly. 'There's a thief on the plantation, Tong Chou. I want you to find out who it is and deal with him. Do you understand me?'

Chen hesitated a moment, taken by surprise by this unexpected demand. Then, realizing he had no choice if he was to get close enough to DeVore to get Karr his proof, he dropped his head.

'As you say, *Shih* Bergson. And when I've dealt with him?'

DeVore laughed. 'Then we'll play again, Tong Chou, and talk about your future.'

When the peasant had gone, DeVore went across to the screens and pulled the curtain back, then switched on the screen that connected him with Berdichev in the House.

'How are things?' he asked as Berdichev's face appeared.

Berdichev laughed excitedly. 'It's early yet, but I think we've done it. Farr's people have come over and the New Legist faction are swaying a little. Barrow calculates that we need only twenty more votes and we've thrown the Seven's veto out.'

'That's good. And afterwards?'

Berdichev smiled. 'You've heard something, then? Well, that's my surprise. Wait and see. That's all I'll say.'

DeVore broke contact. He pulled the curtain to and walked over to the board. The peasant hadn't been a bad player, considering. Not really all that stimulating, yet amusing enough, particularly in the second phase of the game. He would have to give him nine stones next time. He studied the situation a moment. Black had won, by a single stone.

As for Berdichev and his 'surprise'...

DeVore laughed and began to clear the board. As if you could keep such a thing hidden. The albino was the last surprise Soren Berdichev would spring on him. Even so, he admired Soren for having the insight – and the guts – to do what he had done. When the Seven learned of the investigations. And when they saw the end results...

He looked across at the curtained bank of screens. Yes, all hell would break loose when the Seven found out what Soren Berdichev had been up to. And what was so delightful was that it was all legal. All perfectly constitutional. There was nothing they could do about it.

But they *would* do something. He was certain of that. So it was up to him to anticipate it. To find out what they planned and get in first.

And there was no one better at that game than he. No one in the whole of Chung Kuo.

'Why, look, Soren! Look at Lo Yu-Hsiang!' Clarac laughed and spilled wine down his sleeve, but he was oblivious of it, watching the scenes on the big screens overhead.

Berdichev looked where Clarac was pointing and gave a laugh of delight. The camera was in close-up on the Senior Representative's face.

'Gods! He looks as if he's about to have a coronary!'

As the camera panned slowly round the tiers, it could be seen that the look of sheer outrage on Lo Yu-Hsiang's face was mirrored throughout that section of the House. Normally calm patricians bellowed and raged, their eyes bulging with anger.

Douglas came up behind Berdichev and slapped him on the back. 'And there's nothing they can do about it! Well done, Soren! Marvellous! I thought I'd never see the day...'

There was more jubilant laughter from the men gathered in the gallery room, then Douglas called for order and had the servants bring more glasses so they could drink a toast.

'To Soren Berdichev! And *The New Hope!*'

Two dozen voices echoed the toast, then drank, their eyes filled with admiration for the man at the centre of their circle.

Soren Berdichev inclined his head, then, with a smile, turned back to the viewing window and gazed down on the scene below.

The scenes in the House had been unprecedented. In all the years of its existence nothing like this had happened. Not even the murder of Pietr Lehmann had rocked the House so violently. The defeat of the Seven's veto motion – a motion designed to confine *The New Hope* to the Solar System – had been unusual enough, but what had followed had been quite astonishing.

Wild celebrations had greeted the result of the vote. The anti-veto faction had won by a majority of one hundred and eighteen. In the calm that had followed, Under Secretary Barrow had gone quietly to the rostrum and begun speaking.

At first most of the members heard very little of Barrow's speech. They were still busy discussing the implications of the vote. But one by one they fell silent as the full importance of what Barrow was saying began to sweep around the tiers.

Barrow was proposing a special motion, to be passed by a two-thirds majority of the House. A motion for the indictment of certain members of the House. He was outlining the details of investigations that had been made by a secretly convened sub-committee of the House – investigations into corruption, unauthorized practices and the payment of illegal fees.

By the time he paused and looked up from the paper he was reading from, there was complete silence in the House.

Barrow turned, facing a certain section of the tiers, then began to read out a list of names. He was only part way into that long list when the noise from the Han benches drowned his voice.

Every name on his list was a *tai* – a 'pocket' Representative, their positions, their 'loyalty', bought and paid for by the Seven. This, even more than the House's rejection of the starship veto, was a direct challenge upon the authority of the Seven. It was tantamount to a declaration of the House's independence from their T'ang.

Barrow waited while the Secretary of the House called the tiers to order, then, ignoring the list for a moment, began an impassioned speech about the purity of the House and how it had been compromised by the Seven.

The outcry from the *tai* benches was swamped by enthusiastic cheers from all sides of the House. The growing power of the *tai* had been a long-standing bone of contention, even amongst the Han Representatives, and Barrow's indignation reflected their own feelings. It had been different in the old days: then a *tai* had been a man to be respected, but these brash young men were no more than empty mouthpieces for the Seven.

When it came to the vote the margin was as narrow as it could possibly be. Three votes settled it. The eighty-six *tai* named on Barrow's list were to be indicted.

There was uproar. Infuriated *tai* threw bench pillows down at the speaker, while some would have come down the aisles to lay hands on him had not other members blocked their way.

Then, at a signal from the Secretary, House security troops had come into the chamber and had begun to round up the named *tai*, handcuffing them like common criminals and removing their permit cards.

Berdichev watched the end of this process – saw the last few *tai* being led away, protesting violently, down into the cells below the House.

He shivered, exulted. This was a day to remember. A day he had long dreamed of. *The New Hope* was saved and the House strengthened. And later on, after the celebrations, he would begin the next phase of his scheme.

He turned and looked back at the men gathered in the viewing room, knowing instinctively which he could trust and which not, then smiled to himself. It began here, now. A force that all the power of the Seven could not stop. And the Aristotle File would give it a focus, a sense of purpose and direction. When they saw what had been kept from them there would be no turning back. The File would bring an end to the rule of Seven.

Yes. He laughed and raised his glass to Douglas once again. It had begun. And who knew what kind of world it would be when they had done with it?

Chapter 41

THE DARKENING OF THE LIGHT

I t was two in the morning and outside the Berdichev mansion, in the ornamental gardens, the guests were still celebrating noisily. A line of sedans
waited on the far side of the green, beneath the lanterns, their pole-men
and guards in attendance nearby, while closer to the house a temporary
kitchen had been set up. Servants moved busily between the guests, serving
hot bowls of soup or noodles, or offering more wine.

Berdichev stood on the balcony, looking down, studying it all a moment.
Then he moved back inside, smiling a greeting at the twelve men gathered
there.

These were the first of them. The ones he trusted most.

He looked across at the servant, waiting at his request in the doorway,
and gave the signal. The servant – a 'European', like all his staff these days
– returned a moment later with a tray on which was a large, pot-bellied bottle
and thirteen delicate porcelain bowls. The servant placed the tray on the
table, then, with a deep bow, backed away and closed the door after him.

They were alone.

Berdichev's smile broadened. 'You'll drink with me, *Chun t'zu?*' He held up
the bottle – a forty-year-old *Shou Hsing* peach brandy – and was greeted with
a murmur of warm approval.

He poured, then handed out the tiny bowls, conscious that the eyes of the
'gentlemen' would from time to time move to the twelve thick folders laid
out on the table beside the tray.

He raised his bowl. '*Kan pei!*'

'*Kan pei!*' they echoed and downed their brandies in one gulp.

'Beautiful!' said Moore with a small shudder. 'Where did you get it, Soren? I didn't think there was a bottle of *Shou Hsing* left in all Chung Kuo that was over twenty years old.'

Berdichev smiled. 'I have two cases of it, John. Allow me to send you a bottle.' He looked about him, his smile for once unforced, quite natural. 'And all of you *chun t'zu*, of course.'

Their delight was unfeigned. Such a brandy must be fifty thousand yuan a bottle at the least! And Berdichev had just given a case of it away!

'You certainly know how to celebrate, Soren!' said Parr, coming closer and holding his arm a moment. Parr was an old friend and business associate, with dealings in North America.

Berdichev nodded. 'Maybe. But there's much to celebrate tonight. Much more, in fact, than any of you realize. You see, my good friends, tonight is the beginning of something. The start of a new age.'

He saw how their eyes went to the folders again.

'Yes.' He went to the table and picked up one of the folders. 'It has to do with these. You've noticed, I'm sure. Twelve of you and twelve folders.' He looked about the circle of them, studying their faces one last time, making certain before he committed himself.

Yes, these were the men. Important men. Men with important contacts. But friends, too – men he could trust. They would start it for him. A thing that, once begun, would prove irresistible. And, he hoped, irreversible.

'You're all wondering why I brought you up here, away from the celebrations? You're also wondering what it has to do with the folders. Well, I'll keep you wondering no longer. Refill your glasses from the bottle, then take a seat. What I'm about to tell you may call for a stiff drink.'

There was laughter, but it was muted, tense. They knew Soren Berdichev well enough to know that he never played jokes, or made statements he could not support.

When they were settled around the table, Berdichev distributed the folders.

'Before you open them, let me ask each of you something.' He turned and looked at Moore. 'You first, John. Which is more important to you: a little of your time and energy – valuable as that is – or the future of our race, the Europeans?'

Moore laughed. 'You know how I feel about that, Soren.'

Berdichev nodded. 'Okay. Then let me ask you something more specific. If I were to tell you that in that folder in front of you was a document of approximately two hundred thousand words, and that I wanted you to hand-copy it for me, what would you say to that?'

'Unexplained, I'd say you were mad, Soren. Why should I want to hand-copy a document? Why not get some of my people to put it on computer for me?'

'Of course.' Berdichev's smile was harder. He seemed suddenly more his normal self. 'But if I were to tell you that this is a secret document. And not just any small corporate secret, but the secret, would that make it easier to understand?'

Moore sat back slightly. 'What do you mean, the secret? What's in the file, Soren?'

'I'll come to that. First, though, do you trust me? Is there anyone here who doesn't trust me?'

There was a murmuring and a shaking of heads. Parr spoke for them all. 'You know there's not one of us who wouldn't commit half of all they owned on your word.'

Berdichev smiled tightly. 'I know. But what about one hundred per cent? Is anyone here afraid to commit that much?'

Another of them – a tall, thin-faced man named Ecker – answered this time. A native of City Africa, he had strong trading links with Berdichev's company, SimFic.

'Do you mean a financial commitment, Soren, or are you talking of something more personal?'

Berdichev bowed slightly. 'You are all practical men. That's good. I'd not have any other kind of men for friends. But to answer you, in one sense you're correct, Edgar. I do mean something far more personal. That said, which of us here can so easily disentangle their personal from their financial selves?'

There was the laughter of agreement at that. It was true. They were moneyed creatures. The market was in their blood.

'Let me say simply that if any of you choose to open the folder you will be committing yourselves one hundred per cent. Personally and, by inference, financially.' He put out a hand quickly. 'Oh, I don't mean that I'll be coming to you for loans or anything like that. This won't affect your trading positions.'

Parr laughed. 'I've known you more than twenty years now, Soren, and I realize that – like all of us here – you have secrets you would share with few others. But this kind of public indirectness is most unlike you. Why can't you just tell us what's in the folder?'

Berdichev nodded tersely. 'All right. I'll come to it, I promise you, Charles. But this is necessary.' He looked slowly about the table, then bowed his head slightly. 'I want to be fair to you all. To make certain you understand the risks you would be taking in simply opening the folder. Because I want none of you to feel you were pushed into this. That would serve no one here. In fact, I would much rather have anyone who feels uncomfortable with this leave now before he commits himself that far. And no blame attached. Because once you take the first step – once you find out what's inside the folder – your lives will be forfeit.'

Parr leaned forward and tapped the folder. 'I still don't understand, Soren. What's in here? A scheme to assassinate the Seven? What could be so dangerous that simply to know of it could make a man's life forfeit?'

'*The* secret. As I said before. The thing the Han have kept from us all these years. As for why it's dangerous simply to know, let me tell you about a little-known statute that's rarely used these days – and a Ministry whose sole purpose is to create an illusion, which even they have come to believe is how things really are.'

Parr laughed and spread his hands. 'Now you are being enigmatic, Soren. What statute? What Ministry? What illusion?'

'It is called, simply, the Ministry, it is situated in Bremen and Pei Ching, and its only purpose is to guard the secret. Further, it is empowered to arrest and execute anyone knowing of or disseminating information about the secret. As for the illusion...' He laughed sourly. 'Well, you'll understand if you choose to open the folder.'

One of those who hadn't spoken before now sat forward. He was a big, powerful-looking man with a long, unfashionable beard. His name was Ross and he was the owner of a large satellite communications company in East Asia.

'This is treason, then, Soren?'

Berdichev nodded.

Ross stroked his beard thoughtfully and looked about him. Then, almost casually, he opened his folder, took out the stack of papers and began to examine the first page.

A moment later others followed.

Berdichev looked about the table. Twelve folders lay empty, the files removed. He shivered then looked down, a faint smile on his lips.

There was a low whistle from Moore. He looked up at Berdichev, his eyes wide. 'Is this true, Soren? Is this really true?'

Berdichev nodded.

'But this is just so... so fantastic. Like a dream someone's had.'

'It's true,' Berdichev said firmly. They were all watching him now. 'Which of us here has not been down into the Clay and seen the ruins? When the tyrant Tsao Ch'un built his City he buried more than the architecture of the past, he buried its history, too.'

'And built another?' The voice was Parr's.

'Yes. Carefully, painstakingly, over the years. You see, his intention wasn't simply to eradicate all opposition to his rule, he wanted to destroy all knowledge of what had gone before him. As the City grew, so his officials collected all books, all film, all recordings, allowing nothing that was not Han to enter their great City. Most of what they collected was simply burned. But not everything. Much was adapted. You see, Tsao Ch'un's advisors were too clever simply to create a gap. That, they knew, would have attracted curiosity. What they did was far more subtle and, in the long run, far more persuasive to the great mass of people. They set about reconstructing the history of the world – placing Chung Kuo at the centre of everything, back in its rightful place, as they saw it.'

He drew a breath, then continued, conscious momentarily of noises from the party in the gardens outside. 'It was a lie, but a lie to which everyone subscribed, for in the first decades of the City merely to question their version of the past – even to suggest it might have happened otherwise – was punishable by death. But the lie was complex and powerful, and people soon forgot. New generations arose who knew little of the real past. To them the whispers and rumours seemed mere fantasy in the face of the reality they had been taught and saw all about them. The media fed them the illusion daily until the illusion became, even to those responsible for its creation, quite *real*.'

'And this – this Aristotle File... is this the truth Tsao Ch'un suppressed?'

'Yes.'

'How did you come upon it?'

Berdichev smiled. 'Slowly. Piece by piece. For the last fifteen years I've been searching – making my own discreet investigations. Following up clues. And this – this file – is the end result of all that searching.'

Ross sat back. 'I'm impressed. More than that, Soren, I'm astonished! Truly, for the first time in my life I'm astonished. This is...' He laughed strangely. 'Well, it's hard to take it in. Perhaps it's the brandy but...'

There was laughter at that, but all eyes were on Ross as he tried to articulate their feelings.

'Well... I know what my friend, John Moore, means. It is fantastic. Perhaps too much so to swallow at a single go like this.' He reached forward and lifted the first few pages, then looked at Berdichev again. 'It's just that I find it all rather hard to believe.'

Berdichev leaned forward, light glinting from the lenses of his glasses. 'That's just what they intended, Michael. And it's one of the reasons why I want you all to hand-write a copy. That way it will get rooted in you all. You will have done more than simply read it. You will have transcribed it. And in doing so the reality of it will strike you forcibly. You will see how it all connects. Its plausibility – no, its truth! – will be written in the blood of every one of you.'

Ross smiled. 'I see that the original of this was written in your own hand, Soren. You ask us to commit ourselves equally?'

Berdichev nodded.

'Then I for one am glad to do so. But what of the copy we make? What should we do with it? Keep it safe?'

Berdichev smiled, meeting his friend's eyes. Ross knew. He had seen it already. 'You will pass your copy on. To a man you trust like a brother. As I trust you. He, in his turn, will make another copy and pass it on to one he trusts. And so on, forging a chain, until there are many who know. And then...' He sat back. 'Well, then you will see what will happen. But this – this here tonight – is the beginning of it. We are the first. From here the seed goes out. But harvest time will come, I promise you all. Harvest time will come.'

'*Hung Mao* or Han, what does it matter? They're Above. They despise us Clayborn.'

The three boys were sitting on the edge of the pool, their feet hanging out over the water.

Kim was looking down into the mirror of the water, his eyes tracing the patterns of the stars reflected from the Tun Huang map overhead. He had been silent for some while, listening to the others speak, but now he interrupted them.

'I know what you mean, Anton, but it's not always like that. There are some...'

'Like Chan Shui?'

Kim nodded. He had told them what had happened in the Casting Shop. 'Yes, like Chan Shui.'

Anton laughed. 'You probably amuse him. Either that or he thinks that he can benefit somehow by looking after you. As for liking you...'

Kim shook his head. 'No. It's not like that. Chan Shui...'

Josef cut in. 'Be honest, Kim. They hate us. I mean, what has this Chan Shui done that's really cost him anything? He's stood up to a bully. Fine. And that's impressed you. That and all that claptrap T'ai Cho has fed you about Han justice. But it's all a sham. All of it. It's like Anton says. He's figured you must be important – something special – and he's reckoned that if he looks after you there might be something in it for him.'

Again Kim shook his head. 'You don't understand. You really don't.'

Anton laughed dismissively. 'We understand. But it seems like you're going to have to learn it the hard way. They don't want us, Kim. Not for ourselves, anyway – only for what we are. They use us like machines, and if we malfunction they throw us away. That's the truth of the matter.'

Kim shrugged. There was a kind of truth to that, but it wasn't the whole truth. He thought of Matyas and Janko. What distinguished them? They were both bullies. It had not mattered that he, Kim, was Clay like Matyas. Neither was it anything Kim had done to him. It was simply that he was different. So it was with Janko. But to some that difference did not matter. T'ai Cho, for instance, and Chan Shui. And there would be others.

'It's them and us,' said Anton, laughing bitterly. 'That's how it is. That's how it'll always be.'

'No!' Kim was insistent now. 'You're wrong. Them and us. It isn't like that. Sometimes, yes, but not always.'

Anton shook his head. 'Always. Deep down it's always there. You should ask him, this Chan Shui. Ask him if he'd let you marry his sister.'

'He hasn't got a sister.'

'You miss my point.'

Kim looked away, unconsciously stroking the bruise on his neck. Shame and guilt. It was always there in them, just beneath the skin. But why did they let these things shape them? Why couldn't they break the mould and make new creatures of themselves?

'Maybe I miss your point, but I'd rather think well of Chan Shui than succumb to the bleakness of your view.' His voice was colder, more hostile than he had intended, and he regretted his words at once – true as they were.

Anton stood up slowly, then looked down coldly at his fellow. 'Come on, Josef. I don't think we're wanted here any more.'

'I didn't mean...'

But it was too late. They were gone.

Kim sat there a while longer, distressed by what had happened. But maybe it was unavoidable. Maybe he could only have delayed the moment. Because he *was* different – even from his own kind.

He laughed. There! He had betrayed himself: had caught himself in his own twisted logic. For either they were all of one single kind – Han, *Hung Mao* and Clay – or he was wrong. And he could not be wrong. His soul cried out not to be wrong.

He looked up at the dull gold ceiling, stretching and easing his neck, then shivered violently. But what if he *was*? What if Anton was right?

'No.' He was determined. 'They'll not make me think like that. Not now. Not ever.' He looked down at his clenched fists and slowly let the anger drain from him. Then he stood and began to make his way back. Another morning in the Casting Shop lay ahead.

The machine flexed its eight limbs, then seemed to squat and hatch a chair from nothingness.

Kim laughed. 'It seems like it's really alive sometimes.'

Chan Shui, balanced on his haunches at Kim's side, turned his head to look at him, joining in with his laughter. 'I know what you mean. It's that final little movement, isn't it?'

'An arachnoid. That's what it is, Shui!' Kim nodded to himself, studying the now-inert machine. Then he turned and saw the puzzlement in the older boy's face.

'It's just a name I thought of for them. Spiders – they're arachnids. And machines that mimic life – those are often called androids. Put the two together and...'

Chan Shui's face lit up. It was a rounded, pleasant face. A handsome, uncomplicated face, framed by neat black hair.

Kim looked at him a moment, wondering, then, keeping his voice low, asked the question he had been keeping back all morning. 'Do you like me, Chan Shui?'

There was no change in Chan Shui's face. It smiled back at him, perfectly open, the dark eyes clear. 'What an absurd question. What do you think?'

Kim bowed his head, embarrassed, but before he could say anything more, Chan Shui had changed the subject.

'Do you know what they call a spider in Han, Kim?'

Kim met his eyes again. 'Chih chu, isn't it?'

Chan Shui seemed pleased. 'That's right. But did you know that we have other, more flowery names for them? You see, for us they have always been creatures of good omen. When a spider lowers itself from its web they say, "Good luck descends from heaven."'

Kim laughed, delighted. 'Are there many spiders where you are, Chan Shui?'

Chan shook his head, then stood up and began examining the control panel. 'There are no spiders. Not nowadays. Only caged birds and fish in artificial ponds.' He looked back at Kim, a rueful smile returning to his lips. 'Oh, and us.'

His bitterness had been momentary, yet it was telling. No spiders? How was that? Then Kim understood. Of course. There would be no insects of any kind within the City proper – the quarantine gates of the Net would see to that.

Chan Shui pulled the tiny phial from its slot in the panel and shook it. 'Looks like we're out of ice. I'll get some more.'

Kim touched his arm. 'I'll get it, Chan Shui. Where do I go?'

The Han hesitated, then smiled. 'Okay. It's over there, on the far side. There's a refill tank – see it? – yes, that's it. All you have to do is take this empty phial back, slip it into the hole in the panel at the bottom of the tank and punch in the machine number. This here.' Chan Shui pointed out the serial number on the arachnoid's panel. 'It'll return the phial after about a minute, full. Okay?'

Kim nodded and set off, threading his way between the benches. Returning, he took another, different path through the machines, imagining himself a spider moving swiftly along the spokes of his web. He was halfway back when he realized he had made a mistake. Chan Shui lay directly ahead of him, but between them stood Janko, beside his machine, a cruel smile on his face.

'Going somewhere, rat's arse?'

He stepped out, blocking Kim's way.

Kim slipped the phial into the top pocket of his scholar's robe, then looked about him. One of the big collection trays had moved along the main gangway and now barred his way back, while to the left and right of him stacks of freshly-manufactured furniture filled the side gangways.

He looked back at Janko, unafraid, concerned only not to break the phial. If he did there would be a fine of a day's wages for both him and Chan Shui. For himself he didn't mind. But for Chan Shui...

'What do you want, Janko?'

Janko turned, facing Chan Shui's challenge. 'It's none of your business, Han! Stay out of this!'

Chan Shui just laughed. 'None of my business, eh? Is that so, you great bag of putrid rice? Why should you think that?'

Surprisingly Janko ignored the insult. He turned his back on Chan Shui, then faced Kim again. His voice barked out. 'Come here, you little rat's arse. Come here and kneel!'

Kim bent his knees slightly, tensing, preparing to run if necessary, but there was no need. Chan Shui had moved forward quickly, silently and had jumped up onto Janko's back, sending him sprawling forward.

Kim moved back sharply.

Janko bellowed and made to get up, but Chan Shui pulled his arm up tightly behind his back and began to press down on it, threatening to break it.

'Now just leave him alone, Janko. Because next time I *will* break your arm. And we'll blame it on one of the machines.'

He gave one last, pain-inducing little push against the arm, then let Janko go, getting up off him.

Janko sat up, red-faced, muttering under his breath.

Chan Shui held out his arm. 'Come on, Kim. He won't touch you, I promise.'

But even as Kim made to pass Janko, Janko lashed out, trying to trip him, then scrambled to his feet quickly, facing Chan Shui.

'Try it to my face, chink.'

Chan Shui laughed. 'Your verbal inventiveness astonishes me, Janko. Where did you learn your English, in the sing-song house where your mother worked?'

Janko roared angrily and rushed at Chan Shui. But the young Han had stepped aside, and when Janko turned awkwardly, flailing out with one arm, Chan Shui caught the arm and twisted, using Janko's weight to lift and throw him against the machine.

Janko banged against the control panel, winding himself, then turned his head, frightened, as the machine reared up over him.

The watching boys laughed, then fell silent. But Janko had heard the laughter. He looked down, wiping his bloodied mouth, then swore under his breath.

At that moment the door at the far end of the Casting Shop slid open and Supervisor Nung came out. As he came down the gangway he seemed distracted, his eyes unfocused. Coming closer he paused, smiling at Kim as if remembering something. 'Is everything okay, Chan Shui?' he asked, seeming not to see Janko lain there against the machine.

Chan Shui bowed his head, suppressing a smile. 'Everything is fine, Supervisor Nung.'

'Good.' Nung moved on.

Back at their machine Kim questioned him about the incident. 'Is Nung okay? He seemed odd.'

Chan Shui laughed briefly, then shook his head. 'Now there's a man who'll be his own ruin.' He looked at Kim. 'Supervisor Nung has a habit. Do you understand me, Kim?'

Kim shook his head.

'He takes drugs. Harmless, mainly, but I think he's getting deeper. These last few weeks... Anyway, hand me that phial.'

Kim passed him the phial, then looked across, letting his eyes rest briefly on Janko's back.

'By the way, thanks for what you did, Shui. I appreciate it. But really, it wasn't necessary. I'm quick. Quicker than you think. He'd never have caught me.'

Chan Shui smiled, then looked up at him again, more thoughtful than before. 'Maybe. But I'd rather be certain. Janko's a bit of a head case. He doesn't know quite when to stop. I'd rather he didn't get near you. Okay?'

Kim smiled and looked down. He felt a warmth like fire in his chest. 'Okay.'

'Is everything all right?'

Kim looked up from his desk console and nodded. 'I'm a little tired, that's all, T'ai Cho.'

'Is the work too much for you?'

Kim smiled. 'No. I've had a few restless nights, that's all.'

'Ah.' That was unusual. T'ai Cho studied the boy a moment. He was a handsome boy now that the feral emaciation of the Clay had gone from his face. A good diet had worked wonders, but it could not undo the damage of those earliest years. T'ai Cho smiled and looked back down at the screen in front of him. What might Kim have been with a proper diet as an infant? With the right food and proper encouragement? T'ai Cho shuddered to think.

T'ai Cho looked up again. 'We'll leave it for now, neh, Kim? A tired brain is a forgetful brain.' He winked. 'Even in your case. Go and have a swim. Then get to bed early. We'll take this up again tomorrow.'

When Kim had gone, he sat there, thinking about the last week. Kim seemed to have settled remarkably well into the routine of the Casting Shop. Supervisor Nung was pleased with him, and Kim himself was uncomplaining. Yet something worried T'ai Cho. There was something happening in Kim – something deep down that perhaps even Kim himself hadn't recognized as yet. And now this. This sleeplessness. Well, he would watch Kim more closely for the next few days and try to fathom what it was.

He got up and went across to Kim's desk, then activated the memory. At once the screen lit up.

T'ai Cho laughed, surprised. Kim had been doodling. He had drawn a web in the centre of the screen. A fine, delicate web from which hung a single thread that dropped off the bottom of the screen.

He scrolled the screen down, then laughed again. 'And here's the spider!'

But then he leaned closer and, adjusting the controls, magnified the image until the spider's features filled the screen: the familiar, dark-eyed features of a child.

T'ai Cho frowned, then switched the machine off. He stood there a moment, deep in thought, then nodded to himself. Yes. He would watch him. Watch him very carefully indeed.

DeVore sat up, startled into wakefulness. He had had the dream three times now. The same dream, almost identical in its detail.

He looked about him at the room. Red dust lay in tiny drifts against the walls, blown in by the airlock.It was a cold, barren room. More cell than resting place.

He blew out a long breath.

In the dream he had been out there – out on the very edge of the void, enfolded in a darkness that no light could ever reach, no warmth ever touch; distant beyond all measure. He had sat there on that iced and barren rock, or rather... *crouched*, for there was something wrong about him. Not that he could get the tiniest glimpse of himself. Only... it felt like he'd been coated with lacquer, like a clay figure fresh from the kiln. It felt...

DeVore shuddered. For once he had no words for it. Only that discomforting sense of otherness. Even now, awake again, he felt it still: that sense of being uncomfortable in his own skin. More than uncomfortable. As if this form of his were somehow alien.

Yes. That was it. One form contained within the other, like Russian dolls. Some other creature, flexing and unflexing within him. Wearing him like a coat. Unnatural. And yet not unfamiliar.

He queried that in his thoughts. As if he could forget a thing like that.

Something dark and hard. Harder than diamonds. Darker than...

No. There was nothing darker than what he'd glimpsed. Nothing colder or more isolate. It went beyond mere seeing.

A dream, he told himself. *Only a dream*. But part of him knew otherwise. Part of him trusted to these messages. Saw the truth in them. And awaited revelation, knowing it would come.

★

Kim floated on his back in the water, his eyes closed. He had been thinking of Chung Kuo, and of the people he had met in the Above. What had any of them in common? Birth, maybe. That and death, and perhaps a mild curiosity about the state between. He smiled. And that was it. That was what astonished him most of all. Their lack of curiosity. He had thought it would be different up here, in the Above. He had believed that simple distance from the Clay would bring enlightenment. But it was not so. There was a difference in them, yes, but that difference was mainly veneer. Scratch away that surface and they proved themselves every bit as dull, every bit as incuriously wedded to their senses, as the most pitiful creature of the Clay.

The smile faded from his lips. Kim turned his body slowly in the water.

The Clay. What was the Clay but a state of mind? An attitude?

That was the trouble. They followed an idea only to a certain stage – pursued its thread only so far – and then let it fall slack, as if satisfied there was no more to see, no more left to discover. Take the Aristotle File. They had been happy to see it only as a game he had devised to test his intellect and stretch himself. They had not looked beyond that. That single explanation was enough for them. But had they pushed it further – had they dealt with it, even hypothetically, as real, even for one moment – they would have seen at once where he had got it from. Even now they might wake to it. But he thought not.

It was strange, because they had explained it to him in the first place; had told him how intricately connected the finances and thus the computer systems of Chung Kuo were. It was they who had explained about 'discrete systems' cut off from all the rest; islands of tight-packed information, walled round with defences. And it was they who had told him that the Project's system was 'discrete'.

He had discovered none of that himself. All he had discovered was that the Project's files were not alone within the walled island of their computer system. There was another file buried inside the system – an old, long-forgotten file that had been there a century or more, dormant, undisturbed, until Kim had found it. And not just any file. This was a library. More than that. It was a world. A world too rich to have been invented, too consistent – even in its errors – to have been anything less than real.

So why had the Seven hidden it? What reason could they have had for burying the past?

Freed from the burden of his secret he had spent the last two nights considering just this. He'd looked at it from every side, trying to see what purpose they'd had in mind. And finally he'd understood. It was to put an end to change. They had lied to end the Western dream of progress. To bring about a timeless age where nothing changed. A golden age.

But that left him with the problem of himself, for what was he if not Change personified? What if not a bacillus of that selfsame virus they had striven so long and hard to eradicate?

Kim opened his eyes and rolled over onto his front, then kicked out for the deeper water.

He saw it clearly now. What he was made him dangerous to them – made him a threat to the Seven and their ways. Yet he was also valuable. He knew, despite their efforts to hide it from him, what SimFic had paid for his contract. But why had they paid so vast a sum? What did they think to use him for?

Change. He was almost certain of it. But how could he be sure?

Push in deeper, he told himself. Be curious. Is SimFic just a faceless force? A mechanism for making profits? Or does it have a personality?

And if so, whose?

The name came instantly. He had heard it often enough of late in the news. Soren Berdichev.

Yes, but who is he? A businessman. Yes. A Dispersionist. That too. But beyond that, what? What kind of man is he? Where does he come from? What does he want? And – most important of all – what does he want of me?

Kim ducked his head beneath the surface then came up again, shaking the water from his hair, the tiredness washed suddenly from his mind. He felt a familiar excitement in his blood and laughed. Yes, that was it! That would be his new task. To find out all he could about the man.

And when he'd found it out?

He drifted, letting the thread fall slack. Best not anticipate so far. Best find out what he could and then decide.

Soren Berdichev sat in the shadowed silence of his study, the two files laid out on the desk in front of him. The *Wu* had just gone, though the sweet, sickly scent of his perfume lingered in the air. The message of the yarrow stalks was written on the slip of paper Berdichev had screwed into a ball and thrown to the far side of the room. Yet he could see it clearly even so.

> The light has sunk into the earth:
> The image of darkening of the light.
> Thus does the superior man live with the great mass:
> He veils his light, yet still shines.

He banged the desk angrily. This threw all of his deliberations out. He had decided on his course of action and called upon the *Wu* merely to confirm what he had planned. But the *Wu* had contradicted him. And now he must decide again.

He could hear the *Wu*'s scratchy voice even now as the old man looked up from the stalks; could remember how his watery eyes had widened; how his wispy grey beard had stuck out stiffly from his chin.

'*K'un*, the Earth, in the above, *Li*, the Fire, down below. It is *Ming I*, the darkening of the light.'

It had meant the boy. He was certain of it. The fire from the earth. *He veils his light, yet still he shines.*

'Is this a warning?' he had asked, surprising the old man, for he had never before interrupted him in all the years the elder had been casting the *I Ching* for him.

'A warning, *Shih* Berdichev?' The *Wu* had laughed. 'The Book Of Changes does not warn. You mistake its purpose. Yet the hexagram portends harm… injury.'

Berdichev had nodded and fallen silent. But he had known it for what it was. A warning. The signs were too strong to ignore. So now he must decide again.

He laid his glasses on the desk and picked up the newest of the files containing the genotype reports he had had done.

He spread the two charts on the desk before him, beside each other, then touched the pad, underlighting the desk's surface.

There was no doubt about it. Even without the expert's report on the matter, it could be seen at once. The similarities were striking. He traced the mirrored symbols on the spiralling trees of the two double helices and nodded to himself.

'So you *are* Edmund Wyatt's son, Kim Ward. I wonder what Edmund would have made of that?'

He laughed sadly, realizing for the first time how much he missed his dead friend's quiet strengths, then sat back, rubbing his eyes.

The genotyping and the Aristotle File, they were each reason enough in themselves to have Kim terminated. The first meant he was the son of the traitor, Wyatt, the second breached the special Edict that concealed Chung Kuo's true past. Both made Kim's life forfeit under the law, and that made the boy a threat to him. And so, despite the cost – despite the huge potential profit to be made from him – he had decided to play safe and terminate the boy, at the same time erasing all trace of those who had prepared the genotype report for him. But then the *Wu* had come.

The sun in the earth. Yes, it was the boy. There was no doubt about it. And, as he had that first time he had used the services of the *Wu*, he felt the reading could not be ignored. He had to act on it.

A small shiver ran through him, remembering that first time, almost nine years ago now. He had been sceptical and the *Wu* had angered him by laughing at his doubt. But only moments later the *Wu* had shocked him into silence with his reading.

The wind drives over the water:
The image of dispersion.
Thus the kings of old sacrificed to the Lord
And built temples.

It had been the evening before his dinner with Edmund Wyatt and Pietr Lehmann – a meeting at which he was to decide whether or not he should join their new Dispersion faction. And there it was. The fifty-ninth hexagram – *Huan*. He remembered how he had listened, absorbed by the *Wu*'s explanation, convinced by his talk of high goals and the coming of spring after the hardness of winter. It was too close to what they had been talking of to be simple chance or coincidence. Why, even the title of the ancient book seemed suddenly apt, serendipitous – *The Book Of Changes*. He had laughed and bowed and paid the *Wu* handsomely before contacting Edmund at once to tell him yes.

And so it had begun, all those years ago. Neither could he ever think of it without seeing in his mind the movement of the wind upon the water, the budding of leaves upon the branches. So how could he argue with it now – now that he had come to this new beginning?

He switched off the underlighting, slipped the charts back into the folder, then picked up his glasses and stood, folding them and placing them in the pocket of his *pau*.

The sun in the earth... Yes, he would leave the boy for now. But in the morning he would contact his man in the Mid Levels and have him bomb the laboratory where they had prepared the genotypes.

Supervisor Nung sat himself behind his desk and cleared a pile of documents onto the floor before addressing Kim.

'Chan Shui is not here today,' he explained, giving Kim the briefest glance. 'His father has been ill and the boy is taking some time off to look after him. In the circumstances I have asked Tung Lian to look after you until Chan Shui is back with us.'

The office was far more untidy than Kim remembered it. Crates, paper, even clothes, were heaped against one wall, while a pile of boxes had been left in front of the bank of screens.

'Excuse me, Supervisor Nung, but who is Tung Lian?'

Nung looked up again distractedly, then nodded. 'He'll be here any moment.' Then, realizing his tone had been a little too sharp, he smiled at Kim before looking down again.

A moment later there was a knock and a young Han entered. He was a slightly built, slope-shouldered boy a good two or three years younger than Chan Shui. Seeing Kim, he looked down shyly, avoiding his eyes, then moved closer to the desk.

'Ah, Tung Lian. You know what to do.'

Tung Lian gave a jerky bow. Then, making a gesture for Kim to follow him, he turned away.

Walking back through the Casting Shop, Kim looked about him, feeling a slight sense of unease, but there was no sign of Janko. Good. Perhaps he would be lucky. But even if Janko did turn up, he'd be all right. He would simply avoid the older boy: use guile and quickness to keep out of his way.

The machine was much the same as the one he had operated with Chan

Shui and, seeing that the boy did not wish to talk to him, Kim simply got on with things.

He was sitting in the refectory at the mid-morning break when he heard a familiar voice call out to him from the far side of the big room. It was Janko.

He finished his *ch'a* and set the bowl down, then calmly got up from the table.

Janko was standing in the doorway to the Casting Shop, a group of younger boys gathered about him. He was showing them something, but, seeing Kim approach, he wrapped it quickly in a cloth.

Kim had glimpsed something small and white in Janko's hand. Now, as Janko faced him, his pocked face split by an ugly smile, he realized what it had been. A tooth. Janko had lost a tooth in his fight with Chan Shui yesterday.

He smiled and saw Janko's face darken.

'What are you smiling at, rat's arse?'

He almost laughed. He had heard the words in his head a moment before Janko had uttered them. *Predictable*, Kim thought, *that's what you are.* Even so, he remembered what Chan Shui had said about not pushing him too far.

'I'm sorry, Janko. I was just so pleased to see you.'

That was not the right thing, either, but it had come unbidden, as if in challenge, from his darker self.

Janko sneered. 'We'll see how pleased you are...' But as he moved forward, Kim ducked under and round him and was through the doorway before he could turn. 'Come back here!' Janko bellowed, but the bell was sounding and the boys were already filing out to get back to their machines.

For the rest of the morning Janko kept up a constant stream of foul-mouthed taunts and insults, his voice carrying above the hum of the machines to where Kim was at work. But Kim blocked it all out, looking inward, setting himself the task of connecting two of the sections of his star-web – something he had never attempted before. The problems were of a new order of difficulty and absorbed him totally, but finally he did it and, delighted, turned, smiling, to find himself facing Janko again.

'Are you taking the piss, rat's arse?'

Kim's smile faded slowly.

'Didn't you hear the bell?' Janko continued, and the group of boys behind him laughed, as if it was the funniest thing anyone had ever said.

Dull-*wits*, thought Kim, surprised that he had missed the bell. He glanced across at Tung Liang and saw at once how uneasy he was. Strangely, he found himself trying to reassure the young Han. 'It's okay,' he said. 'I'm all right, Tung Lian. Really I am.'

Janko echoed back his words, high-pitched, in what he must have thought was a good imitation of Kim's voice, and the ghouls behind him brayed once more.

He felt a slight twinge of fear at the pit of his stomach, but nothing that cowed him or made him feel daunted in any way by the boy in front of him.

'I don't want to fight with you.'

'Fight?' Janko laughed, surprised, then leaned towards Kim menacingly. 'Who said anything about fighting? I just want to beat the shit out of you, rat's arse!'

Kim looked about him. Boys blocked both his way back and his route to the entrance doorway. He looked up. Yes, he had thought as much. The two overhead cameras were covered over with jackets. He had been set up. They had planned this. Perhaps since they'd heard Chan Shui was absent.

So Janko wasn't alone in hating him. Far from it.

'Please, Janko...' Tung Liang began feebly, but Janko barked at him to be quiet and he did so, moving back out of the way.

So I'm alone, Kim thought. *Just as Anton said I'd be. Them and us. Or, in this case, them and me.* The humour of it pleased him. Made him laugh.

'What's so funny, rat's arse?'

'You,' said Kim, no longer caring what he said. 'You big strutting bag of bird shit.'

But Janko merely smiled. He moved a pace closer, knowing there was nowhere for Kim to run this time.

But run Kim did, not towards the door or back away from Janko, but directly at Janko – up, onto his chest and over the top of him as he fell backwards, his mouth open wide in surprise, then away towards the toilets.

'Stop him!' yelled Janko, clambering to his feet again. 'Block the little bastard off!'

Kim ran, dodging past anyone who tried to stop him. He would lock himself in. Hold out until Nung came out to investigate, or T'ai Cho came up to see why he'd not returned.

But they had pre-empted him. Someone had sealed all the locks to the toilet doors with an ice-based glue. He checked them all quickly, just in case he had been mistaken, then turned. Janko was standing there, as Kim knew he would be, watching him.

Kim looked up. Of course. They had covered the camera here, too. *Very thorough*, Kim thought, and knew from its thoroughness that Janko had not been involved in planning this. This was all far too clever for him. Janko was only the front-man, the gullible dupe who would carry out the plan. No, he wasn't its architect: he had been manipulated to this point by someone else.

The realization made Kim go cold. There was only one of them in the whole Casting Shop capable of planning this. And he was not here...

Janko laughed and began to come at him. Kim could feel the hatred emanating from the boy, like something real, something palpable. And this time his hands weren't empty. This time they held a knife.

'T'ai Cho! T'ai Cho!'

He turned. Director Andersen's secretary was running down the corridor after him.

'What is it?'

'It's Kim...'

'Where is he?'

A slight colour came to her cheek.

'The boy, I mean! Where's the boy?'

She was close to tears. 'I don't know!' she wailed. 'Supervisor Nung's note was only brief. He gave no details.'

'Gods!' T'ai Cho beat his brow with the palm of his left hand, then began to hurry her back towards Director Andersen's offices.

Outside Andersen's door he stopped, then spoke to her slowly, making sure she understood what she had to do.

'I know it's embarrassing, but it'll be more embarrassing for the Director if he doesn't get to hear about this. Whatever sing-song house he's in, get a message to him fast and get him back here. Here! Understand me, woman?'

When she hesitated he barked at her. 'Just do it! I'll go and see how the boy is and sort out things that end. But Director Andersen must be contacted. The whole Project's in jeopardy unless you can get him here.'

The firmness of his instructions seemed to calm her. She bowed and went inside, to do as she'd been told.

T'ai Cho found Nung slumped over his desk. OD'd. He had been ready to lay hands on the supervisor to get at the truth of things but it was too late for that now. The message to Andersen must have been the last thing he managed to do in his worthless life.

He looked about him, then noticed one of the boys hanging about at the far end of the Casting Shop. He ran across to him, grabbing the boy by the arm so that he could not make off.

'Where did they take Kim? You know, the Clayborn? Where did they take him?'

He noticed the strange look of revulsion the boy gave him at the mention of Kim, but held on, shaking the boy until he got some sense from him. Then he threw him aside and ran on, towards the lifts.

They had taken him to the local Security post. Of course! Where else? But he was not thinking straight, he was just acting now, following his instincts, trying to get to Kim before they hurt him any more.

The soldier at the desk told him to sit and wait. He lifted up the barrier and went through anyway, ignoring the shout from behind him. Then, when the soldier laid hands on him from behind, he whirled about and shouted at the man.

'Do you realize who I am, soldier?'

The tone of absolute authority in his voice – a tone he had once used to cower unruly boys fresh from the Clay – worked perfectly. The soldier backed off a pace and began to incline his head. T'ai Cho pressed the advantage before the soldier could begin to think again.

'My uncle is the Junior Minister, T'ai Feng, responsible for Security Subsidies. Lay a finger on me and he'll break you, understand me?'

This time the soldier bowed fully and brought his hand up to his chest in salute.

'Good! Now take me to your commanding officer at once. This is a matter of the utmost urgency both to myself and to my uncle.'

As the soldier bowed again and moved past him, T'ai Cho realized fleetingly that it was his robes that had helped create the right impression. He was wearing his lecturer's *pau* with the bright blue patch, in many ways reminiscent of the sort of gown worn by a high official.

The soldier barely had time to announce him – and no time to turn and query his name – before he burst in behind him and took a chair in front of the Security officer.

This officer was less impressed by tones and gowns and talk of uncles. He asked immediately to see T'ai Cho's permit card. T'ai Cho threw it across the desk at him, then leaned across almost threateningly.

'Where's the boy? The boy from the Clay?'

The officer looked up at him, then down at the permit card. Then he threw the card back at T'ai Cho.

'If I were you, *Shih* T'ai, I'd leave here at once, before you get into any more trouble.'

T'ai Cho ignored the card. He glared at the officer. 'Where's the boy? I'm not leaving until I've seen the boy!'

The officer began to get up from his chair, but T'ai Cho leaned right across and pulled him down.

'Sit down, for the gods' sake, and hear me out!'

T'ai Cho shivered. He had never felt such anger or fear or urgency before. They shaped his every action now.

'*Where is the boy?*' he demanded fiercely.

The officer moved his hand slightly and pressed a pad on the desk, summoning help. He was certain now he had another madman on his hands.

'Understand me, *Shih* T'ai. The boy is in safe hands. We're seeing to the matter. It's a simple case of assault of a citizen by a non-registered being. We'll be terminating the NRB in about an hour or so, once authorization has come down from above.'

'*You're doing what?!*' T'ai Cho screamed. He stood up violently, making the officer do the same; his hands out defensively, expecting attack.

'Please, *Shih* T'ai. Sit down and calm down.'

The door slid open quietly behind T'ai Cho, but he heard it even so and moved around the desk, so that his back was against the wall.

'You have no jurisdiction here,' the officer said, his voice calmer now that he had assistance. 'Whatever your relationship to the boy, I'm afraid the matter is out of your hands.'

T'ai Cho answered him at once. 'It's you who doesn't understand. Kim Ward is not an NRB, as you so ridiculously put it, but one of the most brilliant and important scientific minds in the whole of Chung Kuo. SimFic have negotiated a contract for his services for *ten million yuan*.'

He had said the last three words slowly and clearly and with maximum emphasis and saw the effect the fantastic sum had on them.

'Ten million?' The officer gave a brief, thoughtful laugh. Then he shook his head. 'Oh, no. I don't believe you, Shih T'ai. This is just more of your talk of important uncles!'

T'ai Cho shook his head, then spoke again, his voice ringing with firmness and determination. 'There's one more thing you don't understand. I don't care what happens to me. But you do. That makes me stronger than you. Oh, you can think me a liar or a madman, but just consider – if you ignore my warning and go ahead without checking up, then you'll be liable directly to SimFic for unauthorized destruction of their property.' He laughed, suddenly horrified by this nightmare, sickened that he should even need to do this. Couldn't they see he was only a little boy – a frightened little boy who'd been savagely attacked?

Still the officer hesitated. 'There are certain procedures. I...'

T'ai Cho yelled at the man; using language he had never before in his life used. 'Fuck your procedures! Get on to Director Andersen at once. Unless you really want to be sued for ten million yuan!'

The officer blanched, then consulted his compatriot a second. Swallowing, he turned back to T'ai Cho. 'Would you be willing to wait in a cell for half an hour while we make checks?'

T'ai Cho bowed. 'Of course. That's all I want you to do. Here,' he took a jotpad from the pocket of his robe and, with the stylus from the officer's desk, wrote Andersen's office contact number and his name on the tiny screen. 'You'll find they'll switch you through twice, so hold on. It's a discrete service.'

The officer hesitated, then gave the smallest bow, half-convinced now that T'ai Cho had calmed down.

'Andersen?'

'That's right. He might not be there at once, but keep trying. I've asked his secretary to get him back there as soon as possible.'

An hour later T'ai Cho and four soldiers were taking Kim back to the Project. Kim was heavily sedated and secured in a special carrying harness. It was hard to see what injuries, if any, he had received in the fight with the other boys. His face seemed unmarked. But he was alive and he was not going to be 'terminated', as that bastard in the Security Post had termed it.

Now it was up to Andersen.

Director Andersen met him at the top gate. 'I owe you, T'ai Cho,' he said, slapping the tutor's back. But T'ai Cho turned on him angrily.

'I didn't do it to save your hide, Andersen. Where *were* you?'

Andersen swallowed, noting the open disrespect. 'I... I...' he blustered, then he bowed. 'I'm sorry, T'ai Cho. I know you didn't. Even so, I'm indebted. If there's anything...'

But T'ai Cho simply strode past him, disgusted, thinking of Nung and what had been allowed to happen to Kim. All of it was indirectly Andersen's fault. For not making all the right checks beforehand. If there was any justice, Berdichev would have his hide for it!

Half an hour later he was back in Andersen's office.

'They're what?'

Andersen looked at the package the messenger had delivered ten minutes earlier and repeated what he had said.

'The boy's family are suing us for assault by a property owned by the Project. They've started a suit for fifteen million yuan.'

T'ai Cho sat back, aghast. 'But the boy attacked Kim!'

Andersen laughed bitterly. 'If that's the case, T'ai Cho, why is their boy on the critical list and not Kim? Here, look at these injuries! They're horrific! More than seventeen broken bones and his left ear bitten off. Bitten off! The little savage!'

T'ai Cho glared at him, then looked down at the 2D shots the family's advocate had sent with his package. Gods! he thought, revolted despite himself. Did Kim do this? And he was afraid Matyas would kill *him*!

Andersen was muttering to himself now. 'Fuck him! Fuck the little bastard! Why did he have to go and attack one of them?' He looked at T'ai Cho. 'Why didn't you tell me he was capable of this?'

T'ai Cho went to protest, then thought of all that had been happening the last week or so. Were there warning signs? The restless nights? The problems with Matyas? Should he have foreseen this? Then he rejected all that. He threw the photos down and, with all the angry indignation of the parent of a wronged child, he stood and shouted at Andersen across the table.

'He didn't attack this boy! I *know* he didn't! They attacked him! They must have! Don't you understand that yet?'

Andersen looked up at him scornfully. 'Who gives a shit, eh? We're all out of a job now. There's no way we can contest this. Nung's dead and the cameras were all covered over. There's not a bruise on Kim and the other lad's in critical.' He laughed. 'Who in their right mind would believe Kim was the victim?'

T'ai Cho was watching the Director closely now. 'So what are you going to do?'

Andersen, as ever, had pre-empted him. He saw it in his face.

'I've taken advice already.'

'And?'

Andersen pushed the package aside and leaned across the table. 'The Project's advocate suggests there are ways we can contain the damage. You see, there's not just the matter of the Project's liability to the parents of the injured boy but the question of personal responsibility.' He looked directly at T'ai Cho. 'Yours and mine, in particular. Now, if Kim had actually died in the fight...'

T'ai Cho shook his head in disbelief. His voice, when he found it again, came out as a whisper. 'What have you done, Andersen? What, in the gods' names, have you done?'

Andersen looked away. 'I've signed the order. He'll be terminated in an hour.'

Berdichev went to the cell to see the boy one last time before they sent him on. Kim lay there, pale, his dark eyes closed, the bulky secure-jacket like an incomplete chrysalis, disguising how frail he really was.

Well, well, Berdichev thought, *you have tried your hardest to make my decision an empty one, haven't you?* But perhaps it was just this that the *Wu* had foretold. The darkening of the light.

He knelt and touched the boy's cheek. It was cooler than his own flesh, but still warm. Yes, it was fortunate he had got here in time – before that arsehole Andersen had managed to bugger things up for good and all. He had T'ai Cho to thank for that.

And now it was all his. Kim *and* the Project. And all for the asking price of ten million yuan he had originally contracted purely for the boy.

Berdichev laughed. It had all been rather easy to manage in the circum-stances. The Board had agreed the deal at once, and to help facilitate matters he had offered eight of the ten sitting members an increase in their yearly stipend. The other two he had wanted out anyway, and when the vote went against them he had accepted their resignations without argument. As for the matter of the aggrieved parents, their claim was dropped when they received his counter-claim for two hundred million – his estimate of the potential loss of earnings SimFic would suffer if Kim was permanently brain-damaged. They had been further sweetened by an out-of-court no-liability-accepted settlement of fifty thousand yuan. More than enough in exchange for their dull-witted son.

But what damage had it done? What would Kim be like when the wraps came off and the scars had healed? Not the physical scars, for they were miraculously slight, but the deeper scars – the psychological ones?

He shuddered, feeling suddenly closer to Kim than he had ever been. As if the *Wu*'s reading had connected him somehow to the boy. The sun was buried in the earth once more, but would it rise again? Would Kim become again what he had been? Or was he simple, unawakened Clay?

Ten million yuan. That was how much he had gambled on Kim's full and complete recovery. And the possible return? He laughed. Maybe a thousand times as much! Maybe nothing.

Berdichev got up and wiped his hands on his jacket, then turned to the two SimFic guards, indicating that they should take the boy away. Then, when they had gone, he crossed the cell and looked at its second occupant. This one was also trussed.

He laughed and addressed the corpse of the Director. 'You thought you'd fuck with me, eh, Andersen? Well, no one does that and gets away with it. No one. Not even you.'

Still laughing, he turned and left the cell.

CHUNG KUO

Chapter 42

ICE AND FIRE

Be patient, Li Yuan, we'll not be much longer now!'

Pearl Heart tugged the two wings of his collar together with a show of mock annoyance, then fastened the first of the four tiny catches. He was sitting on the edge of his bed, Pearl Heart kneeling on the floor in front of him, dressing him, while Sweet Rose knelt on the bed, behind him, brushing and braiding his hair.

The younger girl laughed softly. 'Your hair's so long, Li Yuan. Such good, strong hair. It doesn't split easily.' She leaned forward, brushing her nose against it, breathing in its scent. 'I wish I had such hair, dear Yuan.'

He made to turn and speak to her, but Pearl Heart gently brought his head back round, tutting to herself. The last two catches were always the most tricky to fasten.

Li Yuan laughed softly. 'Your hair is lovely too, Sweet Rose. And never more lovely than when it rests across my lap.'

Sweet Rose blushed and looked down, reminded of what they had been up to only hours before. Pearl Heart looked up into his face, amused. 'Perhaps you'd like all five of us next time?'

He looked past her, smiling. 'Perhaps…'

'Still,' she continued, frowning with concentration as she tried to fix the last of the catches. 'It will be good for you to get some exercise.'

Li Yuan laughed, delighted. 'You really think so, Pearl Heart? After last night?'

She leaned back away from him with a sigh, the collar fastened at last, then shook her head, her eyes sparkling.

'You young men. You think you're real horsemen simply because you can keep at it all night long, don't you? But there's more to horsemanship than keeping in the saddle!'

Sweet Rose had gone silent, her head bowed. Pearl Heart looked back. Li Yuan was staring at her strangely. She thought back, then ducked her head, blushing, realizing how she had linked the two things. Li Yuan was about to go out riding with Fei Yen, and there she was saying...

'Forgive me, Prince, I didn't mean...'

But Li Yuan simply leaned forward and took her head between his hands, kissing her forehead before pressing her face down into his lap and closing his legs about her playfully.

She fought up away, enjoying the game, then stood there a few paces off, admiring him. Sweet Rose had finished and had placed a riding hat upon his tight-coiled hair. He was dressed entirely in green, from hat down to boots: a dozen subtle shades of green, yet each of them fresh and bright, reminiscent of the first days of spring, when the snow has just thawed.

'You look...' She laughed and clapped her hands. 'You look like a prince, Li Yuan!'

He laughed with her, then turned to give Sweet Rose a farewell peck before rushing off.

The two maids watched him go, then began to tidy the room. As Pearl Heart stripped the covers from the cushions, she noticed the square of silk beneath one of them. It was a pale lilac with the pictogram of the Yin family in green in one corner. She knew at once whose it was, and lifted it to her nose briefly before returning it, making no mention to Sweet Rose.

'She's beautiful, don't you think, Pearl Heart?'

Sweet Rose was gazing outward through the open doorway, following the figure of Li Yuan as he made his way through the gardens.

'They say there's no one quite as beautiful in all the Families as Fei Yen. But she's a *hua pao*, a flowery panther. She's headstrong and wilful, for all her beauty.'

Sweet Rose sighed and looked back at her older sister. 'And Li Yuan, he seems to love her like a brother.'

Pearl Heart laughed. 'Have you seen how his eyes grow soft at the merest glimpse of her. He's hooked, the poor little one.'

'Ah...' Sweet Rose glanced round once more, then busied herself, disturbed by what Pearl Heart had said. A moment later, while she was gathering up the linen, she stopped suddenly and looked up again, her eyes moist. 'Then I feel pity for him, Pearl Heart. For nothing can come of it.'

Pearl Heart nodded sagely. 'It is our law, Sweet Rose. A man cannot marry his brother's wife. And there's wisdom in that law, mei mei, for think what would come of things were it not so. There are men who would murder their own brothers for the sake of a worthless woman!'

Sweet Rose looked down. 'And yet we are sisters. And we share a man.'

Pearl Heart laughed and began to take the new silk sheets from the drawer. 'Li Yuan's a boy, and they're less complex than men. But in any case, the whole thing's totally different. We are here only to help him and teach him. We must think not of ourselves but of the future T'ang.'

Sweet Rose studied her sister a moment, noting how she busied herself as if unconcerned. But she had heard the undertone of bitterness in her voice and could see the faint trace of regret at the corners of her mouth and in her eyes and knew that, whatever else she said, she too was just a little in love with the young Prince.

'What are you reading?'

Fei Yen half turned her face towards him, then smiled and set the book down on the wooden ledge beside her. 'Ah, Yuan, I wondered when you'd come.'

She was sitting in a bower overlooking one of the garden's tiny water-falls. The interlaced branches of the maple overhead threw her features into shadow as she looked at him, but he could see that her hair had been put up in a complex bun, the dark, fine bunches held there by tiny ivory combs no bigger than his thumb nail. She was wearing a waist-length, curve-edged riding-tunic with a high collar, the satin a delicate lavender with the thinnest edging of black, while her riding breeches were of dark blue silk, cut almost to her figure. Her boots were of kid leather, dyed to match the breeches.

He let his query pass. 'Shall I come and sit with you, Fei Yen?'

'Wait there, Yuan. I'll come out to you. It's rather warm in here. Why don't we walk down to the terrace?'

He bowed, then moved back to let her pass, smelling the scent of her for the first time that day.

Mei hua. Plum blossom.

He fell in beside her on the path. 'How is your father, Yin Tsu?'

She laughed. 'He's fine. As he was yesterday when you asked. And my three brothers too, before you ask.' She stopped and inclined her head towards him. 'Let's drop formality, shall we, Li Yuan? I find it all so tiresome after a while.'

A small bird flitted from branch to branch overhead, distracting them both. When they looked down again their eyes met and they laughed.

'All right,' he said. 'But in public...'

She touched his arm gently. 'In public it shall be as always.' She lifted her chin in imitation of an old, starchy courtier. 'We'll be as tight-laced as a Minister's corsets!'

He giggled, unable to help himself, then saw she was watching him, enjoying his laughter.

'Come, Yuan. Let's go down.'

She let him take her arm. A flight of stone steps snaked steeply downward, following the slope, ending with a tiny bridge of stone. But the bridge was only wide enough for one to cross at a time. Li Yuan went first then turned, holding out his hand to help her across the tiny stream.

She took his hand and let him draw her to him, brushing past him closely, then turned to look back at him, her face in full sunlight for the first time since he had met her in the bower.

'What's that?'

She began to smile, then saw the look on his face. 'It's a *mian ye*. A beauty mark, that's all. Why, don't you like it?'

He made the slightest movement of his head, reluctant to find anything about her less than perfect.

'Here, wipe it off!'

He took the silk handkerchief she offered, realizing at once that it was the twin to the one he had in his room, beneath his pillow. Resisting the temptation to put it to his face, he reached out and made to touch the mark, but Fei Yen laughed and pushed his hand away.

'Come here, Li Yuan! How can you do it from over there? You'll have to hold my cheek while you rub the mark away. It isn't easy, you know!'

He moved closer, then gently took her cheek and turned it, almost fearing to hurt her. His body was touching hers now, brushing against her, and he could feel her warmth and smell the scent of plum blossom on her clothes. He felt a slight shiver pass down his spine, then began, brushing at it, gently at first, then harder, licking the silk then dabbing it against her cheek, until the mark was gone.

And all the while she was watching him, a strange, unreadable expression in her dark, beautiful eyes. He was conscious of her breathing: of her warm breath on his neck; of the soft rise and fall of her breasts beneath the tightly fitting tunic; of the warm pulse of her body where it touched his own.

He shuddered and moved away, bringing his hand back from her face; looking down at it a moment, as if it wasn't his. Then, recollecting himself, he offered her the silk.

Her smile, her answer, made him burn. 'Keep it. Put it with its twin.'

He swallowed, then smiled and gave a small bow of thanks.

On the terrace she stood there, her hands on the balcony, looking out across the lake. 'Do you still want to ride?'

He looked away, a faint colour in his cheeks, remembering what Pearl Heart had said.

'What is it?' she asked, touching his shoulder gently.

'Nothing,' he said, then laughed and changed the subject. 'Do you remember that day here, on the far side of the lake? The day of the reception?'

She looked across and nodded, her mouth opening slightly, showing her perfect white teeth. 'The day I let Han beat me at archery.'

They were silent a moment, a strange mix of emotions in the air between them. Then she turned back to him, smiling.

'Let's go across. I'm not in the mood for riding. Let's walk, and talk of old times, neh, Yuan?'

He looked up shyly at her, then smiled. 'I'd like that very much.'

For a long time after Li Yuan had gone, Fei Yen stood there at the edge of the lake, staring out across the water, deep in thought.

She had thought it would be amusing to play an ancient game: to flirt with him and maybe afterwards, in some secret place away from prying eyes, introduce him to pleasures finer than those his maids could offer. But Li Yuan had wanted more than that. Much more, despite the impossibility of it.

She could still hear his voice echoing in her head.

'Your son will be T'ang.'

Had he seen her surprise? Had he seen how unprepared she was for that? Her laughter had been designed to put him off; to make him think she thought it all a joke, when she could see from his eyes how serious he was.

'Impossible,' she had said when he repeated it. 'You know the law, Li Yuan.'

'You slept with him? Is that what you're saying?'

'What?' She had turned, flustered, shocked by his impropriety. 'What do you mean?'

He seemed obsessed with it; insistent. 'Did you sleep with him? Before the wedding? It is important, Fei Yen. Did you or didn't you?'

She swallowed and looked down, flushing deeply at the neck. 'No! How could I have done? There was never an opportunity. And then...'

Her tears made him relent. But in the breathing space they earned her, she began to understand. The law said that a man could not marry his brother's wife. But was a wife really a wife until the marriage had been consummated?

She had looked up at him, wide-eyed: astonished both that he wanted her and that he was prepared to challenge the law itself to have her.

'You understand me, then, Fei Yen?' he had said and she had nodded, her whole being silenced by the enormity of what he was suggesting to her. His wife. He wanted her to be his wife. But they had had the chance to say no more than that, for then the old servant had come and brought the summons from his father, and he, suddenly more flustered than she, had bowed and gone at once, leaving things unresolved.

Your son will be T'ang.

Yes, she thought, tears of joy coming suddenly to her eyes. *So it shall pass. As it was always meant to be.*

His father's Chancellor, Chung Hu-Yan, met him before the doors to the Hall of Eternal Truth. The huge doors were closed and guarded, the great wheel of the *Ywe Lung* towering over the man as he bowed to the boy.

'What is it, Hu-Yan? What does my father want?'

But Chung Hu-Yan was not his normal smiling self. He looked at Li Yuan strangely, almost sternly, then removed the boy's riding hat and turned him about full circle, inspecting him.

'I was going riding...' Li Yuan began to explain, but the Chancellor shook his head, as if to say, *Be silent, boy.*

Yuan swallowed. What had happened? Why was Hu-yan so stern and formal? Was it the business with the maids? Oh, gods, was it that?

Satisfied, Chung Hu-Yan stepped back and signalled to the guards.

Two bells sounded, the first sweet and clear, the second deep and resonant. Slowly, noiselessly, the great doors swung back.

Yuan stared down the aisle of the great hall and shivered. What was going on? Why did his father not meet with him in his rooms, as he had always done? Why all this sudden ritual?

Li Shai Tung sat on his throne atop the Presence Dais at the far end of the Hall.

'Prostrate yourself, Li Yuan,' Chung Hu-Yan whispered, and Yuan did as he was bid, making the full *k'o t'ou* to his father for the first time since the day of the reception – the day of the archery contest.

He stood slowly, the cold touch of the tiles lingering like a ghostly presence against his brow. Then, with the briefest glance at Chung Hu-Yan, he moved forward, between the pillars, approaching his father.

Halfway down the aisle he noticed the stranger who stood to one side of the Presence Dais at the bottom of the steps. A tall, thin Han with a shaven head, who wore the sienna robes of a scholar, but on whose chest was a patch of office.

He stopped at the foot of the steps and made his obeisance once again, then stood and looked up at the T'ang.

'You asked for me, father?'

His father was dressed in the formal robe he normally wore only for Ministerial audiences, the bright yellow cloth edged in black and decorated with fierce golden dragons. The high-tiered court crown made him seem even taller than he was; more dignified, if that was possible. When Li Yuan addressed him he gave the barest nod of recognition, his face, like Chung Hu-Yan's, curiously stern, uncompromising. This was not how he usually greeted his son.

Li Shai Tung studied his son a moment, then leaned forward and pointed to the Han who stood below the steps.

'This is Ssu Lu Shan. He has something to tell you about the world. Go with him, Li Yuan.'

Li Yuan turned to the man and gently inclined his head, showing his respect. At once the scholar bowed low, acknowledging Li Yuan's status as a prince. Li Yuan turned back, facing his father, waiting, expecting more, then understood the audience was at an end. He made his k'o t'ou a third and final time, then backed away, puzzled and deeply troubled by the strict formality of his father's greeting, the oddness of his instruction.

Outside, Li Yuan turned and faced the stranger, studying him. He had the thin, pinched face of a New Confucian official; a face made longer by the bareness of the scalp. His eyes, however, were hard and practical. They met Li Yuan's examination unflinchingly.

'Tell me, Ssu Lu Shan. What Ministry is it that you wear the patch of?'

Ssu Lu Shan bowed. 'It is the Ministry, Prince Yuan.' From another it might have seemed cryptic, but Li Yuan understood at once that there was nothing elusive in the man's answer.

'The Ministry?'

'So it is known, Excellency.'

Li Yuan walked on, Ssu Lu Shan keeping up with him, several paces behind, as protocol demanded.

At the doorway to his suite of rooms, Li Yuan stopped and turned to face the man again.

'Do we need privacy for our meeting, Ssu Lu Shan?'

The man bowed. 'It would be best, Excellency. What I have to say is for your ears only. I would prefer it if the doors were locked and the windows closed while I am talking.'

Li Yuan hesitated, feeling a vague unease. But this was what his father wanted; what his father had ordered him to do. And if his father had ordered it, he must trust this man and accommodate him.

When the doors were locked and the windows closed, Ssu Lu Shan turned, facing him. Li Yuan sat in a tall chair by the window overlooking the gardens while the scholar – if that was what he was – stood on the far side of the room, breathing deeply, calmly, preparing himself.

Dust motes floated slowly in the still warm air of the room as Ssu Lu Shan began, his voice deep, authoritative, and clear as polished jade, telling the history of Chung Kuo – the true history – beginning with Pao Chan's arrival on the shores of the Caspian Sea in AD 97, and his subsequent withdrawal, leaving Europe to the Ta Ts'in, the Roman Empire.

Hours passed and still Ssu Lu Shan spoke on, telling of a Europe Li Yuan had never dreamed existed – a Europe racked by Dark Ages and damned by religious bigotry, enlightened by the Renaissance, then torn again by wars of theology, ideology and nationalism; a Europe swept up, finally, by the false ideal of technological progress, born of the Industrial Revolution; an ideal fuelled by the concept of evolution and fanned by population pressures into the fire of Change – Change at any price.

And what had Chung Kuo done meanwhile but enclose itself behind great walls? Like a bloated maggot it had fed upon itself until, when the West had come, it had found the Han Empire weak, corrupt, and ripe for conquest.

So they came to the Century of Change, to the Great Wars, to the long years of revolution in Chung Kuo, and finally to the Pacific Century and the decline and fall of the American Empire, ending in the chaos of the Years of Blood.

This, the closest to the present, was the worst of it for Li Yuan, and as if he sensed this, Ssu Lu Shan's voice grew softer as he told of the tyrant, Tsao Ch'un and his 'Crusade of Purity'; of the building of the City; of the Ministry and the burning of the books, the burial of the past.

'As you know, Prince Yuan, Tsao Ch'un wished to create an utopia that would last ten thousand years – to bring into being the world beyond the peach-blossom river, as we Han have traditionally known it. But the price of its attainment was high.'

Ssu Lu Shan paused, his eyes momentarily dark with the pain of what he had witnessed on ancient newsreels. Then, slowly, he began again.

'In 2062 Japan, Chung Kuo's chief rival in the East, was the first victim of Tsao Ch'un's barbaric methods when, without warning – after Japanese complaints about Han incursions in Korea – the Han leader bombed Honshu, concentrating his nuclear devices on the major population centres of Tokyo and Kyoto. Over the next eight years three great Han armies swept the smaller islands of Kyushu and Shikoku, destroying everything and killing every Japanese they found, while the rest of Japan was blockaded by sea and air. Over the following twelve years they did the same with the islands of

Honshu and Hokkaido, turning the "islands of the gods" into a wasteland.

'While this was happening, the crumbling Western nation states were looking elsewhere, obsessed with their own seemingly insuperable problems. Chung Kuo alone of all the Earth's nations remained stable, and, as the years passed, grew quickly at the expense of others.

'The eradication of Japan taught Tsao Ch'un many lessons, yet only one other time was he to use similar methods. In future he sought, in his famous phrase, "not to destroy but to exclude" – though his definition of "exclusion" often made it a synonym for destruction. As he built his great City – the huge machines moving slowly outward from Pei Ching, building the living sections – so he peopled it, choosing carefully who was to live within its walls. His criteria, like his methods, were not merely crude but idiosyncratic, reflecting not merely his wish to make his great City free of all those human troubles that had plagued previous social experiments, but also his deeply held hatred of the black and aboriginal races.'

Noting Li Yuan's surprise, Ssu Lu Shan nodded soberly. 'Yes, Prince Yuan, there were once whole races of black men. Men no more different from ourselves than the *Hung Mao*. Billions of them.'

He lowered his eyes, then continued. 'As the City grew so his men went out, questioning, searching among the *Hung Mao* for those who were free from physical disability, political dissidence, religious bigotry and intellectual pride. And where he encountered organized opposition he enlisted the aid of groups sympathetic to his aims. In Southern Africa and North America, in Europe and in the People's Democracy Of Russia, huge popular movements grew up amongst the *Hung Mao* supporting Tsao Ch'un and welcoming his stability after decades of bitter suffering. Many of them were only too pleased to share in his crusade of intolerance – his "Policy of Purity". In the so-called "civilized" West, particularly, Tsao Ch'un often found that his work had been done for him long before his officials arrived.

'Only the Middle East proved problematic. There a great Jihad was launched against the Han, Muslim and Jew casting off millennia of enmity to fight against a common threat. Tsao Ch'un answered them harshly, as he had answered Japan. The Middle East and large parts of the Indian subcontinent were swiftly reduced to the wilderness they remain to this day. But it was in Africa that Tsao Ch'un's policies were most nakedly displayed. There the native peoples were moved on before the encroaching City, and, like cattle in a desert, they starved or died from exhaustion, driven on relentlessly by a brutal Han army.

'Tsao Ch'un's ideal was, he believed, a high one. He sought to eradicate the root causes of human dissidence and fulfil all material needs. Yet in terms of human suffering, his pacification of the Earth was unprecedented. It was a grotesquely flawed ideal, and more than four billion people died as a direct result of his policies.'

Ssu Lu Shan met the young Prince's eyes again, a strange resignation in his own. 'Tsao Ch'un killed the old world. He buried it deep beneath his glacial City. But eventually his brutality and tyranny proved too much even for those who had helped him carry out his scheme. In 2087 his Council of Seven Ministers rose up against him, using North European mercenaries, and overthrew him, setting up a new government. They divided the world – Chung Kuo – amongst themselves, each calling himself T'ang. The rest you know. The rest, since then, is true.'

In the silence that followed, Li Yuan sat there perfectly still, staring blankly at the air in front of him. He could see the stern faces of his father and his father's Chancellor, and understood them now. They had known this moment lay before him. Had known how he would feel.

He shuddered and looked down at his hands where they clasped each other in his lap – so far away from him, they seemed. A million li from the dark, thinking centre of himself. Yes. But what did he feel?

A nothingness. A kind of numbness at the core of him. Almost an absence of feeling. He felt hollow, his limbs brittle like the finest porcelain. He turned his head, facing Ssu Lu Shan again, and even the simple movement of his neck muscles seemed suddenly false, unreal. He shivered and focused on the waiting man.

'Did my brother know of this?'

Ssu Lu Shan shook his head. It was as if he had done with words.

'I see.' He looked down. 'Then why has my father chosen to tell me now? Why should I, at my age, know what Han Ch'in at his did not?'

When Ssu Lu Shan did not answer him, Li Yuan looked up again. He frowned. It was as if the Han were in some kind of trance.

'Ssu Lu Shan?'

The man's eyes focused on him, but still he said nothing.

'Have you done?'

Ssu Lu Shan's sad smile was extraordinary: as if all he was, all he knew, were gathered up into that small, ironic smile. 'Almost,' he answered softly. 'There's one last thing.'

Li Yuan raised a hand, commanding him to be silent. 'A question first. My father sent you, I know. But how do I know that what you've told me today is true? What proof have you?'

Ssu Lu Shan looked down a moment and Li Yuan's eyes followed their movement, then widened as he saw the knife he had drawn from the secret fold in his scholar's *pau*.

'Ssu Lu Shan!' he cried out, jumping up, suddenly alert to the danger he was in, alone in a locked room with an armed stranger.

But Ssu Lu Shan paid him no attention. He lowered himself onto his knees and laid the knife on the floor in front of him. While Li Yuan watched he untied the fastenings of his robe and pulled it up over his head, then bundled it together between his legs. Except for a loincloth he was naked now.

Li Yuan swallowed. 'What is this?' he asked softly.

Ssu Lu Shan looked up at him. 'You ask what proof I have. This now is my proof.' His eyes were smiling strangely, as if with relief at the shedding of a great and heavy burden carried too long. 'This, today, was the purpose of my life. Now I have fulfilled my purpose, and the laws of Chung Kuo deem my life forfeit for the secrets I have uttered in this room. So it is. So it must be. For they are great, grave secrets.'

Li Yuan shivered. 'I understand, Ssu Lu Shan. But surely there is another way?'

Ssu Lu Shan did not answer him. Instead he looked down, taking a long breath that seemed to restore his inner calm. Then, picking up the knife again, he readied himself, breathing deeply, slowly, the whole of him concentrated on the point of the knife where it rested, perfectly still, only a hand's length from his stomach.

Li Yuan wanted to cry out; to step forward and stop Ssu Lu Shan, but he knew this too was part of it. Part of the lesson. To engrave it in his memory. *For they are great, grave secrets.* He shivered violently. Yes, he understood. Even this.

'May your spirit soul rise up to Heaven,' he said, blessing Ssu Lu Shan. He knelt and bowed deeply to him, honouring him for what he was about to do.

'Thank you, Prince Yuan,' Ssu Lu Shan said softly, almost in a whisper, pride at the honour the young prince did him making his smile widen momentarily. Then, with a sharp intake of breath, he thrust the knife deep into his flesh.

It was not until halfway through the fourth game that DeVore raised the matter.

'Well, Tong Chou? Have you dealt with our thief?'

Chen met the Overseer's eyes and gave the briefest nod. It had been a dreadful job and it was not pleasant to be reminded of it. He had been made to feel unclean; a brother to the Tengs of the world.

'Good,' DeVore said. He leaned forward and connected two of his groups, then turned the board about. 'Play white from here, Tong Chou.'

It was the fourth time it had happened and DeVore had yet to lose a game, despite being each time in what seemed an impossible position as black.

Yes, Chen thought. *Karr was right after all. But you're not just a Master at this game – it is as if the game were invented for one like you.* He smiled inwardly and placed the first of his stones as white.

There was the same ruthlessness in him. The same cold calculation. DeVore did not think in terms of love and hate and relationships but in terms of advantage and groups and sacrifice. He played life as if it was one big game of *wei chi*.

And perhaps that's your weakness, Chen thought, studying him a moment. *Perhaps that's where you're inflexible. For men are not stones, and life is not a game. You cannot order it thus and thus and thus, or connect it thus and thus and thus. Neither does your game take account of accident or chance.*

Chen looked down again, studying the board, looking for the move or sequence of moves that would make his position safe. White had three corners and at least forty points advantage. It was his strongest position yet: how could he lose from this?

Even so, he knew that he *would* lose. He sighed and sat back. It was as if he were looking at a different board from the one DeVore was studying. It was as if the other man saw through to the far side of the board, on which were placed – suspended in the darkness – the stones yet to be played.

He shivered, feeling suddenly uneasy, and looked down at the tube he had brought with him.

'By the way, Tong Chou, what *is* that thing?'

DeVore had been watching him; had seen where his eyes went.

Chen picked it up and hefted it, then handed it across. He had been surprised DeVore had not insisted on looking at the thing straight away. This was his first mention of it in almost two hours.

'It's something I thought might amuse you. I brought it with me from the Above. It's a viewing tube. You manipulate the end of it and place your eye to the lens at this end.'

'Like this?'

Chen held his breath. There! It was done! DeVore had placed his eye against the lens! The imprint would be perfect! Chen let his breath out slowly, afraid to give away his excitement.

'Interesting,' said DeVore and set it down again, this time on his side of the board. 'I wonder who she was.'

The image was of a high-class *Hung Mao* lady, her dress drawn up about her waist, being 'tupped' from the rear by one of the GenSyn ox-men, its huge, fifteen inch member sliding in and out of her while she grimaced ecstatically.

Chen stared at the tube for a time, wondering whether to ask for it back, then decided not to. The imprint might be perfect, but it was better to lose the evidence than have DeVore suspicious.

For a while he concentrated on the game. Already it was beginning to slip from him, the tide to turn towards the black. He made a desperate play in the centre of the board, trying to link, and found himself cut not once but twice.

DeVore laughed. 'I must make those structures stronger next time,' he said. 'It's unfair of me to pass on such weaknesses to you.'

Chen swallowed, suddenly understanding. At some point in the last few games he had become, if not superfluous, then certainly secondary to the game DeVore was playing against himself.

Like a machine with a slight unpredictability factor built into its circuits.

He let his eyes rest on the tube a moment, then looked up at DeVore. 'Does my play bore you, *Shih* Bergson?'

DeVore sniffed. 'What do you think, Tong Chou?'

Chen met his eyes, letting a degree of genuine admiration colour his expression. 'I think my play much too limited for you, Overseer Bergson. I am but a humble player, but you, *Shih* Bergson, are a Master. It would not surprise me to find you were the First Hand Supreme in all Chung Kuo.'

DeVore laughed. 'In this, as in all things, there are levels, Tong Chou. It is true, I find your game limited, predictable, and perhaps I have tired of it already. But I am not quite what you make me out to be. There are others – a dozen, maybe more – who can better me at this game, and of them there is one, a man named Tuan Ti Fo, who was once to me as I am to you. He alone deserves the title you conferred on me just now.'

DeVore sat back, relaxed. 'But you are right, Tong Chou. You lost the game two moves back. It would not do to labour the point, neh?' He half turned in his chair and leaned back into the darkness. 'Well, Stefan? What do you think?'

The albino stepped out from the shadows at the far end of the room and came towards the table.

Chen's heart missed a beat. Gods! How long had *he* been there?

He edged back, instinctively afraid of the youth, and when the albino picked up the viewing tube and studied it, Chen tensed, believing himself discovered – certain, for that brief moment, that DeVore had merely been toying with him; that he had known him from the first.

'These GenSyn ox-men are ugly beasts, aren't they? Yet there's something human about them, even so.'

The pale youth set the tube down then stared at Chen a moment: his pink eyes so cruel, so utterly inhuman in their appraisal, Chen felt the hairs on his neck stand on end.

'Well?' DeVore had sat back, watching the young man.

The albino turned to DeVore and gave the slightest shrug. 'What do I know, Overseer Bergson? Make him Field Supervisor if it suits you. Someone must do the job.'

His voice, like his flesh, was colourless. Even so, there was something strangely, disturbingly familiar about it. Something Chen could not, for the life of him, put his finger on just then.

DeVore watched the youth a moment longer, then turned, facing Chen again. 'Well, Tong Chou. It seems the job is yours. You understand the duties?'

Chen nodded, forcing his face into a mask of gratitude; but the presence of the young albino had thrown him badly. He stood up awkwardly, almost upsetting the board, then backed off, bowing deeply.

'Should I leave, Overseer?'

DeVore was watching him almost absently. 'Yes. Go now, Tong Chou. I think we're done.'

Chen turned and took a step towards the door.

'Oh, and, Tong Chou?'

He turned back slowly, facing DeVore again, fear tightening his chest and making his heart pound violently. Was this it? Was this the moment when he turned the board about?

But no. The Overseer was holding out the viewing tube, offering it to him across the board.

'Take this and burn it. Understand me? I'll have no filth on this planta-tion!'

When the peasant had gone, Lehmann came across and sat in the vacant seat, facing DeVore.

DeVore looked up at him. 'Will you play, Stefan?'

Lehmann shook his head curtly. 'What was all that for?'

DeVore smiled and continued transferring the stones into the bowls. 'I had a hunch, that's all. I thought he might be something more, but it seems I'm wrong. He's just a stupid peasant.'

'How do you know?'

DeVore gave a short laugh. 'The way he plays this game, for an opener. He's not pretending to be awkward, he is! You've seen his face when he concentrates on the board!'

DeVore pulled down his eyes at the corners and stretched his mouth exaggeratedly.

'So? He can't play *wei chi*. What does that mean?'

DeVore had finished clearing the board. Taking a cloth from the pocket of his *pau* , he wiped the wood. 'It means he's not Security. Even the basest recruit would play better than Tong Chou.' He yawned and sat back, stretching out his arms behind him, his fingers interlaced. 'I was just being a little paranoid, that's all.'

'Again, I thought it was your policy to trust no one?'

DeVore smiled, his eyes half-lidded now. 'Yes. That's why I'm having his background checked out.'

'Ah...' Lehmann sat back, still watching him, his eyes never blinking, his stare quite unrelenting. 'And the tube?'

DeVore shook his head. 'That was nothing. He was just trying to impress me. These Han are strange, Stefan. They think all *Hung Mao* are beasts, with the appetites of beasts. Maybe it's true of some.'

Yes, but he had wondered for a moment: had waited to see if Tong Chou would clamour for it back.

'You're certain of him, then?'

DeVore looked sharply at the youth. 'And you're not?'

Lehmann shook his head. 'You said you had a hunch. Why not trust to it? Have you ever been wrong?'

DeVore hesitated, reluctant to say, then nodded. 'Once or twice. But never about something so important.'

'Then why trust to luck now?'

When Lehmann was gone, he went upstairs and sat at his desk, beneath the sharp glare of the single lamp, thinking about what the albino had said. The unease he felt was understandable. Everything was in flux at present – *The New Hope*, the fortresses, the recent events in the House, all these demanded his concentration, night and day. Little wonder, then, that he should display a little paranoia now and then. Even so, the boy was right. It was wrong to ignore a hunch simply because the evidence wasn't there to back it up. Hunches were signs from the subconscious – reports from a game played deep down in the darkness.

Normally he would have had the man killed and thought nothing of it, but there were good reasons not to kill Tong Chou just now. Reports of unrest were serious enough as it was, and had brought enquiries from Duchek's own office. Another death was sure to bring things to a head. But it was important that things were kept quiet for the next few days, until his scheme to pay that bastard Duchek back was finalised and the funds transferred from his accounts.

Yes. And he wanted to get even with Administrator Duchek. Because Duchek had let him down badly when he had refused to launder the funds for the Swiss Wilds fortresses through his accounts. Had let them all down.

Even so, there was a way that he could deal with Tong Chou. An indirect way that would cause the very minimum of fuss.

The dead thief had three brothers. They, certainly, would be keen to know who it was had put their brother in the ground. And who was to say who had left the anonymous note?

DeVore smiled, satisfied that he had found the solution to one of his problems, then leaned forward and tapped out the combination of the discrete line that connected him directly with Berdichev.

'Do you know what time it is, Howard?'

'Two-twenty. Why? Were you sleeping, Soren?'

Berdichev waved his wife, Ylva, away, then locked the door behind her and came back to the screen. 'What's so urgent?'

'We need to talk.'

'What about?'

DeVore paused, conscious of the possibility the call was being traced – especially after the events of the past few days. 'I'll tell you when I see you.'

'Which is when?'

'In an hour and a half.'

'Ah...' Berdichev removed his glasses and rubbed at his eyes, then looked up again and nodded. 'Okay.' Then he cut contact. There was no need to say where they would meet. Both knew.

An hour and a half later they stood there on the mountainside below the landing dome at Landeck Base. The huge valley seemed mysterious and threatening in the moonlight, the distant mountains strange and unreal. It was like being on another planet. Berdichev had brought furs against the cold, even so he felt chilled to the bone, his face numbed by the thin, frigid air. He faced DeVore, noting how little the other man seemed to be wearing.

'So? What do we need to talk about?'

His voice seemed small and hollow; dwarfed by the immensity of their surroundings.

'About everything. But mainly about Duchek. Have you heard from Weis?'

Berdichev nodded, wishing he could see DeVore's face better. He had expected DeVore to be angry, maybe even to have had Duchek killed for what he had done. 'I was disappointed in him, Howard.'

'Good. I'd hate to think you were pleased.'

Berdichev smiled tightly. 'What did you want to do?'

'Wrong question, Soren. Try "What have you done?"'

'So?'

'He's dead. Two days from now. Next time he visits his favourite sing-song house. But there's something else I want to warn you about. I've got a team switching funds from the plantation accounts here. At the same time Duchek greets his ancestors there'll be a big fire in the Distribution Centre at Lodz. It'll spread and destroy the computer records there. I thought I'd warn you, in case it hurts any of our investors. It'll be messy and there'll doubtlessly be a few hiccups before they can reconstruct things from duplicate records.'

'Is that wise, Howard?'

DeVore smiled. 'My experts estimate it'll take them between six and eight weeks to sort out the bulk of it. By that time I'll be out of here and the funds will have been tunnelled away, so to speak. Then we cut Weis out of it.'

Berdichev narrowed his eyes. 'Cut Weis out?'

'Yes. He's the weak link. We both know it. Duchek's betrayal gives me the excuse to deal with them both.'

Berdichev considered a moment, then nodded, seeing the sense in it. With Weis dead, the trail covered and the fortresses funded, what did it matter if they traced the missing plantation funds to Duchek? Because beyond Duchek there would be a vacuum. And Duchek himself would be dead.

'How much is involved?'

'Three billion. Maybe three and a half.'

'Three billion. Hmm. With that we could take some of the pressure off our investors.'

DeVore shook his head. 'No. That would just alert Weis. I gave him the distinct impression that we were grabbing for every *fen* we could lay our hands on. If we start making refunds he'll know we've got funding from elsewhere and he'll start looking for it. No, I want you to go to him with the begging bowl again. Make him think things are working out over budget.'

Berdichev frowned. 'And if he says it can't be done?'

DeVore laughed and reached out to touch his arm. 'Be persuasive.'

'Right. You want me to pressure him?'

DeVore nodded. 'How are things otherwise?'

'Things are good. Under Secretary Barrow tells me that the *tai* are to face impeachment charges next week. Until then they're suspended from the House. That gives our coalition an effective majority. Lo Yu-Hsiang read out a strongly worded protest from the Seven yesterday, along with an announce-ment that funding in certain areas was to be cut. But we expected as much. Beyond that they're impotent to act – as we knew they would be. The House is humming with it, Howard. They've had a taste of real power for once and they like it. They like it a lot.'

'Good. And the File?'

For a moment Berdichev thought to play dumb. Then, seeing how things stood, he shrugged inwardly, making a mental note to find out how DeVore had come to know of it. It was fortunate that, for once, he had prepared for such an eventuality. 'I've a copy in my craft for you, Howard. I'll hand it to you before we go.'

'Excellent. And the boy? Kim, isn't it? Have you sorted out your problems there?'

Berdichev felt his stomach tighten. Was there anything DeVore hadn't heard about? 'It's no problem,' he said defensively.

'Good. Because we don't want problems. Not for the next few days, anyway.'

Berdichev took a deep breath, forcing himself to relax. 'And how is young Stefan? How is he settling in?'

DeVore turned his head away, staring out at the mountains, the moon-light momentarily revealing his neat, rather handsome features. 'Fine. Absolutely fine. He's quiet, but I rather like that. It shows he has depths.' He looked back, giving Berdichev the briefest glimpse of a smile.

Yes, thought Berdichev, recalling the two appalling weeks the boy had spent with them as a house guest, *he has depths all right – vacuous depths.*

'I see. But has he learned anything from you, Howard? Anything useful?'

DeVore laughed, then looked away thoughtfully. 'Who knows, Soren? Who knows?'

The huge bed was draped with veils of silk-white *voile*, the thin, gauze-like cotton decorated with butterflies and delicate, tall-stemmed irises. It filled one end of the large, sumptuously decorated room, like the cocoon of some vast, exotic insect.

The air in the room was close, the sweet, almost sickly scent of old perfumes masking another, darker odour.

The woman lay on the bed, amidst a heap of pale cream and salmon pink satin cushions that blended with the colours of the silk *shui t'an i* camisole she wore. As he came closer, she raised her head. The simple movement seemed to cost her dearly, as if her head were weighted down with bronze.

'Who is it?'

Her voice had a slightly brittle edge to it, a huskiness beneath its silken surface.

He stood where he was, looking about the room, noting with disgust its excesses. 'I am from *Shih* Bergson, *Fu Jen* Maitland.'

'You're new...' she said sleepily, a faintly seductive intonation entering her voice. 'Come here where I can see you, boy.'

He went across and climbed the three small steps that led up to the bed, then drew the veil aside, looking down at her.

She was a tall, long-limbed woman with knife-sharp, nervous facial features, their glass-like fragility accentuated rather than hidden by the heavy pancake of make-up she was wearing. She looked old before her time, the web of lines about each eye like the cracked earth of a dried-up stream, her eyeballs protruding slightly beneath their thin veils of flesh. The darkness of her hair, he knew at once, had been achieved artificially, for the skin of her neck and arms had the pallor of albinism.

Yes, he could see now where his own colouring came from.

Bracelets of fine gold wire were bunched about her narrow wrists, jewelled rings clustered on her long, fragile fingers. About her stretched and bony neck she wore a garishly large *ying luo*, the fake rubies and emeralds like pigeons' eggs. Her hair was unkempt from troubled sleep, her silks creased. She looked what she was – a rich Han's concubine. A kept woman.

He watched her turn her head slowly and open her eyes. Pale, watery blue eyes that had to make an effort before they focused on him.

'Ugh... Pale as a worm. Still...' She closed her eyes again, letting her head sink back amongst the cushions. 'What's your name?'

'Mikhail,' he said, adopting the alias he had stolen from DeVore. 'Mikhail Böden.'

She was silent a moment, then gave a small, shuddering sigh and turned slightly, raising herself onto her elbows, looking at him again. The movement made her camisole fall open slightly at the front, exposing her small, pale breasts.

'Come here. Sit beside me, boy.'

He did as he was bade, the perfumed reek of her filling his nostrils, sickening him. It was like her jewellery, her silks and satins, the make-up and nail paint. All this – this ostentation – offended him deeply. He himself wore nothing decorative. His belief was in purity. In *essence*.

Her hand went to his face, then moved down until it rested on his shoulder.

'You have it?'

He took the two packets from his jacket pocket and threw them down onto the bed beside her. If she noticed his rudeness, she said nothing, but leaned forward urgently, scrabbling for the tiny sachets, then tore one open with her small, pointed teeth and swallowed its contents down quickly.

It was as he had thought. She was an addict.

He watched her close her eyes again, breathing deeply, letting the drug take hold of her. When she turned her head and looked at him again she seemed more human, more animated, a slight playfulness in her eyes revealing how attractive she must once have been. But it was only a shadow. A shadow in a darkened room.

'Your eyes,' she said, letting her hand rest on his chest again. 'They seem... wrong somehow.'

'Yes.' He put a finger to each eye, popping out the contact lenses he had borrowed from DeVore's drawer, then looked back at her, noting her surprise.

'Hello, mother.'

'I have no...' she began, then laughed strangely, understanding. 'So. You're Pietr's son.'

He saw how the muscles beneath her eyes betrayed her. But there was no love there. How could there be? She had killed him long ago. Before he was born.

'What do you want?'

In answer he leaned forward and held her to him, embracing her. *DeVore is right*, he thought. *Trust no one. For there's only yourself in the end.*

He let her fall back amongst the satin cushions, the tiny, poisoned blade left embedded at the base of her spine. Then he stood and looked at her again. His mother. A woman he had never met before today.

Carefully, almost tenderly, he took the device from his pocket, set it, then laid it on the bed beside her. In sixty seconds it would catch fire, kindling the silks and satins, igniting the gauze-like layers of voile, cleansing the room of every trace of her.

Lehmann moved back, away, pausing momentarily, wishing he could see it, then turned and left, locking the door behind him, knowing that no one now had any hold on him. Especially not DeVore.

Li Yuan lay there in the darkness, listening to the rain falling in the garden beyond the open windows, letting his heartbeat slow, his breathing return to normal. The dream was fading now and with it the overwhelming fear which had made him cry out and struggle back to consciousness, but still he could see its final image, stretching from horizon to horizon, vast and hideously white.

He shuddered, then heard the door ease open, a soft tread on the tiled floor.

'Do you want company, Li Yuan?'

He sighed, then rolled over and looked across to where she stood, shadowed and naked, at the foot of his bed.

'Not now, Sweet Rose...'

He sensed, rather than saw her hesitation. Then she was gone.

He got up, knowing he would not sleep now, and went to the window, staring out into the moonlit garden. Then, taking a gown from the side, he wrapped it about him and went to the double doors that led out, pulling them open.

For a while Li Yuan stood there, his eyes closed, breathing in the fresh, sweet, night scents of the garden, then he went outside, onto the balcony, the coldness of the marble flags beneath his feet making him look down, surprised.

'Prince Yuan?'

He waved the guard away, then went down, barefoot, into the garden. In the deep shadow of the bower he paused, looking about him, then searched blindly until he came upon it.

'Ah!' he said softly, finding the book there, on the side, where she had laid it only hours before. It had been in the dream, together with the horse, the silks, the scent of plum blossom. The thought made his throat dry again. He shivered and picked the book up, feeling at once how heavy it was, the cover warped, ruined by the rain. He was about to go back out when his fingers found, then read, the pictograms embossed into the sodden surface of the cover.

Yu T'ai Hsin Yang.

He moved his fingers over the figures once again, making sure, then laughed shortly, understanding. It was a book of love poetry. The sixth century collection, *New Songs From A Jade Terrace*. He had not read the book himself, but he had heard of it. Moving out from the bower he turned it over and held it out, under the moonlight, trying to make out the page she had been reading. It was a poem by Chiang Yen. 'Lady Pan's *Poem on the Fan.*'

White silk like a round moon
Appearing from the loom's white silk.
Its picture shows the King of Ch'in's daughter
Riding a lovebird toward smoky mists.
Vivid colour is what the world prefers,
Yet the new will never replace the old.
In secret I fear cold winds coming
To blow on my jade steps tree
And, before your sweet love has ended,
Make it shed midway.

He shivered and closed the book abruptly. It was like the dream, too close, too portentous to ignore. He looked up at the three-quarters moon and felt its coldness touch him to the core. It was almost autumn, the season of executions, when the moon was traditionally associated with criminals.

The moon... A chill thread of fear ran down his spine, making him drop the book. In contrast to the sun, the new moon rose first in the west. Yes, it was from the west that *Chang-e*, the goddess of the Moon, first made herself known.

Chang-e... The association of the English and the Mandarin was surely fanciful – yet he was too much the Han, the suggestive resonances of sounds and words too deeply embedded in his bloodstream, to ignore it.

Li Yuan bent down and retrieved the book, then straightened up and looked about him. The garden was a mosaic of moonlight and shadows, unreal and somehow threatening. It was as if, at any moment, its vague patterning of silver and black would take on a clearer, more articulate shape; forming letters or a face, as in his dream. Slowly, fearful now, he moved back towards the palace, shuddering at the slightest touch of branch or leaf, until he was inside again, the doors securely locked behind him.

He stood there a while, his heart pounding, fighting back the dark, irrational fears that had threatened to engulf him once again. Then, throwing the book down on his bed, he went through quickly, almost running down the corridors, until he came to the entrance to his father's suite of rooms.

The four elite guards stationed outside the door bowed deeply to him but blocked his way. A moment later, Wang Ta Chuan, Master of The Inner Palace, appeared from within, bowing deeply to him.

'What is it, Prince Yuan?'

'I wish to see my father, Master Wang.'

Wang bowed again. 'Forgive me, Excellency, but your father is asleep. Could this not wait until the morning?'

Li Yuan shuddered, then shook his head. His voice was soft but insistent. 'I must see him now, Master Wang. This cannot wait.'

Wang stared at him, concerned and puzzled by his behaviour. Then he averted his eyes and bowed a third time. 'Please wait, Prince Yuan. I will go and wake your father.'

He had not long to wait. Perhaps his father had been awake already and had heard the noises at his door. Whatever, it was only a few seconds later that Li Shai Tung appeared, alone, a silk *pau* pulled about his tall frame, his feet, like his son's, bare.

'Can't you sleep, Yuan?'

Li Yuan bowed, remembering the last time he had spoken to his father, in the Hall of Eternal Truth, after his audience with Ssu Lu Shan. Then he had been too full of contradictions, too shocked, certainly too confused to be able to articulate what he was feeling. But now he knew. The dream had freed his tongue and he must talk of it.

'I had a dream, father. An awful, horrible dream.'

His father studied him a moment, then nodded. 'I see.' He put a hand out, indicating the way. 'Let us go through to your great-grandfather's room, Yuan. We'll talk there.'

The room was cold, the fire empty. Li Shai Tung looked about him, then turned and smiled at his son. 'Here, come help me, Yuan. We'll make a fire and sit about it, you there, I here.' He pointed to the two big armchairs.

Li Yuan hesitated, surprised by his father's suggestion. He had never seen the T'ang do anything but be a T'ang. Yet, kneeling there, helping him make up the fire, then leaning down to blow the spark into a flame, it felt to him as if he had always shared this with his father. He looked up, surprised to find his father watching him, smiling, his hands resting loosely on his knees.

'There. Now let's talk, neh?'

The fire crackled, the flames spreading quicker now. In its flickering light the T'ang sat, facing his son.

'Well, Yuan? You say you had a dream?'

Much of the early part of the dream evaded him now that he tried to recall its details, and there were some things – things related too closely to Fei Yen and his feelings for her – that he kept back from the telling. Yet the dream's ending was still vivid in his mind and he could feel that strange, dark sense of terror returning as he spoke of it.

'I was high up, overlooking the plain where the City had been. But the City was no longer there. Instead, in its place, was a mountain of bones. A great mound of sun-bleached bones, taller than the City, stretching from horizon to horizon. I looked up and the sky was strangely dark, the moon huge and full and bloated, blazing down with a cold, fierce radiance as though it were the sun. And as I looked a voice behind me said, "This is history." Yet when I turned there was no one there, and I realized that the voice had been my own.'

He fell silent, then looked down with a shudder, overcome once more by the power of the dream.

Across from him the T'ang stretched his long body in the chair, clearly discomfited by what his son had seen. For a time he too was silent, then he nodded to himself. 'You dream of Tsao Ch'un, my son. Of the terrible things he did. But all that is in our past now. We must learn from it. Learn not to let it happen again.'

Li Yuan looked up, his eyes burning strangely. 'No... It's not the past. Can't you see that, father? It is what we are, right now. What we represent. We are the custodians of that great white mountain – the gaolers of Tsao Ch'un's City.'

Normally Li Shai Tung would have lectured his son about his manners, the tone in which he spoke, yet this was different: this was a time for open speaking.

'What Tsao Ch'un did was horrible. Yet think of the alternatives, Yuan, and ask yourself what else could he have done? Change had become an evil god, destroying all it touched. Things seemed beyond redemption. There was a saying back then which expressed the fatalism people felt – E hsing hsun huan. Bad nature follows a cycle; a vicious circle, if you like. Tsao Ch'un broke that circle – fought one kind of badness with another and ended the cycle. And so it has been ever since. Until now, that is, when others wish to come and set the Wheel in motion once again.'

Li Yuan spoke softly, quietly. 'Maybe so, father, yet what Tsao Ch'un did is still inside us. I can see it now. My eyes are opened to it. We are the creatures of his environment – the product of his uncompromising thought.'

But Li Shai Tung was shaking his head. 'No, Yuan. We are not what he created. We are our own men.' He paused, staring at his son, trying to understand what he was feeling at that moment, recollecting what he himself had felt. But it was difficult. He had been much older when he had learned the truth of things.

'It is true, Yuan – the world we find ourselves born into is not what we would have it be in our heart of hearts, yet it is surely not so awful or evil a world as your dream would have it? True, it might limit our choices, but those choices are still ours to make.'

Li Yuan looked up. 'Then why do we keep the truth from them? What are we afraid of? That it might make them think other than we wish them to think? That they might make other choices than the ones we wish them to make?'

The T'ang nodded, firelight and shadow halving his face from brow to chin. 'Perhaps. You know the saying, Yuan. To shuo hua pu ju shao.'

Li Yuan shivered, thinking of the moonlight on the garden. He knew the saying: Speech is silver, silence is golden. Sun and moon again. Silver and gold. 'Maybe so,' he said, yet it seemed more convenient than true.

'In time, Yuan, you will see it more clearly. The shock, I know, is great. But do not let the power of your dream misguide you. It was, when all's considered, only a dream.'

Only a dream. Li Yuan looked up, meeting his father's eyes again. 'Maybe so. But tell me this, father, are we good or evil men?'

★

Chen looked up from where he was sitting on the stool outside the equipment barn to see whose shadow had fallen across him.

'Do I know you?'

The three Han had ugly, vicious expressions on their faces. Two of them were holding thick staves threateningly in both hands. The third – the one whose shadow had fallen across him – brandished a knife. They were dressed in the same drab brown as himself.

'Ah...' Chen said, seeing the likeness in their faces. So the thief had brothers. He got up slowly. 'You have a score to settle?'

The momentary smile on the eldest brother's face turned quickly to a scowl of hatred. Chen could see how tense the man was and nervous, but also how determined.

Chen let the hoe he had been repairing drop, then stood there, empty-handed, facing the man, watching him carefully now, knowing how dangerous he was. A careless, boastful man would often talk too much or betray himself into ill-considered movements, but these three were still and silent. They had not come to talk, or to impress him. They had come for one thing only. To kill him.

He glanced across and saw, in the distance, outlined against the lip of the irrigation dyke, the Overseer's man, Teng. So. That was how they knew. He looked back, weighing the three up, letting his thoughts grow still, his breathing normalize. His pulse was high, but that was good. It was a sign that his body was preparing itself for the fight to come.

'Your brother was a thief,' he said, moving to his right, away from the stool, putting the sun to one side of him.

The eldest made a sound of disgust.

Yes, thought Chen, *I understand you. And maybe another time, in different circumstances, I'd have let you kill me for what I've done. But there are more important things just now. Like DeVore. Though you'd not understand that, would you?*

Chen saw the man's movement a fraction of a second before he made it, the sudden action betrayed by a tensing of the muscles, a slight movement in his eyes. Chen bunched his fist and knocked the big knife aside, then followed through with a kick to the man's stomach that left him on his knees, badly winded.

The other two yelled and charged him, their staves raised.

Chen moved quickly to one side, making them wheel about, one of the brothers momentarily hidden behind the other. Taking his opportunity, Chen ducked and moved inside the stave's wild swing, his forearm lifting the man's chin and hurling him back into his brother.

At once Chen was standing over them, kicking, punching down at them, his breath hissing from him sharply with each blow, until the two men lay there, unconscious.

The eldest had rolled over, groaning, still gasping for his breath. As Chen turned, facing him again, his eyes widened with fear and he made to crawl away. But Chen simply stood there, his hands on his hips, getting his breath, and shook his head.

'I'm sorry. I did what I had to do. Do you understand me? I have no quarrel with you. But if you come again – if *any* of you come again – I will kill you all.'

Chen bowed then walked back to the barn, picking up the hoe. Only then did he see Pavel, watching from the doorway.

'You saw, then, Pavel?'

The young man's eyes were wide with astonishment. 'I saw, *Shih Tong*, but I'm not sure I believe what I saw. I thought they'd kill you.'

Chen smiled. 'Yes. And so did Teng. I must deal with him, before he can tell others.'

Pavel's eyes narrowed, then, as if he had made up his mind about something, he took Chen's arm and began to turn him about.

Chen shook him off. 'What are you doing?'

Pavel stared at him. 'You said you must deal with Teng. Well, he's gone already. As soon as he saw what you could do. If you want to catch him you had best come with me. I know a quicker way.'

Chen laughed. 'A quicker way?'

Pavel grabbed his arm again. 'Yes. Now don't argue with me. Come on! We'll cut the bastard off.'

At the lip of the dyke, Pavel didn't stop but went over the top and down. Chen followed, splashing through the shallow water, then following Pavel up the other bank, pulling himself up a rough, indented ladder which had been cut into the side of the dyke.

'Teng will go by the bridges,' Pavel explained breathlessly as they ran across the field towards the intersection. 'He won't want to get his uniform muddy. But that means he has to go along and across. We, however, can go diagonally. We can catch him at the fourth west bridge.'

'Where's Chang Yan?' Chen asked, not slowing his pace. 'I thought those two bastards were inseparable!'

'Chang Yan's on leave in Lodz. Which is where Teng should be. But it looks like he wanted to see the outcome of his trouble-making before he went.'

Yes, thought Chen. *But DeVore's behind it. I knew it. I felt he was up to something the other evening.*

The fourth west bridge consisted of four long, thick planks of wood, embedded into the earth on either side of the irrigation canal. Chen waited, hidden among the man-tall stand of super-wheat to one side of the path, while Pavel stayed down below, in the water beneath the bridge.

Teng was wheezing when he came to the bridge. He slowed and wiped his brow, then came out onto the wooden planking.

'Teng Fu,' said Chen, stepping out onto the pathway. 'How fortunate to meet you here.'

Teng blinked furiously, then turned, looking about him. The sun was low now. The fields on every side were empty.

He turned back, facing Chen, slipping the rifle from his shoulder and holding it out before him threateningly. But it was clear he was shaken.

'Get out of my way, Tong Chou! I'll kill you if you don't!'

Chen laughed scornfully. 'It's Chen, by the way. Kao Chen. But that aside, why should I move? You've seen too much, Teng. If I let you go, you'll say what you've seen, and I can't have that. Anyway, it was you set those poor bastards onto me, wasn't it? You who told them. Well... this will be for them. And for their brother. Oh, and for Pavel, too.'

Teng turned too late. Pavel had climbed the bank and come up behind him. As the Overseer's man turned, hearing someone behind him, Pavel launched himself forward and pushed. Teng fell awkwardly, going headlong into the shallow stream, the gun falling away from him.

Chen ran forward, then jumped from the bridge into the water. Pavel followed him a fraction of a second later.

Teng rolled over, lifting his head from the water, spluttering, his eyes wide with surprise, only to find himself thrust down again. He was a big man and struggled hard, straining with his arms and neck to free himself, his feet kicking desperately beneath him, but the two men gritted their teeth and held him down beneath the water until, after one final, violent spasm of activity, Teng's body went limp.

Pavel shuddered, then stood up in the water, looking down at what he had done.

'Gods…' he said softly. 'We've killed him.'

'Yes,' said Chen, steeling himself, recognizing the pain in the young man's twisted face. Oh, Pavel had hated him beforehand – had hated him even enough to kill him – but now that it was done the boy saw Teng clearer, as another man. A man he had robbed of life. 'Come on,' he said, getting to his feet. 'We have to hide the body.'

For a moment Pavel just stared at the lifeless body that now floated, face down, in the shallow water; then he seemed to come to himself. He swallowed deeply, then looked back at Chen. 'What?'

'We have to hide the body,' Chen repeated, careful to be gentle with the boy. 'Do you know a place, Pavel?'

The light was failing fast. They would not be missed at once, but if they delayed too long…

Pavel shivered again, then nodded. 'Yes. There's a place. Farther along.'

They towed the heavy body between them, pulling it by its arms, moving as quickly as they could against the resistance of the water, until they came to a place where the reeds on one side of the canal threatened to spill right across and block the stream. There Pavel halted.

'Here,' he said, indicating a vague patch of darkness against the bank.

Chen heaved the body round, then, with Pavel's help, moved it in amongst the tall reeds. There, behind the cover of the reeds, a small cave had been carved out of the bank. Inside, it was curiously dry. Small niches, like tiny, primitive ovens, had been cut into the walls on either side. Pavel turned and reached into one. A moment later, Chen saw the flicker of a flint.

Pavel turned, a lighted candle in his hand, and looked down at the body floating there between them.

'I don't like it, but it's the only place.'

Chen looked about him, astonished. The walls were painted, red and green and yellow, the openings lined with coloured tiles. Tiny statues were placed in each of the niches, about which were placed small pieces of paper and the remains of tiny finger candles. It was a shrine. A secret shrine.

'Kuan Yin preserve us!'

Pavel nodded vehemently, then let out another shuddering breath. 'How will we anchor him?'

Chen looked about him, then hit upon the best solution. 'We'll lift him up. Jam his head and shoulders into one of the niches. That should hold him long enough for us to decide what to do with him.'

Pavel looked at him, wide-eyed, then swallowed again.

'What *are* you, Kao Chen? What are you doing here?'

Chen looked down, then decided to tell Pavel the truth. It was that now or kill him, and he didn't think he *could* kill the boy, even to get DeVore.

'What I am doesn't really matter. But I'm here to get Overseer Bergson. To trap him and bring him to justice. Will you help me, Pavel? Will you help me get the bastard?'

Pavel looked again at the body of the man he had helped to kill, then looked up at Chen again, the candle wavering in his hand, throwing shadows about the tiny space. He smiled and offered his hand. 'Okay, Kao Chen. I'll help you.'

Karr stood at the window, looking down at the vast apron of Nanking spaceport, then turned, smiling. 'Well, General, it seems we must play our final card.'

The old man nodded, returning Karr's smile openly. 'So it seems. Unless they change their minds. You're prepared?'

'I know what I have to do.'

'Good.' Tolonen went across and stood beside Karr, then, unexpectedly, embraced him. He did not expect to see the big man again.

Karr held Tolonen's upper arms a moment, his smile undiminished. 'Don't be sad, General. Remember what you said to me. I'm a winner.'

Tolonen sighed, then smiled. 'I hope it's so, my friend. Never more than now.'

Karr turned his head, looking outward again, watching a craft rise slowly on the far side of the field. The noise reached them a moment later – a deep, rumbling reverberation that went down the register.

'You know, General. I'd love to see their faces. Especially DeVore's.' He paused, then, on another track, added. 'Chen has his back-up?'

'Of course. The best I could arrange.'

Karr turned back. 'That's good.' He went across and took something from the top of his pack and brought it back across, handing it to Tolonen.

'What's this?'

'For Chen. Just in case.'

Tolonen laughed. 'So you are human, after all. I was beginning to wonder.'

'Oh, yes,' Karr answered, his smile fading momentarily. 'And I'll tell you this, General. What I'm about to do frightens me. More than anything I've ever done before. But I'll do it. Or die trying.'

Tolonen looked at him, admiring him, then bowed his head respectfully.

'Good luck. And may heaven favour you, Gregor Karr.'

The journey to Tongjiang took Tolonen an hour. Li Shai Tung was waiting for him in his study, the authority on the desk beside him, signed and witnessed – the seven tiny *Ywe Lung* seals imprinted into the wax in the whiteness on the left-hand side of the document.

'Your man is on his way, Knut?' the T'ang asked, handing Tolonen the parchment, then waving away his secretary.

'He is, *Chieh Hsia*. We should know by tomorrow evening how things stand.'

'And the other matter? The business with DeVore?'

Tolonen smiled. 'That will be settled sooner, *Chieh Hsia*. The agent concerned, Kao Chen, passed vital evidence back through channels yesterday. It has been verified that the suspect, Overseer Bergson is, in reality, the traitor, DeVore.'

'Have we arrested the man?'

'I have arranged things already, *Chieh Hsia*. We will capture the man this evening. Within the next few hours, in fact.'

'Good. That, at least, eases my mind.' The T'ang sniffed, his expression grave, then got up slowly from his desk. 'A great storm is coming, Knut, and we shall have made enemies enough before it blows itself out. DeVore is one I'd rather have in hand, not loose and making mischief for us.'

Yes, thought Tolonen. *And Berdichev, too. But that would have to wait a day or two. Until after Karr had done his stuff.* He looked down at the document in his hands, feeling a great sense of pride at being at the centre of things this night. He had foreseen this long ago, of course. Had known the day would come when the Seven could no longer sit on their hands and do nothing.

Now they would shake Chung Kuo to its roots. Shake it hard, as it needed to be shaken.

Tolonen smiled and then bowed to his T'ang, acknowledging his dismissal; feeling a deep satisfaction at the way things had gone. The days of *wuwei* – of passive acceptance – were past. The dragon had woken and had bared its claws.

And now it would strike, its seven heads raised, magnificent, like tigers, making the *hsiao jen* – the little men – scuttle to their holes and hide, like the vermin that they were.

Yes. They would clean the world of them. And then? His smile broadened. *Then summer would come again.*

Li Shai Tung sat at his desk, brooding. What had he done? What was set in motion? He shuddered, disturbed by the implications of his actions.

What if it cracked Chung Kuo itself apart? It was possible. Things were balanced delicately now. Worse, what if it brought it all tumbling down – levelling the levels?

He laughed sourly, then turned at a sound. It was Li Yuan. He was standing in the doorway, his shoes removed, awaiting his father's permission to enter. Li Shai Tung nodded and beckoned his son to him.

'Bitter laughter, father. Is there something wrong?'

Too wise. Too young to be so old and knowing.

'Nothing. Just a play of words.'

Li Yuan bowed, then turned away slightly: a gesture of indirectness his father could read perfectly. It was something difficult. A request of some kind. But awkward. Not easy to ask. Li Shai Tung waited, wondering how Li Yuan would breach the matter. It was an opportunity to study his son: to assess his strengths, his weaknesses.

'I've been much troubled, father.'

Li Yuan had looked up before he spoke. A direct, almost defiant look. He had resolved the matter and chosen to present it with firmness and authority. *Yes*, the old man thought, *Li Yuan would make a fine T'ang. When it was time.*

'Is it your dream again, Yuan?'

Li Yuan hesitated, then shook his head.

'Then tell me what it is.'

He stood and went across to the pool, then stood there, looking down at the dim shapes moving in the depths of the water, waiting for his son to join him there.

Unexpectedly, Li Yuan came right up to him, then went down onto his knees at his feet, his eyes fixed upon the floor as he made his request.

'I want to ask your permission to marry, father.'

Li Shai Tung turned sharply, surprised, then laughed and bent down, lifting Li Yuan's face, his hand cupping his son's chin, making him look up at him.

'But you're only twelve, Yuan! There's more than enough time to think of such matters. A good four years or more. I never meant for you to...'

'I know, father. But I already know what I want. Who I want.'

There was such certainty, such fierce certainty in the words, that the T'ang released his hold and stepped back, his hand stroking his plaited beard thoughtfully. 'Go on,' he said. 'Tell me who it is.'

Li Yuan took a deep breath, then answered him. 'Fei Yen. I want Fei Yen.'

Li Shai Tung stared at his son in disbelief. 'Impossible! She was Han's wife, Yuan. You know the law.'

The boy's eyes stared back at him intently. 'Yes, and by our law Fei Yen was never Han Ch'in's wife.'

Li Shai Tung laughed, amazed. 'How so, when the seals of Yin Tsu and I are on the marriage contract? Have you left your senses, Yuan? Of course she was Han's wife!'

But Li Yuan was insistent. 'The documents were nullified with Han's death. Think, father! What does our law actually say? That a marriage is not a marriage until it has been consummated. Well, Han Ch'in and Fei Yen...'

'Enough!' The T'ang's roar took Li Yuan by surprise. 'This is wrong, Li Yuan. Even to talk of it like this...'

He shook his head sadly. It was not done. It simply was not done. Not only was she too old for him, she was his brother's bride.

'No, Yuan. She isn't right for you.'

'Fei Yen, father. I know who I want.'

Again that intensity of tone, that certainty. Such certainty impressed Li Shai Tung, despite himself. He looked down into the pool again.

'You could not marry her for four years at the least, Yuan. You'll change your mind. See if you don't! No, find some other girl to be your bride. Don't rush into this foolishness!'

Li Yuan shook his head. 'It's her I want. I've known it since Han Ch'in was killed. And she'll take me. I know she will.'

Li Shai Tung smiled bitterly. What use was such knowledge? In four years Chung Kuo would have changed. Perhaps beyond recognition. Li Yuan did not know what was to be: what had been decided. Even so, he saw how determined his son was in this matter and relented.

'All right. I will talk to her parents, Yuan. But I promise you no more than that for now.'

It seemed enough. Li Yuan smiled broadly and reached out to take and kiss his father's hand. 'Thank you, father. Thank you. I shall make her a good husband.'

When Yuan had gone, he stood there, staring down into the darkness of the water, watching the carp move slowly in the depths, like thought itself. Then, when he felt himself at rest again, he went back into his study, relaxed, resigned almost to what was to come.

Let the sky fall, he thought: *What can I, a single man, do against fate?*

Nothing, came the answer. For the die had been cast. Already it was out of their hands.

Bamboo. A three-quarter moon. Bright water. The sweet, high notes of an *erhu*. Chen looked about himself, at ease, enjoying the warmth of the evening. Pavel brought him a beer and he took a sip from it, then looked across at the dancers, seeing how their faces shone, their dark eyes laughed brightly in the fire's light. At a bench to one side sat the bride and groom, red-faced and laughing, listening to the friendly banter of their fellow peasants.

Two great fires had been built in the grassy square formed by the three long dormitory huts. Benches had been set up on all sides and, at one end, a temporary kitchen. Close by, a four-piece band had set up their instruments on the tail-piece of an electric hay wagon: *yueh ch'in, ti tsu, erhu* and *p'i p'a* – the ancient mix of strings and flutes enchanting on the warm night air.

There were people everywhere, young and old, packing the benches, crowded about the kitchen, dancing or simply standing about in groups, smoking clay pipes and talking. Hundreds of people, maybe a thousand or more in all.

He turned, looking at Pavel. 'Is it true, Pavel? Have you no girl?'

Pavel looked down, then drained his jug. 'No one here, Kao Chen,' he answered softly, leaning towards him as he spoke.

'Then why not come back with me? There are girls in the levels would jump at you.'

Pavel shivered, then shook his head. 'You are kind, my friend. But...' He tilted his shoulder slightly, indicating his bent back. 'T'o they call me here. What girl would want such a man?'

'T'o?'

Pavel laughed, for a moment his twisted face attractive. 'Camel-backed.'

Chen frowned, not understanding.

'It was an animal, so I'm told. Before the City.'

'Ah...' Chen looked past the young man, watching the dancers a moment. Then he looked back. 'You could buy a bride. I would give you the means...'

Pavel's voice cut into his words. 'I thank you, Kao Chen, but...' He looked up, his dark eyes strangely pained. 'It's not that, you see. Or not only that. It's just... well, I think I would die in there. No fields. No open air. No wind. No running water. No sun. No moon. No changing seasons. Nothing. Nothing but walls.'

The young man's unconscious echo of DeVore's words made Chen shiver and look away. Yet perhaps the boy was right. He looked back at the dancers circling the fires and nodded to himself. For the first time since he had been amongst them, Chen had seen the shadow lift from them and knew how different they were from his first conception of them. He saw how happy they could be. So simple it was. It took so little to make them happy.

He stared about him, fascinated. When they danced, they danced with such fiery abandon, as if released from themselves – no longer drab and brown and faceless, but huge and colourful, overbrimming with their own vitality, their coal dark eyes burning in their round, peasant faces, their feet pounding the bare earth carelessly, their arms waving wildly, their bodies twirling lightly through the air as they made their way about the fire.

As if they were enchanted.

He shivered, wishing that Wang Ti were there with him, partnering him in the dance; then with him in the darkness afterwards, her breath sweet with wine, her body opening to him.

He sighed and looked down into his jug, seeing the moon reflected there in the dark, sour liquid. In an hour it would begin. And afterwards he would be gone from here. Maybe forever.

The thought sobered him. He took a large swallow of the beer, then wiped his mouth and turned to face Pavel again. 'You're right. Stay here, Pavel. Find yourself a girl. Work hard and get on.' He smiled, liking the young man. 'Things will be much better here when Bergson is gone.'

Yes, he thought, *and maybe one day I'll come back, and bring Wang Ti with me, and Jyan and the new child. They'd like it here. I know they would.*

He saw Pavel was watching him and laughed. 'What is it, boy?'

Pavel looked down. 'You think life's simple here, don't you? But let me tell you about my birth.'

'Go on,' said Chen softly, noting the sudden change in him. It was as if Pavel had shed a mask. As if the experience they had shared, beneath the fourth west bridge, had pared a skin from the young man, making him suddenly more vulnerable, more open.

'I had a hard childhood,' he began. 'I was born the fifth child of two casual workers. Hirelings – like yourself – who come on the land only at harvest time. During the harvest things were fine. They could feed me. But when it was time to go back to the City, they left me here in the fields to die. Back in the levels they could not afford me, you understand. It is often so, even today. People here accept it as the way. Some say the new seed must be fertilized with the bones of young children. I, however, did not die.'

Pavel licked at his lips, then carried on, his downcast eyes staring back into the past.

'Oh, I had nothing to do with it. *Mei fa tzu,* they say. It is fate. And my fate was to be found by a childless woman and taken in. I was lucky. She was a good woman. A Han. Chang Lu was her name. For a time things were good. Her man, Wen, never took to me, but at least he didn't beat me or mistreat me, and she loved me as her own. But when I was seven they died. A dyke collapsed on top of them while they were repairing it. And I was left alone.'

Pavel was silent a moment, then he looked up, a sad smile lighting his face briefly.

'I missed her bitterly. But bitterness does not fill the belly. I had to work, and work hard. There is never quite enough, you see. Each family takes care of its own. But I had no family. And so I strove from dawn until dusk each day, carrying heavy loads out into the fields, the long, thick carrying pole pressing down on my shoulders, bending my back until I became as you see me now.' He gave a short laugh. 'It was necessity that shaped me thus, you might say, Kao Chen. Necessity and the dark earth of Chung Kuo.'

'I'm sorry,' Chen began. 'I didn't know...' But Pavel interrupted him once more.

'There's something else.' The young man hesitated, then shivered and went on. 'It's the way you look at us, Kao Chen. I noticed it before. But now I think I understand. It's like we're a dream to you, isn't it? Not quite real. Something picturesque...'

Chen was about to say no, to tell the boy that it was just the opposite – that all of this was real, and all the rest, inside, no more than a hideous dream to which he must return – but Pavel was looking at him strangely, shaking his head; denying him before he had begun.

'Maybe,' he said finally, setting his jug down. But he still meant no. He had only to close his eyes and feel the movement of the air on his cheeks...

'You came at the best time,' Pavel said, looking away from him, back towards the dancers. 'Just now the air smells sweet and the evenings are warm. But the winters are hard here. And the stench sometimes...'

He glanced back at Chen then laughed, seeing incomprehension there.

'What do you think the City does with all its waste?'

Chen sipped at his beer, then shrugged. 'I'd never thought...'

Pavel turned, facing him again. 'No. No one ever does. But think of it. Over thirty billion, they say. So much shit. What do they do with it?'

Chen saw what he was saying and began to laugh. 'You mean... ?'

Pavel nodded. 'They waste none of it. Its stored in vast wells and used on the fields. You should see it, Kao Chen. Vast, lake-like reservoirs of it, there are. Imagine!' He laughed strangely, then looked away. 'In a week from now the fields will be dotted with honey-carts, each with its load of sweet dark liquid to deposit on the land. Black gold, they call it. Without it the crop would fail and Chung Kuo itself would fall.'

'I always thought...'

Chen stopped and looked across. The dull murmur of talk had fallen off abruptly; the music faltered and then died. He searched among the figures, suddenly alert, then saw them. Guards! The Overseer's guards were in the square!

Pavel had turned and was staring at him, fear blazing in his eyes. 'It's Teng!' he said softly. 'They must have found Teng!'

'No...' Chen shook his head and reached out to touch the young man's arm to calm him. No, not Teng. But maybe something worse.

The guards came through, then stood there in a rough line behind their leader, a tall *Hung Mao*.

'Who's that?' whispered Chen.

'That's Peskova. He's Bergson's lieutenant.'

'Gods... I wonder what he wants?'

It was quiet now. Only the crackle of the fires broke the silence. Peskova looked about him, then took a handset from his tunic pocket, pressed for display and began to read from it.

'By the order of Overseer Bergson, I have a warrant for the arrest of the following men...'

Chen saw the guards begin to fan out amongst the peasants, pushing through the crowd roughly, their guns in front of them, searching for the faces of those Peskova was naming, and wondered whether he should run, taking his chance. But as the list of names went on, he realized Tong Chou was not amongst them.

'What's going on?' he asked Pavel.

'I don't know. But they all seem to be friends of Field Supervisor Sung and his wife. Maybe they forced him to make a list before they killed him.'

Chen watched the guards gather the fifteen named men together and begin to lead them away, then looked about him, realizing how quickly the shadow had fallen once again.

'An hour,' he said softly, more to himself than to Pavel. 'If they can only wait an hour.'

The bodies lay heaped up against the wall. They were naked and lay as they had fallen. Some still seemed to climb the barrier of stone, their bodies stretched and twisted, their limbs contorted. Others had knelt, bowing to their murderers, facing the inevitability of death. Chen looked about him, sickened by the sight. Pavel stood beside him, breathing noisily. 'Why?' he asked after a moment. 'In the gods' names, why? What had they done?'

Chen turned and looked to his left. The moon was high, a half-moon part obscured by cloud. Beneath it, like the jagged shadow of a knife, the Overseer's House rose from the great plain. *Where are you?* thought Chen, searching the sky. *Where the fuck are you?* It was so unlike Karr.

It was two hours since the arrests. Two hours and still no sign of them. But even if they had come a half hour early it would have been too late to save these men. All fifteen were dead. They had all heard it, standing there about the guttering fires. Heard the shots ring out across the fields. Heard the screams and then the awful silence afterwards.

'Peskova,' Pavel said, bending down and gently touching the arm of one of the dead men. 'It was Peskova. He always hated us.'

Chen turned back, staring down at the boy, surprised, realizing what he was saying. Pavel thought of himself as Han. When he said 'us' he didn't mean the peasants, the *ko* who worked the great ten thousand *mou* squares, but the Han. *Yes,* he thought, *but DeVore is the hand behind this. It was he who gave permission. And I will kill him. T'ang's orders or no, I will kill him now for what he's done.*

He looked back. There was a shadow against the moon. As he watched it passed, followed a moment later by a second.

'Quickly, Pavel,' he said, hurrying forward. 'They've come.'

The four big Security transporters set down almost silently in the fields surrounding the Overseer's House. Chen ran to greet the nearest of them, expecting Karr, but it wasn't the big man who jumped down from the strut, it was Hans Ebert.

'Captain Ebert,' he said, bowing, bringing his hand up to his chest in salute, the movement awkward, unpractised. Ebert, the 'Hero of Hammerfest' and heir to the giant GenSyn corporation, was the last officer Chen had expected.

'Kao Chen,' Ebert answered him in a crisp, businesslike fashion, ignoring the fact of Chen's rank. 'Are they all inside the house?'

Chen nodded, letting the insult pass. 'As far as I know, sir. The Overseer's craft is still on the landing pad, so I assume DeVore is in there.'

Ebert stared across the fields towards the house, then turned back to him, looking him up and down. He gave a short, mocking laugh. 'The costume suits you, Kao Chen. You should become a peasant!'

'Sir!' He tried to keep the sourness from his voice, but it was hard. He knew instinctively that Ebert was the reason for the delay. He could imagine him waiting until he had finished dining. Or whoring, maybe. He had heard such tales of him. Karr would never have done that. Karr would have been there when he'd said.

Men jumped down from the craft behind Ebert. Special unit guards, their hands and faces blacked up. One of them came over to Ebert and handed him a clipboard.

Chen recognized him from the old newscasts about the Hammerfest massacre. It was Ebert's chief lieutenant, Auden.

Ebert studied the board a moment, then looked up at Chen again. 'You know the layout of the Overseer's House?'

Chen bowed his head. 'I do, sir.'

'Good. Then you can play scout for us, Kao Chen. Auden here will be in command, but you'll take them in, understand?'

Chen kept his head lowered. 'Forgive me, Captain, but I am unarmed.'

'Of course...' Ebert reached down and drew the ten-shot handgun from his holster. 'Here.'

Chen took the weapon and stared at it in disbelief. 'Forgive me, sir. But they've automatics and lasers in there.'

Ebert was looking at him coldly. 'It's all you'll need.'

Chen hesitated, wondering how far to push it, when Ebert barked at him.

'Are you refusing my orders, Kao Chen?'

In answer, Chen bowed to the waist, then turned to Auden. 'Come. We'd best move quickly now.'

Halfway across the field a figure came towards them. Auden stopped, raising his gun, but Chen put a hand out to stop him.

'It's all right,' he said urgently. 'I know him. He's a friend.'

Auden lowered his gun. The figure came on, until he stood only a few paces from them. It was Pavel.

'What do you want?' Chen asked.

'I want to come with you.'

He had found himself a hoe and held it tightly. There was anger in his twisted face. Anger and an awful, urgent need.

'No,' said Chen after a moment. 'It's too dangerous.'

'I know. But I want to.'

Chen turned and looked at Auden, who shrugged. 'It's his neck, Lieutenant Kao. He can do what he likes. But if he gets in our way we'll shoot him, understand?'

Chen looked back at Pavel. The young man smiled fiercely, then nodded. 'Okay. I understand.'

'Good,' said Auden. 'Then let's get into position. The other squad is going in five minutes from now.'

They waited in the shadows at the bottom of the ramp, the main door to the house above them. The windows of the house were dark, as if the men inside were asleep, but Chen, crouched there, staring up at the great three-tiered pagoda, knew they would be awake, celebrating the night's events. He watched the vague shadows of the assault troops climbing the ropes high overhead, nursing his anger, knowing it would not be long now.

Pavel was crouched beside him in the darkness. Chen turned and whispered to him. 'Keep close to me, Pavel. And don't take risks. They're killers.'

Pavel's mouth sought his ear. 'I know.'

They waited. Then, suddenly, the silence was broken. With a loud crash the assault troops swung through the windows of the second tier. It was the signal to go in. Chen leapt up onto the ramp and began to run toward the door, his handgun drawn, Pavel, Auden and his squad close behind.

He was only ten ch'i or so from the door when it slid back suddenly, spilling light.

'Down!' he yelled as the figure in the doorway opened fire. But it was only a moment before the man fell back, answering fire from behind Chen ripping through his chest.

There were shouts from within, then two more men appeared, their automatics stuttering. Chen watched them fall, then scrambled up and ran for the door.

He stood in the doorway, searching the first room at a glance, the handgun following each movement of his eyes. As he'd thought, the three men had been the duty squad. Close by the door a table had been upset and mah jong tiles lay scattered about the floor. He stepped over the dead man and went inside.

Up above there was the sound of further shots, then a burst of automatic fire. Chen turned, nodding to Auden as the veteran came into the room, pleased to see Pavel, unharmed, behind him in the doorway.

'They'll defend the stairwell,' Chen said quietly, pointing to the door at the far end of the room. 'There's a second guardpost at the top, then DeVore's offices beyond that.'

'Right.' Auden went across and stood by the doorway, forming his squad up either side of it. He tried the door. It was unlocked.

Chen took Pavel's arm. 'Here,' he said, drawing him aside. 'Let them do this. It's what they're trained for.'

Pavel stared back at him. 'And you, Kao Chen? You're one of them? A lieutenant?'

Chen nodded, then turned in time to see Auden tug the door aside and crouch there, the big automatic blazing in his lap.

The noise was deafening. There was a moment's silence, then four of the squad moved past him, climbing the stairs quickly. But they were only halfway up when the firing began again, this time from above.

Chen started forward, but Auden was already in charge. He was climbing the stairs over his fallen men, his gun firing ceaselessly, picking off anything that dared show itself up above.

Chen went up after him. Two of the Overseer's men had been guarding the stairs. One lay to one side, dead. The other was slumped over a makeshift barrier, badly wounded. Auden took a new clip from his band and fitted it in the gun, then tugged the man's head back and looked across at Chen. 'Who is he? Is he important?'

Chen shrugged, not recognizing the Han, then said. 'No... he's only a guard.'

Auden nodded, then put his gun to the man's head and pulled the trigger savagely. 'Come on,' he said, letting the body fall away.

He was about to turn, when the door behind him burst open.

Chen opened up without thinking, firing off three shots rapidly, the big handgun kicking violently.

The man looked at him wide-eyed, as if surprised, then fell to his knees, clutching his ruined chest, his gun falling away from him. He toppled forward and lay still.

Auden looked at Chen strangely. 'Thanks,' he said coldly, almost brutally. Then he turned and went through the door, the big gun chattering deafeningly in his hands.

Chen followed him through, into DeVore's office.

The place was a mess. The *wei chi* board was broken, the stones scattered over the floor. The bank of screens had been smashed, as if in a drunken orgy. He frowned, not understanding. Auden couldn't have made all of this mess. It was too thorough. Too all inclusive. It had the look of systematic destruction.

And where was DeVore?

One man lay dead beneath the screens. Two others were kneeling in the far corner of the room, their weapons discarded, their brows pressed to the floor in a gesture of submission. Auden glanced at them dismissively, then waved one of his men over to bind them and take them away. Pavel had come into the room. As the captives passed him, the young man leaned close and spat into their faces.

'For Supervisor Sung,' he said, his voice hard, bitter.

Chen watched him a moment, then turned to Auden. 'Something's wrong,' he said, indicating the screens, the broken board.

Auden looked back at him. 'What do you mean?'

Chen looked about him, uncertain. 'I don't know. It's just...'

Auden turned away, impatient. 'Come on, Kao Chen. No more foolishness. Let's finish the job.'

Chen stared at him a moment, angered, then did as he was bid. *But there is something wrong*, he thought. *The killings in the field. The broken screens. They mean something.*

In the corridor outside Auden had stopped and was talking to the sergeant from the second squad.

'They're holed up at the top of the house, sir,' the sergeant was saying. 'About eight of them. Peskova's there. But not DeVore.'

'What?' Auden turned and glared at Chen. 'I thought you said...'

Chen shivered. So that was it. He'd gone already. It explained the killings, the board, the broken screens. He had known it earlier – some part of him had sensed it. But where? Where could he have gone to?

Chen turned and banged his fist against the wall, all his anger and frustration spilling out. 'Shit!'

Auden blinked, surprised, then looked back at the sergeant. 'Okay. Keep them covered, but pull most of the men back. We'll offer terms.'

He watched the sergeant go, then turned and met Chen's eyes. 'What's eating you, Kao Chen?'

Chen laughed bitterly. 'You think I wanted DeVore to get away?'

'That's if he has. We've only their word. One of those eight could be him.'

Chen shook his head. 'I doubt it. He's too good a player.'

Auden shrugged, not understanding, then went through. Chen followed.

There was a space at the foot of the narrow stairs where the corridor widened out, forming a kind of small room without doors. Two men were stationed there, guns at their shoulders, keeping the door at the top of the steps covered. It was the only way in to the upper room and the stairs themselves were too narrow for more than a single man to use at any one time.

'What have they got?' Auden asked his sergeant.

'Guns. One or two *deng* rifles, maybe. But that's all.'

'You're sure?'

'It's all they're issued with out here. These peasants never riot.'

Auden laughed. 'Lucky them!'

Waving one of the men away, he took his position on the left, half sheltered by the wall, then called out to the men above.

'My name is Lieutenant Auden of the T'ang's Security forces. As you know, you're totally surrounded by my men. Worse than that, you're in a bad situation. The Overseer, the man you knew as Bergson – his real name was DeVore. Yes, DeVore, the traitor. Which means that in helping him you too are traitors. Dead men. Understand me? But the T'ang has empowered me to make a deal with you. To be lenient. Surrender now and we deal with you lightly. If you come out, unarmed and with your arms raised where we can see them, we'll treat this whole matter as a mistake. Okay? Any tricks, however, and you're *all* dead.'

Chen crouched by the back wall, watching. He had heard the sudden murmur of voices from above at the revelation of Bergson's true identity. *So now you know,* he thought. *But what are you going to do?*

The door slid open a fraction.

'Good,' said Auden, turning to Chen. 'They're coming out...'

Chen heard the grenade bump-bump-bump down the stairs before he saw it, and threw himself to the side, his handgun clattering away from him across the floor. He tensed, fearing the worst, but instead of an explosion, there was a tiny pop and then a furious hissing.

'Gas...'

It was a riot gas; a thick, choking gas that billowed out of the split canister, spreading quickly in the tiny space. He had to get up, above it. Forgetting his gun, Chen crawled quickly on his hands and knees, his breath held, making for the stairs. But they were quicker than him.

Chen glanced up. The first of them was already halfway down the narrow stairs. He was wearing a breathing mask and held a stiletto in his right hand. Seeing Chen, his eyes narrowed and he crouched, preparing to spring. But Chen moved quickly. As he jumped, Chen rolled to the side.

The man landed next to him and turned, slashing out wildly with the knife. It flashed past Chen's face, only a hand's width from his eyes. Chen scrambled backward, cursing softly to himself.

More masked men were coming down the stairs now, spilling out into the tiny smoke-filled space, while from the two side corridors Auden's men emerged, their knives drawn, afraid to use their guns in the confusion.

Chen's man had turned, looking for him. He took a step towards Chen, his knife raised, then, with a small strangled noise, he staggered forward, collapsing to his knees. Behind him Auden smiled fiercely through his mask, then quickly turned away, rejoining the fight.

Chen's eyes were streaming now, his throat on fire. He had to get air. He dragged himself forward, making for the stairs, then stopped.

'No-o!'

Pavel was halfway up the stairs, his hoe held out before him. He turned, surprised, looking back down at Chen. 'It's Peskova!' he said hoarsely, as if that explained it all. Then his face changed and he fell forward slowly, a knife protruding from his back.

For a moment Chen struggled to get to his feet, then he fell back, a wave of blackness overwhelming him.

It seemed only a moment before he came to again, but the corridor was almost clear of gas, and five bodies lay neatly to one side. Three men sat trussed and gagged in one corner. The door at the top of the stairs was locked again, the stairway covered by the sergeant.

Chen sat up, his head pounding, then remembered.

Pavel! He mouthed the word, his heart wrenched from him.

He crawled across to where they had lain the bodies, and saw him at once.

Chen pulled the young man's body up into his arms and cradled him a moment. He was still warm. 'You silly bastard!' he moaned softly. 'You poor, silly bastard!' He shuddered and straightened up, looking across to where Auden was standing, watching him. Chen's cheeks were wet with tears, but it didn't matter. It was like losing a son, a brother. He felt a black rage sweep through him.

'What are you waiting for? You told him what would happen! All dead if they played any tricks. That's what you said.'

Auden glanced across at the stairs, then looked back at Chen. 'I've offered our friend Peaskova a new deal. He's thinking it over.'

Chen shuddered again, then looked down again. Pavel's face was ugly, his twisted features set in a final snarl of pain. Even in death he had been denied the peace that most men found. *Damn you, Pavel!* he thought, torn by the sight. *It was supposed to be a job. Just a simple infiltration job.*

He turned sharply. The door at the head of the stairs had opened slightly. A moment later there was a clattering on the steps. Chen looked. Two weapons lay there at the sergeant's feet – a rifle and a knife.

'Okay,' Peskova called down. 'I'll do what you say.'

Chen turned back, swallowing drily. His stomach had tightened to a cold, hard knot. A deal. They were going to make a deal with the bastard. He lowered Pavel gently, carefully, then turned back, looking across at Auden. But Auden had turned away. He had forgotten him already.

'All right,' Auden was saying. 'I'm coming up. Throw the door open wide, then go to the far side of the room and stay there with your hands in the air. If I see *any* movement I'll open fire. Understand me?'

'I understand.'

Chen pushed his hands together to stop them shaking, then pulled himself up onto his feet. The effort made him double up, coughing. For a moment his head swam and he almost fell, but then it cleared. He straightened up, wheezing for breath, and looked across.

Auden was halfway up the stairs now, moving slowly, cautiously, one step every few seconds, his gun tracking from side to side. Then he was at the top, framed by the doorway. Without turning, he called his sergeant up after him.

Chen stood there a moment, breathing deeply, slowly, getting his strength back. He swallowed painfully, then looked about him. Where... ? Then he saw it. There, on the floor by the wall where they had lain him. His handgun.

He went across and picked it up, then turned back, following two of Auden's men up into the top room.

Peskova stood against the back wall, his hands resting loosely on his head. He was looking across at Auden, his chin raised arrogantly, his eyes smiling cruelly, almost triumphantly, knowing he was safe.

Chen shivered and looked away, sickened by the sight of the man, barely in control of himself now. He wanted to smash that arrogant face. To wipe the smile from those coldly mocking eyes. But it was not Peskova he wanted. Not really. It was DeVore.

He lifted his head, forcing himself to look at him again. Yes. He could see the pale shadow of the man in this lesser creature. Could see the same indifference behind the eyes. A kind of absence. Nothing that a retinal print could capture, but there nonetheless. Like his master, Peskova had nothing but contempt for his fellow creatures. All he did was shaped by a cold and absolute dismissal of their separate existence. They were things for his amusement. *Things...*

Chen looked down again, the trembling in him so marked now that he had to clench his left fist again and again to control it.

Such power DeVore had. Such awful power, to cast so many in his own dark image.

'Kuan Yin! Look at this!'

The sergeant had been moving about the room, searching. In the far corner he had come across a large shape covered by a sheet. Now he turned, facing them, the colour drained from his face.

'Watch him closely!' Auden said to the man at his side, then went across to where his sergeant stood. Chen followed.

He was not sure what he'd expected, but it wasn't this. The man was stretched naked over the saddle, his hands and feet bound tightly to the stirrups. Dark smears of congealed blood coated his legs and arms and the lower part of his back, and he was split from arse to stomach.

'Gods...' Auden said softly, walking about the body. 'I'd heard of this, but I never dreamed...' He fell silent.

Chen felt the bile rise to his throat. The man's eyes bulged, but they were lifeless now. He had choked to death. Not surprisingly. His balls had been cut from him and stitched into his mouth.

'Who is this?' Auden asked, looking across at Peskova.

Peskova stared back coldly, almost defiantly. 'A guard. His name was Chang Yan. He had been stealing...'

'Stealing...' Auden made to shake his head, then turned away. 'Cover it up,' he said to his sergeant, meeting his eyes a moment, a look of disgust passing between them.

'You made a deal,' said Chen, glaring at Auden. 'Was this a part of it?'

Auden glanced at him, then turned away, moving back towards Peskova. 'I made a deal.'

Chen followed him across, something still and cold and hard growing in the depths of him.

Auden stopped, three, four paces from Peskova, looking about the room. Then he turned and looked directly at the man. There was something like a smile on his lips. 'Is that how you deal with thieves out here?'

Peskova's face had hardened. He had been worried momentarily. Now, seeing that hint of a smile, he relaxed again, misinterpreting it. His own smile widened. 'Not always.'

'So it was special?'

Peskova looked down. 'You could say that. Mind you, I'm only sorry it wasn't his friend, Teng. I would have liked to have seen that bastard beg for mercy.' He looked up again, laughing, as if it was a joke only he and Auden could share. 'These Han...'

Chen stared at him coldly. 'And Pavel? What about him? He wasn't Han...'

Peskova turned and smiled at him contemptuously. An awful, smirking smile. 'Why split hairs? Anyway, that little shit deserved what he got...'

Chen shuddered violently. Then, without thinking, he lunged forward and grabbed Peskova, forcing the man's jaw open, thrusting the handgun into his open mouth. He sensed, rather than saw, Auden move forward to stop him, but it was too late – he had already pulled the trigger.

The explosion seemed to go off in his own head. Peskova jerked back away from him, his skull shattered, his brains spattered across the wall behind like rotten fruit.

Chen stepped back, looking down at the fallen man, Then Auden had hold of him and had yanked him round roughly. 'You stupid bastard!' he shouted into his face. 'Didn't you understand? We needed him alive!'

Chen stared back at him blankly, shivering, his jaw set. 'He killed my friend.'

Auden hesitated, his face changing, then he let him go. 'Yes,' he said quietly. 'Yes.' Then, angrily, 'But we're even now, Kao Chen. Understand me? You saved my life downstairs. But this... We're even now. A life for a life.'

Chen stared at him, then looked away, disgusted. 'Even,' he said, and laughed sourly. 'Sure. It's all even now.'

Ebert was waiting for them at the bottom of the ramp.

'Well?' he demanded. 'Where is he? I'd like to see to him once more, before we send him on. He was a good officer, whatever else he's done.'

Chen looked down, astonished. A good officer!

Beside him Auden hesitated, then met his Captain's eyes. 'I'm afraid there's no sign of him, sir. We're taking the place apart now, but I don't think he's hiding in there. One of the guards says he flew off earlier this evening, but if so it wasn't in his own craft. That's still here, as Kao Chen said.'

Ebert turned on Chen, furious. 'Where the fuck is he, Chen? You were supposed to be keeping an eye on him!'

It was unfair. It also wasn't true, but Chen bowed his head anyway. 'I'm sorry...' he began, but was interrupted.

'Captain Ebert! Captain Ebert!'

It was the communications officer from Ebert's transporter.

'What is it, Hoenig?'

The young man bowed deeply, then handed him the report.

Ebert turned and looked back towards the west. There, in the distance, the sky was glowing faintly. 'Gods...' he said softly. 'Then it's true.'

'What is it, sir?' Auden asked, knowing at once that something was badly wrong.

Ebert laughed strangely, then shook his head. 'It's the Lodz garrison. It's on fire. What's more, Administrator Duchek's dead. Assassinated thirty minutes back.' Then he laughed again; a laugh of grudging admiration. 'It seems DeVore's outwitted us again.'

Fei Yen stood there in her rooms, naked behind the heavy silk screen, her maids surrounding her. Her father, Yin Tsu, stood on the other side of the screen, his high-pitched voice filled with an unusual animation. As he talked, one of Fei Yen's maids rubbed scented oils into her skin, while another dried and combed her long, dark hair. A third and fourth brought clothes for her to decide upon, hurrying back and forth, trying to please her whim.

He had called upon her unexpectedly, while she was in her bath, excited by his news, and had had to be physically dissuaded from going straight in.

'But she is my daughter!' he had complained when the maids had barred his way.

'Yes, but I am a woman now, father, not a girl!' Fei Yen had called out sweetly from within. 'Please wait. I'll not be long.'

He had begged her forgiveness, then, impatient to impart his news, had launched into his story anyhow. Li Shai Tung, it seemed, had been in touch.

'I'm almost certain it's to tell me there's an appointment at court for your eldest brother, Sung. I petitioned the T'ang more than a year ago now. But what post, I wonder? Something in the T'ang's household, do you think? Or perhaps a position in the secretariat?' He laughed nervously, then continued hurriedly. 'No. Not that. The T'ang would not bother with such trivial news. It must be a post in the ministry. Something important. A junior minister's post, at the very least. Yes. I'm almost certain of it. But tell me, Fei Yen, what do you think?'

It was strange how he always came to her when he had news. Never to Sung or Chan or her younger brother Wei. Perhaps it was because she reminded him so closely of her dead mother, to whom Yin Tsu had always confided when she was alive.

'What if it has nothing to do with Sung, father? What if it's something else?'

'Ah, no, foolish girl. Of course it will be Sung. I feel it in my bones!' He laughed. 'And then, perhaps, I can see to the question of your marriage at long last. Tuan Wu has been asking after you. He would make a good husband, Fei Yen. He comes from a good line. His uncle is the third son of the late Tuan Chung-Ho and the Tuans are a rich family.'

Fei Yen looked down, smiling to herself. Tuan Wu was a fool, a gambler and a womanizer, in no particular order. But she had no worries about Tuan Wu. Let her father ramble on – she knew why Li Shai Tung was coming to see them. Li Yuan had spoken to his father. Had done what she had thought impossible.

'I know what you're thinking, Fei Yen, but a woman should have a proper husband. Your youth is spilling from you, like sand from a glass. Soon there will be no more sand. And then?'

She laughed. 'Dearest father, what a ridiculous image!' Again she laughed and, after a moment, his laughter joined with hers.

'Whatever...' he began again, 'my mind is made up. We must talk seriously about this.'

'Of course.' Her agreement surprised him into momentary silence.

'Good. Then I shall see you in my rooms in three hours. The T'ang has asked to see us all. It might be an opportune time to discuss your re-marriage.'

When he had gone she pushed aside her maids, then hurried across the room and stood there, studying herself in the full-length dragon mirror. *Yes, she thought, you are a T'ang's wife, Fei Yen. You always were a T'ang's wife, from the day you were born.* She laughed and threw her head back, admiring her taut, full breasts, the sleekness of her thighs and stomach, the dark beauty of her eyes. Yes, and you shall have a proper husband. But not just any fool or Minor Family reprobate. My man shall be a T'ang. My son a T'ang.

She shivered, then turned from the mirror, letting her maids lead her back to her place behind the screens.

But make it soon, she thought. *Very soon.*

Karr drifted in from the darkside, the solar sail fully extended, slowing his speed as he approached. His craft was undetectable – just another piece of space junk.

They would have no warning.

Twenty *li* out he detached himself and floated in, a dark hunched shape, lost against the backdrop of space. As planned he landed on the blind spot of the huge ship, the curved layers of transparent ice beneath his boots.

He stood there a moment, enjoying the view. The moon vast and full above him, Chung Kuo far to his right and below him, the sun between, magnificent even through the visor of his suit. It surprised him how much he felt in his element, standing there on the curved hull of the starship, staring fearlessly into the furnace of creation, the void pressing in upon him. He laughed soundlessly and then ducked down, his movements slow at first as he climbed toward the airlock, then more fluent as he caught the proper rhythm.

He slowed himself with the double rail, then pushed into the semicircular depression. Beside the hexagonal door-hatch was a numbered touch-pad. He fingered the combination quickly, almost thoughtlessly, then leaned back as the hatch irised, its six segments folding back upon themselves.

As expected, there was no guard. He pulled himself inside and closed the hatch.

This part was easy. He had done it a hundred, two hundred times in simulation. He had been trained to do this thoughtlessly. But at some point he would need to act on his own: to use his discretion and react with immediacy. Until then he went by rote, knowing every inch of the huge craft as if he had built it.

The airlock filled and the inner door activated. He went through quickly, his weapon searching for targets, finding nothing, no one. But somewhere an alarm would be flashing. Unauthorized entry at airlock seven. A matter for investigation. Security would be buzzing already. There would be guards at the next junction of the corridor.

Karr removed the two heat-seeking darts from his belt and pressed a button on his suit. In seconds the ice of his suit was minus ten. He hurled the darts ahead of him and raced down the corridor after them.

Explosions punctuated the silence up ahead. The darts had found their targets. Coming to the ruined corpses he leaped over them without stopping and ran on, taking the corridor to his left and going through the two quick-irising doors before he paused and anchored himself to the ceiling, the short, securing chain attached to the back of his sturdy helmet.

He swung up and kicked. The inspection hatch moved but did not open. His second kick shifted it back and he hooked his feet through, scrambling up into the narrow space, releasing the anchor chain.

Here his size was a handicap. He turned awkwardly, putting back the hatch, knowing he had only seconds to spare.

He had cut it fine. He heard guards pass by below only a moment later, their confusion apparent. Good. It was going well.

Karr smiled, enjoying himself.

He moved quickly now, crawling along the inspection channel. Then, at the next intersection, he swung out over the space and dropped.

He landed and turned about immediately, crouching down then working his way awkwardly into a second channel. This one came out at the back of the Security desk. Timing was crucial. In a minute or so they would have guessed what he had done.

Maybe they had already and were waiting.

He shrugged and poised himself over the hatch, setting the charge. Then he went along to the second hatch. The explosion would blow a hole in the room next door to Security – a sort of recreation room. There would be no one there at present, but it would distract them while he climbed down.

He lifted the hatch cover a fraction of a second before the charge blew and was climbing down even as the guards turned below him, surprised by the explosion.

He landed on the neck of one of them and shot two others before they knew he was there amongst them. Another of the guards, panicking, helped Karr by burning two more of his colleagues.

Confusion. That too was a weapon.

Karr shot the panicking guard and rolled a smoke bomb into the corridor outside. Then he turned and blasted the Security communications desk. The screens went dead.

He waited a moment. The screens flickered into brief life, showing scenes of chaos in corridors and rooms throughout the starship, then they died again, the backups failing. The inside man had done his job.

Good, thought Karr. *Now to conclude.*

He went out into the corridor, moving fast, jumping over bodies, knocking aside confused, struggling guards. All they saw was a giant in a dark, eerily glowing suit, moving like an athlete down the corridor, unaffected by the thick, black choking smoke.

He went right and right again, then fastened himself to the inner wall of the corridor, rolling a small charge against the hull.

The spiked charge almost tore his anchorage away. He was tugged violently towards the breach. The outer skin of the starship shuddered but held, beginning to seal itself. But it had bled air badly. It was down to half an atmosphere. Debris cluttered about the sealing hole.

He released the anchor chain and ran on down the corridor, meeting no resistance. Guards lay unconscious everywhere. Many had been thrown against walls or doorways and were dead or badly wounded. It was complete chaos.

The engine was inside, in the inner shell. A breach of the hull could not affect it.

This was the difficult part. They would be expecting him now. But he had a few tricks left to show them before he was done.

He ignored the inner shell airlock and moved on to one of the ducts. It would have shut down the instant the outer hull was breached, making the inner shell airtight. Thick layers of ice were interlaced like huge fingers the length of a man's arm. Above them a laser-protected sensor registered the atmospheric pressure of the outer shell.

Karr unclipped a rectangular container from his belt and took two small packages from it. The first was a one-atmosphere 'pocket'. He fitted it over the sensor quickly, ignoring the brief, warning sting from the laser. The second of the packages he treated with a care that seemed exaggerated. It was ice-wire: a long thread of the deadly cutting material. He drew it out cautiously and pulled it taut, then swiftly used it to cut the securing bolts on each of the six sides of the duct.

The whole thing dropped a hand's length as the lasers blinked out. There was a soft exhalation of air. The sound a lift makes when it stops.

Karr waited a moment, then began cutting into the casing with small, diagonal movements that removed pieces of the ice like chunks of soft cheese. As the gap widened he cut deeper into the case and then pulled back and set the thread down.

He climbed up onto the casing and kicked. Three of the segments fell away. He eased himself down into the gap.

It was far narrower than he had anticipated and for a moment he thought he was going to be stuck. The segments had wedged against the internal mechanism of the duct at an awkward angle, leaving him barely enough room to squeeze by. He managed, just, but his right arm was trapped against the wall and he couldn't reach the device taped to his chest.

He shifted his weight and stood on tiptoe, edging about until his hand and lower arm were free, then reached up and unstrapped the bomb from his chest.

Another problem presented itself. He could not reach down and place the device against the inner casing of the duct. There was no way he could fasten it.

Did it matter? He decided that it didn't. He would strengthen the upper casing when he was out. The explosion would be forced inward.

It was such a small device. So delicate a thing. And yet so crude in its power.

He placed the bomb between his knee and the duct wall, then let it slide down between leg and wall, catching it with his foot.

He didn't want it to go up with him there.

He touched the timer with his boot and saw it glow red. Eight minutes to get out.

He began to haul himself up the sides of the duct, using brute force, legs and back braced, his thickly muscled arms straining to free himself from the tight-packed hole.

At the top he paused and looked around. What could he use? He bent down and picked up the ice-wire, then went to a nearby room and cut machinery away from the desks, then brought it back and piled it up beside the breached duct.

Three minutes thirty seconds gone. He went to the doorway and cut a huge rectangle of ice from the wall. It was thin – insubstantial almost – but strong. It weighed nothing in itself but he could pile all the heavy machinery up on top of it.

It would have to do.

There was just short of two minutes left to get out.

Time for his last trick. He ran for his life. Back the way he'd come. Without pause he pulled the last of his bombs from his belt and threw it, pressing the stud at his belt as he did so.

The outer wall exploded, then buckled inward.

Karr, his life processes suspended, was thrown out through the rent in the starship's outer skin; a dark, larval pip spat out violently.

The pip drifted out from the giant sphere, a thin trail of dust and iced air in its trail. Seconds later the outer skin rippled and then collapsed, lit from within. It shrivelled, like a ball of paper in a fire, then, with a suddenness that surprised the distant, watching eyes, lit up like a tiny sun, long arms of vivid fire burning a crown of thorns in the blackness of space.

It had been done. War had been declared.

EPILOGUE **MOSAICS**

SUMMER 2203

What is it whose closing causes the dark
and whose opening causes the light?
Where does the Bright God hide before the
Horn proclaims the dawning of the day?'
—*T'ien Wen* ('Heavenly Questions') by Ch'u Yuan,
from the Ch'u Tz'u ('Songs Of The South'),
second century BC

CHUNG KUO

A BRIDGE OVER NOTHINGNESS

And so they began, burying the dark; capping the well of memory with a stone too vast, too heavy to move. The machine watched them at their work, seeing many things their frailer, time-bound eyes were prone to miss – subtle changes of state it had come to recognize as significant. At times the full intensity of its awareness was poured into the problem of the boy, Kim. For a full second, maybe two, it thought of nothing else. Several lifetimes of normal human consciousness passed this way. And afterwards it would make a motion in its complex circuitry – unseen, unregistered on any monitoring screen – approximate to a nod of understanding.

While the two theoreticians began the job of mapping out a new mosaic – a new ideal configuration for the boy's mental state, his personality – the Builder returned to the cell and to the boy. His eyes, the small, unconscious movements of his body, revealed his unease, his uncertainty. As he administered the first of the drug treatments to the boy he could not hide the concern, the *doubt* he felt.

It watched, uncommenting, as the drugs began to have their desired effect. It saw how they systematically blocked off all pathways that led into the boy's past, noting the formulae of the drugs they used, deriving a kind of mathematical pleasure from the subtle evolving variations as they fine-tuned the process of erasure. There was an art to what they did. The machine saw this and, in its own manner, appreciated it.

It was a process of reduction different in kind from what they had attempted earlier. This time they did not seek to cower him but to strip him of every last vestige of that which made him a personality, a *being*. In long sessions on the operating table, the two theoreticians probed the boy's mind, sliding micro-thin wires into the boy's shaven skull, then administering fine dosages of chemicals, until, at last, they had achieved their end.

In developing awareness the machine had developed memory. Not memory as another machine might have defined it – that, to the conscious entity that tended these isolated decks, was merely 'storage', the bulk of things known. No, memory was something else. Its function was unpredictable. It threw up odd items of data – emphasized certain images, certain words and phrases over others. And it was inextricably bound up with the sensation of self-awareness. Indeed, it *was* self-awareness, for the one could not exist without the eccentric behaviour of the other. Yet it was also much more than the thing these humans considered memory – for the full power of the machine's ability to reason and the frighteningly encyclopaedic range of its knowledge *informed* these eccentric upwellings of words and images.

One image that it held important occurred shortly after they had completed their work and capped the well of memory in Kim. It was when the boy woke in his cell after the last of the operations. At first he lay there, his eyes open, a glistening wetness at the corner of his part-open mouth. Then, as though instinct were taking hold – some vestige of the body's remembered language of actions shaping the attempt – he tried to sit up.

It was to the next few moments that the machine returned, time and again, sifting the stored images through the most intense process of scrutiny.

The boy had lifted his head. One of his arms bent and moved, as if to support and lift his weight, but the other had been beneath him as he lay and the muscles were 'asleep'. He fell forward and lay there, chin, cheek and eye pressed close against the floor. Like that he stayed, his visible eye registering only a flicker of confusion before the pupil settled and the lid half closed. For a long time afterwards there was only blankness in that eye. A nothingness. Like the eye of a corpse, unconnected to the seeing world.

Later, when, in the midst of treatment, the boy would suddenly stop and look about him, that same look would return, followed by a moment of sheer, blind panic that would take minutes to fully subside. And though, in the months that followed, the boy grew in confidence, it was like building a bridge over nothingness. From time to time the boy would step up to the edge and look over. Then would come that look, and the machine would remember the first time it had seen it. It was the look of a machine. Of a thing without life.

They began their rehabilitation with simple exercises, training the body in new ways, new mannerisms, avoiding if they could the old patterns of behaviour. Even so, there were times when far older responses showed through. Then the boy's motor activities would be locked into a cycle of meaningless repetition – like a malfunctioning robot – until an injection of drugs brought him out of it.

For the mind they devised a set of simple but subtle games to make it learn again. At first it was resistant to these, and there were days when the team were clearly in despair, thinking they had failed. But then, almost abruptly, in mid-session, this changed. The boy began to respond again. That night the three men got drunk together in the observation room.

Progress was swift once the breakthrough was made. In three months the boy had a complete command of language again. He was numerate to a sophisticated degree, coping with complex logic problems easily. His spatial awareness was perfect: he had a strong sense of patterns and connections. It seemed then, all tests done, that the treatment had worked and the *mode* of his mind – that quick, intuitive talent unique to the boy – had emerged unscathed from the process of walling in his personality. With regard to his personality, however, he demonstrated many of the classic symptoms of incurable amnesia. In his new incarnation he was a colourless figure, uncertain in his relationships, colder, distanced from things – somehow less human than he'd been. There was a machine-like, functional aspect to him. Yet even in this respect there were signs of change – of a softening of the hard outlines of the personality they had grafted onto him.

Nine months into the programme it seemed that the gamble had paid off. When the team met that night in the observation room they agreed it was time to report back on their progress. A message was sent uplevel. Two days later they had their reply. Berdichev was coming. He wanted to see the boy.

Soren Berdichev waited at the security checkpoint, straight-backed and severe, his bodyguards to either side of him, and thought of his wife. It was more than a month now since her death, but he still had not recovered from it. The doctors had found nothing wrong with her in their autopsy report, but that meant little. They had killed her. The Seven. He didn't know how, but there was no other explanation. A healthy woman like Ylva didn't just die like that. Her heart had been strong. She had been fit – in her middle-aged prime. There had been no reason for her heart to fail.

As they passed him through he found himself going over the same ground again, no nearer than before to finding a solution. Had it been someone near to her – someone he trusted? And how had they managed it? A fast-acting drug that left no trace? Some physical means? He was no nearer now than he had been in that dreadful moment when he had discovered her. And the pain of her absence gnawed at him. He hadn't known how much he was going to miss her until she was gone. He had thought he could live without her...

The corridor ended at a second security door. It opened as he approached it and a dark-haired man with a goatee beard stood there, his hand out in welcome.

Berdichev ignored the offered hand and waited while one of his guards went through. A team of his men had checked the place out only hours before, but he was taking no chances. Administrator Jouanne had been killed only a week ago and things were heating up daily. The guard returned a moment later and gave the all-clear signal. Only then did he go inside.

The official turned and followed Berdichev into the centre of the room. 'The boy is upstairs, sir. The Builder is with him, to make introductions. Otherwise...'

Berdichev turned and cut the man off in mid-sentence. 'Bring me the Architect. I want to talk to him before I see the boy.'

The official bowed and turned away.

While he waited, he looked about him, noting the spartan austerity of the place. Employees were standing about awkwardly. He could sense the intensity of their curiosity about him, though when he looked at them they would hasten to avert their eyes. It was common knowledge that he was one of the chief opponents of the Seven, that his wife had died and that he himself was in constant danger. There was a dark glamour to all of this and he recognized it, but today his mood was sour. Perhaps seeing the boy would shake him from its grip.

The official returned with the Architect in tow. Berdichev waved the official away, then took the Architect by the arm and led him across the room, away from the others. For a moment he studied the man. Then, leaning forward, he spoke, his voice low but clear.

'How stable is the new mental configuration? How reliable?'

The Architect looked down, considering. 'We think it's firm. But it's hard to tell as yet. There's the possibility that he'll revert. Only a slender chance, but one that must be recognized.'

Berdichev nodded, at one and the same time satisfied with the man's honesty and disappointed that there was yet this area of doubt.

'But taking this possibility into consideration, is it possible to...' he pursed his lips momentarily, then said it, '... to *use* the boy?'

'Use him?' The Architect stared at him. 'How do you mean?'

'Harness his talents. Use his unique abilities. *Use* him.' Berdichev shrugged. He didn't want to be too specific.

The Architect seemed to understand. He smiled bleakly and shook his head. 'Impossible. You'd destroy him if you *used* him now.' There was a deliberate, meaningful emphasis on the word.

'How soon, then?'

'You don't understand. With respect, *Shih* Berdichev, this is only the beginning of the process. We reconstruct the house, but it has to be lived in for some time before we can discover its faults and flaws. It'll be years before we know that the treatment has worked properly.'

'Then why did you contact me?'

Berdichev frowned. He felt suddenly that he had been brought here under false pretences. When he'd received the news he had seen at once how the boy might be used. He had planned to take the boy with him, back into the Clay. And there he would have honed him; made him the perfect weapon against the Seven. The means of destroying them. The very cutting edge of knowledge.

The Architect was explaining things, but Berdichev was barely listening. He interrupted. 'Just show me the boy. I want to see him.'

The Architect led him through, the bodyguards following.

'We've moved him. His new quarters are more spacious, better equipped. Once he's settled in we'll begin the next stage.'

Berdichev glanced at the psychiatrist. 'The next stage?'

'He needs to be resocialized. Taught basic social skills. At present he has very few defences. He's vulnerable. Highly sensitive. A kind of hothouse plant. But he needs to be desensitized if he's to survive uplevel.'

Berdichev slowed. 'You mean the whole socialization programme has to be gone through from scratch?'

'Not exactly. You see, it's a different process here. A slow widening of his circle of contacts. And no chance of him mixing outside this unit until we're certain he can fit in. It'll take three years, maybe longer.'

'Three years?'

'At least.'

Berdichev stared at the man, but he hardly saw him. He was thinking of how much things would have changed in three years. On top of everything else, this was a real disappointment.

'And there's no way of hastening this?'

'None we can guarantee.'

He stood there, calculating. Was it worth risking the boy on a chance? He had gambled once and – if these men were right – had won. But did he want to risk what had been achieved?

For a moment longer he hesitated, then signalled to the Architect to move on again. He would see for himself and then decide.

Berdichev sat on a chair in the middle of the room, the boy stood in front of him, no more than an arm's length away. The child seemed calm and answered his questions without hesitating, without once glancing towards the Builder who sat away to the side of him. His eyes met Berdichev's without fear. As though he had no real conception of fear.

He was not so much like his father now. Berdichev studied the boy a long time, looking for that resemblance he had seen so clearly – so shockingly – that first time, but there was little sign of Edmund Wyatt in him now – and certainly no indication of the child he might have been. The diet of the Clay had long ago distorted the potential of the genes, refashioning his physical frame. He seemed subdued, quiet. There was little movement of his head, his hands, no sign of restlessness. Yet beyond what was seen – behind the surfaces presented to the eye – was a sense of great intensity. The same could be said of his eyes. They too were calm, reflective; yet at the back of them was a darkness that was profound, impenetrable. It was like staring into a mirror and finding the vast emptiness of space there behind the familiar, reflected image.

Now that he faced the boy he could see what the Architect had meant. The child was totally vulnerable. He had been reconstructed without defences. Like Adam, innocent, he stood there, facing, if not his Creator, then, in his new shape, his Instigator. The boy knew nothing of that. Neither did he understand the significance of this encounter. But Berdichev, studying him, came to his decision. He would leave well alone. Would let them shape the boy further. And then, in three, maybe four years' time, would come back for him. That was, if either he or the boy was still alive.

The camera turned, following Berdichev's tall, aristocratic figure as it left the room, looking for signs of the man it had heard about. For the machine Outside was a mosaic formed from the broken shards of rumour. In its isolation, it had no knowledge of the City and its ways other than what it overheard, fitting these imperfect glimpses into an ever-widening picture. When the guards talked, it listened, sifting and sorting what they said, formulating its own version of events. And when something happened in that bigger world beyond itself, it would watch the ripples spread, and form its own opinion.

Assassinations and reprisals; this seemed the pattern of the War-that-wasn't-a-War. No armies clashed. No missiles fell on innocents. The City was too complex, too tightly interwoven for such things. Yet there was darkness and deceit in plenitude. And death. Each day seemed to bring its freight of names. The mighty fallen. And in the deep, unseen levels of its consciousness, the machine saw how all of this fitted with its task here in the Unit – saw how the two things formed a whole: mosaics of violence and repression.

It watched as Berdichev stood there in the outer room, giving instructions to the Unit's Head. This was a different man from the one he had expected. Deeper, more subtle than the foolish, arrogant villain the men had drawn between them. More dangerous and, in some strange way, more *kingly* than they would have had him be.

It had seen how Berdichev had looked at the boy, as if recognizing another of his own kind. As if, amongst men, there were also levels. And this the highest; the level of Shapers and Doers – Architects and Builders not of a single mind but of the vast hive of minds that was the City. The thought recurred, and from somewhere drifted up a phrase it had often heard spoken – 'the Kings of the City'. How well the old word sat on such men, for they moved and acted as a king might. There was the shadow of power behind their smallest motion. Power and death.

It watched them all. Saw how their faces said what in words could not be uttered. Saw each small betraying detail clearly, knowing them for what they were; all desire and doubt open to its all-seeing eye. Kings and peasants all, it saw the things that shaped each one of them. Variations on a theme. The same game played at a different level, for different stakes. All this was old knowledge, but for the machine it was new. Isolated, unasked, it viewed the world outside with a knowing innocence. Saw the dark heart of things. And stored the knowledge.

When they felt it was time, they taught him about his past. Or what they knew of it. Heavily edited, they returned to him the history of the person he had been. Names, pictures and events. But not the experience.

Kim learned his lessons well. Once told he could not forget. But that was not to say they gave him back his self. The new child was a pale imitation of the old. He had not lived and suffered and dreamed. What was dark in him was hidden; was walled-off and inaccessible. In its place he had a fiction; a story learned by rote. Something to fill the gap; to assuage the feeling of emptiness that gripped him whenever he looked back.

It was fifteen months into the programme when they brought T'ai Cho to the small suite of five rooms Kim had come to know as home. Kim knew the stranger by his face; knew both his history and what he had done for him. He greeted him warmly, as duty demanded, but his eyes saw only a stranger's face. He had no real feeling for the man.

T'ai Cho cried and held the boy tightly, fiercely to him. He had been told how things were, but it was hard for him. Hard to feel the boy's hands barely touching his back when he held him. Hard to see love replaced by curiosity in those eyes. He had been warned – had steeled himself – yet his disappointment, his sense of hurt, was great nonetheless.

In a nearby room the team watched tensely, talking amongst themselves,

pleased that the boy was showing so little sign of emotion or excitement. A
camera focused on the boy's eyes, showing the smallest sign of movement
in the pupils. A monitoring unit attached to the back of the boy's neck traced
more subtle changes in the brain's activity. All seemed normal. Stable. There
was no indication that the boy had any memory of the man other than those
implanted by the team.

It was just as they'd hoped. Kim had passed the test. Now they could
progress – move on to the next stage of his treatment. The house, once
empty, had been furnished. It was time now to fill the rooms with life. Time
to test the mosaic for flaws.

In the room the man turned away from the boy and picked up his jacket
from the chair. For a moment he turned back, looking at him, hopeful to
the last that some small flicker of recognition would light those eyes with
their old familiar warmth. But there was nothing. The child he had known
was dead. Even so, he felt a kind of love for the form, the flesh, and so he
went across and held him one last time before he left. For old times' sake.
Then he turned and went, saying nothing. Finding nothing left to say.

CHUNG KUO

A GIFT OF STONES

In the Hall of the Eight Immortals, the smallest, most intimate of the eighty-one Halls in the Palace of Tongjiang, the guests had gathered for the betrothal ceremony of the young prince Li Yuan to the beautiful Fei Yen. As these events went it was only a tiny gathering; there were less than a hundred people in the lavishly decorated room – the tight circle of those who were known and trusted by the T'ang.

The room was silent now, the guests attentive as Li Shai Tung took the great seal from the cushion his Chancellor held out to him, then, both his hands taking its weight, turned to face the table. The seal – the Family 'chop', a huge square thing, more shield than simple stamp – had been inked before-hand and, as the great T'ang turned, the four Mandarin characters that quartered the seal glistened redly in the lamplight.

On the low table before him was the contract of marriage, which would link the T'ang's clan once more with that of Yin Tsu. Two servants, their shaven heads lowered, their eyes averted, held the great scroll open as the T'ang positioned the seal above the silken paper and then leaned forward, placing his full weight on the ornate handle.

Satisfied, he stepped back, letting an official lift the seal with an almost pedantic care and replace it on the cushion. For a moment he stared at the vivid imprint on the paper, remembering another day. Yin Tsu's much smaller chop lay beneath his own, the ink half-dried.

They had annulled the previous marriage earlier in the day, all seven T'ang setting their rings to the wax of the document. There had been smiles then, and celebration, but in all their hearts, he knew, there remained a degree of unease. Something unspoken lay behind every eye.

Dark Wei followed in his brother's footsteps and the Lord of You-yi was stirred against him...

The words of the 'Heavenly Questions' had kept running through his mind all morning, like a curse, darkening his mood. So it was sometimes. And though he knew the words meant nothing – that his son, Yuan, was no adulterer – still he felt wrong about this. A wife was like the clothes a man wore in life. And did one put on one's dead brother's clothes?

Han Ch'in... Had five years really passed since Han had died? He felt a twinge of pain at the memory. This was like burying his son again. For a moment he felt the darkness well up in him, threatening to mist his eyes and spoil things for his younger son. Then it passed. It was Li Yuan now. Yuan was his son, his only son, his heir. And maybe it was right that he should marry his dead brother's wife – maybe it *was* what the gods wanted.

He sniffed, then turned, smiling, to face Yin Tsu, and opened his arms, embracing the old man warmly.

'I am glad our families are to be joined again, Yin Tsu,' he said softly in his ear. 'It has grieved me that you and I had no grandson to sweeten our old age.'

As they moved apart, the T'ang saw the effect his words had had on the old man. Yin Tsu bowed deeply, torn between joy and a fierce pride, the muscles of his face struggling to keep control. His eyes were moist and his hands shook as they held the T'ang's briefly.

'I am honoured, *Chieh Hsia*. Deeply honoured.'

Behind Yin Tsu his three sons looked on, tall yet somehow colourless young men. And beside them, her eyes lowered, demure in her pink and cream silks, Fei Yen herself, her outward appearance unchanged from that day when she had stood beside Han Ch'in and spoken her vows.

Li Shai Tung studied her a moment, thoughtful. She looked so frail, so fragile, yet he had seen for himself how spirited she was. It was almost as if all the strength that should have gone into Yin Tsu's sons had been stolen – spirited away – by her. Like the thousand-year-old fox in the Ming novel, *Feng-shen Yen-I*, that took the form of the beautiful Tan Chi and bemused and misled the last of the great Shang Emperors...

He sniffed. No. These were only an old man's foolish fears – dark reflections of his anxiety at how things were. Such things were not real. Were only stories.

Li Shai Tung turned, one hand extended, and looked across at his son. 'Li Yuan... bring the presents for your future wife.'

The Shepherd boy stood apart from the others, staring up at the painting that hung between the two dragon pillars on the far side of the Hall. Li Yuan had noticed him earlier – had noted his strange separateness from every-thing – and had remarked on it to Fei Yen.

'Why don't you go across and speak to him?' she had whispered. But he had held back. Now, however, his curiosity had got the better of him. Maybe it was the sheer intensity of the boy that drew him, or some curious feeling of fellowship; a sense that – for all his father had said of Ben's aversion to it – they were meant to be companions, like Hal and his father. T'ang and Advisor. They had been bred so. And yet...

'Forgive me, General,' he said, smiling at Nocenzi, 'but I must speak with Hal's son. I have not met him before and he will be gone in an hour. If you'll excuse me.'

The circle gathered about the General bowed low as he moved away, then resumed their conversation, an added degree of urgency marking their talk now that the prince was no longer amongst them.

Li Yuan, meanwhile, made his way across the room and stopped, a pace behind the boy, almost at his shoulder, looking up past him at the painting.

'Ben?'

The boy turned his head and looked at him. 'Li Yuan...' He smiled and lowered his head the tiniest amount, more acknowledgment than bow. 'You are to be congratulated. Your future wife is beautiful.'

Li Yuan returned the smile, feeling a slight warmth at his neck. The boy's gaze was so direct, so self-contained. It made him recall what his father had told him of the boy.

'I'm glad you could come. My father tells me you are an excellent painter.'

'He does?' Again the words, like the gesture, seemed only a token; the very minimum of social response. Ben turned his head away, looking up at the painting once again, the forcefulness of his gaze making Li Yuan lift his eyes as if to try to see what Shepherd was seeing.

It was a landscape – a *shan shui* study of 'mountains and water' – by the Sung painter, Kuo Hsi. The original of his *Early Spring*, painted in 1072.

'I was watching you,' Li Yuan said. 'From across the room. I saw how you were drawn to this.'

'It's the only *living* painting here,' Ben answered, his eyes never leaving the painting. 'The rest...'

His shrug was the very symbol of dismissiveness.

'What do you mean?'

'I mean, the rest of it's dead. Mere mechanical gesture. The kind of thing a machine might produce. But this is different.'

Li Yuan looked back at Ben, studying him intently, fascinated by him. No one had ever spoken to him like this; as if it did not matter who he was. But it was not simply that there was no flattery in Ben's words, no concession to the fact that he, Li Yuan was Prince and heir; Ben seemed to have no conception of those 'levels' other men took so much for granted. Even his father, Hal, was not like this.

Li Yuan laughed, surprised; not sure whether he was pleased or otherwise. 'How is it different?'

'For a start it's aggressive. Look at the muscular shapes of those trees, the violent tumble of those rocks. There's nothing soft, nothing tame about it. The very forms are powerful. But it's more than that – the artist captured the *essence* – the very pulse of life – in all he saw.' Ben laughed shortly, then turned and looked at him. 'I've seen such trees, such rocks...'

'In your valley?'

Ben shook his head, his eyes holding Li Yuan's almost insolently. 'In my dreams.'

'*Your dreams?*'

Ben seemed about to answer, but then he smiled and looked past Li Yuan. 'Fei Yen...'

Li Yuan turned to welcome his betrothed.

She came and stood beside him, touching his arm briefly, almost tenderly. 'I see you two have found each other at last.'

'Found?' Ben said quietly. 'I don't follow you.'

Fei Yen laughed softly, the fan moving slowly in her hand. Her perfume filled the air about them. 'Li Yuan said earlier how much he wanted to speak to you.'

'I see...'

Li Yuan saw how Ben looked at her and felt a pang of jealousy. It was as if he saw her clearly, perfectly; those dark, intense eyes of his taking in everything at a glance.

What do you see? he wondered. *You seem to see so much, Ben Shepherd. Ah, but would you tell me? Would even you be that open?*

'Ben lives outside,' he said after a moment. 'In the Domain. It's a valley in the Western Island.'

'It must be beautiful,' she said, lowering her eyes. 'Like Tongjiang.'

'Oh, it is,' Ben said, his eyes very still, watching her. 'It's another world. But small. Very small. You could see it all in an afternoon.'

Then, changing tack, he smiled and turned his attention to Li Yuan again. 'I wanted to give you something, Prince Yuan. A gift of some kind. But I didn't know quite what.'

It was unexpected. Li Yuan hesitated, his mind a blank, but Fei Yen answered for him.

'Why not draw him for me?'

Ben's smile widened, as if in response to her beauty, then slowly faded from his lips. 'Why not?'

They went through to the anteroom while servants were sent to bring paper and brushes and inks, but when it arrived Ben waved the pots and brushes aside and, taking a pencil from his jacket pocket, sat at the table, pulling a piece of paper up before him.

'Where shall I sit?' Li Yuan asked, knowing from experience how much fuss was made by artists. The light, the background – everything had to be just so. 'Here, by the window? Or over here by the kang?'

Ben glanced up at him. 'There's no need. I have you. Here.' He tapped his forehead, then lowered his head again, his hand moving swiftly, decisively across the paper's surface.

Fei Yen laughed and looked at him, then, taking his hand, began to lead him away. 'We'll come back,' she said. 'When he's finished.'

But Li Yuan hesitated. 'No,' he said gently, so as not to offend her. 'I'd like to see. It interests me...'

Ben looked up again, indicating that he should come across. Again it was a strange, unexpected thing to do, for who but a T'ang would beckon a prince in that manner? And yet, for once, it seemed quite natural.

'Stand there,' Ben said. 'Out of my light. Yes. That's it.'

He watched. Saw how the figures appeared, like ghosts out of nothingness, onto the whiteness of the paper. Slowly the paper filled. A tree, a clutch of birds, a moon. And then, to the left, a figure on a horse. An archer. He caught his breath as the face took form. It was himself. A tiny mirror-image of his face.

'Why have you drawn me like that?' he asked, when it was done. 'What does it mean?'

Ben looked up. On the far side of the table Fei Yen was staring down at the paper, her lips parted in astonishment. 'Yes,' she said, echoing her future husband. 'What does it mean?'

'The tree,' Ben said. 'That's the legendary *fu sang*, the hollow mulberry tree – the dwelling place of kings and the hiding place of the sun. In the tree are ten birds. They represent the ten suns of legend which the great archer, the Lord Shen Yi, did battle with. You recall the legend? Mankind was in danger from the intense heat of the ten suns. But the Lord Yi shot down nine of the suns, leaving only the one we know today.'

Li Yuan laughed, surprised that he had not seen the allusion. 'And I... I am meant to be the Lord Yi?'

He stared at the drawing, fascinated, astonished by the simple power of the composition. It was as if he could feel the horse rearing beneath him, his knees digging into its flanks as he leaned forward to release the arrow, the bird pierced through its chest as it rose, silhouetted against the great white backdrop of the moon. Yes, there was no doubting it. It was a masterpiece. And he had watched it shimmer into being.

He looked back at Ben, bowing his head, acknowledging the sheer mastery of the work. But his admiration was tainted. For all its excellence there was something disturbing, almost frightening about the piece.

'Why this?' he asked, staring openly at Ben now, frowning, ignoring the others who had gathered to see what was happening.

Ben signed the corner of the paper, then set the pencil down. 'Because I dreamt of you like this.'

'You dreamt... ?' Li Yuan laughed uneasily. They had come to this point before. 'You dream a lot, Ben Shepherd.'

'No more than any man...'

'But this... Why did you dream this?'

Ben laughed. 'How can I tell? What a man dreams – surely he has no control over that?'

'Maybe so...' But he was thinking, *Why this?* For he knew the rest of the story – how Lord Yi's wife, Chang-e, goddess of the moon, had stolen the herb of immortality and fled to the moon. There, for her sins, she had turned into a toad, the dark shadow of which could be seen against the full moon's whiteness. And Lord Yi? Was he hero or monster? The legends were unclear, contradictory, for though he had completed all of the great tasks set him by Pan Ku, the Creator of All, yet he was an usurper who had stolen the wives of many other men.

Ben surely knew the myth. He knew so much, how could he not know the rest of it? Was this then some subtle insult? Some clever, knowing comment on his forthcoming marriage to Fei Yen? Or was it as he said – the innocent setting down of a dream?

He could not say. Neither was there any certain way of telling. He stared at the drawing a moment longer, conscious of the silence that had grown about him, then, looking back at Ben, he laughed.

'You know us too well, Ben Shepherd. What you were talking of – the essence behind the form. Our faces are masks, yet you're not fooled by them, are you? You see right through them.'

Ben met his eyes and smiled. 'To the bone.'

Yes, thought Li Yuan. *My father was right about you. You would be the perfect match for me. The rest are but distorting mirrors, even the finest of them, returning a pleasing image to their lord. But you... you would be the perfect glass. Who else would dare to reflect me back so true?*

He looked down, letting his fingers trace the form of the archer, then nodded to himself. 'A dream...'

Klaus Ebert roared with laughter, then reached up and drew his son's head down so that all could see. 'There! See! And he's proud of it!'

Hans Ebert straightened up again, grinning, looking about him at the smiling faces. He was in full uniform for the occasion, his new rank of major clearly displayed, but that was not what his father had been making all the fuss over – it was the small metal plate he wore, embedded in the back of his skull; a memento of the attack on Hammerfest.

'The trouble is, it's right at the back,' he said. 'I can't see it in the mirror. But I get my orderly to polish it every morning. Boots, belt and head, I say to him. In that order.'

The men in the circle laughed, at ease for the first time in many months. Things were at a dangerous pass in the world outside, but here at Tongjiang it was as if time had stood still. From here the War seemed something distant, illusory. Even so, their conversation returned to it time and again; as if there were nothing else for them to talk of.

'Is there any news of Berdichev?' Li Feng Chiang, the T'ang's second brother, asked. His half-brothers, Li Yun-Ti and Li Ch'i Chun, stood beside him, all three of Li Yuan's uncles dressed in the same calf-length powder blue surcoats; their clothes badges of their rank as Councillors to the T'ang.

'Rumours have it that he's on Mars,' General Nocenzi answered, stroking his chin thoughtfully. 'There have been other sightings, too, but none of them confirmed. Sometimes I think the rumours are started by our enemies, simply to confuse us.'

'Well,' Tolonen said. 'Wherever he is, my man Karr will find him.'

Tolonen was back in uniform, the patch of Marshal on his chest, the four pictograms – *Lu Chun Yuan Shuai* – emblazoned in red on white. It had been the unanimous decision of the Council of Generals, three months before. The appointment had instilled new life into the old man and he seemed his fierce old self again, fired with limitless energy. But it was true also what the younger officers said: in old age his features had taken on the look of something ageless and eternal, like rock sculpted by the wind and rain.

Klaus Ebert, too, had been promoted. Like Li Yuan's uncles, he wore the powder blue of a Councillor proudly, in open defiance of those of his acquaintance who said a *Hung Mao* should not ape a Han. For him it was an honour – the outward sign of what he felt. He smiled at his old friend and leaned across to touch his arm.

'Let us hope so, eh, Knut? The world would be a better place without that carrion, Berdichev, in it. But tell me, have you heard of this new development? These "messengers", as they're called?'

There was a low murmur and a nodding of heads. They had been in the news a great deal these last few weeks.

Ebert shook his head, his features a mask of horrified bemusement, then spoke again. 'I mean, what could make a man do such a thing? They say that they wrap explosives about themselves, and then, when they're admitted to the presence of their victims, trigger them.'

'Money,' Tolonen answered soberly. 'These are low-level types you're talking of, Klaus. They have nothing to lose. It's a way of ensuring their families can climb the levels. They think it a small price to pay for such a thing.'

Again Ebert shook his head, as if the concept were beyond him. 'Are things so desperate?'

'Some think they are.'

But Tolonen was thinking of all he had seen these last few months. By comparison with some of it, these 'messengers' were decency itself.

A junior minister and his wife had had their six-month-old baby stolen and sent back in a jar, boiled and then pickled, its eyes like bloated eggs in the raw pinkness of its face. Another man – a rich *Hung Mao* who had refused to cooperate with the rebels – had had his son taken and sold back to him, less his eyes. That was bad enough, but the kidnappers had sewn insects into the hollowed sockets, beneath the lids. The ten-year old was mad when they got him back: as good as dead.

And the culprits? Tolonen shuddered. The inventiveness of their cruelty never ceased to amaze and sicken him. They were no better than the half-men in the Clay. He felt no remorse in tracking down such men and killing them.

'Marshal Tolonen?'

He half turned. One of the T'ang's house-servants was standing there, his head bowed low.

'Yes?'

'Forgive me, Excellency, but your daughter is here. At the gatehouse.'

Tolonen turned back and excused himself, then followed the servant through and out into the great courtyard.

Jelka was waiting by the ornamental pool. She stood there in the shade of the ancient willow, dropping pebbles into the water and watching the ripples spread. Tolonen stopped, looking across at his daughter, his whole being lit by the sight of her. She was standing with her back to him, the white-gold fall of her hair spilling out across the velvet blue of her full-length cloak. Her two bodyguards stood nearby, looking about them casually, but as Tolonen came nearer they came to attention smartly.

Jelka turned at the sound and, seeing him, dropped the stones and ran across, a great beam of a smile on her face. Tolonen hugged her to him, lift-ing her up off the ground and closing his eyes to savour the feel of her arms about his back, the softness of her kisses against his neck. It was a full week since they had seen each other last.

He kissed her brow, then set her down, laughing softly.

'What is it?' she said, looking up at him, smiling.

'Just that you're growing so quickly. I won't be able to do that much longer, will I?'

'No...' Her face clouded a moment, then brightened again. 'I've brought Li Yuan and his betrothed a gift. Erkki has it...' She turned and one of the two young guards came across. Taking a small package from his inner pocket, he handed it to her. She smiled her thanks at him, then turned back to her father, showing him the present. It fitted easily into her palm, the silk-paper a bright crimson – the colour of good luck and weddings.

'What is it?' he asked, letting her take his arm as they began the walk back to the palace buildings.

'You'll have to wait,' she teased him. 'I chose them myself.'

He laughed. 'And who paid for them, may I ask?'

'You, of course,' she said, squeezing his arm. 'But that's not the point. I want it to be a surprise, and you're useless at keeping secrets!'

'Me?' He mimed outrage, then roared with laughter. 'Ah, but don't let the T'ang know that, my love, or your father will be out of a job!'

She beamed up at him, hitting him playfully. 'You know what I mean. Not the big ones – the little secrets...'

They had come to the main entrance to the Halls. While a servant took Jelka's cloak, Tolonen held the tiny package. He sniffed at it, then put it to his ear and shook it.

'It rattles...'

She turned and took it back off him, her face stern, admonishing him. 'Don't! They're delicate.'

'They?' He looked at her, his face a mask of curiosity, but she only laughed and shook her head.

'Just wait. It won't be long...'

Her voice trailed off, her eyes drawn to something behind him.

'What is it?' he said quietly, suddenly very still, seeing how intent her eyes were, as if something dangerous and deadly were at his back.

'Just something you were saying, the last time General Nocenzi came for dinner. About all the ways there are of killing people.'

He wanted to turn – to confront whatever it was – but her eyes seemed to keep him there. 'And?' he said, the hairs at his neck bristling now.

'And Nocenzi said the simplest ways are always the most effective.'

'So?'

'So behind you there's a table. And on the table is what looks like another gift. But I'm wondering what a gift is doing, lying there neglected on that table. And why it should be wrapped as it is, in white silk.'

Tolonen turned and caught his breath. 'Gods...'

It was huge, like the great seal the T'ang had lifted earlier, but masked in the whiteness of death.

'Guard!' he barked, turning to look across at the soldier in the doorway.

'Sir?'

'Who left this here?'

The look of utter bemusement on the soldier's face confirmed it. It was a bomb. Someone had smuggled a bomb into the Palace.

'No one's been here,' the soldier began. 'Only the T'ang's own servants...'

Tolonen turned away, looking back up the corridor. There were three other guards, stationed along the corridor. He yelled at them. 'Here! All of you! Now!'

He watched as they carried the thing outside, their bodies forming a barrier about the package. Then, his heart pounding in his chest, he turned to Jelka, kneeling down and drawing her close to him.

'Go in. Tell the T'ang what has happened. Then tell Nocenzi to get everyone into the cellars. At once. Interrupt if you must. Li Shai Tung will forgive you this once, my little one.'

He kissed her brow, his chest rising and falling heavily, then got up. She smiled back at him, then ran off to do as he had told her. He watched her go – saw her childish, slender figure disappear into the Hall – then turned and marched off towards the Gatehouse, not knowing if he would ever see her again.

Nocenzi and young Ebert met him returning from the Gatehouse.

'Is it a bomb?' Nocenzi asked, his face grim.

'No...' Tolonen answered distractedly, but his face was drawn, all colour gone from it.

Nocenzi gave a short laugh of relief. 'Then what is it?'

Tolonen turned momentarily, looking back, then faced them again, shaking his head. 'They're bringing it now. But come. I have to speak to the T'ang. Before he sees it.'

Li Shai Tung got up from his chair as Tolonen entered and came across the room. 'Well, Knut, what is it?'

'Chieh Hsia...' Tolonen looked about him at the sea of faces gathered in the huge, lantern-lit cellar, then bowed his head. 'If I might speak to you alone.'

'Is there any danger?'

'No, Chieh Hsia.'

The T'ang breathed deeply, then turned to his son. 'Yuan. Take our guests back upstairs. I will join you all in a moment.'

They waited, the T'ang, Tolonen, Nocenzi and the young Major, as the guests filed out, each stopping to bow to the T'ang before they left. Then they were alone in the huge, echoing cellar.

'It was not a bomb, then, Knut?'

Tolonen straightened up, his face grave, his eyes strangely pained. 'No, Chieh Hsia. It was a gift. A present for your son and his future bride.'

Li Shai Tung frowned. 'Then why this?'

'Because I felt it was something you would not want Li Yuan to have. Perhaps not even to know about.'

The T'ang stared at him a moment, then looked away, taking two steps then turning to face him again.

'Why? What kind of gift is it?'

Tolonen looked past him. There were faint noises on the steps leading down to the great cellar. 'It's here now, Chieh Hsia. Judge for yourself.'

They brought it in and set it down on the floor in front of Li Shai Tung. The wrapping lay over the present loosely, the white silk cut in several places.

'Was there a card?' The T'ang asked, looking up from it.

Tolonen bowed his head. 'There was, Chieh Hsia.'

'I see... But I must guess, eh?' There was a hint of mild impatience in the T'ang's voice that made Tolonen start forward.

'Forgive me, *Chieh Hsia*. Here...'

Li Shai Tung studied the card a moment, reading the brief, unsigned message, then looked back at Tolonen. He was silent a moment, thoughtful, then, almost impatiently, he crouched down on his haunches and threw the silk back.

Li Shai Tung looked across at Tolonen. The Marshal, like Nocenzi and young Ebert, had knelt, so as not to be above the T'ang.

The T'ang's eyes were filled with puzzlement. 'But this is a *wei* chi board, Knut. And a good one, too. Why should Li Yuan not have this or know of it?'

In answer Tolonen reached out and took the lids from the two wooden pots that held the stones.

'But that's wrong...' the T'ang began.

Wei chi was played with black and white stones: one hundred and eighty-one black stones and one hundred and eighty white. Enough to fill the nineteen by nineteen board completely. But this set was different.

Li Shai Tung dipped his hands into each of the bowls and scattered the stones across the board. They were all white. Every last one. He lifted the bowls and upended them, letting the stones spill out onto the board, filling it.

'They feel odd,' he said, rubbing one of the stones between thumb and forefinger, then met Tolonen's eyes again. 'They're not glass.'

'No, *Chieh Hsia*. They're bone. Human bone.'

The T'ang nodded, then got up slowly, clearly shaken. His fingers pulled at his plaited beard distractedly.

'You were right, Knut. This is not something I would wish Yuan to know of.'

He turned, hearing a noise behind him. It was Klaus Ebert. The old man bowed low. 'Forgive me for intruding, Chieh Hsia, but I felt you would want to know at once. It seems we have unearthed part of the mystery.'

Li Shai Tung frowned. 'Go on...'

Ebert glanced up, his eyes taking in the sight of the *wei chi* board and the scattered stones. 'The search of the palace Marshal Tolonen ordered has borne fruit. We have discovered who placed the present on the table.'

'And is he dead or alive?'

'Dead, I'm afraid, *Chieh Hsia*. He was found in one of the small scullery cupboards in the kitchens. Poisoned, it seems. By his own hand.'

The T'ang glanced at Tolonen, his eyes suddenly black with fury. 'Who was it? Who would *dare* to bring such a thing into my household?'

'One of your bondservants, *Chieh Hsia*,' Ebert answered. 'The one you knew as Chung Hsin.'

Li Shai Tung's eyes widened, then he shook his head in disbelief. 'Chung Hsin...' It was inconceivable. Why, Li Shai Tung had raised him from a three-year-old in this household. Had named him for his strongest quality.

Yes, *Chung Hsin*, he'd named him. *Loyalty*.

'Why?' he groaned. 'In the gods' names, why?'

Ebert was staring at the board now, frowning, not understanding. He looked across at Tolonen. 'Is that what he delivered?'

Tolonen nodded tersely, more concerned for the state of his T'ang than in answering his old friend.

'Then why did he kill himself?'

It was the T'ang who answered Ebert's question. 'Because of the message he delivered.'

'Message?' Old Man Ebert looked back at his T'ang, bewildered.

Li Shai Tung pointed down at the board, the scattered stones.

'The board... that is Chung Kuo. And the white stones...' He shuddered and wet his lips before continuing. 'They represent death. It is a message, you see. From our friend, DeVore. It says he means to kill us all. To fill Chung Kuo with the dead.'

Tolonen looked up sharply at mention of DeVore. So the T'ang understood that too. Of course...

Ebert was staring at the board now, horrified. 'But I thought stones were symbols of longevity?'

'Yes...' The T'ang's laughter was bitter. 'But Knut has had them tested. These stones are made of human bone. They will outlast you and I, certainly, but they symbolize nothing but themselves. Nothing but death.'

'And yet it might have been worse, surely? It could have been a bomb.'

Li Shai Tung studied his Councillor a moment, then slowly shook his head. 'No. No bomb could have been quite as eloquent as this.' He sighed, then turned to Nocenzi. 'Take it away and destroy it, General. And, Klaus...' He turned back. 'Say nothing of this to anyone. Understand me? If Li Yuan should get to hear of this...'

Ebert bowed his head. 'As you wish, *Chieh Hsia*.'

★

Li Yuan had been watching for his father. He had seen the guards come and go with the mystery package; had seen both Old Man Ebert and the Marshal emerge from the cellar, grim-faced and silent, and knew, without being told, that something dreadful must have happened.

When Li Shai Tung finally came from the cellar, Yuan went across to him, stopping three paces from him to kneel, his head bowed.

'Is there anything I can do, father?'

His father seemed immensely tired. 'Thank you, my son, but there is nothing to be done. It was all a mistake, that's all.'

'And Chung Hsin... ?'

His father was quiet a moment, then he sighed. 'That was unfortunate. I grieve for him. He must have been very unhappy.'

'Ah...' Yuan lowered his head again, wondering whether he should ask directly what had been beneath the white silk. But he sensed his father would not answer him. And to ask a question that could not be answered would merely anger him, so he held his tongue.

He searched for a way to lighten the mood of things, and as he did so his fingers closed upon the eight tiny pieces in the pocket of his ceremonial jacket.

He looked up, smiling. 'Can I show you something, father?'

Li Shai Tung smiled bleakly back at him. 'Yes... But get off your knees, Yuan. Please... This is your day. We are here to honour you.'

Yuan bowed his head, then stood and moved closer to his father. 'Hold out your hand, father. They're small, so it's best if you look at them closely. They're what the Marshal's daughter gave us for a betrothal gift. Aren't they beautiful?'

Li Shai Tung stared at the tiny figures in his hand. And then he laughed. A loud, ringing laughter of delight.

'Knut!' he said, looking past his son at the old Marshal. 'Why didn't you say? Why didn't you tell me what your daughter had brought?'

Tolonen glanced at his daughter, then stepped forward, puzzled.

'What is it, *Chieh Hsia?*'

'You mean you do not know?'

Tolonen shook his head.

'Then look. They are the eight heroes. The eight honourable men.'

Tolonen stared at the tiny, sculpted pieces that rested in the T'ang's palm, then laughed, delighted. 'It's an omen,' he said, meeting the T'ang's eyes. 'What else can it be?'

The T'ang nodded and then began to laugh again, his laughter picked up by those nearest until it filled the Hall.

He looked down at the tiny figures in his palm. How many times had he seen them on the stage, their faces blacked to represent their honour? And now here they were, sculpted from eight black stones! It was as Knut said; it was an omen. A sign from the gods. These eight to set against the vast, colourless armies of the dead.

Yuan was standing nearby, his mouth open in astonishment. 'What is it?' he asked. 'What have I missed?'

In answer the T'ang placed the pieces back in his son's palm and closed his fingers tightly over them.

'Guard these well, Yuan. Keep them with you at all times. Let them be your talisman.'

His son stared back at him, wide-eyed, then, with the vaguest shake of the head, he bowed low. 'As my father wishes...'

But Li Shai Tung had let his head fall back again, a great gust of laughter rippling out from him, like a huge stone dropped into the centre of a pond.

Let him hear of this, he thought. *Let DeVore's spy report to him how the T'ang laughed in his face defiantly. And let him learn, too, of the second gift of stones – of the eight dark heroes; the eight men of honour.*

Let him hear. For I will place the last stone on his grave.

END OF BOOK FOUR

IN TIMES TO COME...

Chung Kuo: *Ice And Fire* is the fourth volume of a vast dynastic saga that covers more than half a century of this vividly realized future world. In the sixteen volumes that follow, the Great Wheel of fate turns through a full historical cycle, transforming the social climate of Chung Kuo utterly. *Chung Kuo* is the portrait of these turbulent – and often apocalyptic – times and the people who lived through them.

The story of the young prince, Li Yuan – his love for the beautiful Fei Yen, his accession to the throne, and his long, relentless struggle against the traitorous DeVore – is interwoven with the tales of many others, among them the brilliant young scientist Kim Ward, whose 'web' will one day make it possible at last for Mankind to reach the stars, and the artist Ben Shepherd, whose development of a completely new art form – the Shell – will revolutionize the culture of Chung Kuo.

This epic tale continues in Book Five, *The Art Of War*. Five years after the destruction of the starship *The New Hope*, the Council of Seven is preparing to meet and discuss the way ahead. In the long and bitter war they have just fought they have emerged triumphant but greatly weakened. The days of speaking with one voice are past and there is dissension among them. But DeVore thrives on such dissension and, ruthlessly casting off his First Level co-conspirators, makes a new alliance among those disinherited billions in the lowest levels of the City.

The problems for the Seven are vast. Even so, there is one solution that – even if it leaves the underlying malaise untreated – might yet prove successful.

Li Yuan's plan is to 'wire up' the whole population of Chung Kuo; placing delicate electronics in every citizen's head that would enable the Seven to trace and thus control them. Among those brought in to try to make the 'wire' a reality is the young Clayborn boy, Kim Ward.

Ben Shepherd, meanwhile, discovers an artistic vocation, and soon the unexpected happens – this cold and seemingly distant young man falls in love. For the young Prince, too, love is a distraction from his work, the fulfilment of a long cherished dream. But his love is far from the fragile, compliant creature she outwardly appears.

In *Chung Kuo: The Art Of War* the Great Wheel turns into a new, more dangerous phase – from which no one will escape unscathed.

CHARACTER LISTING

MAJOR CHARACTERS

DeVore, Howard
A major in the Security forces of the T'ang, Li Shai Tung, he is also the leading figure in the struggle against the Seven. A highly intelligent and coldly logical man, he is the puppet master behind the scenes as the great 'War of the Two Directions' begins.

Ebert, Hans
Son of Klaus Ebert and heir to the vast GenSyn Corporation, he is a captain in the Security forces, admired and trusted by his superiors. Ebert is a complex young man: a brave and intelligent officer, he also has a selfish, dissolute and rather cruel streak.

Fei Yen
Daughter of Yin Tsu, one of the heads of the 'Twenty-Nine', the minor aristocratic families of Chung Kuo. The classically beautiful 'Flying Swallow' is engaged to Li Han Ch'in, prince and heir to City Europe. Fragile in appearance, she is surprisingly strong-willed and fiery.

Kao Chen
Once an assassin from the Net, the lowest levels of the great City, Chen is to raise himself from his humble beginnings to become a captain in the T'ang's Security forces, and, as friend and helper to Gregor Karr, he is to be one of the foot soldiers in the war against DeVore.

Karr, Gregor
He was recruited by Marshal Tolonen from the Net. In his youth he was an athlete and, later, a 'blood' – a to-the-death combat fighter. A giant of a man, he is to become the 'hawk' Li Shai Tung will fly against his adversary, DeVore.

Li Shai Tung	T'ang of City Europe and one of the Seven, the ruling Council of Chung Kuo, Li Shai Tung is now in his seventies. For many years he was the fulcrum of the Council and unofficial spokesman for the Seven, representing their strong determination to prevent Change at all costs.
Li Yuan	Second son of Li Shai Tung, he is considered to be old before his time. His cold, thoughtful manner conceals a passionate nature, expressed in his love for his brother's bride, Fei Yen.
Shepherd, Ben	Son of Hal Shepherd, the T'ang's chief advisor, and great-great-grandson of City Earth's architect, Shepherd is born and brought up outside the City in the Domain, an idyllic valley in the South-West of England. There, in childhood, he begins his artistic explorations which are to one day lead to the creation of a whole new art form, the Shell, which will have a cataclysmic effect on Chung Kuo's society.
Tolonen, Jelka	Daughter of Marshal Tolonen, Jelka has been brought up in a very masculine environment, lacking a mother's influence. However, her genuine interest in martial arts and in weaponry and strategy mask a very different side to her nature; a side which will be brought out by violent circumstances.
Tolonen, Knut	General to Li Shai Tung, Tolonen is a big, granite-jawed man and the staunchest supporter of the values and ideals of the Seven. Possessed of a fiery, fearless nature, he will stop at nothing to protect his masters.
Tsu Ma	T'ang of West Asia and one of the Seven, the ruling Council of Chung Kuo, Tsu Ma has thrown off his former dissolute ways to support his father in Council. A strong, handsome man, he has still, however, a weakness in his nature – one that will almost prove his undoing.
Wang Sau-leyan	Fourth and youngest son of Wang Hsien, T'ang of Africa, the murder of his two eldest brothers has placed him closer to the centre of political events. Thought of as a wastrel, he is, in fact, a shrewd and highly capable political being who is set – through circumstances of his own devising – to become the harbinger of Change inside the Council of Seven.
Ward, Kim	Born in the Clay, that dark wasteland beneath the great City's foundations, Kim has a quick and unusual bent of mind. His vision of a giant web,

formulated in the darkness, has driven him into the
light of the Above. Rescued from oblivion, he begins
to show his true potential as the most promising
young scientist in the whole of Chung Kuo.

THE SEVEN AND THE FAMILIES

Chi Hu Wei	T'ang of the Australias
Hou Ti	T'ang of South America
Li Ch'i Chun	brother of and advisor to Li Shai Tung
Li Feng Chiang	brother and advisor to Li Shai Tung
Li Shai Tung	T'ang of City Europe
Li Yuan	second son of Li Shai Tung and heir to City Europe
Li Yun-Ti	brother of and advisor to Li Shai Tung
Pei Ro-hen	head of the Pei family, one of the 'Twenty Nine' Minor Families
Tsu Ma	son of Tsu Tiao, and T'ang of West Asia
Tsu Tao Chu	third son of Tsu Chang, deceased first son of Tsu Tiao
Wang Hsien	T'ang of Africa
Wang Sau-leyan	fourth son of Wang Hsien
Wei Feng	T'ang of East Asia
Wu Shih	T'ang of North America
Yin Chang	older brother of Fei Yen
Yin Fei Yen	'Flying Swallow, Minor Family Princess and daughter of Yin Tsu
Yin Sung	eldest brother of Fei Yen
Yin Tsu	head of the Yin family, one of the 'Twenty Nine' Minor Families
Yin Wei	younger brother of Fei Yen

FRIENDS AND RETAINERS OF THE SEVEN

Auden, William	captain in Security
Chung Hsin	'Loyalty' bondservant to Li Shai Tung
Chung Hu-Yan	Chancellor to Li Shai Tung
DeVore, Howard	major in Li Shai Tung's Security forces
Ebert, Hans	captain in Security and heir to the GenSyn Corporation
Ebert, Klaus Stefan	Head of GenSyn (Genetic Synthetics) and advisor to Li Shai Tung
Erkki	guard to Jelka Tolonen

Fest, Edgar	captain in Security and friend of Hans Ebert
Haavikko, Axel	lieutenant in Security
Haavikko, Vesa	sister of Axel Haavikko
Heng Chi-po	Minister of Transportation for City Europe
Heng Yu	son of Heng Fan and nephew of Heng Chi-po
Hung Feng-Chan	Li Shai Tung's chief groom
Karr, Gregor	'Blood' (to-the-death fighter) and major in Security
Kirov, Alexander	Marshal to the Seven head of the Council of Generals
Nan Ho	Li Yuan's Master of the Inner Chambers
Nocenzi, Vittorio	major in Security, City Europe
Pearl Heart	maid to Li Yuan
Pi Ch'ien	Third Secretary to Junior Minister, Yang Lai
Rosten	captain of Security in the Domain
Shepherd, Ben	son of Hal Shepherd
Shepherd, Beth	wife of Hal Shepherd
Shepherd, Hal	chief advisor to Li Shai Tung and head of the Shepherd family
Shepherd, Meg	daughter of Hal Shepherd
Shiao Shi-we	martial arts tutor to the Li children
Ssu Lu Shan	official of the Ministry
Sweet Rose	maid to Li Yuan
Tolonen, Jelka	daughter of Knut Tolonen
Tolonen, Knut	general of Security, City Europe, and Father of Jelka Tolonen
Wang Ta Chuan	master of the Inner Palace at Tongjiang
Yang Lai	minister under Li Shai Tung

DISPERSIONISTS

Barrow, Chao	representative of the House in Weimar
Berdichev, Soren	Head of SimFic (Simulated Fictions)
Berdichev, Ylva	wife of Soren Berdichev
Blake, Peter	head of personnel for Berdichev's SimFic Corporation
Cho Hsiang	subordinate to Hong Cao and middleman for Pietr Lehmann
Clarac, Armand	director of the 'New Hope' project
Douglas, John	company head
Duchek, Albert	administrator of Lodz
Ecker, Michael	company head
Hong Cao	middleman for Pietr Lehmann

Lehmann, Pietr	leader of the Dispersionists and senior representative in The House at Weimar
Lehmann, Stefan	albino son of Pietr Lehmann
Moore, John	company head
Moore, Paul	senior executive of Berdichev's SimFic Corporation
Parr, Charles	company head
Ross, Alexander	company head
Scott	alias of DeVore
Weiss, Anton	banker

OTHER CHARACTERS

Andersen, Leonid	director of the Recruitment Project
Anton	friend of Kim Ward on the Recruitment Project
The Architect	one of the psych team on the Recruitment Project
Baxi	chief of the tribe in the Clay
Bergson	overseer on the plantation; alias for DeVore
The Builder	part of the psych team on the Recruitment Project
Carl	'Sucker'; one of Matyas's gang
Chang Yan	plantation guard
Chan Shui	young worker in the Casting Shop
Chu Heng	'Kwai' or hired knife, a hireling of DeVore's
Crimson Lotus	sing-song girl in Mu Chua's
Endfors, Pietr	best friend of Knut Tolonen
Fang Hui	guard on the plantation
Golden Heart	young prostitute purchased by Hans Ebert for his household
Gosse	Security soldier
Hong	'Hsien' or District Judge
Hwa	'Blood', or fighter, beneath the Net
Janko	bully in the Casting Shop
Josef	friend of Kim Ward's on the Recruitment Project
Kao Chen	'kwai' (knife) and assassin
Kao Jyan	assassin
Krenek, Henryk	senior representative of the Martian Colonies
Krenek, Irina	wife of Henryk Krenek
Krenek, Josef	company head
Krenek, Maria	wife of Josef Krenek
Lo Ying	'Panchang' or Supervisor friend of Kao Chen
Lo Yu-Hsiang	senior representative in the House at Weimar
Lu Ming Shao	'Whiskers Lu' – Tong Boss in the Net
Maitland, Idris	mother of Stefan Lehmann

Matyas	Clayborn boy in the Recruitment Project
Mu Chua	'Madam' of the House of the Ninth Ecastasy, a singsong house, or brothel
Nung	supervisor of the Casting Shop
Pavel	young man on the plantation
Peng Yu-wei	tutor to the Shepherd children
Peskova	lieutenant of the guards on the plantation
Seidemann	guard on the plantations
Shang Li-Yen	tutor on the Recruitment Project
Siang	Jelka Tolonen's martial arts instructor
Si Wu Ya	'Silk Raven', wife of Supervisor Sung
Sung	Supervisor on the plantation
Sweet Honey	singsong girl in Mu Chua's house
T'ai Cho	tutor and guardian to Kim Ward
Teng Fu	plantation guard
Tolonen, Hannah	aunt to Knut Tolonen
Tom	'Greaser', part of Matyas's gang
Tong Chou	assassin and 'kwai' – hired knife, and alias of Kao Chen
Tung Liang	boy in the Casting Shop
Wang Ti	wife of Kao Chen
Ward, Kim	'Clayborn', orphan and scientist
White Orchid	singsong girl in Mu Chua's house
Wolfe	security guard on the Domain
Yu, Madam	First Level socialite
Yung Pi-chi	head of the Yung family
Zhakar	speaker of the House of Representatives

THE DEAD

Aaltonen	marshal and head of Security for City Europe
Anders	a mercenary
Bakke	marshal in Security
Beatrice	daughter of Cathy Hubbard granddaughter of Mary Reed
Big Wen	a 'landowner'
Boss Yang	an exploiter of the people
Buck, John	head of development at the Ministry of Contracts
Chang Hsuan	Han painter from the 8th Century
Chang Lai-hsun	nephew of Chang Yi Wei
Chang Li Chen	Junior Dragon, in charge of drafting the Edict of Technological Control

Chang Lui	woman who adopted Pavel
Chang Yi Wei	senior brother of the Chang clan owners of MicroData
Chang Yu	Tsao Ch'un's appointment as First Dragon
Chao Ni Tsu	Grand Master of wei chi and computer genius servant Of Tsao Ch'un
Ch'eng I	Minor Family prince and son of Ch'eng So Yuan
Ch'eng So Yuan	Minor Family Head
Chen So I	head of the Ministry of Contracts
Chen Yu	steward to Tsao Ch'un in Pei Ch'ing
Cheng Yu	one of the original Seven advisor to Tsao Ch'un
Chi Fei Yu	an usurer
Chi Lin Lin	legal assistant to Yang Hong Yu
Ching Su	friend of Jiang Lei
Chiu Fa	media commentator on the Mids news channel
Cho Yi Yi	Master of the Bedchamber at Tongjiang
Chun Hua	wife of Jiang Lei
Croft, Rebecca	'Becky', daughter of Leopold, with the lazy eye
Curtis, Tim	Head of Human Resources for GenSyn
Dag	a mercenary
Dick, Philip Kindred	American science fiction writer
Ebert, Gustav	genetics genius and co-founder of GenSyn (Genetic Synthetics)
Ebert, Ludovic	son of Gustav Ebert and a GenSyn director
Ebert, Wolfgang	financial genius and co-founder of GenSyn (Genetic Synthetics)
Einar	a mercenary
Endfors, Jenny	wife of Knut Tolonen and mother of Jelka
Fan Chang	one of the original Seven; advisor to Tsao Ch'un
Fan Cho	son of Fan Chang
Fan Lin	son of Fan Chang
Fan Peng	eldest wife of Fan Chang
Fan Ti Yu	son of Fan Chang
Feng I	colonel in charge of Tsao Ch'un's elite force
Grant, Thomas	captain in Security
Griffin, James B	sixtieth President of the United States of America
Haavikko, Knut	major in Security
Henrik	a mercenary
Ho	steward to Jiang Lei
Hou Hsin-Fa	one of the original Seven; advisor to Tsao Ch'un
Hsu Jung	friend of Jiang Lei
Hubbard, Beth	daughter of Tom and Mary Hubbard

Hubbard, Cathy	daughter of Tom and Mary Hubbard
Hubbard, Mary	wife of Tom Hubbard and mother of Cathy, Meg and Beth. Second wife of Jake Reed
Hubbard, Meg	daughter of Tom and Mary Hubbard
Hubbard, Tom	farmer, resident in Church Knowle, husband of Mary Hubbard and father of Beth, Meg and Cathy. Best friend to Jake Reed
Hui	receptionist for GenSyn
Hui Chang Ye	senior legal advocate for the Chang family
Hung	Tsao Ch'un's spy in Jiang Lei's camp
Jiang Ch'iao-chieh	eldest daughter of Jiang Lei
Jiang Lei	general of Tsao Ch'un's Eighteenth Banner Army, also known as Nai Liu
Jiang Lo Wen	granddaughter of Jiang Lei
Jiang San-chieh	youngest daughter of Jiang Lei
Jung	steward to Tobias Lahm
Karl	a mercenary
Ku	marshal of the Fourth Banner Army
Kurt	chief technician for GenSyn
Lahm, Tobias	Eighth Dragon at the Ministry ('The Thousand Eyes')
Lao Jen	junior minister to Li Shai Tung
Li Chang So	sixth son of Li Chao Ch'in
Li Chao Ch'in	one of the original Seven' advisor to Tsao Ch'un
Li Fu Jen	third son of Li Chao Ch'in
Li Han Ch'in	first son of Li Shai Tung and heir to City Europe
Li Kuang	fifth son of Li Chao Ch'in
Li Peng	eldest son of Li Chao Ch'in
Li Shen	second son of Li Chao Ch'in
Li Weng	fourth son of Li Chao Ch'in
Lin Yua	first wife of Li Shai Tung
Ling	steward at the Black Tower
Ludd, Drew	biggest grossing actor in Hollywood and star of Ubik
Lung Ti	secretary to Edmund Wyatt
Lwo Kang	son of Lwo Chun-yi and Li Shai Tung's Minister of the Edict of Technological Control
Ma Shao Tu	senior servant to Li Chao Ch'in
Mao Tse T'ung	first Ko Ming emperor (ruled AD 1948 to 1976)
Melfi, Charles	father of Alexandra Shepherd
Ming Hsin-far	senior advocate for GenSyn
Nai Liu	'Enduring Willow' pen name of Jiang Lei and the most popular Han poet of his time
Palmer, Joshua	'Old Josh', father of Will and record collector

Pan Chao	the great hero of Chung Kuo, who conquered Asia in the first century AD
Pan Tsung-yen	friend of Jiang Lei
Pei Ko	one of the original Seven; advisor to Tsao Ch'un
Pei Lin-Yi	eldest son of Pei Ko
P'eng Chuan	Sixth Dragon at the Ministry (The Thousand Eyes')
P'eng K'ai-chi	nephew of P'eng Chuan
Ragnar	a mercenary
Raikkonen	marshal in Security
Reed, Anne	first wife of Jake Reed; mother of Peter Reed and sister of Mary Hubbard (Jake's second wife)
Reed, Jake	'Login' or 'webdancer' for Hinton Industries. Father of Peter and Tom Reed
Reed, Mary	sister of Jake Reed
Reed, Peter	son of Jake and Anne Reed GenSyn executive
Reed, Tom	son of Jake and Mary Reed
Rheinhardt	Media Liaison Officer for GenSyn
Schwartz	aide to Marshal Aaltonen
Shao Shu	First Steward at Chun Hua's mansion
Shao Yen	major in Security friend of Meng Hsin-far
Shen Chen	son of Shen Fu
Shen Fu	The First Dragon, Head of the Ministry ('The Thousand Eyes')
Shepherd, Alexandra	wife of Amos Shepherd and daughter of Charles Melfi
Shepherd, Amos	great-great grandfather of Hal Shepherd chief advisor to Tsao Chj'un and architect of City Earth
Shepherd, Augustus	son of Amos Shepherd
Shepherd, Augustus Raedwald	great grandfather of Hal Shepherd
Shepherd, Beth	daughter of Amos Shepherd
Shu Liang	senior legal advocate
Shu San	junior minister to Lwo Kang
Su Tung-p'o	Han official and poet of the eleventh century
Svensson	Marshal in Security
Tai Yu	'Moonflower', maid to Gustav Ebert a GenSyn clone
Teng	common citizen of Chung Kuo
Teng Liang	Minor Family princess betrothed to Prince Ch'eng I
Trish	artificial intelligence 'filter avatar' in Jake Reed's penthouse apartment
Ts'ao Pi	'Number Three' steward at Tsao Ch'un's court in Pei Ch'ing
Tsao Ch'I Yuan	youngest son of Tsao Ch'un

Tsao Ch'un	ex-member of the Chinese politburo and architect of 'the Collapse'. Mass murderer and tyrant, 'creator' of Chung Kuo
Tsao Heng	second son of Tsao Ch'un
Tsao Hsiao	Tsao Ch'un's elder brother
Tsao Wang-po	eldest son of Tsao Ch'un
Tsu Chen	one of the original Seven advisor to Tsao Ch'un
Tsu Lin	eldest son of Tsu Chen
Tsu Shi	steward to Gustav Ebert a GenSyn clone
Tsu Tiao	T'ang of West Asia
Tu Mu	assistant to Alison Winter at GenSyn
Wang An-Shih	Han official and poet of the eleventh century
Wang Hui So	one of the original Seven advisor to Tsao Ch'un
Wang Lung	eldest son of Wang Hui So
Wang Yu-lai	cadre and servant of the Ministry ('The Thousand Eyes'). Instructed to report back on Jiang Lei
Wei	a judge
Weo Shao	chancellor to Tsao Ch'un
Wen P'ing	Tsao Ch'un's man. A bully
Winter, Alison	Jake Reed's girlfriend at New College and evaluation executive at GenSyn
Winter, Jake	Son of Alison Winter
Wu Chi	AI (Artificial Intelligence) to Tobias Lahm
Wu Hsien	one of the original Seven; advisor to Tsao Ch'un
Wyatt, Edmund	businessman and (unknown to him) father of Kim Ward
Yang Hong Yu	legal advocate
Yo Jou His	a judge
Yu Ch'o	family retainer to Wang Hui So

GLOSSARY OF MANDARIN TERMS

The transcription of standard Mandarin into a European alphabetical form was first achieved in the seventeenth century by the Italian, Matteo Ricci, who founded and ran the first Jesuit Mission in China from 1583 until his death in 1610. Since then several dozen attempts have been made to reduce the original Chinese sounds, represented by some tens of thousands of separate pictograms, into readily understandable phonetics for Western use. For a long time, however, three systems dominated-those used by the three major Western powers vying for influence in the corrupt and crumbling Chinese Empire of the nineteenth century: Great Britain; France; and Germany. These systems were the Wade-Giles (Great Britain and America – sometimes known as the Wade System), the Ecole francaise d'Extrême-Orient (France) and the Lessing (Germany).

Since 1958, however, the Chinese themselves have sought to create one single phonetic form, based on the German system, which they termed the *hanyu pinyin fang'an* (Scheme for a Chinese Phonetic Alphabet), known more commonly as pinyin, and in all foreign language books published in China since 1 January 1979 pinyin has been used, as well as being taught now in schools alongside the standard Chinese characters. For this work, however, I have chosen to use the older, and to my mind, far more elegant transcription system, the Wade-Giles (in modified form). For those now used to the harder forms of pinyin the following may serve as a basic conversion guide, the Wade-Giles first, the pinyin after.

p for b	ch' for q
ts' for c	j for r
ch' for ch	t' for t
t for d	hs for x
k for g	ts for z
ch for j	ch for zh

The effect is, I hope, to render the softer, more poetic side of the original Mandarin, ill-served, I feel, by modern pinyin.

It is not intended to belabour the reader with a whole mass of arcane Han expressions here. Some – usually the more specific – are explained in context. However, as a number of Mandarin terms are used naturally in the text, I've thought it best to provide a brief explanation of these terms.

aiya!	a common expression of surprise or dismay
amah	a domestic maidservant
Amo Li Jia	the Chinese gave this name to North America when they first arrived in the 1840s. Its literal meaning is 'The Land Without Ghosts'
an	a saddle. This has the same sound as the word for peace, and thus is associated in the Chinese mind with peace
catty	the colloquial term for a unit of measure formally called a *jin*. One catty – as used here – equals roughly 1.1. pounds (avoirdupois), or (exactly) 500 grams. Before 1949 and the standardization of Chinese measures to a metric standard, this measure varied district by district, but was generally regarded as equalling about 1.33 pounds (avoirdupois)
ch'a	tea. It might be noted that *ch'a shu*, the Chinese art of tea, is an ancient forebear of the Japanese tea ceremony *chanoyu*. *Hsiang p'ien* are flower teas, *Ch'ing ch'a* are green, unfermented teas
ch'a hao t'ai	literally, a 'directory'
ch'a shu	the art of tea, adopted later by the Japanese in their tea ceremony. The *ch'a* god is Lu Yu and his image can be seen on banners outside teahouses throughout Chung Kuo
chan shih	a 'fighter', here denoting a *tong* soldier
chang	ten *ch'i*, thus about 12 feet (Western)

Chang-e	the goddess of the Moon, and younger sister of the Spirit of the Waters. The moon represents the very essence of the female principal, *Yin*, in opposition to the Sun, which is *Yang*. Legend has it that Chang-e stole the elixir of immortality from her husband, the great archer *Shen I*, then fled to the Moon for safety. There she was transformed into a toad, which, so it is said, can still be seen against the whiteness of the moon's surface
chang shan	literally 'long dress', which fastens to the right. Worn by both sexes. The woman's version is a fitted, calf-length dress similar to the *chi pao*. A south China fashion, it is also known as a *cheung sam*
chao tai hui	an 'entertainment', usually, within *Chung Kuo*, of an expensive and sophisticated kind
chen yen	true words; the Chinese equivalent of a mantra
ch'eng	the word means both 'City' and 'Wall'
Ch'eng Ou Chou	City Europe
Ch'eng Hsiang	'Chancellor', a post first established in the Ch'in court more than two thousand years ago
ch'i	a Chinese 'foot'; approximately 14.4 inches
ch'i	'inner strength'; one of the two fundamental 'entities' from which everything is composed. Li is the 'form' or 'law', or (to cite Joseph Needham) the 'principle of organization' behind things, whereas *ch'i* is the 'matter-energy' or 'spirit' within material things, equating loosely to the *Pneuma* of the Greeks and the *prana* of the ancient Hindus. As the sage Chu Hsi (AD 1130–1200) said, 'The *li* is the *Tao* that pertains to "what is above shapes" and is the source from which all things are produced. The *ch'i* is the material [literally instrument] that pertains to "what is within shapes", and is the means whereby things are produced... Throughout the universe there is no *ch'i* without *li*, or *li* without *ch'i*.'
chi ch'i	common workers; but used here mainly to denote the antlike employees of the Ministry of Distribution
Chia Ch'eng	Honorary Assistant to the Royal Household
chi'an	a general term for money
chiao tzu	a traditional North Chinese meal of meat-filled dumplings eaten with a hot spicy sauce
Chieh Hsia	term meaning 'Your Majesty', derived from the expression 'Below the Steps'. It was the formal way of addressing the Emperor, through his Ministers, who stood 'below the steps'
chi pao	literally 'banner gown'; a one-piece gown of Manchu origin, usually sleeveless, worn by women

chih chu	a spider
ch'in	a long (120 cm) narrow, lacquered zither with a smooth top surface and sound holes beneath, seven silk strings and thirteen studs marking the harmonic positions on the strings. Early examples have been unearthed from fifth century BC tombs, but it probably evolved in the fourteenth or thirteenth century BC. It is the most honoured of Chinese instruments and has a lovely mellow tone
Chin P'ing Mei	*The Golden Lotus*, an erotic novel, written by an unknown scholar – possibly anonymously by the writer Wang Shih-chen – at the beginning of the seventeenth century as a continuation of the *Shui Hui Chuan*, or 'Warriors of the Marsh', expanding chapters 23 to 25 of the *Shan Hui*, which relate the story of how Wu Sung became a bandit. Extending the story beyond this point, the *Golden Lotus* has been accused of being China's great licentious (even, perhaps, pornographic) novel. But as C.P. Fitzgerald says, 'If this book is indecent in parts, it is only because, telling a story of domestic life, it leaves out nothing.' It is available in a three-volume English-language translation
ch'ing	pure
ching	literally 'mirror'; here used also to denote a perfect GenSyn copy of a man. Under the Edict of Technological Control, these are limited to copies of the ruling T'ang and their closest relatives. However, mirrors were also popularly believed to have certain strange properties, one of which was to make spirits visible. Buddhist priests used special 'magic mirrors' to show believers the form into which they would be reborn. Moreover, if a man looks into one of these mirrors and fails to recognise his own face, it is a sign that his own death is not far off. [See also *hu hsin chung*.]
ch'ing ch'a	green, unfermented teas
Ch'ing Ming	the Festival of Brightness and Purity, when the graves are swept and offerings made to the deceased. Also known as the Festival of Tombs, it occurs at the end of the second moon and is used for the purpose of celebrating the Spring, a time for rekindling the cooking fires after a three-day period in which the fires were extinguished and only cold food eaten
Chou	literally, 'State', but here used as the name of a card game based on the politics of Chung Kuo. See 'The Feast Of The Dead' in Book Four
chow mein	this, like chop suey, is neither a Chinese nor a Western dish, but a special meal created by the Chinese in North America

for the Western palate. A transliteration of *chao mian* (fried noodles) it is a distant relation of the *liang mian huang* served in Suchow

ch'u
the west

chun hua
literally, 'Spring Pictures'. These are, in fact, pornographic 'pillow books', meant for the instruction of newly-weds

ch'un tzu
an ancient Chinese term from the Warring States period, describing a certain class of noblemen, controlled by a code of chivalry and morality known as the *li*, or rites. Here the term is roughly, and sometimes ironically, translated as 'gentlemen', The *ch'un tzu* is as much an ideal state of behaviour – as specified by Confucius in the *Analects* – as an actual class in Chung Kuo, though a degree of financial independence and a high standard of education are assumed a prerequisite

chung
a lidded ceramic serving bowl for *ch'a*

chung hsin
loyalty

E hsing hsun huan
a saying: 'Bad nature follows a cycle'

er
two

erh tzu
son

erhu
a traditional Chinese instrument

fa
punishment

fen
a unit of currency; see *yuan*. It has another meaning, that of a 'minute' of clock time, but that usage is avoided here to prevent any confusion

feng yu
a 'phoenix chair', canopied and decorated with silver birds. Coloured scarlet and gold, this is the traditional carriage for a bride as she is carried to her wedding ceremony

fu jen
'Madam', used here as opposed to *t'ai t'ai*, 'Mrs'

fu sang
the hollow mulberry tree; according to ancient Chinese cosmology this tree stands where the sun rises and is the dwelling place of rulers. *Sang* (mulberry), however, has the same sound as sang (sorrow) in Chinese

Han
term used by the Chinese to describe their own race, the 'black-haired people', dating back to the Han dynasty (210 BC – AD 220). It is estimated that some ninety-four per cent of modern China's population are *Han* racially

Hei
literally 'black'. The Chinese pictogram for this represents a man wearing war paint and tattoos. Here it refers specifically to the genetically manufactured half-men, made by GenSyn and used as riot police to quell uprisings in the lower levels of the City

ho yeh	Nelumbo Nucifera, or lotus, the seeds of which are used in Chinese medicine to cure insomnia
Hoi Po	the corrupt officials who dealt with the European traders in the nineteenth century, more commonly known as 'hoppos'
Hsia	a crab
hsiang p'en	flower *ch'a*
hsiao	filial piety. The character for *hsiao* is comprised of two parts, the upper part meaning 'old', the lower meaning 'son' or 'child'. This dutiful submission of the young to the old is at the heart of Confucianism and Chinese culture generally
Hsiao chieh	'Miss', or an unmarried woman. An alternative to *nu shi*
hsiao jen	'little man/men'. In the *Analects*, Book XIV, Confucius writes, 'The gentleman gets through to what is up above; the small man gets through to what is down below.' This distinction between 'gentlemen' (*ch'un tzu*) and 'little men' (*hsiao jen*), false even in Confucius's time, is no less a matter of social perspective in Chung Kuo
hsien	historically an administrative district of variable size. Here the term is used to denote a very specific administrative area; one of ten stacks – each stack composed of 30 decks. Each deck is a hexagonal living unit of ten levels, two *li*, or approximately one kilometre, in diameter. A stack can be imagined as one honeycomb in the great hive that is the City. Each *hsien* of the city elects one Representative to sit in the House at Weimar
Hsien Ling	Chief Magistrate, in charge of a *Hsien*. In Chung Kuo these officials are the T'ang's representatives and law enforcers for the individual *hsien*. In times of peace each *hsien* would also elect one Representative to sit in the House at Weimar
hsueh pai	'snow white'; a derogatory term here for *Hung Mao* women
Hu pu	the T'ang's Finance Ministry
hu hsin chung	see *ching*, re Buddhist magic mirrors, for which this was the name. The power of such mirrors was said to protect the owner from evil. It was also said that one might see the secrets of futurity in such a mirror. See the chapter 'Mirrors' in *The White Mountain* for further information
hu t'ieh	a butterfly. Anyone wishing to follow up on this tale of Chuang Tzu's might look to the sage's writings and specifically the chapter, 'Discussion on Making All Things Equal'
hua pen	literally ' story roots', these were précis guidebooks used by the street corner storytellers in China for the past two thousand years. The main events of the story were written

down in the *hua pen* for the benefit of those storytellers who had not yet mastered their art. During the Yuan or Mongol dynasty (AD 1280–1368) these *hua pen* developed into plays, and, later on – during the Ming dynasty (AD 1368–1644) into the form of popular novels, of which the *Shui Hu Chuan*, or 'Outlaws Of The Marsh', remains one of the most popular. Any reader interested in following this up might purchase Pearl Buck's translation, rendered as *All Men Are Brothers* and first published in 1933

Huang-ti   originally Huang-ti was the last of the 'Three Sovereigns' and the first of the 'Five Emperors' of ancient Chinese tradition. Huang-ti, the Yellow Emperor, was the earliest ruler recognized by the historian Ssu-ma Ch'ien (136–85 BC) in his great historical work, the *Shih Chi*. Traditionally, all subsequent rulers (and would-be rulers) of China have claimed descent from the Yellow Emperor, the 'Son of Heaven' himself, who first brought civilization to the black-haired people. His name is now synonymous with the term 'emperor'

hun   the higher soul or 'spirit soul', which, the Chinese believe, ascends to Heaven at death, joins Shang Ti, the Supreme Ancestor, and lives in his court for ever more. The *hun* is believed to come into existence at the moment of conception (see also *p'o*)

hun tun   'the Chou believed that Heaven and Earth were once inextricably mixed together in a state of undifferentiated chaos, like a chicken's egg. *Hun Tun* they called that state' (*The Broken Wheel*, Chapter 37). It is also the name of a meal of tiny sack-like dumplings

Hung Lou Meng   *The Dream of Red Mansions*, also known as *The Story Of The Stone*, a lengthy novel written in the middle of the eighteenth century. Like the *Chin Ping Mei*, it deals with the affairs of a single Chinese family. According to experts the first eighty chapters are the work of Ts'ao Hsueh-ch'in, and the last forty belong to Kao Ou. It is, without doubt, the masterpiece of Chinese literature, and is available from Penguin in the UK in a five volume edition

Hung Mao   literally 'redheads', the name the Chinese gave to the Dutch (and later English) seafarers who attempted to trade with China in the seventeenth century. Because of the piratical nature of their endeavours (which often meant plundering Chinese shipping and ports) the name continues to retain connotations of piracy

Hung Mun   the Secret Societies or, more specifically, the Triads

huo jen	literally, 'fire men'
I Lung	The 'First Dragon', Senior Minister and Great Lord of the 'Ministry', also known as 'the Thousand Eyes'
jou tung wu	literally 'meat animal': 'It was a huge mountain of flesh, a hundred *ch'i* to a side and almost twenty *ch'i* in height. Along one side of it, like the teats of a giant pig, three dozen heads jutted from the flesh, long, eyeless snouts with shovel jaws that snuffled and gobbled in the conveyor-belt trough...'
kai t'ou	a thin cloth of red and gold that veils a new bride's face. Worn by the *Ch'ing* empresses for almost three centuries
kan pei!	'good health!' or 'cheers!' – a drinking toast
kang	the Chinese hearth, serving also as oven and, in the cold of winter, as a sleeping platform
K'ang hsi	a *Ch'ing* (or Manchu) emperor whose long reign (AD 1662–1722) is considered a golden age for the art of porcelain-making
kao liang	a strong Chinese liquor
Ko Ming	'revolutionary'. The *Tien Ming* is the Mandate of Heaven, supposedly handed down from Shang Ti, the Supreme Ancestor, to his earthly counterpart, the Emperor (*Huang-ti*). This Mandate could be enjoyed only so long as the Emperor was worthy of it, and rebellion against a tyrant – who broke the Mandate through his lack of justice, benevolence and sincerity – was deemed not criminal but a rightful expression of Heaven's anger
k'o t'ou	the fifth stage of respect, according to the 'Book of Ceremonies', involves kneeling and striking the head against the floor. This ritual has become more commonly known in the West as kowtow
ku li	'bitter strength'. These two words, used to describe the condition of farm labourers who, after severe droughts or catastrophic floods, moved off their land and into the towns to look for work of any kind – however hard and onerous – spawned the word 'coolie' by which the West more commonly knows the Chinese labourer. Such men were described as 'men of bitter strength', or simply 'ku li'
Kuan Hua	Mandarin, the language spoken in mainland China. Also known as *kuo yu* and *pai hua*
Kuan Yin	the Goddess of Mercy. Originally the Buddhist male bodhisattva, Avalokitsevara (translated into Han as 'He who listens to the sounds of the world', or 'Kuan Yin'), the Han mistook the well-developed breasts of the saint for a woman's and, since the ninth century, have worshipped

	Kuan Yin as such. Effigies of Kuan Yin will show her usually as the Eastern Madonna, cradling a child in her arms. She is also sometimes seen as the wife of *Kuan Kung*, the Chinese God of War
Kuei Chuan	'Running Dog', here the name of a Triad
kuo yu	Mandarin, the language spoken in most of Mainland China. Also rendered here as *kuan hua* and *pai hua*
kwai	an abbreviation of *kwai tao*, a 'sharp knife' or 'fast knife'. It can also mean to be sharp or fast (as a knife). An associated meaning is that of a 'clod' or 'lump of earth'. Here it is used to denote a class of fighters from below the Net, whose ability and self-discipline separate them from the usual run of hired knives
Lan Tian	'Blue Sky'
Lang	a covered walkway
lao chu	sing-song girls, slightly more respectable than the common *men hu*
lao jen	'old man' (also *weng*); used normally as a term of respect
lao kuan	a 'Great Official', often used ironically
lao shih	term that denotes a genuine and straightforward man – bluff and honest
lao wai	an outsider
li	a Chinese 'mile', approximating to half a kilometre or one third of a mile. Until 1949, when metric measures were adopted in China, the li could vary from place to place
Li	'Propriety'. See the Li Ching or 'Book Of Rites' for the fullest definition
Li Ching	'The Book Of Rites', one of the five ancient classics
liang	a Chinese ounce of roughly 32g. 16 *liang* form a *catty*
liu k'ou	the seventh stage of respect, according to the 'Book of Ceremonies'. Two stages above the more familiarly known 'k'o t'ou' (kowtow) it involves kneeling and striking the forehead three times against the floor, rising on to one's feet again, then kneeling and repeating the prostration with three touches of the forehead to the ground. Only the *san kuei chiu k'ou* – involving three prostrations – was more elaborate and was reserved for Heaven and its son, the Emperor (see also *san k'ou*)
liumang	punks
lu nan jen	literally 'oven man'; title of the official who is responsible for cremating all of the dead bodies

lueh	'that invaluable quality of producing a piece of art casually, almost uncaringly'
lung t'ing	'dragon pavilions'; small sedan chairs carried by servants and containing a pile of dowry gifts
Luoshu	the Chinese legend relates that in ancient times a turtle crawled from a river in Luoshu province, the patterns on its shell forming a three by three grid of numeric pictograms, the numbers of which – both down and across – equalled the same total of fifteen. Since the time of the Shang (three thousand-plus years ago) tortoise shells were used in divination, and the Luoshu diagram is considered magic and is often used as a charm for easing childbirth
ma kua	a waist-length ceremonial jacket
mah jong	Whilst, in its modern form, the 'game of the four winds' was introduced towards the end of the nineteenth century to Westerners trading in the thriving city of Shanghai, it was developed from a card game that existed as long ago as AD 960. Using 144 tiles, it is generally played by four players. The tiles have numbers and also suits – winds, dragons, bamboos and circles
mao	a unit of currency. See yuan
mao tai	a strong, sorghum-based liquor
mei fa tzu	common saying, 'It is fate!'
mei hua	'plum blossom'
mei mei	sister
mei yu jen wen	'sub humans'. Used in Chung Kuo by those in the City's uppermost levels to denote anyone living in the lower hundred
men hu	literally, 'the one standing in the door'. The most common (and cheapest) of prostitutes
min	literally 'the people'; used (as here) by the Minor Families in a pejorative sense, as an equivalent to 'plebeian'
Ming	the Dynasty that ruled China from 1368 to 1644. Literally, the name means 'Bright' or 'Clear' or 'Brilliant'. It carries connotations of cleansing
mou	A Chinese 'acre' of approximately 7,260 square feet. There are roughly six mou to a Western acre, and a 10,000-mou field would approximate to 1666 acres, or just over two and a half square miles
Mu Ch'in	'Mother'; a general term commonly addressed to any older woman
mui tsai	rendered in Cantonese as 'mooi-jai'. Colloquially it means either 'little sister' or 'slave girl'; though generally, as here,

the latter. Other Mandarin terms used for the same status are *pei-nu* and *yatou*. Technically, guardianship of the girl involved is legally signed over in return for money

nan jen	common term for 'Man'
Ni Hao?	'How are you?'
niao	literally 'bird', but here, as often, it is used euphemistically as a term for the penis, often as an expletive
nu er	daughter
nu shi	an unmarried woman; a term equating to 'Miss'
Pa shi yi	literally 'Eighty-One'; here referring specifically to the Central Council of the New Confucian officialdom
pai nan jen	literally 'white man'
pai pi	'hundred pens'; term used for the artificial reality experiments renamed 'shells' by Ben Shepherd.
pan chang	supervisor
pao yun	a 'jewelled cloud' *ch'a*
pau	a simple long garment worn by men
pau shuai ch'i	the technical scientific term for 'half-life'
p'i p'a	a four-stringed lute used in traditional Chinese music
Pien Hua!	Change!
p'ing	an apple, symbol of peace
ping	the east
Ping Fa	Sun Tzu's *The Art Of War*, written over two thousand years ago. The best English translation is probably Samuel B. Griffith's 1963 edition. It was a book Chairman Mao frequently referred to
Ping Tiao	levelling. To bring down or make flat. Here, in Chung Kuo, it is also a terrorist organization
p'o	the 'animal soul' which, at death, remains in the tomb with the corpse and takes its nourishment from the grave offerings. The *p'o* decays with the corpse, sinking down into the underworld (beneath the Yellow Springs) where – as a shadow – it continues an existence of a kind. The *p'o* is believed to come into existence at the moment of birth (see also *hun*)
sam fu	an upper garment (part shirt, part jacket) worn originally by both males and females, in imitation of Manchu styles; later on a wide-sleeved, calf-length version was worn by women alone
san	three
San chang	the three palaces

san kuei chiu k'ou	the eighth and final stage of respect, according to the 'Book Of Ceremonies', it involves kneeling three times, each time striking the forehead three times against the ground before rising from one's knees (in k'ou t'ou one strikes the forehead but once). This most elaborate form of ritual was reserved for Heaven and its son, the Emperor. See also liu k'ou
san k'ou	abbreviated form of *san kuei chiu k'ou*
San Kuo Yan Yi	*The Romance of The Three Kingdoms*, also known as the *San Kuo Chih Yen I*. China's great historical novel, running to 120 chapters, it covers the period from AD 168 to AD 265. Written by Lo Kuan-chung in the early Ming dynasty. Its heroes, Liu Pei, Kuan Chung and Chang Fei, together with its villain, Ts'ao Ts'ao, are all historical personages. It is still one of the most popular stories in modern China
sao mu	the 'Feast of the Dead'
shang	the south
shanshui	the literal meaning is 'mountains and water', but the term is normally associated with a style of landscape painting that depicts rugged mountain scenery with river valleys in the foreground. It is a highly popular form, first established in the T'ang Dynasty, back in the seventh to ninth centuries AD
shao lin	specially trained assassins, named after the monks of the *shao lin* monastery
shao nai nai	literally, 'little grandmother'. A young girl who has been given the responsibility of looking after her siblings
she t'ou	a 'tongue' or taster, whose task is to safeguard his master from poisoning
shen chung	'caution'
shen nu	'god girls' – superior prostitutes
shen t'se	special elite force, named after the 'palace armies' of the late T'ang dynasty
Shih	'Master'. Here used as a term of respect somewhat equivalent to our use of 'Mister'. The term was originally used for the lowest level of civil servants, to distinguish them socially from the run-of-the-mill 'Misters' (*hsian sheng*) below them and the gentlemen (*ch'un tzu*) above
shou hsing	a peach brandy
Shui Hu Chuan	*Outlaws of the Marsh*, a long historical novel, attributed to Lo Kuan-chung, but re-cast in the early siteenth century by 'Shih Nai-an', a scholar. Set in the eleventh century, it is a saga of bandits, warlords and heroes. Written in pure *pai hua* – colloquial Chinese – it is the tale of how its heroes became

	bandits. Its revolutionary nature made it deeply unpopular with both the Ming and Manchu dynasties, but it remains one of the most popular adventures among the Chinese populus
siang chi	Chinese chess; a very different game from its Western counterpart
Ta	'Beat', here a heavily amplified form of Chinese folk music, popular amongst the young
ta lien	an elaborate girdle pouch
Ta Ssu Nung	the Superintendancy of Agriculture
tai	literally 'pockets' but here denoting Representatives in the House at Weimar. 'Owned' financially by the Seven, historically such *tai* have served a double function in the House, counterbalancing the strong mercantile tendencies of the House and serving as a conduit for the views of the Seven. Traditionally they had been elderly, well-respected men, but more recently their replacements were young, brash and very corrupt, more like the hoppoes of the Opium Wars period
t'ai chi	the Original, or One, from which the duality of all things (*yin* and *yang*) developed, according to Chinese cosmology. We generally associate the *t'ai chi* with the Taoist symbol, that swirling circle of dark and light supposedly representing an egg (perhaps the *Hun Tun*), the yolk and the white differentiated
tai hsiao	a white wool flower, worn in the hair
Tai Huo	'Great Fire'
T'ai Shan	Mount T'ai, the highest and most sacred of China's mountains, located in Shantung province. A stone pathway of 6293 steps leads to the summit and, for thousands of years, the ruling emperor has made ritual sacrifices at its foot, accompanied by their full retinue, presenting evidence of their virtue. T'ai Shan is one of the five Taoist holy mountains, and symbolizes the very centre of China. It is the mountain of the sun, symbolizing the bright male force (*yang*). 'As safe as T'ai Shan' is a popular saying, denoting the ultimate in solidity and certainty
Tai Shih Lung	Court Astrologer, a title that goes back to the Han Dynasty
T'ang	literally, 'beautiful and imposing'. It is the title chosen by the Seven, who were originally the chief advisors to Tsao Ch'un, the tyrant. Since overthrowing Tsao Ch'un, it has effectively had the meaning of 'emperor'

Ta Ts'in	the Chinese name for the Roman Empire. They also knew Rome as Li Chien and as 'the land West of the Sea'. The Romans themselves they termed the 'Big Ts'in' – the Ts'in being the name the Chinese gave themselves during the Ts'in dynasty (AD 265–316).
te	'spiritual power', 'true virtue' or 'virtuality', defined by Alan Watts as 'the realisation or expression of the Tao in actual living'
t'e an tsan	'innocent westerners'. For 'innocent' perhaps read naïve
ti tsu	a bamboo flute, used both as a solo instrument and as part of an ensemble, playing traditional Chinese music
ti yu	the 'earth prison' or underworld of Chinese legend. There are ten main Chinese Hells, the first being the courtroom in which the sinner is sentenced and the last being that place where they are reborn as human beings. In between are a vast number of sub-Hells, each with its own Judge and staff of cruel warders. In Hell, it is always dark, with no differentiation between night and day
Tian	'Heaven', also, 'the dome of the sky'
tian-fang	literally 'to fill the place of the dead wife'; used to signify the upgrading of a concubine to the more respectable position of wife
tiao tuo	bracelets of gold and jade
T'ieh Lo-han	'Iron Goddess of Mercy', a ch'a
T'ieh Pi Pu Kai	literally, 'the iron pen changes not', this is the final phrase used at the end of all Chinese government proclamations for the last three thousand years
ting	an open-sided pavilion in a Chinese garden. Designed as a focal point in a garden, it is said to symbolize man's essential place in the natural order of things
T'ing Wei	The Superintendancy of Trials, an institution that dates back to the T'ang dynasty. See Book Six, The White Mountain, for an instance of how this department of government – responsible for black propaganda – functions
T'o	'camel-backed'; a Chinese term for 'hunch-backed'
tong	a gang. In China and Europe these are usually smaller and thus subsidiary to the Triads, but in North America the term has generally taken the place of Triad
tou chi	Glycine Max, or the black soybean, used in Chinese herbal medicine to cure insomnia
Tsai Chien!	'Until we meet again!'
Tsou Tsai Hei	'the Walker in the Darkness'
tsu	the north

tsu kuo	the motherland
ts'un	a Chinese 'inch' of approximately 1.4 Western inches. Ten ts'un form one *ch'i*
Tu	Earth
tzu	'Elder Sister'
wan wu	literally 'the ten thousand things'; used generally to include everything in creation, or, as the Chinese say, 'all things in Heaven and Earth'
Wei	Commandant of Security
wei chi	'the surrounding game', known more commonly in the West by its Japanese name of Go. It is said that the game was invented by the legendary Chinese Emperor Yao in the year 2350 BC to train the mind of his son, Tan Chu, and teach him to think like an emperor
wen ming	a term used to denote Civilization, or written culture
wen ren	the scholar-artist; very much an ideal state, striven for by all creative Chinese
weng	'Old man'. Usually a term of respect
Wu	a diviner; traditionally these were 'mediums' who claimed to have special pyshic powers. Wu could be either male or female
Wu	'non-being'. As Lao Tzu says: 'Once the block is carved, there are names.' But the Tao is un-nameable (*wu-ming*) and before Being (*yu*) is Non-Being (*wu*). Not to have existence, or form, or a name, that is *wu*
Wu Ching	the 'Five Classics' studied by all Confucian scholars, comprising the *Shu Ching* (Book Of History), the *Shih Ching* (Book of Songs), the *I Ching* (Book of Changes), the *Li Ching* (Book of Rites, actually three books in all), and the *Ch'un Chui* (The Spring And Autumn Annals of the State of Lu)
wu fu	the five gods of good luck.
wu tu	the 'five noxious creatures – which are: toad, scorpion, snake, centipede and gecko (wall lizard)
Wushu	the Chinese word for Martial Arts. It refers to any of several hundred schools. *Kung fu* is a school within this, meaning 'skill that transcends mere surface beauty'
wuwei	nonaction; an old Taoist concept. It means keeping harmony with the flow of things – doing nothing to break the flow
ya	homosexual. Sometimes the term 'a yellow eel' is used
yamen	the official building in a Chinese community
yang	the 'male principle' of Chinese cosmology, which, with its complementary opposite, the female *yin*, forms the *t'ai ch'i*,

derived from the Primeval One. From the union of *yin* and *yang* arise the 'five elements' (water, fire, earth, metal, wood) from which the 'ten thousand things' (the *wan wu*) are generated. Yang signifies Heaven and the South, the Sun and Warmth, Light, Vigour, Maleness, Penetration, odd numbers, and the Dragon. Mountains are *yang*

yang kuei tzu	Chinese name for foreigners, 'Ocean Devils'. It also is synonymous with 'Barbarians'
yang mei ping	'willow plum sickness', the Chinese term for syphilis, provides an apt description of the male sexual organ in the extreme of this sickness
yi	the number one
yin	the 'female principle' of Chinese cosmology (see *yang*). Yin signifies Earth and the North, the Moon and Cold, Darkness, Quiescence, Femaleness, Absorption, even numbers, and the Tiger. The *yin* lies in the shadow of the mountain
yin mao	pubic hair
Ying kuo	English, the language
ying tao	'baby peach', a term of endearment here
ying tzu	'shadows' – trained specialists of various kinds, contracted out to gangland bosses
yu	literally 'fish', but, because of its phonetic equivalence to the word for 'abundance', the fish symbolises wealth. Yet there is also a saying that when the fish swim upriver it is a portent of social unrest and rebellion
yu ko	a 'Jade Barge'; here a type of luxury sedan
Yu Kung	'Foolish Old Man!'
yu ya	deep elegance
yuan	the basic currency of Chung Kuo (and modern-day China). Colloquially (though not here) it can also be termed *kuai* – 'piece' or 'lump'. Ten *mao* (or, formally, *jiao*) make up one *yuan*, while 100 *fen* (or 'cents') comprise one *yuan*
yueh ch'in	a Chinese dulcimer; one of the principal instruments of the Chinese orchestra
Ywe Lung	literally 'The Moon Dragon', the wheel of seven dragons that is the symbol of the ruling Seven throughout Chung Kuo: 'At its centre the snouts of the regal beasts met, forming a rose-like hub, huge rubies burning fiercely in each eye. Their lithe, powerful bodies curved outward like the spokes of a giant wheel while at the edge their tails were intertwined to form the rim.' (Chapter Four of *The Middle Kingdom*)

CHUNG KUO

AUTHOR'S NOTE AND ACKNOWLEDGEMENTS

Thanks must go to all those who have read and criticized parts of the many different drafts of *Chung Kuo* over the twenty-eight years of its creating: to my good friends and 'Writers' Bloc' companions – Chris Evans, David Garnett, Rob Holdstock, Garry Kilworth, Bobbie Lamming, Lisa Tuttle and Geoff Ryman – for honing the cutting edge; to John Murry – alias Richard Cowper – both for sharing what he knew, and for long years of patient husbandry; to my brother Ian, much-loved, ever-enthusiastic; to Ritchie Smith, dear friend, drinking companion and 'Great Man'; to Andrew Motion – for finding 'A Perfect Art' not so perfect and giving good reasons; and to my agents, Hilary Rubinstein, Clarissa Rushdie and Diana Tyler. Their comments and advice have helped me avoid many pitfalls and – without doubt – given shape to the final manuscript.

I would also like to offer thanks to Bruce Sterling for the inspiration given by his excellent novel, *Schismatrix...* and for five of his words, now embedded in my text.

I reserve special thanks for two friends whose encouragement, advice and criticism throughout have been invaluable: Brian Griffin for unerringly knowing (better than me sometimes) what I'm up to; and Robert Carter not merely for the introduction to *Wei Chi* and his patient and astute reading of the emergent book but for all the long years of friendship. To you both, *Kan Pei!*

To my editors, Nick Sayers at New English Library and Brian DeFiore at Delacorte, Nic Cheetham of Corvus and now to Sara O'Keeffe for taking over

CREDITS

The version of the I Ching or Book of Changes quoted from throughout is the Richard Wilhelm translation, rendered into English by Cary F. Baynes and published by Routledge & Kegan Paul, London, 1951.

The translation of Ch'u Yuan's T'ien Wen, or 'Heavenly Questions' is by David Hawkes from The Songs of the South, An Anthology of Ancient Chinese Poems, published by Penguin Books, London, 1985.

The translation of Chiang Yen's 'Lady Pan's "Poem on the Fan"', from the Yu T'ai Hsin Yung, is by Anne Birrell, from her annotated version of New Songs From A Jade Terrace, published by George Allen & Unwin, London, 1982.

The quotation from Rainer Maria Rilke's Duino Elegies is from the Hogarth Press, fourth edition, 1968, translated by J. B. Leighman and Stephen Spender.

The game of Wei Chi mentioned throughout this volume is, incidentally, more commonly known by its Japanese name of Go, and is not merely the world's oldest game but its most elegant. As far as this author knows it has no connection to the trigram of the same name in the I Ching – the sixty-fourth, 'Before Completion', but a playful similarity of the kind beloved of the Han might possibly be noted.

Finally, The Game of Wei Chi by D. Pecorini and T. Shu (with a Foreword by Professor H. A. Giles) is a real book and was published by Longmans, Green & Co. in 1929. It was, alas, long out of print, and I have Brian Aldiss to thank for my much-treasured copy. It was my fond hope that its use herein might some day lead to the re-publication of this slender classic, as proved the case.

David Wingrove
December 1988/April 2011

at the helm – I can only say thanks for the many kindnesses, and for making the whole business of editing so enjoyable. Their patience, cheerfulness and encouragement were more than I could ever have hoped for.

To Christian Vander and Magma, for the music...

Finally, thanks to my partner-in-crime, Brian Aldiss. If anyone's shadow lies behind this work, I guess it's yours. This is delivery on the Planetarium speech that time!

David Wingrove
December 1988/May 2012